REED FARREL COLEMAN

GUN CHURCH

TYRUS BOOKS

F+W Media, Inc.

Published by
TYRUS BOOKS
an imprint of F+W Media, Inc.
10151 Carver Road, Suite 200, Blue Ash, Ohio 45242
www.tyrusbooks.com

Hardcover ISBN 10: 1-4405-5170-7
Hardcover ISBN 13: 978-1-4405-5170-3
Trade Paperback ISBN 10: 1-4405-5199-5
Trade Paperback ISBN 13: 978-1-4405-5199-4
eISBN 10: 1-4405-5171-5
eISBN 13: 978-1-4405-5171-0

Printed in the United States of America.

10   9   8   7   6   5   4   3   2   1

Library of Congress Cataloging-in-Publication Data

Coleman, Reed Farrel.
Gun church / Reed Farrel Coleman.
    p. cm.
ISBN-13: 978-1-4405-5170-3 (hardcover)
ISBN-10: 1-4405-5170-7 (hardcover)
ISBN-13: 978-1-4405-5199-4 (pbk.)
ISBN-10: 1-4405-5199-5 (pbk.)
[etc.]
    1. College teachers–Fiction. 2. University towns–Fiction. 3. Clubs–Fiction. I. Title.
PS3553.O47445G86 2012
813'.54–dc23
                                        2012023899

This book is available at quantity discounts for bulk purchases.
For information, please call 1-800-289-0963.

For Peter Spiegelman

"Rather than love, than fame, give me truth."

—Thoreau

"Stardom isn't a profession; it's an accident."

—Lauren Bacall

With his roaring debut, *Beatnik Soufflé*, Kip Weiler displays prodigious talent. He somehow manages to meld the drug-infused bohemian mania of the Beats with the polyester hedonism of today's disco generation. In one deliciously cruel attack on the Beats, Weiler describes the aging Ginsberg-like poet, Moses Gold, dressed in double knits and platform shoes, mimicking the dance steps from *Saturday Night Fever*. Disgusted with himself not for his raging pedophilia but for his dance and polyester fetish, Gold lashes himself with a mace while reciting Blake's "The Garden of Love." While a bit overambitious and undisciplined, this is a fine and entertaining first novel. Kip Weiler is a writer to watch.

—JACKSON DRUM, THE MERTON REVIEW

One

Black Lung

My fifteen minutes had come and gone. Unfortunately, I probably had a few decades more to live out. Prufrock had coffee spoons. I measured my remaining days from shrinking royalty check to shrinking royalty check, from term to term. I achieved what all artists dread: I had outlived most of my money and all of my talent. As I once told an interviewer from *Publishers Weekly*, "My career's like a road flare. It burns hot and oh so brightly." Total cocaine-speak. The cocaine did a lot of talking for me back then, some of the writing too. Maybe most of it.

I smiled, dropping the change on the newsstand counter at the student union, recalling how I'd bedded that chick from *PW*, how her fangirl innocence stuck out from beneath her journalistic veneer like . . . like . . . I stopped smiling. I'd lost or squandered what I once had. The talent, the muse, the knack, the gift, the craft, the skill, the magic, the art, the whatever-the-hell-it-was was gone. Gone. Goodbye. Farewell. Adieu. That ship done sailed, Mr. Hemingway. I didn't regret the coke so much as the road flare analogy. Well, no, not the analogy itself. The truth of the analogy, the spot on-ness of it. *That* I surely regretted.

Thirty odd years ago, I was gold, a literary wunderkind, one of the '80s big three bad boys: Bart Stanton Meyers, Jake McNulty, and Kip Weiler. The Jewtheran, Nutly, and me, the Kipster: that's how we referred to ourselves back in those heady days when Dom was our fallback champagne, and Vassar and Brandeis girls knelt at our altar. Us three lads had homesteaded the Upper West Side of Manhattan, holding court at the Hunt Club or, as Nutly was wont to call it, the Cunt Club. Nutly: always so refined, always the articulate one. Now those days seem as far away to me as Atlantis, and much more like memories from one of my protagonists' lives than my own. Bart and Jake had had their ups and downs too, but had managed to adapt to things like the end of the Cold War, safe sex, and the Christian Right.

Now it was just a dull ache to bear when I clicked through the cable channels and would come upon VH1 airing one of those *I Love the '80s* nightmares. The Kipster—it's difficult not to think of that me in the third person—is usually featured wearing a "Hey, look at me: I'm so high right now!" smile frozen on his face and an anorexic blond on his arm. Was the Kipster ever that young? Was I? It isn't only a nightmare in retrospect. Back when I was actually sleeping with those blonds, the sex was only middling and none of the relationships lasted more than three dates and a bj. I often thought the blonds so brittle they might snap if I humped them hard enough.

These days I didn't worry about snapping anybody in two. My sex life consisted of the very occasional coed or adjunct lecturer whose boredom was surpassed only by my own. Desire had so little to do with it anymore that it seemed I should reclassify the physical act of sex as something else, something between an oil change and a stress test. I felt closer to the skin of my left palm than to any woman I'd been with in many years. That last year

Amy and I were together we hardly fucked, and when we did it was about rage and disappointment.

I didn't have rage in me anymore. That skipped town shortly after my talent. At the very least you needed the vestiges of passion to have rage. I could likely still provoke it, though. I snickered to myself sometimes, imagining Amy watching *I Love the '80s*. She probably seizured at the sight of me and the brittle blonds on screen. Amy: the Jew goddess from Bloomfield Hills. Amy could do rage, all right. She could bend, fold, and shape it like an origami butterfly and make it flap its wings. The stir I felt just thinking about Amy surprised me. I guess maybe I wasn't so close to numb as I hoped. I wasn't sure I liked that. I had assumed seven years of teaching English to the rural yahoos at Brixton County Community College had pretty much removed the notion of surprise from my life.

Brixton County's two most abundant natural resources were bituminous coal and pine trees. So when the early fall breezes blew just right, the air smelled like Christmas trees being hot-dipped in roofing tar. I hadn't ever quite gotten used to the Pine-Sol and petroleum bouquet of Brixton County's lush green hills. As far as I could tell, the county's third biggest export behind coal and lumber was black lung.

What Brixton didn't have in abundance was creative writing talent. On its face, this didn't make BCCC unique. On the contrary, since my first visiting teaching position at Columbia—a job Amy urged me to take, noticing my discipline heading up my nose and my sales heading out my ass—I had been searching for one student with the magic. That I taught creative writing at all was a complete sham. In what now passed for my soul, I knew that writing was a born gift, that you could teach illusion, but not magic. The farther away from Columbia I roamed, even illusion got harder and harder to teach. These days I gave passing grades to any remotely original assignment written in something resembling comprehensible English. I had long ago abandoned all hope of discovering a diamond in the rough. In Brixton County, the rough was deep and the coal too soft to produce diamonds.

Christ, I dreaded days like today, days when I would hand back the class's first take-home assignments. Although, I had to confess that out of the sixteen I received, four didn't make me want to stick needles in my eyes. Two weren't half bad. This was the best ratio in my sad tenure at BCCC. One of the papers was from Renee Svoboda, a fairly spectacular blond who—in spite of her obvious Slavic roots—I had come to think of as the St. Pauli Girl. I'd jerked off thinking about her after the first class. I gave her paper a B-/A; the B- was for the paper itself, the A for the orgasms she induced.

The other respectable effort came from Jim Trimble, a square-jawed kid with coppery eyes and skin like a cave wall. Unlike most of the zombies that took up class space, Jim actually answered questions in class. Still, he'd been a pain in the ass, a brown-noser trying to prove how well he knew my work. Boy, someone needed to tell him that was not the way to my heart or to an A. At least his writing wasn't terrible and it contained distant echoes of my older, better work. The other two passable papers were notable only in that they included commas and periods, occasionally in the right places.

"Okay, folks, it's the day we've all been so looking forward to." I tried not to sound completely suicidal. "Time to return your papers and discuss them. When I call your name, please come up and retrieve your masterpieces. Mr. Kranski . . . Miss Hall . . . Miss Svoboda . . . Good work, Renee."

"Thank you, Professor Weiler." The St. Pauli Girl's smile was broad and white, and hinted at more than simple appreciation.

Her impossible cheekbones and blue suede eyes put exclamation points to the hints. I smiled back with half my mouth. That half smile had gotten me a fair share of women back in the day. "Nice jacket," she said, brushing her hand over the brown corduroy sleeve. "My grandpa has one just like it."

So much for my fantasies of the St. Pauli Girl. It was bad enough to be compared to their fathers, but grandfathers! I'd hit a new penis-shriveling low.

"Thanks, Renee. This jacket's probably older than your grandpa."

I was exaggerating, but not wildly. My mom had gotten me the brown corduroy blazer on the day in late '79 when my first novel, *Beatnik Soufflé*, had been bought by the legendary Moira Blanco at Ferris, Ledoux. Moira was legendary for more than her editorial skills. She had a writing stable full of the decade's angriest young men shuttling in and out of her offices and bedroom. As she got older, the men got younger, less angry, and less talented. I was amazed that the jacket, which smelled of ancient chalk dust and was worn shiny at the elbows, still fit like it did the day I got it.

"Mr. Crable . . . Mr. Trimble . . . Good job, Jim."

"Thanks, Professor Weiler." Jim didn't brush my sleeve or offer a flirtatious smile. Good thing, as I didn't think I had much more shrivel room left.

"Mr. Vuchovich . . ."

Frank Vuchovich came to collect his paper, but never left. He was a small, wispy kid who cast a bigger shadow across my desk than his stature might have suggested.

I looked up, really looking at Vuchovich for the first time. He had inky black hair, a twisted beak of a nose, and opaque eyes that peered through slits in a mournful Slavic face. There were many such faces in Brixton and neighboring counties. A large percentage of the local population was descended from the families of the Eastern and Central Europeans who had come to work the area mines over a century ago. Most of the men still worked the mines or in the paper mills.

"Is there something else, Mr. Vuchovich?"

The kid didn't move, didn't speak, but screwed his face into a red twisted mess that was only vaguely human. Just because I no longer had the rage in me didn't mean I was blind to it. And once I recognized it, I forced myself to look away from Vuchovich's face and scan down. The kid was dressed in military fatigues covered by an oversized black trench coat. As I focused more carefully, I noticed an elastic strap and a leather band slung under the kid's left arm.

"Shit!" I thought I heard myself say.

Before the word was fully out of my mouth, Frank had pulled a dark blue hunk of metal out from under his coat and was now pointing it at my nose. It took a second for me to accept what was going on. The world was at a standstill. I was lightheaded. My hearing took on that bizarre windy quality like when I was a kid and I'd hold two empty cardboard towel rolls up to my ears. I could make out distinct noises: the scraping of grit trapped between the chairs and the tile floor, the scuffling of feet, the snapping of gum, the hammer clicking back under Vuchovich's thumb. As distinct as they all were, they sounded as far away as my old life. That all changed when Vuchovich squeezed the trigger.

Royal Blue

I was still alive and, all things considered, I was in better shape than the blackboard. Unfortunately, my left ear hadn't stopped ringing and the burn on my cheek was hurting like a bastard. The stink of my singed hair was masked by the puff of gun powder residue that came in the immediate wake of the shot. My initial reaction, after the kid had inched the barrel away from my nose and put a hole in the blackboard, was relief: relief I hadn't shit my pants or pissed down my sock. I had had all the indignity I could handle for one lifetime, thank you very much. The last twenty years hadn't left much pride in the tank and there was nowhere left to fall after BCCC.

The acrid scent of spent powder, the sickening stink of singed hair, and burnt skin brought it all back to me: the smell of my dad's suicide. Suddenly, I was twelve years old again at the summer house on the lake. My mom and sister were in town shopping when I heard it. I didn't know what it was exactly. I knew what it wasn't. Why would my dad light a firecracker inside the house anyway? He was at his desk, but it wasn't him I looked at. What I remembered most vividly was first staring at the curtains: those fussy, frilly, white lace curtains that my mother adored and he detested. They were splattered with his blood like a sneering last "Fuck you!" to my mom. His head was thrown back over the ledge of the chair as if he were studying the morning sun through the shattered window behind him. The image of him, of the curtains, of the gun on the planked floor, comes back to me sometimes, but I had shut away the fresh smell of his death the way a kid buries something in his backyard and forgets about it.

About two hours had passed since the first shot. In the meantime, the brooding Mr. Vuchovich hadn't put another round in anything more threatening than an overhead light fixture. He'd herded the other students and me into a corner at the back of the classroom, away from the windows. The kid had planted himself in the opposite corner, across from the door. Anyone making a run for it or attempting to storm the classroom via the door would've been quite dead quite quickly. The state and local police had done as expected. They had cell-phoned, texted, bull-horned, cajoled, coaxed, negotiated in all manner and forms. They had offered him food, friendship, psychiatric help, a bus, a car, a helicopter, a lawyer, his priest, his mom, his dad, his stepdad, and his ex-girlfriend. They'd offered up everything short of hookers and an all-expense-paid trip to Vegas, but the problem wasn't theirs. Apparently, Frank Vuchovich didn't seem interested in doing much of anything except brooding.

Given the minor nature of my injuries and my close proximity to Renee, I suppose things could have been worse, much worse. The St. Pauli Girl had had her arm looped through mine, her head pressed against my chest. It probably made her feel safe, like being close to Grandpa. Whatever the reason, I was glad for the touch. The brief affairs I had managed since coming to Brixton were of the roll-over-and-feign-sleep or take-a-shower-and-get-the-fuck-outta-there variety. However hopefully my dalliances would begin, they always ended in disappointment.

With the coeds, the disappointment was categorically mutual. The adjuncts were another matter. The adjuncts had usually read me or at least heard of me. The ones who'd read me expected . . . I didn't know what the hell they expected. Maybe the Kipster, maybe somebody more like one of my ultra-hip '80s cool-boy protagonists: greedy, coked out, and horny, with a taste for ruby port and tawny pussy. They certainly didn't expect me: a bitter, talentless, middle-aged boor. The ones who had only heard of me expected some hard-drinking romantic hybrid of Hemingway (pre-shotgun) and Mailer (post-stabbing). I'm not sure what I expected—probably very little—but I always hoped for Amy. Disappointment was inevitable.

I tried engaging Vuchovich in conversation, which netted the reply, "Shut the fuck up and get back in the corner."

Hey, I didn't need to be told twice. I guess I felt some responsibility for the students, but I wasn't exactly overwhelmed by it. Look, I didn't know these kids and they sure didn't know me. They were in community college, for fuck's sake—the academic equivalent of jerking off. What the hell did these kids think they were going to get out of this? They were sleepwalking in the land of denial. It was a land I was well familiar with. Maybe if we got out alive, I'd draw them a road map.

I may not have had any attachment to my students, but I didn't *want* anything to happen to them. They had as much right to fuck up their lives as I'd had, even if they were apt to do it in less spectacular fashion. I had once been good with people. "A real schmoozer," Bart Meyers used to say. But that was a long time ago, before I'd become disconnected from my wife, my life, and my talent. I was struggling with how to approach Vuchovich when circumstance forced the issue.

Jim Trimble jumped to his feet. "This is bullshit!" he growled.

That impressed the hell out of me. While I hadn't stooped to begging Frank for my life and the lives of my students, I hadn't exactly acted very heroically either. I decided right then and there, that if we came through this, to give Jim a second chance.

"Sit down, Jim!" I got up, stepping between Vuchovich and Jim. "Sit down!" I repeated, actually shoving Jim away. "Go sit next to Renee." .

I took a few tentative steps toward Vuchovich. Frank raised his weapon, but he was sufficiently sharp not to move out of his corner. After spending the last two hours with him, I figured Tom Clancy novels were probably Frank's favorite masturbation material. No doubt he was acutely aware of the snipers on the adjoining roofs. I was sure he knew what kind of rifles and ammo they used. He was probably hard thinking about it.

A ray of light from the afternoon sun caught the raised revolver just right. Until then, I hadn't paid it much mind. It had bullets and it went "bang." I'd seen close up what guns could do to the human skull. What else did I need to know? But now as its blue finish gleamed in the sunlight and its unusual shadow was cast against the blackboard, I had an idea. One that, if my drug- and alcohol-atrophied brain fucked up, would likely get me killed.

"Colt Python, right? Royal Blue finish, eight-, no, six-inch barrel."

The kid didn't say anything, but his eyes got big and his right index finger eased off the trigger onto the trigger guard.

I kept going. "That thing on top of the barrel, that's a ventilated rib."

Frank was impressed. "That's right."

"Colt Python, the Rolls-Royce of American handguns." I said, repeating verbatim the words Bart Meyers had said to me twenty years earlier. Truth was I knew more about the location of Schrödinger's cat than handguns. Let's just say that since the day I found my father, I hadn't been especially keen on guns. That was until I needed to write about them.

I had outlined a chapter in my second novel, *Flashing Pandora*, where my tragically cool futures-trading prince, Kant Huxley, and the eponymous Pandora are confronted outside CBGB by the gun-toting Harper Marx, one of Huxley's ruined partners. Kant Huxley and Harper Marx, indeed! Christ, I used to think I was so fucking witty. Could I have been any more pretentious? I heard Joe Heller thought I was a schmuck for riffing on what he'd done with names in *Catch-22*. He was right.

In any case, I had foreshadowed that scene earlier in the book when Kant is forced to improvise a new trading strategy as a crisis in the Middle East—*yeah, like that could ever happen*—forces oil prices to soar. Pandora, who up until that point had been cool to Huxley's advances, gets totally hot for him while watching him ad-lib a new strategy with billions of dollars on the line. Later in the book, when Kant feels Pandora slipping away, he pays the desperate Marx to act the role of the vengeful partner. Of course it all goes wrong in the end.

"It has to be a distinctive-looking gun," I had told Bart.

Bart, who was a complete gun nut, had first selected a Luger. "Behold!" he said, carefully removing the Luger from its original packaging, handling it as delicately as a slippery newborn. He laid it across the palms of his white gloves. "Fine German craftsmanship and machining; an intricate firing mechanism, beautifully balanced, and its shape ... Kipster, there are few things on this earth as immediately recognizable simply by its shape than a Luger."

"No, Bart. I want something brutal and American, the firearms equivalent of a muscle car."

"I've got just the thing: an elegant beast." With that, he curled the fingers of my left hand around the grip of a hefty, blue metal revolver with a weird-looking barrel. "Meet the Colt Python .357 Magnum: the Rolls-Royce of American handguns. That's a 1955, one of the first Royal Blues with a six-inch barrel off the production line."

Now as I stood across the classroom from Vuchovich, I struggled to remember what else Bart had taught me that day nearly three decades back and how I had used it in the book. Problem was he hadn't told me much.

I played for time. "Is the Python yours?"

A smile. "It's mine now."

Good. This was progress. I gave myself an invisible pat on the back.

"A 1955?"

"Maybe, maybe not," said Vuchovich, his cold eyes receding into their original broody slits. "*You* tell me, since you seem to know so much."

This was not progress. In the span of a few seconds I'd changed the dynamic from common ground into a pissing contest.

"That's a trick question, Mr. Vuchovich," I said, inching slowly closer. "I'd have to see the serial number."

The smile turned malevolent, detached—a smile as disconnected from joy as a legless man's collection of spare shoes. His finger was back on the trigger. "You think you're pretty clever, don't you?"

Clever! I hated the word. Clever is what my father used to call me. I wasn't smart or bright or talented. I was clever. Drunk as he was most of the time, I suppose I should have been pleased he noticed I was alive.

I found that I was no longer inching toward Vuchovich, but taking full strides. The room got deadly silent.

"Hold the gun out into the light again!" I barked at the kid.

He complied, extending his arm and lifting the Colt so that it was once again captured by the sun. I was now no more than a few feet away and on a very, very lonely island.

The scene in *Flashing Pandora*, as originally conceived, had Harper Marx angrily waving the gun at Kant and Pandora. Kant, as always, would act like he had everything under control, which—having paid Marx off to load the burly gun with blanks—Kant would assume he had. Already rendered impotent, literally and figuratively, by his financial ruination and impending trial, Marx had different plans. There would be no blanks in this gun. He meant to kill Pandora, the only possession in Kant's life that was more to him than just another proper noun. I needed a way for Kant Huxley to prevent Harper Marx from taking a shot at him after shooting Pandora.

"That's easy, Kipster," Bart said. "Have Kant grab the cylinder and hold it tight against the gun frame."

"Grab the cylinder? That's fucking crazy!"

"Here, try it. There's not a person alive who can exert enough trigger pressure to make the cylinder spin if it's being held properly. Pull the hammer back and then when I grab the cylinder, try to pull the trigger. Ready?"

. ... Kant's ears were still ringing from the shot. Harper Marx's eyes were as loving as a shark's, black and cold as the sea at night. He turned and saw Pandora slumped against the soot-stained Bowery brick, her blood turning pink in the rain.

"Too bad it's raining, Huxley, old chum," Marx snickered. "You'll never hail a cab in this weather. Let me save you the trouble."

Kant grabbed the gun.

Bart grabbed the gun.

I grabbed the gun.

It dawned on me, perhaps a little too late, that this was hand to weapon and not words on the page. I peeked over my shoulder to see my students frozen in place, still huddled in the opposite corner.

"Run! Get the fuck out of here!"

Now there was a mad rush, the pressure that had built up in the room over the last several hours exploding out the door in a single panicked burst. It all happened so fast that I half expected the chairs and textbooks to be sucked out the door in the wash. I felt myself smile, thinking about the St. Pauli Girl being proud of Grandpa.

Outside the door someone was screaming, "Go! Go! Go! Go!"

Vuchovich, who like the rest of the class had seemed momentarily stunned by my newly grown balls, had scrambled to his feet and was tugging on the gun. I clamped my other hand on the gun and leaned back for leverage. Vuchovich lost his balance. As he pitched forward, I stumbled backward, reflexively throwing out my arms to cushion the fall. On the way down I had the following thoughts:

Fuck!

I hope I don't fall on my wallet.

I wonder where Amy is right now?

It's amazing what you think about sometimes.

The ironic thing about the "Passion Play" chapter in *Flashing Pandora* was that I never used it. Moira Blanco hated it.

"It's too facile, too off the shelf, Kipling." That's what she used to call me. "You want to take Pandora away from Kant without killing her. Her death would be painful for Kant, but not crippling. You want to cripple Kant, to punish him for his transgressions. If you want to cripple him, she must survive and live just beyond his reach."

She was right. Moira, in contrast to her angry young men, had lived a little. She felt her job was to introduce subtlety to the young writer's palette.

"Men get older, Kipling, but they never do grow up."

She was right about that too. I was living testament to it.

I edited the chapter so that Harper Marx lures both Kant and Pandora up to the roof of his old loft building in SoHo. He holds them at bay with a chef's knife, explaining in excruciating detail to Pandora how Kant ruined him, how Kant had paid him to play the part of the vengeful partner, how he was supposed to menace them the following night at CBGB. When Marx sees that Pandora believes him in spite of Kant's feverish denials, Marx leans over the edge of the building and plunges to his death. Like the smell of my father's suicide, I hadn't thought about that chapter in decades.

I peered up at Frank Vuchovich standing over me, that blue hunk of metal in his hand. He looked more perplexed than angry, as if he hadn't ever considered the endgame. He just sort of stared at the gun as if it held the answer about what to do next. He might just as well have clicked the heels of his ruby slippers or strung together all his blown-out birthday candle wishes for the good it would do him.

"Frank, put it—"

A window shattered. I felt the spray of warm liquid on my face before I could make sense of it. Another window broke and the kid sat down on stringless legs; his head making a sickening thud as it smacked against the tile floor. I scrambled over to him, but it was no use. The shots had ripped holes through his heart and liver. Death had come so quickly that Frank Vuchovich hadn't had time to rearrange his expression. He was puzzled even in death. And in that second I felt every feeling I'd ever felt, including things that hadn't stirred in me for a very long time.

Three

Keith Richards

"Lazy, undisciplined, untalented writers who can't figure out bridge scenes—how to get from point A to point B—employ dream sequences."

I never forgot Professor Archer Knox's admonition, although I stopped quoting it to my own classes a long time ago. The Kipster was a lot of things, but he wasn't a hypocrite. By the advent of the '90s, I was Archer Knox's poster boy. Money had made me lazy. Coke made me undisciplined. And who the fuck knew what disappeared my talent?

I had included dream sequences in my last three novels and they were some of the best things in the books. That's when I knew my career had come to utter shit. Talk about work destined for the remainder bin! If it hadn't been for Meg Donovan, I wouldn't have even bothered retrieving the rights to those books.

"Christz, Meg, it's like asking the surgeon for the tumor back." •

"Don't be so dramatic, Weiler. You can't afford it."

"Says who?"

"Says me, your agent."

"Who in their right mind is going to pay me to put out new editions of this puke? If no one liked lunch going down, they're not going to like it any better coming back up."

"This is publishing, Kip! Since when does logic have anything to do with it?"

I may have written my final dream sequence many years earlier, but I seemed to have been living in an extended one these last couple of weeks. I had appeared on all the network morning shows. I had done the circuit before in the '80s, many times; although, my memories of those spots ranged from vague to nonexistent. I was usually hung over, sometimes drunk, and often lit up like a Christmas tree. By '89, I was live television poison and my on-air comments about the size and shape of Jane Pauley's ass hadn't exactly helped my cause.

Meg had hoped to slap some sense into me by sharing with me what the head publicist at Ferris, Ledoux had told her about trying to book me on the morning shows.

"Kip, a producer at GMA told your head publicist to go fuck herself. She said that watching Capote self-destruct on air was one thing, that him doing it was Greek tragedy, but that you were an incoherent clown. 'If I want incoherence, I'll book Keith Richards. If I want a clown, I'll book Bozo. When your guy writes *In Cold Blood*, I'll think about it.' That's what she said."

But I laughed it off as I laughed everything off in those days because I'd yet to hit bottom. I had no way of knowing the terminus would be Grand Central Nowhere and that it would smell of pine tar and asphalt.

For now, all the satellite trucks had gone back to the state capital or New York City or whatever termite mound they crawled out of. The *Newsweek, Time,* and *People* reporters were history. Even the local rags had moved on to the next school shooting and photos of the county's biggest pumpkin. School was back in session. Frank Vuchovich was buried. The police had finished up their investigations, such as they were. Cashiers, who for weeks had refused my attempts to pay for my meals, were once again accepting my money. My bottomless cup of coffee was drying up. But not everything had returned to the rocky depths of normalcy.

I hadn't slept soundly for two weeks, which, I suppose, wasn't altogether a bad thing because at some point every night I would find myself in front of my laptop. There was one night when my shaking hand had gone to Documents and I'd double clicked on the file saved as McGuinn.doc. It wasn't exactly cause for celebration. The file was nearly as empty as my soul.

McGuinn.doc was nothing more than a collection of feeble first lines from a book I had wanted to write for many years. Problem was that by the time the inspiration train pulled into the station, the train with my talent aboard had long since pulled out. So over the course of the last decade and a half, I would, upon occasion, sit and cringe at what I'd written:

Terry McGuinn
Terry McGuinn killed.
Terry McGuinn was a killer.
Terry McGuinn was an assassin.
What Terry McGuinn did could not be called a living.
He was a nondescript man of no discernable age who drank like he
I met the ghost of Terry McGuinn in a pub in Deptford High
Street and

That one there, the one about the ghost of Terry McGuinn was the one with the most promise, but I had no promise. I had nothing to add after the *and*. I cursed the day I met the man who I always thought of as Terry McGuinn; rather, I cursed the timing of it. He'd actually never told me his name.

It was during that period in my life when simple downward momentum had succumbed to gravity and it was all going to shit—when my world was a blur of cocaine, alcohol, and fading celebrity. You can't imagine how desperately you want to hang on to celebrity until it begins to fade. Bill Septan, a friend of mine at *Rolling Stone*, wanted to assign someone to do a long piece on the Troubles in Northern Ireland, but he said he was sick to death of the unremittingly dark tales of woe that came out of the place. For some bizarre reason, he seemed to think the Kipster's biting cynicism was a good fit for the piece. The whole idea was madness, of course. I jumped at the chance. It offered all sorts of things that appealed to my worst instincts: money, escape, and a chance to fuck up on the big stage.

I didn't disappoint. Not only did I have nothing fresh to write, I had no juice in the tank with which to write it. No one who spent five minutes in that bubbling caldron of religious hatred, political radicalism, and violence would question why the reporting from the North was categorically dark, moody, and full of woe. But I had to write something in order to collect the kill fee from the magazine. The only thing I could be cynical about was my own pathetic life, so that's exactly what I wrote about: my endless pub crawl from the Catholic ghettos of Belfast to the streets of London. Naturally, the day after I faxed my piece to *Rolling Stone*, I met a nameless man in a bar in Deptford.

I was in Deptford because I vaguely remembered—I suppose all of my memories from those days were vague—that the Elizabethan playwright Christopher Marlowe had been murdered there and because the band Squeeze came from there. I liked Squeeze a lot more than Marlowe, frankly: more danceable, catchier lyrics. Some literary genius I turned out to be, huh? I was just getting started on my afternoon drunk when a man walked over to my booth.

"Yer Weiler, then? Would ya mind if I pulled in the snug next to ya there?" He didn't wait for an answer.

His charming introduction aside, his voice lacked any hint of the disarming lilt Americans associate with an Irish brogue. On the contrary, there was menace in his alcohol-thick voice and a distance in his stare that stretched light years. At about five eight with a pot belly, sandy hair going thin and gray, a rough and ruddy complexion, and bad teeth, he was utterly unremarkable: a laborer or lorry driver, not an assassin, certainly.

I offered him my hand. "What should I call you?"

"Whatever ya fancy."

"How about McGuinn?" I said, picking a name out of the air.

"Good a name as any."

We drank to it.

He said, "I hear ya've been to the North looking for a story."

"And you have one?"

"We'll see about that, lad," he said. "Come 'round the church-yard at St. Nicholas half ten and we'll chat."

The meeting with McGuinn all those years ago, that's what I was thinking about when the doorbell rang.

It was late. Then again, late was a relative concept. Back in the day, I'd just be firing up the engine about now and the brittle blonds with their vampire complexions and C-note nostrils would just about be rising from their cocaine coffins. These days, "late" was defined by the local news. And local news doesn't get more local than in a place like Brixton. The bell rang again; my laptop screen still displaying the sum total of my literary output over the last decade-plus: seven first lines of a book never to be written. I figured I'd better get the door.

I trudged down the stairs and through the vestibule to the front door. In spite of having rented this big old house on Spruce Path for the past six years, I felt a strange unease in the place. I was an apartment rat by temperament. House-living fit me like a fat man's coveralls. I was lost in space. Around Brixton there were more synagogues (one) and mosques (one under construction) than rentable apartments. The closest rentable apartments were over the state line and if I'd been willing to pay state income tax, I would have made the move and done the daily commute. But at the whopping salary of $37,400 per annum, I could afford neither the luxury of more taxes nor the extra gas. Besides, what I paid per year for a three-bedroom house with a garage on a few acres would just about pay the security deposit for a one-bedroom in Chelsea.

I pulled back the front door.

"Renee!"

The St. Pauli Girl stood on the porch dressed in low-cut denim skin, a midriff top, and a brown hoodie. Her navel was pierced—a small silver cross dangling on a short chain. Her nipples asserted themselves in the chilly night air. She stared directly into my eyes, her rapid breaths visible in the moonlight. Without a word, she kissed me softly on the mouth. I might have said something vaguely romantic if I could have separated my thoughts from my desire.

"Aren't you cold? Would you like to come in?"

"Shhhhh," she said, placing her index finger across my lips. "Thank you for saving me." She handed me a slip of paper. "Please come."

I stood there, frozen, watching her retreat down the porch steps. I listened to the crunch of her footfalls, the slamming of a car door, tires spitting up gravel. I followed her taillights until they became red pinpoints darting through the trees like deer eyes. When I lost sight of her car, I looked down at the piece of paper. Somehow I couldn't quite focus.

Four

Gun Smoke and Blood

I thought I was lost.

Given the lack of nightlife in Brixton, you'd think seven years here might have afforded me more than adequate opportunity to chart every square inch of this green and unpleasant land. I suppose had I gotten a personality transplant somewhere along the way, I might have been willing to explore the corners of purgatory. Frankly, I was more interested in contracting malaria than exploring the Brixton environs. Part of me knew I should've been grateful to have a teaching job, any teaching job, and that there was no less writing talent here than most anywhere else I'd taught, but all I had for the place was a bellyful of resentment.

I was in exile and complicit in my ignorance of Elba. I knew how to get to and from school, to and from the five local restaurants, to and from the multiplex in Stateline. I also used to know the to-and-from for Hendricks Motor Court—a motor court! How fucking quaint is that? *See the USA in a Chevrolet*—and both area bars. And yes, one was called the Dew Drop Inn. The other one wasn't. I hadn't been to Hendricks in quite some time. My trysting had suffered since Janice Nadir and her husband, Jerry, had gotten appointments at a four-year college upstate some-where. Just as well. It was getting to the point where I enjoyed playing cards with Jerry more than I liked boning his wife.

About a year ago, I got this silly notion in my head that I wanted Amy back. I had always wanted Amy back, but she wouldn't have me back. That much was clear the day after the divorce. I'd burned bridges between us that had yet to be built. It dawned on me dur-ing a rare moment of clarity that I wanted to be worthy of Amy's respect and that sleeping with other men's wives wasn't the way to go about it. I wanted to be worthy of Amy's respect even if she would never know it. So I stopped smoking, cut way back on my drinking, and tried—rather too successfully—to keep my dick in my pants.

Before coming to Brixton, two bouts of detox and rehab had pretty much cured me of my coke habit. Blow actually proved easy to stay away from once I'd put some time and distance between me and the rock. A smoker with a chest full of cancer can spend the rest of his days lighting one half-smoked cigarette with another, perspective being beside the point. My dependency was different because when I came out the other end, I had the thoroughly mixed blessing of getting to survey the scorched land-scape of what had once been my promising life. It was nearly depressing enough to make me start using again. But no, I had myriad ways of punishing myself without sliding back down into that particular hell.

I wasn't as lost as I thought I was, and kept checking the invi-tation the St. Pauli Girl had delivered me. I hadn't made a wrong turn after all. That too was a change. Till I got to Brixton, I was defined by my wrong turns. Then, when I came over one last hill I saw a cluster of squat buildings on what had to be the flattest stretch of land in the county. At the bottom of the hill, the road sign let me know I was getting close.

While the letters RSVP were nowhere to be found on the piece of paper Renee had slipped into my hand after she kissed me, I couldn't quite imagine that I'd been invited to anything but a party. It didn't really matter. With the way the St. Pauli Girl had kissed me on the porch that night, I would have come even if it were a cockroach rodeo. That simple little kiss had been the object of my obsession for several days now and there were limits to how much self-denial I was willing to put up with in the name of Amy's unknowing respect. From the moment that Renee had walked into my classroom, she had been testing those limits.

The old industrial park was about as welcoming as a clenched fist. The six-building complex was strictly Warsaw Pact chic: drab, impersonal, desolate. This place was nowhere in the middle of nowhere. I didn't want to perseverate on the implications of that for me.

I put my car in first gear and rolled into the old industrial park, listening for any sign of life. Mostly I heard the *tha-dump tha-dump* of my tires rolling across the cracked pavement. That was another thing about Brixton: it was a mostly silent place. You'd hear whistles from the mines, the distant buzz of cars along the interstate, the blaring horns of freight trains, but the cars never seemed to stop here. Brixton was somewhere to pass by, not through, a blur in the rearview mirror: a faceless place not worthy of forgetting. I remembered my inability to adjust to the silence when I first moved here. Even Manhattan, Kansas, and Bloomington, Indiana, were loud enough to drown out the not inconsiderable noise in my head. That first year in Brixton I spent a lot of time with the Jack brothers—Yukon Jack and Jack Daniel's—adjusting to the silence.

I stopped the car along the rear border of the industrial park. A tall cyclone fence topped with curls of razor wire marked the boundary. The fence seemed to have no end, disappearing into opposite edges of the night. Somehow the abject desolation of the place made the night seem that much darker on the other side of the fence.

When the silence broke, it broke hard.

There was a loud rapping on the passenger door window. My heart leapt into my throat. The St. Pauli Girl waved at me, amused at the sight of me jumping out of my seat. She let herself into my old Porsche, trying and failing to suppress her laughter.

"Glad you find me so funny."

She did that *shhhh* thing again, pressing her finger across my mouth. "I thought you'd never get here. We're going to be a little late." She brushed the back of her hand against my cheek.

"Late for what?"

"You'll see."

Before I could ask the next question, her tongue was pushing through my lips and her right hand was unbuckling my belt. I forgot the question.

When she was done, Renee looked up at me.

"Was that all right?"

I smiled. It was my turn to shush her. I stroked her hair as she rested her head on my thigh. I wanted to tell her that she was more than all right, but how was I supposed to explain that the only thing standing between her and perfection was the memories of my ex-wife?

"Let's go," she said.

"Go where?"

She rose up, kissing me softly on the lips; my taste still on her breath. "Just drive," she whispered. "Drive."

●

I wasn't wrong about the darkness on the other side of the fence. There wasn't a light anywhere but in the night sky. That was one thing about Brixton; you could see stars, millions of them. I wasn't the star-gazing type, nor, it seemed, was Renee. She didn't need a star to guide the way.

"What is this place?"

"Hardentine Air Force Base. They flew, like, tankers and cargo planes out of here. Some fighter planes too, I guess."

"Not quite Area 51, huh?"

"You're the closest thing we got to an alien around here, Professor Weiler."

I stopped the car. "Look, Renee, given what just happened, I think you're going to have to call me Kip or Ken, at least outside of class."

"I'll try."

We drove for what felt like another half hour, but was probably no more than ten minutes. In between the occasional "turn right here" and "loop around these huts," Renee explained that the base had closed in the late '90s. Hardentine AFB and I shared a common history: we'd both gone fully into the crapper at roughly the same time.

"Jim's dad—"

"Jim Trimble?"

"Yeah, his dad was a colonel here, but when they closed the base, Jim and his mom stayed behind. Jim hates his dad."

"Jim's got some writing talent," I said, still rushing on my orgasm and feeling magnanimous.

"Oh, my god, he'll like freak when you tell him that. It'll mean so much to him."

"Are you two close?" There was a jealous edge to my voice that only I seemed to notice.

"We went out for a while, but it didn't work. We're friends."

We zigged and zagged a few more times before she said, "We're almost there."

Ahead of us, I could make out the shape of several aircraft hangars rising up out of the night. When we got closer, the St. Pauli Girl had me turn into a narrow alley between two of the vacant behemoths. The gap wasn't actually narrow at all, but the darkness and the huge scale of the hangars just made it feel claustrophobic. I was paying too much attention to the soaring walls surrounding us when Renee shouted for me to stop. There, parked in front of us, were about ten other vehicles: pickup trucks, mostly.

"Come on," she said, kissing me again, then giving me a little shove towards my door. "Let's go."

Now outside the car, I detected the first sounds of activity since Renee's soft moans and my own strained sighs. There was engine noise coming from somewhere close by and the comforting smell of spent gasoline blew upwind into our faces. We shimmied our way past the pickups. As we walked, the engine noise grew louder, the odor of the fumes more pronounced. After about twenty yards, I spotted a gas-powered generator coughing out a small but steady stream of exhaust. Renee walked ahead, seeming to follow two heavy-duty orange extension cords leading away from the generator. We came to a door held ajar by the extension cords. She shouldered the door open and we stepped inside.

I'm not sure what I expected: music at least, hip-hop or country. Maybe a cloud of pot or cigarette smoke. Maybe a sow's head on a stick. Whatever I might've expected, I didn't get it. The hangar was cold and cavernous as a giant's empty crypt. It was dark, but not lightless. Beyond the door, the two extension cords separated by a few feet and ran a parallel course straight ahead of us. Every ten feet or so, caged bulbs—the type mechanics use when checking the undercarriage of your car—lit the way. Appropriate to our surroundings, the path looked kind of like a runway at dusk. And while it wasn't exactly the Yellow Brick Road, we followed it just the same, our footsteps echoing as we walked.

Twenty yards ahead of us, rising up from the hangar floor was an incongruous rectangular structure with ten-foot-high walls made of concrete blocks. Painted a stark white, it didn't seem to have any contextual relationship to the rest of the vacant hangar.

"What's that?" I asked, pointing at the concrete blockhouse.

She didn't answer, instead walking quickly ahead of me. As I trotted to catch up to her, I noticed an elaborately carved wooden door built into the white concrete wall. The door seemed as out of place on that blockhouse as I did in Brixton.

"Ken, come over here." Renee beckoned, standing off to the side of the structure. "I need to get you ready."

"Ready. Ready for what?" I asked, as I came to where she stood.

"You'll see. Take your jacket and sweater off and put this on," she said, handing me a clean white T-shirt about one size too large.

I did as she asked, dropping my jacket to the floor, my sweater on top of it, and donning the tee. Renee removed her jacket too. Beneath it, she too was wearing a white tee that fit loosely over the curves of her upper body. Her T-shirt was faded with age and covered in gray-black smudges. There was one more rather stark difference between her shirt and the pristine one I wore. The front of her shirt was marked in small, blood-red crosses.

I pointed at the crosses. "What are those about?"

"Soon," she said, "soon." She knelt down to the floor, reached behind her, and came up holding a coffee can in her left palm. She dipped her right thumb into the can and pressed her thumb to my forehead above the bridge of my nose. She dipped her thumb again, only this time she pressed it to her own forehead, leaving a gray smudge.

I opened my mouth, but the St. Pauli Girl put her finger across her lips.

"Ashes," she whispered.

I thought I heard muted human voices coming from inside the blockhouse and caught a whiff of rank beer. I also caught the scent of something else. It had a sharp metallic tang. The odor gnawed at me, but I couldn't or wouldn't place it. I turned, reached for the handle on the carved door.

Renee grabbed my arm. "Not yet."

Standing there, her hand on my forearm, the smell filling up my nose, it came to me. Suddenly I was twelve again, standing there at my father's desk, enveloped in that sickening and intoxicating cloud of gun smoke and blood, my stomach twisted in knots. Then time shifted like sand under my feet and I was in my classroom, standing over Frank Vuchovich's body; his warm blood running out onto the cool tile floor, his face utterly confused.

Suddenly I was overwhelmed with the need to see behind that door, and grabbed the handle.

Five

Resurrection

From the second I pulled back that door and stepped toward the smell of the spent gunpowder, I was on my way to getting hooked. Getting hooked, that was something I knew a little bit about. Vuchovich's death had stirred things up in me that hadn't seen the light of day in a long time. Now the smell of the gunpowder had opened up that clogged vein once again. I couldn't get inside fast enough, but behind the door my path was blocked by a wall of thick padding. I squeezed myself through a seam in the padding like the world's most impatient baby determined to be born. Finally through, I was born, but into what?

It was much brighter inside the blockhouse. Portable stand lights were rigged all around the room. The room itself was not like any I'd seen before. All four interior walls were covered from floor to top ledge with ratty old mattresses. The ceiling itself was nothing more than a blue plastic tarp that sagged in the middle out of habit. On either side of me were two rows of salvage-yard church pews. There were people seated in the pews, their faces barely registering. But it was what my eyes beheld before me that got my full attention. Jim Trimble, a gun-shaped hunk of metal in his hand and wearing a white T-shirt like the St. Pauli Girl's, stood twenty feet ahead of me to my right. To my left, thirty feet in front of Jim, stood a white-shirted fat kid, gun in hand.

Someone yelled "Go!" And my old world blew apart with two explosions that came so close together they were nearly one. The padded walls did little to dampen the noise. Jim and the fat kid were down. Frozen in place at first, I talked myself into moving forward.

Jim Trimble lay motionless on the gray industrial floor. As I approached, I saw a Luger clutched in his hand. A gun-smoke ghost lingered above his body like a waiting cab and then drifted away. There were those knots in my belly. I was time traveling yet again. It was like a weird logical progression from my father's suicide to Frank's death to here to now. The fat kid was red-faced and rolling around on the floor, hugging his ribs, a pistol at his feet. He made honking noises as he struggled to catch his breath. Was I scared for Jim lying motionless—maybe dead—there on the cold floor? Yeah, I was scared for him and for myself a little bit, too. I had stepped through a wooden door into another world, but it didn't matter.

That vein had been opened all the way now and I was feeling things again, things other than the self-pity and resentment that had sustained me. I was buzzing, humming. I was my own generator. I was electric. Every inch of me felt alive for the first time in nearly two decades. It was that revulsion/revelation push and pull all junkies know from when they stand at the precipice before taking the dive; that *don't look/I can't look away* tug of war we all suffer through as we pass slowly by the scene of a car accident.

But just as suddenly as the rush had come, the bottom dropped out. It is the writer's curse, I think, standing back to observe and record. I got very close to Jim's body when I saw that there wasn't a spot of blood anywhere. Just as I thought I was getting a sense

of things, the ground crumbled beneath me. The current sur-
reality shifted away from his bloodless body to the cheering of
the assembled crowd. My senses were being pushed and pulled
all over the place. I'd barely noticed the others in the room to
begin with, but now they were all I could see, all I heard. They
were shaking up cans of Bud, popping the tops, and showering
each other with the spray. While their faces remained feature-
less blurs, I saw that they all sported the gray forehead smudges
and that their white shirts were covered in those red crosses. A
few of them embraced. Some kissed. The absurdity of the setting,
the audience's whoops and high-fives, their whistles and applause
were like a Dr. Strangelove tent revival. The only missing elements were sideshow freaks and a calliope.

I willed my eyes to focus and I recognized some of the faces
in the crowd, if none of their names. There was a snaggle-toothed
girl with bad skin I'd seen drifting through the halls at school like
a faint shadow, and this skater boy who boarded around campus
with a duct-taped backpack slung over his shoulders. There was
the bald, barrel-chested man from the BCCC maintenance crew
who reeked of stale cigarettes. Not all the faces I recognized were
from school. There was the short-order cook from Stan's Diner; a
nondescript local nobody who worked at the copy center in town;
and a deputy sheriff whose main duty seemed to be hitting on
high school girls. And there was even a guy in uniform: a rent-a-
cop security guard with a 9mm strapped to his thigh. I couldn't
place any of the other people besides Renee and Jim.

I'd forgotten about the St. Pauli Girl. Turning, I saw she was
lending Jim a hand, helping him to his feet. I witnessed the resurrection. Jim stared me directly in the eye as he stood, smiling
the most unnerving smile: *I know all about you.* I froze in place,
pinned but not wriggling. Jim broke his stare and went over to the

fat kid, offering his hand, pulling him up. They did a fist pound and embraced hard.

Suddenly—without any cue I could see or hear—things turned again. An eerie silence settled over the blockhouse, the smiles falling away from everyone's faces. Jim and the fat kid stepped back from one another and, using their index fingers, drew invisible crosses on each other's chests. As they did so, they recited in unison: "Stop doubting and believe." Next, the crowd formed a straight line in front of the pews. Renee tugged my arm and whispered for me to sit and watch. The deputy was at one end of the line, Renee at the other. Jim and the fat kid turned to face the line. Jim walked up to the deputy. The deputy reached out and placed his finger on Jim's chest above his heart and recited, "Stop doubting and believe." Jim remained silent. When Jim moved on, the fat kid approached the deputy and the ritual was repeated. And so it went until they had both stopped by everyone in line. When it was over, Jim and the fat kid removed their T-shirts and handed them to the snaggle-toothed girl. The silence broke.

Beneath their shirts they wore protective Kevlar vests. It struck me that neither of them wore head or eye protection, or anything to cover their limbs. This was madness and I was sick with the need to know what was going on. I pushed my way between Jim and the fat boy, no one seeming to mind.

"Hey, Professor Weiler!" Jim slapped my back. He winced in pain. "Glad you could make it. The professor doesn't have a beer. Somebody get Professor Weiler a beer!" Then he took my right hand and curled my fingers around the butt of the Luger. "You ever hold one of these before?"

"As a matter of fact, Jim, I have."

He smiled that smile again and for an instant it felt like we were the only ones in the room. Then the St. Pauli Girl handed me a Bud.

"Would you like to try it sometime?" Jim asked, letting the question dangle.

"How about someone explaining to me what's going on?" I tried to sound aloof, but it came out flat and unconvincing.

"Sure, Professor Weiler. You saved my life. Anything for you. Come on."

We walked back out through the seam in the mattresses, through the door. I followed Jim through the hangar and up some stairs into a dimly lit locker room. I sat down on a narrow wooden bench that ran between two rows of facing lockers. I noticed the Luger was still in my hand and that I didn't seem to want to put it down.

Jim removed his vest and not without difficulty. Even in the low light, I could see the angry bruise on his chest where the bullet must have hit his vest. It wasn't so much the fresh bruise that caught my eye. No, Jim's well-muscled body was a testament to old wounds, a map drawn in discolored blotches and scar tissue. All that was missing was a legend to help me understand the scale of the hurt. Some of the scars on his body were pink and waxy. Some were jagged, others symmetrical. Lines of cross-hatched stitches were scattered on his chest and abs, their color fading like half-buried railroad spurs.

"You're staring, Professor."

I said, "It would be hard not to stare."

"The scars on my back are mostly from my daddy. He used to take the belt to me a lot when I was a kid. It was tough being his son, but when I found your books I had a place to go to be safe, a world far away from Brixton." Jim shrugged. "This one here's from a bullet," he said, pointing at a particularly ragged scar halfway between his right hip and navel. "I stitched it up myself. Hurt like a son of a bitch."

"What's all this about, Jim?"

"*This?*" He seemed not to understand.

"This! Tonight."

"It's what matters," he said as if that explained it.

"What matters?"

"What matters to us," he said, wincing in pain as he tried to pull a hooded BCCC sweatshirt over his head.

I put the beer and the Luger down and helped him get the sweatshirt on.

"C'mon," he said, grabbing the Luger and tucking it in his pants. "Let's get back out to the party. We'll need to talk about this another time. We can meet at Stan's Diner or something."

"Sounds like a plan. Stan's for lunch tomorrow?"

"Make it a few days. I'm gonna be pretty sore." He turned to go and then stopped to face me. "One thing, Professor Weiler . . ."

"What's that?"

"We don't talk about what goes on here, not with anyone, not even with each other, okay?"

"Like in *Fight Club*," I said. "The first rule of Fight Club is you do not talk about Fight Club."

Jim's shoulders slumped. "Yeah, like that. And we don't use names, at least not while we're here. 'Course they all know who you are."

As we walked back to the bunker, my mind was zooming in another direction. I was still off balance, contemplating Jim's wounds, remembering my own wounds—self-inflicted or otherwise. Words began forming in my head. I could see my list of seven first lines, could hear them in my own voice, repeating and repeating. There might be a second line in there somewhere, I thought, maybe even a third, maybe a paragraph. The rush of it was even more intense than it had been with the St. Pauli Girl. I swear I was hard. I felt like a writer again. I was Kipster come from the dead. Jim's wasn't the only resurrection of the evening.

Six

Looking Glass

My bedroom was heavy with the St. Pauli Girl's scent and it wasn't lost on me that my entire universe once smelled this way, of blonds and possibility. Peeking over the edge of my laptop, I studied the St. Pauli Girl's curves. Her shape, like her scent, was still raw: curing, not cured. She was a demon in bed and it seemed to me she slept as fiercely as she fucked. Her orgasms may not have moved the earth, but they sure as shit moved me. Now fast asleep, Renee was squeezing the feathers out of my pillows and plowing over quilted mountain ranges with a sweep of her bare leg. There was nothing brittle about the blond in my bed tonight. Yet, I couldn't help but wonder about where such ferocity had come from in such a young woman.

Funny thing about her was that she wasn't quite so spectacular to look at without her clothes on. Don't misunderstand, she was by far the hottest woman I'd been with since Amy. Amy was lush and moody and seductive. She had those gold-flecked green eyes that were just unfair, but Amy wasn't head-turning. I think that's what turned my head. When I was at the height of my fame and this week's batch of blonds was taking numbers like at the supermarket deli counter, Amy couldn't be bothered. The first time we met at Puffy's in Tribeca, her clothes and hands were speckled and splattered with paint, and she was about as impressed by me as by a moth. Maybe less so. When Amy's clothes came off, her imperfections blended into a kind of fleshy magic. Renee's looks were nearly perfect and therefore less interesting. It was a puzzlement, a paradox. The exploration of paradox was why I thought I'd become a writer.

Once I lost my gift, I realized writing wasn't about paradox at all, but about words. I had been in love with words my whole life and I didn't think I could love anything more. When I got famous, I didn't think there was anything I could love more than fame. Then I met Amy and I didn't think I could love anything more than Amy. Cocaine proved me wrong and proved easier to love than words or fame or Amy.

When I was certain the St. Pauli Girl had settled down into a still sleep, I started typing:

From the moment McGuinn stepped off the bus and into the belly of a depot that was straight out of the B movies his aul wan favored, he knew he was well through the looking glass. Not even a man as accomplished at murder as himself could foresee the dangers awaiting him in this faceless, generic town on the fringes of the map of the States. He'd been to America before, many times, when he'd have to disappear for a while to let things settle down back home. But those other trips had been spent in Boston or New York, and in the bosom of the Republican underground. Here in this nowhere, he was wholly on his own, exposed without a coat against the chill, and felt as if everyone he passed walking from the bus depot was staring at him with accusation in their eyes.

While peace in the North was not quite at hand, it was on the horizon and McGuinn knew it. Someday soon, there would be handshakes and smiles between ancient enemies, promises of disarmament, and amnesty. Good news for everyone but the likes of himself, for there were sins not destined for forgiving and secrets never intended for telling. That was why he was in this godforsaken shite hole, because his own people would be as anxious to kill him as the Brits, maybe more so. Still, he hadn't fully come to terms with it until he'd had a sit-down with Old Jack Byrnes.

"So, you'll be bobbling off then, Terry McGuinn."

"Can I not now enjoy the fruits of me labors, Old Jack?"

"If history's taught us any lesson, boyo, it's that the need for revolutionaries ends with the revolution."

"Revolutionary! Is that what I am?"

"Were, lad, were. Yer tense is thoroughly past."

"Haven't I a say in me own life?"

"It hasn't been yer own life from the moment ya took another man's in the name of the cause."

"Where did I sign on fer that, Jack?"

"Terry, after all these years, have ya no more sense than a can a piss? The peace will come and the hoors will sing songs of brotherhood and understanding, but the Brits and Prods would sooner sip shite-flavored tea than forgive ya fer what ya've done."

"It's not the Brits and Prods that worry me."

"Ya speak the truth, lad. 'Tis our own boyos you've most to fear." Old Jack pointed from his own eyes to Terry's and back again. "Ya've seen too much. Ya know too many things about the men behind the men who'll share power in this land. Yer a potential embarrassment that can't be afforded."

"Surely, Jack, I'm owed."

"Owed! Owed what and by whom? Yer a killer, son, one who's outlived his brief, if ya take my meaning. Listen to me, Terrence; many are the casualties of war that will come after the peace. So be gone. When I go, look under the table."

"What's there to see?"

"A short reprieve from your date at the knacker's yard. Now, give us a kiss, lad. We won't be seeing each other again in this world."

McGuinn held tightly to the man who had been a father and mentor to him, but who had also brought the curse down on him. With the embrace finally broken, he watched Old Jack limp off, disappearing into a veil of bodies and smoke. McGuinn looked under the table and found an envelope thick with American money. He tucked the envelope away and headed out the back of the boozer into the alley. He didn't return to his flat that night and hadn't looked back until now . . .

According to the man I met at St. Nicholas' churchyard in the Deptford section of London that night all those years ago, he had good reason to see accusation in the eyes of passersby. He told me that he had started killing before the age of fourteen and that he had been killing ever since.

"That first one was easy," he said, in his peculiar monotone, "a man twice me age with a fierce reputation for mayhem of his own. A few of the lads diverted his attention with a brawl and I stepped right close beside him and put two through his liver."

I said, "You don't look like much of a killer."

"Really? What the fook do ya suppose a killer looks like?"

"Not like you."

"Well, then, Weiler, have a good look in the mirror and behold." He laughed a cool, distant laugh. "Come now; stroll with me."

McGuinn did very little talking about himself as we walked. He seemed far more interested in me and, narcissist that I was, I was only too happy to oblige him.

"Ya are a bit of a bastard, Weiler, aren't ya?" It was a rhetorical question.

"More than a bit, but what's that got to do with the story you've got to tell?"

"Everything."

He reached his right arm around his back under his jacket and I froze. If he had taken any longer, I would have pissed myself.

"Take this," he said, handing me a tattered spiral notebook. "Make something more of it than what's there."

"And what *is* there?"

"Me life, Weiler. Don't cock it up."

In the music business there's an affectionate little niche for one-hit wonders; but, paradoxically, have two or three hits and you're forgotten. It's akin to being the second person to swim the English Channel or fly across the Atlantic. You are trivia. Maybe less. Kip had a gift none of us could touch, but he pissed it away. I cannot sometimes help but think he might have achieved literary immortality had he pulled a Harper Lee.

—BART STANTON MEYERS, *GQ*

Seven

Guns, Metaphysics, and the Art of Golf

Logging and mining towns are rough and tumble places. Brixton was no exception. It was the kind of place where even the emo kids had grown up hunting and field dressing deer. None of the locals wasted time mourning Frank Vuchovich. They crossed themselves and moved on. Brixtonians were stoic and not given to hand wringing or calling Child Protective Services. The parish priest was their first responder of choice. So, yeah, I fit right in here, like a foot in a glove.

I didn't exactly have my choice of jobs when I moved to Brixton. The only reason I got this dream job was because I once charity-fucked Ellen Gershowitz, a new girl in the publicity department at Ferris, Ledoux. The head of PR had arranged for five journalists to have lunch with me at The Quilted Giraffe—an aptly pretentious venue for the decade of wretched pretension. The luncheon was a big deal at the time because I had stopped giving interviews. The moratorium was a total bullshit publicity stunt in order to create some hype for *Flashing Pandora*. Unfortunately, no one had cued in Ellen G, who had arranged for me to give an interview to her alma mater's newspaper that morning.

Needless to say, Miss Gershowitz received the reaming of her life and was forced to apologize to me in person prior to the luncheon. That she had to throw herself on my mercy was indicative of just how low on the totem pole poor Miss Gershowitz was. Readers have some peculiar notions about the status of writers, the most foolish of which is that writers are treated like royalty by their publishers. *Yeah, right!* By the time *Clown Car Bounce* was published, I couldn't get the PR department to return my calls. When I complained to the head of publicity that they misspelled my last name in the press release for *Curley Takes Five*, the editor in chief at Ferris called me up and told me to concern myself less with other people's spelling and to concentrate more vigorously on my own vanquished skills. I was royalty, all right: King Shit.

Ellen Gershowitz was pleasant enough on the eyes when she wasn't crying and apologizing. God, she was so miserable that day I think I would have slept with her even if she'd been a beast. Women aren't the only suckers for wounded lovers and I was particularly vulnerable to tits and tears. I was never quite sure if she was more grateful for the mercy fuck or for the interview I gave her college newspaper the following day. I was too vain to ask. Regardless, a few more months of abuse at Ferris, Ledoux cured Ellen Gershowitz of publishing and drove her straight back to graduate school and a life in academia.

It's not like my academic travails were closely guarded secrets. On the contrary, my deconstruction had been quite a public affair. The issue was that the newsworthiness of my plummet from grace had diminished in direct proportion to my sales. No one cared. I wasn't old news. I was no news. I was forgotten. Better to be dead than forgotten. Just ask my father. That I'd suffered through seven years in Brixton without throwing myself into an industrial meat grinder was testament to my narcissism. People often mistook my egregious lack of pride for poor self-esteem. That wasn't it at all. At the bitter end of our marriage, Amy used to say I was born with an ego in place of a heart. I didn't disagree. Generally, writers are the most appalling narcissists.

When Ellen Gershowitz contacted me after hearing about my being run out of yet another job, I was amazed anyone had taken notice. I doubted colleges could get any more obscure than the schools I'd been thrown out of. My mistake was projecting my utter lack of pride onto those schools. When you're fourth-rung material, even third-rung schools look down their noses at you. Ellen, who had passed through Brixton as an adjunct and was a friend of the chairman of the English department, got me the job. Only very recently have I stopped regretting that long-ago mercy fuck and forgiven her.

While Brixton was not a college town, per se, the area in the immediate proximity of the campus was a bit softer at the edges than the rest of the place. Although I thought BCCC a beshitten little pimple, kids came to school here from all around the state. I still wasn't quite sure why, but I knew it wasn't for the English department. After the Nadirs left and since our current chairman was a Cajun, I was the only member of the English department faculty on cordial terms with the mother tongue. Stan's Diner was kind of the crossroads—the one place where the two area populations met.

When I walked in, Jim Trimble was seated in a booth at the back of the diner reading a yellowed, dog-eared copy of *Beatnik Soufflé*.

"That stuff'll rot your brain," I said, sliding in across from him. "A lot more dangerous than guns."

"Hey, Professor Weiler." He put the book down and shook my hand. "I've read it so many times I can recite whole passages. Listen . . ."

With that, Jim handed me the book, pointed to his place so I could follow, and recited, verbatim, an entire page. I don't mean just any page. It was a page where the protagonist, Moses Gold, recites a long, complex poem. Man, I'd forgotten most of it and here was this kid reciting it from memory. Very scary stuff. It reminded me of the crazy kid in the movie *Diner* who only spoke in dialogue from the movie *Sweet Smell of Success*. I couldn't help but wonder how deep his obsession with the Kipster went.

I bowed with false humility. Was there any other kind? At least now I understood the faint echoes of my old style in Jim's assignments. Imitating voice is what nascent writers do. Imitating mine was a death wish.

"I've read everything you've ever written."

"Not to put too fine a point on it, but you've read everything I've published, not written. If you'd read everything I'd ever written, you'd still be throwing up."

He smiled that disconcerting smile of his. "I don't care what you say. You're a great writer." There was a level of admiration in Jim's voice that bordered on fanboy gushing. I'd once been quite used to the sound of it, once liked it, once expected it. Now it made me feel like a fraud.

"I was pretty good thirty years ago."

"And just so *you* understand, Professor, it's not the guns that are dangerous, it's not the bullets. It's the man holding the gun." There was a subtle, but immodest bend at the corners of his mouth.

Just then, Stan Petrovic hobbled over to take our order. Stan, the son of a Brixton miner, was an ex-Cleveland Browns linebacker and special-teamer who'd spent time enough in the NFL during the late '70s and '80s to permanently fuck up his knees, and to save the money to buy the diner. Petrovic was fond of self-medication and his small-town celebrity. Over the years, as the generations churned and his celebrity lost most of its luster, his need for self-medication increased. Neither the loss of status nor the alcohol had done much to improve Stan's famously surly personality.

"If it ain't the local hero and the local zero," he said, tossing menus at us.

Petrovic had always been a bit of a dick to me, but since the shooting incident at school, his distaste for me had ratcheted up another notch. He seemed to take my recent notoriety as a personal affront. Like I said, you only realize how intoxicating celebrity is after you begin losing it; so while I didn't much like him, I could empathize with Stan. Jim was not as forgiving.

"Better than being the local hero that became the local zero. Who knows, Stan, a few more years and maybe they'll vote you into the Football Hall of Lame."

"Watch your mouth, kid."

Jim persisted. "Did they have face masks when you played or were you born like that?"

Petrovic's cheek twitched, his pock-marked, leathery skin flushing red, but he just limped away without a word and sent over a waitress.

When we were done ordering, I asked, "What's with you and Stan?"

"We don't like each other much."

"No shit? I never would have guessed. Took balls to talk to him like that."

"Grabbing a loaded Colt from Frank Vuchovich's hand, that took balls. What I just did was nothing. Stan's a bully. Bullies are naked once you stand up to them."

"Just the same, you should be careful."

"Don't worry about me, Professor. Stan won't touch me. He dated my mom a few times and he's still hung up on her. But he really doesn't seem to like you very much."

"It's been that way from the day I showed up here and it's degenerated since what happened with Frank."

There was fire in the kid's eyes. "Listen, Professor Weiler, you've stared down the barrel of a gun. Me too, more than a few times. Once you've done that, bullies like Stan don't scare you. That's the thing with guns: they are what they seem. You'll see."

"Is that what the other night was all about, staring down the barrel of a gun?"

He swiveled his head about to make sure no one was in earshot. "That's a part of it. Look at it this way, Professor—"

"For chrissakes, Jim, outside of class call me Kip or Ken."

Now the kid was smiling like the circus was in town. I half expected him to say *golly gee* and ask to blow me. "Really, I can call you Kip?"

"If you'd like."

He leaned across the table, his whispers conspiratorial. "Well, it's like I said the other night: it didn't start out as anything. Me and some friends would go out into the woods above the Crooked River rapids and shoot at shit. 'Round here, that's no big thing. Every group of friends in these parts shoots out in the woods somewhere. If you haven't noticed, there isn't much to do in Brixton."

"Tell me about it."

"But you have your head to live in," he said. "The rest of us aren't that lucky."

"Jim, you've got a peculiar definition of luck."

He looked wounded.

"Sorry," I said. "Go on."

"Most guys take rifles. We did, too. Rifles are what you grow up with, but I have all these guns from the Colonel's collection."

"The Colonel?"

"My daddy. That's what he used to make me and my mom call him, the Colonel. He had his guns and I had your books. Anyways, my mom said he cared more for his guns than he ever cared for us, so she made sure she got them in the divorce settlement. She said that if she couldn't have his balls, his guns were the next best thing."

"Remind me not to piss off your mom."

He liked that. "Anyways, we stopped taking rifles and only took handguns with us into the woods."

"So you stopped taking rifles . . ."

"Yeah, between all of us, we had access to all sorts of sidearms and we got real good with them, but we were ignorant of the guns themselves. I mean, we knew how they worked and everything, but we were ignorant of their nature. It was only when we got so good with them that it became boring that I began to understand."

"Understand?"

"Understand their nature."

"I'm sorry, Jim, but you lost me."

He thought about that. "Okay, let's say you have this beautiful, custom-fitted set of golf clubs, but all you ever did with them was go out and hit balls into a net in your backyard. And let's say the government said that the most you could ever do with those clubs was to go to some driving range somewhere. Sure, the driving range is better than hitting balls into a net in your backyard, but how much better? Golf clubs aren't made for driving ranges. Nets and ranges and such are untrue to the nature of the clubs and to the man who owns them. The nature of the clubs is to be used to play the game. To be satisfied to hit balls into a net or to go to a range is like a sin in the scheme of things."

Guns, Metaphysics, and the Art of Golf, by Jim Trimble. Was this kid for real? I felt like a character in a Woody Allen movie and not one of the good ones, either. Come to think of it, fuck Woody Allen! Talk about a guy who lost his muse and got tens of millions of dollars worth of second chances. So, yeah, I wrote a few bad books and broke a few university rules, but I hadn't been fucking my own stepdaughter. Even the Kipster had his limits.

"Golf, Jim? Do they even have golf courses in Brixton?"

"Two, up by Mirror Lake. The mine executives need something to do when they're not counting their money."

"Good line, I'll have to steal it." Uh oh, he got that *aw-shucks-can-I-blow-you* look on his face again. I'd have to watch how I worked this kid. "But why golf as allegory?"

"Because I know you play," he said. "You were captain of your high school golf team."

"That's right, I was, wasn't I? I forgot about that. Forgetting is a skill you're still too young to appreciate."

He shrugged. "But you can see the analogy, right?"

"Sure."

"When we reached the point where we were bored by how good we'd gotten at hitting targets, it dawned on me. I understood. It was like a revelation from the Bible. We were bored because, like with the golf clubs, we were hitting balls into a net. That's not what handguns are for."

"No, they're for killing people."

"Exactly!"

At that moment, the waitress delivered our food. "Fries with gravy for you," she said, sliding the plate in front of Jim. "And a burger for you, Professor Weiler."

She wasn't as enthusiastic about serving me as she'd been only a few weeks ago. All fame is fleeting. The waitress's once-pretty face had plumped up and frayed with time. She looked like she'd been squeezed into her polyester uniform by a blind sausage maker. Funny, she'd been working here since the day I arrived in Brixton, but I never really noticed her before. I mean, really noticed her.

"Do you know our waitress?" I asked Jim as she walked away.

"Irina? Sure. Everybody knows Irina. You must've seen her in here."

"But what's her deal?"

"She was Stan's high school girlfriend. He knocked her up, made her get an abortion, and then he split for Penn State."

"At least Stan is a consistent asshole, but how do you know about Irina and him? That had to be before you were born."

"C'mon, Kip, I haven't been much of anywhere, but I don't think places get much smaller than Brixton. Everybody knows everybody else's business 'round here."

"Sounds like publishing."

He laughed, but didn't know why.

I realized that I had lived in Brixton for seven years and not only didn't I know the lay of the land, I didn't know the people. Sure, I knew about Stan Petrovic, but only because he wore his surliness like clown makeup. I didn't know the place or the people because I hadn't wanted to know. I held myself apart. I didn't know anything about the women I slept with. It wasn't like they didn't try to tell me. Christ, Janice Nadir would've told me the pet names for her vagina had I shown the least bit of interest.

"You going to eat your burger?" Jim asked, stuffing a handful of gravy fries in his mouth. "You seem kinda distracted."

I bit into the burger only to heave it right back up. The meat was cold and raw. When I looked up, I saw Stan Petrovic, his eyes twinkling, his crooked lips bent into a smug, self-congratulatory smile. I removed the top of the bun from the burger to confirm what my taste buds and gag reflex had already told me.

"What an asshole!" Jim jumped up like he'd done that day in class.

I grabbed his arm. "Sit down, Jim. This is my fight."

As I walked up to Petrovic, I took notice of what a nasty package he really was. The bad knees, the alcohol and bitterness, the fried and fatty food had turned him into a pitiable-looking fat man; but I knew there was an angry, second team All-American linebacker still living inside his blubber suit. By the time I got close to him, he'd swapped his smile for a sneer. He was puffed up, the fingers on both his hands twitching in anticipation. The diner was silent except for the bubbling and hissing of oil in the fry-o-lator.

I'd done a little boxing in college—just enough to know that fights never went the way you expected and to know when I was going to get my ass kicked. Short of a miracle, I was about to get my ass kicked.

"Hey, hero, what you think you're gonna do to me? I ain't no college kid with a gun in his hand and there ain't no SWAT team here to save your faggoty ass."

"I guess I could kick you in the balls, but that would require you to have some."

He snickered, but said nothing. His now clenching fists were going to do the rest of his talking, so I let mine get in the first word. I feinted with my left shoulder, but threw my right hand. Stan lifted his arms to protect his face as my trunk twisted to power the punch. Too bad for him I wasn't going for his head. I caught him flush in the liver with the hook. I figured the liver was as good a target as any. Given his intake of vodka and deep fried food, it must've been foie gras central.

That bent him over and the rush of air that went out of him was pretty impressive. But instead of following up, I did what I always do: I spent too much time playing to the crowd. Stan, still bent over, charged me, his left shoulder burying itself in my ribs. I tried keeping my feet, but it was no good. I was going down. My left hand spun off a counter stool and that was my last moment of verticality.

Petrovic was on me, pulling at my legs trying to get me out from between the stools. But I'd hitched my arms around the stool poles on either side of me to anchor myself and I kicked out my legs. My left heel connected with something hard. His jaw, I hoped. Whatever it was just pissed him off. He gave up on my legs and brought his right forearm down across my diaphragm and abdomen. Something big and spongy, my left lung probably, caught in my throat and I gasped for air. Suddenly that first punch I threw didn't seem like such a brilliant move. I tried turning on my side and curled into a ball like a hedgehog, but I lacked protective quills. Petrovic kicked me in the back, but it didn't land with much force as his foot deflected off one of the poles.

The front door opened; the string of sleigh bells tied to the handle clanged against the glass. I felt a gush of cool, fresh air and I saw a pair of polished black boots walking my way. Christmas coming early. Maybe Santa was bringing me a shotgun.

"That's enough, Stan!" Black Boots barked. Petrovic disagreed, stomping instead of kicking me. This time his shoe didn't deflect off anything but my ribs. Good thing I already couldn't breathe or it might've really hurt.

"Enough!"

I recognized the voice. It was the deputy sheriff who'd been at the Air Force base three nights ago. I guess he was taking a break from high school skirt patrol. Still, I was wary enough of Stan to brace myself against another stomp. It never came. Arms were pulling me up and I was standing—well, sort of standing—between Deputy Dog and Jim Trimble. I managed some shallow breaths.

"You all right, Professor Weiler?" the deputy wanted to know.

Do I look all right, you yokel motherfucker? "Fine. I'm fine." I straightened myself out and noticed Petrovic about ten feet away over by the front door. He was snarling. I can't say that I'd ever actually seen a human snarling before. "Somebody get Stan a bone or some Liv-A-Snaps or something before he goes batshit."

"Fuck you, asshole. This isn't over."

"Shut up, Stan," the deputy said. "And, Professor, I think we could use a little less of your lip at the current moment. Okay?"

"Okay."

"Now what the hell was goin' on here?"

"Nothing," I said.

"Stan?"

"Nothing."

"So, that's the way it's gonna be, huh?" the deputy said, shaking his head. "Have it your way, boys, but next time I'll haul both your asses in. Professor, why don't you take this opportunity to depart?" It wasn't a suggestion.

Jim made sure to keep himself between Petrovic and me as I walked out.

"Remember, hero, this ain't over," Stan said as we passed.

I caught a glimpse of Jim's face. He wanted me to say something. I could see it in his eyes and for some reason it was suddenly important for me not to disappoint the kid.

"Yeah, you're right, Stan. It isn't over. You started it, but I'll finish it. Next time it won't be me they're peeling off the floor. Remember that."

Out on the street, I took a few deep lungfuls of Brixton's best. Jim was holding on to my elbow, walking me away from the diner.

"That was great in there, Kip," he said.

"The part where I curled up in a ball like an insect?"

"The first punch. Do you know how many people in this town would like to pop Stan Petrovic one? You actually did it."

"Yeah, Jim, but you heard him in there. He's going to kick my ass sooner or later."

"Or, like you said, maybe you'll kick his."

"That was just my anger talking."

"No way," he gushed. "Are you on campus tomorrow?"

"Freshman Comp at nine fifteen," I said.

"Meet me by the student union after class."

"Why?"

"So we can go hit some balls."

Eight

Fifteen Minutes

My writing didn't suck. I couldn't believe it, but it really didn't suck. I read and reread and re-reread the pages I put down in between the long bouts in bed with the St. Pauli Girl. It didn't suck because what I was reading wasn't recognizable as the Kipster's, and that was all to the good. The Kipster was dead, not risen, and I was all that remained in his place.

The Kipster was a cynical bastard, full of high sentence, but never obtuse: a poet, a prince looking down upon the great unwashed with only contempt. He was above it all, untouchable and untouched. He was master of his instrument, so much so that it was all an inside joke to him. I didn't recognize the writing because it came from a very different place than from where the Kipster's art had come. It all came too easily for the Kipster, which is why he foundered when the words stopped coming to him on the cusp of the '90s. I had nothing to hold on to but the empty shell of the Kipster. His old protagonists were whimsies and straw men, put up like bowling pins only to be knocked down. They were sacrifices meant as meat for elitist snobs. His protagonists were soulless, ironic follies to be run up the flagpole like a fat girl's underthings.

Other than a complete loss of talent, one of the reasons I'd managed but seven first lines in all these years was the very nature of the man I thought of as McGuinn. He was a real man, not a construct. There was nothing about his bloody and violent life that even remotely resembled Kant Huxley's or any of the other cool-boy protagonists that had flowed from the Kipster's fingertips. The other things that had daunted me for so long were setting and form.

I wasn't a biographer, not in temperament or by training, but what McGuinn had given me was basically the details for the biography of a murderer. The killings—their mechanics, the reasons and rationalizations behind them, the stories of the victims—as fascinating as some readers might have found those things, weren't what interested me. Nor, do I think, were they what motivated McGuinn. It was his emotional journey and evolution from teenage murderer to soldier to assassin to target that got my attention. Besides, I'd spent all of two months in Ireland and the North. I didn't know the place or the people, and I certainly had only a superficial understanding of the conflict. I'd been a glorified tourist, nothing more. A mostly drunk one at that. Even if I'd been up to the writing, I didn't understand the context.

Just because I lost my talent for writing didn't mean I'd lost my instinct for good work and a good story. I still had an eye and ear for fine ingredients even if I had lost the recipe. And McGuinn's life had all the best ingredients. Whenever I imagined the book, I imagined it as fiction with Terry McGuinn in an alien setting. What could I have added to something set on the streets of Belfast? Nothing. If I wanted to give meaning to this man's journey, he needed to be a stranger in a strange land. But until the St. Pauli Girl brought me to that old hangar and anointed me with gunpowder, I had no idea of where that strange land would be. It was those shots—the sight of Jim Trimble's still body and the fat kid rolling around, the church pews, the spray of beer, the landscape of Jim's scars—that had, after so long, helped me to arrive at a destination.

What a perfect concept, I thought. An assassin being hunted by his enemies and his brothers alike ends up hiding in an unremarkable place in the center of nowhere. Yet even in this netherworld, he cannot escape the blood. The contrast was delicious, because the violence McGuinn finds isn't born of passion or religious hatred, but of boredom and sport. A man who was certain he understood violence and blood as well as any who had ever lived is thrust into a world he can't fathom. Now that was something I understood, being exiled in a world that defied my comprehension.

It was a place to start, but I wouldn't be satisfied to simply use what little I had seen at Hardentine Air Force Base, nor did I want to confine my characters in a concrete bunker. No, the fictionalized McGuinn needed to operate against the backdrop of the real world, even if it was a withered and tiny speck of the world. He was too large a character to stick in a box somewhere and duel like a gentleman. Red crosses on dirty T-shirts might have been dramatic enough for the boys and girls from Brixton, but they would not suffice for a killer like McGuinn. In my novel, there would be blood, lots of blood, and very little of it spilled for a good cause. First things first. I had to get McGuinn involved with the wrong people. No better way to do that, I thought, than with the noir conceit of a beautiful woman.

He thought he'd go feckin' mad, did Terry McGuinn. He could put a rifle round through a man's ear hole at several hundred meters or build an IED out of household chemicals and a plastic bottle, but he was banjaxed by his loneliness. It was his curse to have been born a social sort. The Prods would say it was a curse he was born at all. When he'd been forced to lay low in the States in the past, there was always someone to share a pint of the black stuff. As an honored soldier of the Republic, he was seen to. Now he was a scurrying rat, hiding from the shadows in his bedsit above a novelty shop. And just lately the walls of the bedsit had been closing in on him.

Och ocon—"woe is me" were the words that had recently seeped into his thoughts, and he despised himself for letting them in. McGuinn was not a man to rue the trail of blood that followed him across the Atlantic, nor to pray the rosary before a shrine to his victims. Soldiers and innocents, it was all the same shite. In the end, we all got off the train at the same station. But even assassins fall prey to the blues and he had 'em fierce. "Jaysus," he thought. What he wouldn't give for a pint and a chat without having to look over his shoulder.

Some of the wee Mexicans at the slaughterhouse were friendly sorts, though nary a one spoke twenty words of English. McGuinn could manage a bit of Basque, but his Spanish was crap. No matter. He couldn't envision himself and a bunch of Pedros sitting around passing the poteen. Besides, those lads were as busy keeping their heads down as was he.

He was so wrecked, he'd gone out of pocket for a bit of flange. Never before had he paid for a woman. A point of pride, that. No longer. McGuinn had killed in coldest blood without giving a toss, but could not forgive himself for the sin of paying for a piece of skirt.

"Escort service, me arse," he snarled, shredding the postcard advert into confetti. "In the photos they all look like Christie Brinkley. Bollix! When they showed up at your door they look like buckets of snot." But desperation improved their looks and never did he turn them away.

Christ on his cross, now he was talking to himself. Worse, he was showing his age. Though still a fine-looking flah, Christie Brinkley was older than his own self. He had to get out of there, now. Taking a bullet could be no worse than this lonely hell. He tucked the Sig in the small of his back and walked out into the night.

The first two pubs he tried were woeful disappointments—as if that was news in this town, the disappointment mecca of America—but McGuinn thought he spotted some promise in the twitchy neon sign above Ralph and Jim's Bar and Grill. Dark lit and moody with a single ceiling fan that turned with the urgency of a sloth, the establishment was not without its charms. The bar surface was so pitted it was positively lunar and the red vinyl snugs were held together by duct tape and prayers.

McGuinn waved a twenty to get the bartender's attention. "A scotch neat and a burger with chips."

"I can do the scotch," the barman said, "but the kitchen's been closed since Jim took sick."

"And when was that?"

"The second Eisenhower administration. Ralph and Jim were dead before I was born."

McGuinn paid for his scotch and moved over to the juke-box, which was a bit of a revelation itself. That it was an authentic juke with real vinyl to play was shock enough, but that it contained Thin Lizzy tunes was brilliant. He stuffed in quarters.

"Tonight there's gonna be a jailbreak," he sang along, pumping his fist in the air.

"Who is this?" A siren's voice interrupted his reverie.

The voice belonged to a diabolical blond with untamable tresses and eyes that fairly glowed blue in the dim-lit bar. She was thirty years his junior with curves in abundance where the Almighty had planned them to go. Her skirt was short; her legs long and tanned. And her smile was white and inviting, but it was her eyes that held McGuinn's attention.

"Have ya never heard of Thin Lizzy?"

"Tin Lizzy?"

McGuinn laughed his first honest laugh since he'd arrived in this beshitten town and there was more than a bit of nervousness to it.

"That's Thin Lizzy—T-h-i-n—Thin. Great Irish band."

"Like U2?"

"Not likely. Phil Lynott was a Dubliner, not a poser like Bono. Citizen of the world, me arse. He's a singer in a feckin' rock band, not Ghandi." He finished his drink in a gulp. "I'm empty. Can I get ya a drink?"

"A Bud."

"What's yer name, darlin'?"

"Zoe."

"Lovely name for a stunning woman," McGuinn said, feeling almost human again. "Guard the juke with yer life. Any bollocks tries to play U2, come fetch me."

As he stepped back to the bar and beyond the power of Zoe's eyes, his radar popped on. Something was amiss. Of all the lads in the bar, why, he wondered, had the looker approached him, the one fella near old enough to be her aul da? Somehow he didn't think it was his thinning hair, pot-belly, or Phil Lynott's singing that had called to her.

Waiting patiently to be served, McGuinn used the mirror behind the bar to study what was going on at his back. The fair Zoe kept a poker face, and a beautiful one it was.

Her focus seemed fully on the juke, but he knew that if he watched her long enough, she would give herself away. One way or another, he supposed, women were always giving themselves away. Ah, just there, a subtle swivel of her head to the left and a shift in her gaze. As slight as her movements were, Zoe might just as well have painted a bull's-eye on the poor fooker's chest . . .

So entranced by what I'd written, I nearly jumped out of my skin when the phone rang. The phone hadn't done much ringing since the day Janice Nadir moved upstate.

I picked up after catching my breath. "Yeah."

"You're such an asshole, Weiler. Don't you ever return phone calls?"

Technically, I guess Meg Donovan was still my agent, a position her colleagues no doubt coveted as much as receiving placebos in a late-stage cancer study. Although I hadn't seen her in years, Meg was still more friend than agent, really. She was my only remaining link to the Kipster.

"It was you who called?" I asked, pretending I'd noticed the red message light flashing. I hadn't.

"You haven't listened to the message yet?"

"Come on, Donovan. You know how it is with me and the phone. The last time someone called with good news, the Mets won the World Series."

"You're an asshole."

"Yeah, well, I've spent the better part of my life lending credence to that assertion."

"Shut up and listen. Your second fifteen minutes of fame might pay off."

"A reality show? Survival of the Fittest Has-beens? I'll kick Webster's little black ass."

"Very cute, but no. Besides, my money would be on the dwarf."

"Isn't it your job to be on my side, Meg?"

"It's a lonely place, being on your side. My job's to tell you the truth."

"Agents and the truth, now there's unexplored territory."

"If you haven't managed to alienate me after all these years, you're not going to do it now."

"Okay, Meg, what are we talking about?"

"A book deal."

Book deal: those two words made me weak. If I'd been born with a vagina, it would have been wet.

"What kind of book deal?" I asked.

"Haskell Brown at Travers Legacy has had a big Eighties retrospective series in the works for a year or so and—"

"A year, huh? And this is the first I'm hearing about it?"

"Don't be a dunce cap, Weiler."

"So I wasn't part of the original retrospective."

"Very good. You should take the *Jeopardy* home challenge. Now can we talk money?"

"Who was in the original deal?"

"Don't do this to yourself, Kip."

"If I don't, who will? Names, ranks, and serial numbers, please."

"The usual suspects: Bart, Nutly, Kate Silva, Marty Castronieves ..."

I couldn't believe how much hearing those names hurt me. Surely the omission of my name should have come as no shock. I think maybe it was that I knew the Kipster had once been able to write circles around them all, even his Highness, Marty Castronieves.

"Earth to Planet Weiler, are you reading me? Over."

"Sorry, Meg. I was lost there for a minute. Do the others know I wasn't part of the original package?"

She hesitated. "Come on, Kip, of course they know. Publishing makes *Oedipus Rex* look like a play about distant cousins. Now can we stop talking about what was and get to what is? This could be a nice paycheck for us both."

"Sure."

Meg wasn't exaggerating. Travers Legacy was willing to pay me big bucks for my backlist, which—not having published a novel in about fifteen years—was all the wares I had to sell.

"They're going to do big print runs on your first three novels and might send you guys out on tour. Lots of press, lots of stores, even late night TV. Think of it: you, Bart, and Nutly back on the road together, and you could get away from that dreadful Garden State Brickface Community College."

"Yeah, it could be just like one of those British Invasion tours with Freddie and the Dreamers, Gerry and the Pacemakers, and the Swinging Blue Jeans."

"Weiler, this is your chance to get out of Dodge."

"Maybe I don't want to get out of Dodge."

"What?"

"It's a rights deal, not a book deal," I said.

"It's a money deal."

"I don't know."

"What's not to know? No one's pounding down the door for you, honey. I'm the one who parlayed your saving those kids into this deal and, trust me, it wasn't easy. You may have really straightened yourself out, but it's the Kipster people remember in this town. Around here, you're still that boorish, coked-up horn dog who turned his silk purse talent into a sow's asshole."

"And," I said, "if the sales numbers were good on *Clown Car Bounce*, *The Devil's Understudy*, and *Curley Takes Five*, they'd still be lining up to suck my dick."

"If my bowling ball had square corners, it wouldn't roll. If, if, if..."

"Look, Meg, I'm not ungrateful and I know it's a miracle you still talk to me after all the bullshit and heartache I put you through, but can you stall them a little while? Tell them I want to be sure I can handle the road again."

"Fine. I'll tell them whatever I have to, but other than pissing away a lot of my hard work and a fat payday, why exactly am I doing it?"

"So you can think of a way to have the deal include a clause for a new book."

There was dead silence on the other end of the phone. At least I didn't hear her collapse to the floor or beg me to call 911.

"A new book?" she said at last. "You're writing again?"

"Yes, sort of."

"Can I see it?"

"Not yet."

"So you're willing to blow the biggest money offer we've had since MTV actually played videos because you're sort of writing again?"

"Something like that, yeah."

"This ain't old times, Kip. I've got lots of other clients who pay my various mortgages, but you're all you've got."

"I know."

"There won't be any more offers like this."

"I know that too."

"Okay, I'll ask, but they might think you're being difficult like the Kipster they all know and hate. This might queer the whole deal. You understand that? Are you sure this is what you want me to do?"

"Strangely enough, Meg, it is."

When she clicked off at the other end, my hands were shaking. It had been many years since I'd burned a bridge, and I remembered it being much easier as the Kipster.

Nine

Lipitor

About an hour after I got off the phone with Meg, the St. Pauli Girl showed up on my doorstep with three bags of groceries. Did I have mixed feelings? Fuck no, especially when I saw her smile. It was like a love letter in the *Times Book Review.* Those smiles, the lighting up when you came into view, the brush of fingers against cheek, the first desperate hug, that first kiss are more powerful than a locomotive. But the flip side is always more insipid, because you don't notice the individual aspects of attraction when they're going, only when they're gone. You can feel yourself falling in love, not out of it. By the time you've noticed the fading, all the color's been bleached out.

Love? *Who was I kidding?* I'd be bored with Renee soon enough. I always got bored. It was in my nature. My fame, even the frayed and threadbare variety with which I was now afflicted, guaranteed me a steady stream of eager young women like Renee or bored women like Janice Nadir. I may well have been a self-absorbed prick, but I wasn't so shut off that I didn't recognize the underlying current of anger in my boredom. Every first kiss, every orgasm—genuine or suspect—was a reminder of persistence and loss: the persistence of my inconsequential fame and the loss of my talent.

Still, I smiled back at the St. Pauli Girl. She had already occupied my attention longer than anyone in my sorry tenure at Brixton, with the exception of Janice Nadir. And why not? Renee was easy to look at, fucked like a demon, and was as yet untouched by the bitterness of age. No pillow talk of limp penises for the St. Pauli Girl. My inevitable boredom didn't prevent me from enjoying the onset of romance, no matter how brief or ill-fated. I was an asshole, not anhedonic. And when I smiled back at Renee, I was smiling as much at the three bags of groceries as at her.

Other women had tried this sort of mothering, you-look-like-you-could-use-a-good-home-cooked-meal approach on me before with little or no success. Sometimes I enjoyed the meal, sometimes the sex. Seldom both. On those most rare occasions when I did, my partner didn't. Janice Nadir tried this routine early on, but abandoned it almost immediately. She was a bright woman. I hoped the St. Pauli Girl would catch on quickly too.

When I opened the door for her, she put the groceries down on the table, felt my smile with her fingertips, and kissed me hard on the mouth. I returned the favor.

"What's on the menu?"

"Me," she said without a hint of guile. "I thought we could work up an appetite."

Smart girl.

●

The fucking was spectacular, if not quite as ferocious as it had been the last few nights. As soon as we hit the sheets, I realized I had been too quick to dismiss the meaning of the grocery bags. Even as we were otherwise engaged, I detected subtle, barely perceptible signs that tenderness was already seeping into the relationship. There was warmth in her sighs, less urgency in my thrusting, gentle caresses. And when the St. Pauli Girl nuzzled her cheek against my chest and fairly pulled my arm over her back for a post-coital cuddle, I was sure of it. I managed not to run screaming. It was actually kind of nice. Maybe it was too early and there was still too much ground to cover for me to get bored.

She made us grilled chorizo, avocado, queso fresco omelets with chipotle salsa and garnished with chopped cilantro. This wasn't your typical Brixton fare, not by a long shot. Brixton was your basic ham, eggs, grits, scrapple, bacon, American cheese, and ketchup kind of place. Around here, if you didn't need to chase it down with Lipitor and baby aspirin, it wasn't food. And when she pulled the bottle of fine French Chardonnay from my fridge, I knew the St. Pauli Girl meant business. She might've been able to scrape together the omelet ingredients from stores in surrounding towns, but she definitely had to go to Stateline to get the wine. During dinner, I had actually reached my hand across the table and placed it atop hers.

"I heard you had some trouble at the diner today," she said, while doing the dishes.

"You talk to Jim?"

"Come on, Ken, the whole town knew five minutes after you left Stan's place. Are you okay?"

"You would know."

She walked away from the sink, threaded herself into my arms and sat in my lap. "Much better than okay," she whispered, her lips touching my ear. Then she kissed me gently. When our lips separated, she just sort of stared at me.

"Stan Petrovic isn't the kind of man you should be messing with."

"*He* messed with me."

"I heard, but you punched him."

An involuntary smile appeared on my face. "I guess I did."

Renee frowned. "If Jim wasn't there, would you have . . . you know, would you have done that?"

I jerked my head back. "What are you getting at?"

Her body stiffened. "Nothing." She stood up and went back to the sink to finish the dishes. "I'm not getting at anything. I just don't want you to get hurt."

I walked up behind her and put my arms around her. "Too late for that."

"I guess."

I told her about the call from Meg Donovan and the Travers Legacy deal. That seemed to excite her.

"They offered you *how* much?"

"You heard me. It's a lot more than I make teaching here."

"And what did you say?"

"Maybe."

"Why didn't you just take it?"

"I'm not sure I can explain it in a way that will make much sense to you."

Renee actually slammed the dishes in the sink and pulled out of my grasp. "I'm young, not stupid."

"I'm sorry. That's not what I meant. The thing is I'm not sure I can explain it to myself in a way that makes any real sense."

"Try."

"It's not that I don't want the money. I do. It's that all the other people included in this deal, they're still writing. Go into any book store, go on Amazon and you'll find their books. Mine are so long out of print you can't even find them on the discount racks. My agent got me included in the deal because Frank Vuchovich got himself killed."

She turned to me, brushed the back of her hand across my cheek. "But it's still your work, Ken. What does it matter why someone buys it or reads it as long as they read it?"

I winked. "Spoken like an agent. You could have a bright future in the business."

"Brixtonians don't have futures."

Christ, what do you say to that?

She saw the question in my eyes and rescued me. "You didn't answer me. Why does it matter to you why they included your books in the deal?"

"Because in New York, I'm still a joke. No, I'm not even a joke. I'm a punch line to a bad joke."

"You're not a joke to me," she said in that earnest way only the young can and not sound ridiculous. The St. Pauli Girl rested her head on my shoulder. "You're here, not there. I can't hear them laughing."

"I can. I couldn't before Meg called, but I can now."

"Listen, Ken . . . you should take the money and get as far away from here as fast as you can."

"Hey, you, where's this coming from all of a sudden?" I asked, staring into her eyes. There was a depth to them I'd never seen in twenty-year-old eyes. "If I leave now, where would that leave us?"

"Us? I told you, I'm young, not stupid. Take the money, get out of this place, and never look back."

"Don't worry, kiddo, nothing's going to happen with Stan Petrovic. He's a bully. I've had the shit kicked out of me by better men than him. Besides, I stood up to him. I'll be fine."

"Is that what Jim says?"

"What's this got to do with Jim?"

"Just forget it," she said. "I've got to go."

She grew quiet, quickly finished the dishes, and left, but I knew she'd be back. They always came back. All except for Amy.

Ten

Magician's Hat

I met Jim after school as agreed, my old golf bag and clubs slung over my shoulder. He drove a beat-up Ford F-150 pickup. There wasn't anything unusual in that. Pickups were *de rigueur* in Brixton. Took me a year to figure out that the parking lot at Wal-Mart wasn't the staging area for a monster truck show. I didn't say much of anything after I got into the cab. I figured to let the kid do the talking. He did some, but he was decidedly less expansive about the essential nature of handguns than he had been previously. He seemed far more interested in discussing what a prick Stan Petrovic had been and how cool it was that I stood up to him.

Even as Jim bragged on me, the St. Pauli Girl's question rattled around in my head: *"If Jim wasn't there, would you have . . . you know, done that?"* Smart question, that. She knew and I knew the answer was no.

Hero worship is a potent drug. I knew firsthand that it could make both the worshipper and worshippee do some fairly risky things. Just ask the assistant editors and PR girls who'd slept with me, or the society fans who fucked me in bathrooms at parties with their husbands in the next room. Sometimes I wonder what those PR girls, the assistant editors, and the society dames think of me these days. There probably isn't enough chewing gum or mouthwash in the world for them to rinse away the taste of those memories, if they remember at all. I laughed to myself, imagining them telling their middle-aged friends about having blown the great Kip Weiler. *Kip who?* Exactly, ladies. Kip who?

"What are you smiling at, Kip?" Jim asked, smiling himself.

"Just reminiscing."

"Do you think about the old days much?"

"More recently. Since Frank Vuchovich was killed, I've been remembering things I haven't thought about for a long time."

"Like about your dad."

It was as if he'd hit me with a steel pipe. "How did you—you know about that?"

"That he killed himself and that you found him? Yeah, uh huh, I know. Sometimes I think I know more about your life than I do about my own, Kip. If life was college, you'd be my major. So why did your dad do it?"

"Because he was a miserable person. I don't know. He didn't leave a note. Just like him too, not to leave a note. I think he did that just to torture my mother."

We didn't talk again for quite a while.

Every time the truck hit a bump, my old golf clubs smacked into the sidewalls of the pickup box. Not that I really gave a shit about those clubs. Although they weren't quite as old as my brown corduroy blazer, they were woefully out of date. Jim noticed the racket too.

He said, "I guess I should have tied your clubs down."

"They're not my clubs anymore. They're yours now."

"Huh?"

"I didn't know what we were going to do today, but I didn't think you really wanted to go hit golf balls, Jim. If I took a swing in anger after all these years, I'd dislocate both shoulders. I dug those old clubs out for you . . . as a gift."

He pulled the truck over to the side of the road. *Uh oh.* I was a manipulative asshole, but I was much more adept at it with women. I knew just how to play them in the key of me. I was on less steady ground with men. Luckily, he didn't get that goofy *can-I-blow-you-now* look on his face.

"I can have your clubs?"

"If you want them, they're yours."

"Thanks, Kip." He shook the life out of my hand.

"You're welcome. I'm happy to do it."

And I was.

I should have gotten rid of those golf clubs a long time ago. I'd shed every other vestige of my old life except my car. Strange, the things a man clings to. I remembered all too well the last time I had used my clubs. Back then, "CC" at the end of a place name meant country club and not community college. I was teaching at Columbia, my writing career aimed squarely at the abyss. Things with Amy were deteriorating, and the end of my time at Ferris, Ledoux was at hand. Meg Donovan, in a misguided attempt to salvage what was left of my career, had arranged for me to meet with Peter Moreland III, an up-and-coming editor at the Travers Group. His rise through the ranks wasn't hurt by the fact that his family was a majority stockholder in Travers's parent company.

When he called, Moreland was all good cheer and WASPy old-boy charm. He was polite, self-deprecating, and flattered the hell out of me. He just loved Moira Blanco, but supposed a change of editors might do me some good. Chemistry in publishing, he noted, was a fickle thing. He even seemed willing to turn a blind eye to my recent coke-fueled self-sabotage. He said he always appreciated my edginess and hoped his editing could help re-sharpen it.

"Why don't you come up to the club on Sunday? Oh, and please bring the missus," he'd said as if an afterthought.

Afterthought, my balls. Looking back, I can't point to any one thing he said or did after our round of eighteen that betrayed his interest in Amy. He even had the good taste to keep a Daughter of the American Revolution centerfold by his side. Her name was like Zoe Gates-Tilton or Bates-Swinton or some such thing. Bart Meyers would have referred to her as a shiksa goddess.

Moreland didn't ignore Amy. He was properly attentive. He knew her work and that led to a discussion of her more well-known contemporaries. It was as polite and civil a discussion of painting as I'd ever heard. In retrospect, the chat between Peter and Amy may not have been all that polite because I really didn't hear much of it. I was jonesing like mad and my internal voice kept at me to order another scotch or take a run to the bathroom for a toot. To distract myself from my addictional callings, I pondered the full shape and color of the fair Zoe Swinton-Tilton's assertive nipples. The distraction was fleeting because I was scared shitless at the idea of talking future books with Moreland. This was before I'd met the man I would come to think of as McGuinn. Besides, for all my legendary debauchery, I never actually cheated on Amy while she was present. To show you just how fucked up I was, I used to think I deserved credit for that.

Amy recognized the signs of me falling apart and tried valiantly to steer Peter's conversation to my work. She had, by one means or another, been trying to rescue me from my self-destructiveness for years. It wasn't as if Peter Moreland didn't attempt to follow my wife's lead. He tried several times to engage me in talk of new projects, which in turn led me to order another scotch and to turn my boorishness up another notch. Only after I began to speculate aloud about whether Zoe shaved or waxed did things disintegrate.

In the car on the way home Amy asked for a divorce. I don't remember my exact response because I was so thoroughly wasted. I vaguely recall begging her to stick it out with me for a few more years. Junkies get skilled at begging. I remember that she started crying and told me that I couldn't afford her and that she could no longer afford me. She moved into her Tribeca studio that Tuesday night. I think I was at Indiana University when I heard she'd married Moreland.

Jim must've noticed the sick look on my face. "Something wrong?"

"Not now. That's the problem with reminiscing."

"What is?"

"Starts out good, ends badly."

"I know what you mean."

I had seen Jim with his shirt off. The scars on his body from his dad's belt gave me confidence that he knew exactly what I meant.

"We're here," he said, pulling the old Ford off the dirt road we'd been on for the last several minutes. "Come on, Kip."

We were parked on a low bluff near a waterfall, its ambient spray misting the pickup's windshield. From the foot of the falls, the river narrowed and the water churned white as it was squeezed into a smaller course and rushed over large boulders that jutted out of the riverbed. Tall stands of reeds and weepy grasses that had begun to turn a dormant fall-brown stood silent guard along the banks. Except for a huge clearing just beneath the bluff, old pine forests lined both sides of Crooked River and extended well up into the hills as far as the eye could see. With the warming sun overhead and the strong pine scent filling up the air, it was difficult not to find this little corner of Brixton serene and beautiful.

Stepping out of the truck cab, I took an icy cold spray in the face and my ears were assaulted by the roar of the river. After a few seconds, the din of the falls and rapids receded into background noise. I was conscious of Jim watching me.

"Pretty here, isn't it?"

"That it is, Jim. Thanks for showing it to me."

"Just give me a second," he said, unlocking the steel tool carrier affixed to the front end of the truck box. Jim pulled out a stained and faded blue Air Force duffel bag that was as patched as the skin on his back and belly. There was a thin rectangular area near the handle of the bag that had been neatly colored over with a black marking pen. My bet was the Colonel's name was under the black marker. I didn't need to be a seer to guess what was in the bag. "This way." He motioned up the hill. "Come on."

The low bluff was the last flat bit of land my feet touched for the next ten minutes. We spent that time walking up into the hills above the falls and rapids. I slipped a few times on the pine straw carpet thick beneath the trees. Jim seemed to enjoy my unsteadiness, snickering and yelling for me to catch up.

By the time we got to the little clearing between the trees, I was in a full sweat and gasping for breath. Although I'd managed to maintain a fairly consistent weight over the years, I was completely out of shape and probably a good candidate for a massive coronary. Decades of cigarette smoking and drug and alcohol abuse had only enhanced my chances of an early death.

"You don't look so good."

"I feel worse than I look," I said.

"You oughta start running with me."

"I'll take it under advisement."

As I regained my composure, I noticed that the roar of the falls and rapids was somewhat muted, but still remarkably pronounced. I noticed too the old bullet scars on the surrounding trees, and the collection of beer cans, plastic soda bottles, and piles of spent casings. And there was a neatly stacked pile of wood partially covered by a tarp sitting in between some trees. The stack of wood seemed as out of place up here as the blockhouse had seemed in the hangar. Jim saw me staring at the pile.

"The ashes," he said, touching his index finger to his forehead, "from the chapel."

"The chapel? I'm confused."

He tapped his forehead again. "The white building. The other night, remember?"

"Oh, those ashes. Right. Everybody had that smudge."

"That wood is from the first tree we ever used for practice. It's what we burn for the ashes. Can't enter the chapel without the ashes."

"About that, I—"

"In time, Kip. In time. For now, are you ready to shoot?" he asked, reaching into the duffel bag.

I suppose somewhere I'd known this is what Jim was bringing me up here for and I'd be lying if I said I wasn't excited by the prospect. Since that night at the Air Force base, I'd wanted to get on the inside of whatever it was that had gone on in that white concrete blockhouse. In my bones I knew it was where McGuinn was headed in my book, but he couldn't get there if I didn't get there first. I had spent a lot of my time imagining the parameters of the world the character of McGuinn would be thrust into, a world even an experienced killer would find both comfortable and disorienting. Being out here with Jim was the gateway to that world.

I was also a little sick at the idea of shooting. I hadn't liked my father very much, but even if it had been a complete stranger's body I'd found that day when I was a kid, it would have fucked with my head. There's something about the cusp of teenagehood, when the hormones are just beginning to course through you, that makes you especially vulnerable. I sensed that once I took my first shot, there wouldn't be any going back. Maybe it was already too late to go back.

I pointed at the duffel. "That the Colonel's bag?"

"It is."

"What you got there?"

"This look familiar?" Jim asked, unzipping a black nylon and foam gun case.

"Yes, it does." I smiled in spite of myself, because what he held in his hand was a shiny version of the Colt Python that Frank Vuchovich had used to take my class hostage.

"It's nickel plated and newer than the one Frank had." He undid the trigger lock and handed it to me. "Go ahead, take a few shots."

I tried to recall how Bart had taught me to handle a pistol of this size. I held the big revolver with both hands, tried to relax, and squeezed one off. My arms jumped up and back. Brown bark splinters and pieces of juicy white pulp flew from the trunk of the tree about fifteen yards ahead of me. I got an instant reminder of the thunder that thing produced as the report echoed through the woods. Some birds took wing. Water tumbled down the falls. Wind blew back the tops of the trees. Nothing much changed except my heart rate. There it was again. I was rushing. The first snort of coke, the first taste of a woman, the first sip of scotch: every high is different, but somehow the same.

"Very good. Now watch what happens with the second shot," Jim said, that knowing smile on his face.

I took a few deep breaths and calmed myself, then aimed at the same tree and let go the second shot I'd ever taken. No splinters this time, only the echo.

"What happened?"

"Funny thing about shooting, Kip. Before you took your first shot, you didn't know how the Python would recoil. Once you knew, you anticipated. So even before you got the second shot off, you were pulling your arms back. The only thing you were in danger of hitting with that second round there was a red-tailed hawk in the wrong place at the wrong time. Don't fret. You'll get better."

I hoped so, but for now I was perfectly happy to play with all the Colonel's toys. I fired a Luger, a .38 Police Special, a .45 Browning, a .40 Glock, a Walther PPK, and a .25 Beretta. It didn't matter what I shot. I got that same rush every time. The Colonel's duffel bag was like a magician's hat. Each time Jim reached in, he seemed to pull out a different automatic or revolver. Whatever I fired and regardless of how badly I missed what I was aiming for, Jim assured me that I would get better.

"Amateur hour's over, Jim. Now let me see some real shooting," I said, reaching into the bag and handing him the Browning.

He positively beamed, as I knew he would, at the chance to show off for me. Jim surveyed the landscape, picking out a target.

"See that dried pine cone wedged in there between the branch and the trunk," he said, pointing the muzzle of the .45 at a tree about fifty feet away.

"I do, the one—"

Before I got the rest of the words out of my mouth, the round obliterated the pine cone. Shot after shot, no matter the weapon in his hand, Jim hit whatever he set his sights on. Then switching hands, he did much the same thing. He even took a few blind shots and hit most of his targets.

"I can make you better at this," he said, "but I don't think you'll ever get as good as me."

"This is fun, but why would I want to get as good as you?"

"Well, you don't really have to get as good as me, I guess; but you do have to get better, much better."

"Why?"

His expression went through several changes in the course of only a few seconds. At first, he seemed confused, then annoyed, and then he smiled as if finally understanding my question.

"The only reason we came up here was to get you better, so you can come back to the chapel."

"The white blockhouse?"

"Yeah, the chapel. You do want to go back there, don't you?"

He knew I did. A pusher always knows a junkie when he sees one.

"Absolutely."

"Well, Kip, you want to go back to the chapel again . . ." His voice dropped to a whisper as he picked up the little Beretta and snapped back its slide. "You have to shoot."

Then, to underline the point, he swung the freshly loaded Beretta around and put several bullets—*pop, pop, pop, pop, pop, pop, pop*—one on top of the next, into a nearby tree. That I was sitting against the tree and the shots might've parted my hair down the middle had they been a few inches lower was apparently beside the point.

"What the fuck!" I jumped to my feet, rushing on adrenalin. I poked my finger into the hole in the tree.

"*Reach out your hand and put it into my side,*" said Jim. "*Stop—*

"*—doubting and believe,*" I completed the sentence.

He looked pleased. "You remember?"

"From the other night and from the Bible," I said. "That's Jesus to Doubting Thomas. It's been a long time since I recalled scripture."

"Around here, Kip, it's all about the Good Book. It's the only hope people got."

"I imagine the spear in Jesus's side went in a lot deeper than these bullets," I said, only the tip of my finger disappearing into the tree.

He shrugged his shoulders. "What do you expect? It's a .25. No stopping power."

"That wasn't very funny, Jim, shooting above my head that way."

"It wasn't meant to be funny. I wanted to give you a taste of what it feels like to stand in the chapel. It's not fooling around."

"I figured that out the other night. I get it. You're not fucking around."

"So you want back in?" he asked, already knowing the answer.

Fuck yeah! "I guess."

"Then you have to shoot."

"Shoot?"

"Shoot."

I was still a bit dazed. As the effects of the adrenalin faded, I became conscious of the ringing in my ears and a profound weakness in my legs. I sat back down before gravity made the decision for me. I heard what the kid was saying, but couldn't make sense of it. He must've seen the puzzlement in my eyes.

"Shoot," he repeated, voice steady and calm, letting the clip slide out of the Beretta, racking the slide to make sure the little automatic was empty, tossing it into the duffel bag. "You have to face someone else down. That's the rule. No exceptions, not even for you."

"Renee?"

"Renee too. You know those little red crosses on our shirts?"

"I noticed them, yes," I answered. "I was going to ask you about them."

"Those crosses mark how many times we've shot and where we've been hit. If you look closely next time, you'll see that the holes in the shirt have been sewn together."

"But you let me in without—"

"You earned the right by what happened in class, but if you want back in—"

"—I have to shoot. I get it, Jim."

"You understand, but you don't get it. You won't get it until you raise a gun up at someone raising a gun up at you. Until then, regardless of how good you get out here, it won't matter."

"Kind of like hitting golf balls into a net," I heard myself say. "It's not the real thing."

He was beaming again. "Just like that, but different. There's more than just the shooting. The shooting is a means to an end, not an end in itself."

Guns, golf, and metaphysics: I figured we'd get back around to it eventually.

"But what about hunting?"

Jim's face went blank. He stood up, walked to the bag, fished out the Police Special, and loaded it with a single round. Without a word to me about his intentions, Jim scanned the woods. He raised up and fired. A few seconds later, a squirrel tumbled out of a nearby tree.

"My daddy was a cruel man, Kip, but he hated hunting. After we went out shooting a few times, I killed a squirrel like I did just now. The Colonel beat me senseless right out here in these woods. The Colonel liked to say that a sport's only a sport when both sides know they're playing. I never forgot that. For something to matter, both sides have to know." He looked back up into the trees. "Come on. It's getting late."

Eleven

Sissy Loads

My body wasn't as achy as it had been when we began. I had to confess that for the first time since coming to Brixton, I had a routine that required a level of engagement beyond sleepwalking. Having a routine of any kind made me feel less like a fraud. No mean feat, that, but Jim had bigger plans for his hero and his hero had had his fill of disappointing people. So for the last few weeks I was up at 5:00 A.M., writing. Jim would come by at 7:00 A.M. and we'd go running. We hadn't yet made it past a mile, but you wouldn't have been able to tell by the burning soreness in my legs. My lungs . . . forget my lungs. That first week I would begin gasping for breath when I heard the crunch of Jim's tires on the gravel driveway. Yet, there was something incredibly pleasing about the pain, about feeling anything beyond the drip, drip, dripping dull ache of regret for a life flushed down the shitter.

After classes, Jim would pick me up and we'd drive back to the spot above the falls to shoot. For now we worked with the little Beretta because he said it was the most easily tamed. Eventually, Jim felt confident enough in my shooting—or just crazy enough—to stand a few feet to the left or right of the target I was aiming at. I think I probably flinched more than he did. The flinching scared him more than the bullets.

What Jim couldn't know was how hard I was rushing. I was flinching because I could not slow my heart. With the haze and sharp tang of the gun smoke filling the air, it was all I could do not to swoon. I was in four places at once: here, the lake house, my classroom, and the chapel. With each shot I took I was everywhere. It was like one continuous gestalt dream: I was the bloodied curtains, the broken glass, the ashes, the guns, and the bullets. I was my father, Frank, Jim, the fat kid. I was me, watching.

Each squeeze of the trigger was a burst of adrenalin, every shot had a life of its own. Although I could not control my pulse rate, the world seemed to slow down. The more I fired, the slower it got. I swore I could watch the ejected shells spinning, tumbling in space as if gravity were more a suggestion than a law of nature.

When I'd grabbed Frank Vuchovich's gun, I had opened a portal to a different universe, one I thought I'd never get back to; but here I was at the event horizon, almost at the point of falling into the black hole. And I wanted into the darkness. I wanted to reclaim some dignity and I knew in my gut this was the way to do it. It had already fired me up so much that I had produced more work in a few weeks than I had produced in fifteen years, and better work than I had managed in twenty.

"Kip, relax. You keep clenching up like that, you'll hit me. Those bullets are sissy loads, so don't worry too much. There's less powder in the cartridge, so there's less of an explosion and less power at impact. If you hit me with one of them, you probably won't kill me, but it'll require more treatment than rubbing some dirt on it."

I guess I relaxed a little after that because he didn't say another word about it. When we took a break, he rolled up the left leg of his jeans. There was a pink splotch of scar tissue like a wad of chewed bubble gum a few inches up his shin from the top of his boot. His face was aglow with pride.

"If you *had* hit me, Kip, it wouldn't be the first time. What you and me were just doing, you shooting and me standing over near the target, that's how this started out," he said. "There's just something about standing across from someone holding a gun in your direction, even if it's not pointed right at you. It's . . . I don't know how to put it in words. It's like you're scared, but alive, really alive for the first time. And once you feel that, there's no going back. Do you know what I mean?"

Did I. Anyone who's experienced the first fifteen minutes of a good cocaine high knows that feeling. Problem is you spend the rest of the night doing more and more blow getting less and less high. You try to get back to that first rush, but you can't. You can't no matter how hard you try and believe me, I tried.

"This," he said, rubbing the scar like a lucky rabbit's foot, "was the best thing that ever happened to me."

"How do you figure?"

"Opened up my eyes."

"To what?"

"To everything."

"Everything?"

He laughed. "What I'm saying is that I was reborn."

"Jim, no offense, but getting shot in the shin isn't exactly a near-death experience."

"Near enough," he said, his face cold and serious. "Look, I know I'm just some dumb hick from a little mining town, but it doesn't mean I don't think about big things. Before I got shot, I was dead inside. Everybody's dead inside in a place like this. It's a world of the dead. You think we all don't know that community college is a dead end? But what else is there for us growing up around here? We're just wasting time until we get a job mining coal or logging or we enlist. There's no great challenges waiting for us. None of us is growing stem cells in the cellar in our spare time. Our world is built on nothingness. There are no dreams anymore.

"Listen, Kip, people in these parts, they have that ignorant faith in God. In spite of everything they see around them in this fucked-up place where there's nothing waiting for them at the end of the rainbow, they believe. Well, for me, for those of us who shoot, it's a lot easier to believe in guns than God. Guns don't make empty promises, and they answer our prayers. Out here, in this dead world, we're nothing. Look at the bunch of us: a guy who works in a copy center, a cook, an ugly girl. Who are we? Where are we going? Nowhere. But when we're inside the walls of the chapel, we matter and it's the rest of the world that's insignificant. Every gesture has meaning for us. We're only really alive with guns in our hands. Like you wrote in *Flashing Pandora*, there's no meaning of good without bad, no light without the dark. For us, there's no life without the threat of dying."

"A man should think about big things," I said.

He had no doubt spent hours preparing this little speech and had waited for just the right moment to lay it on me. Although I found his philosophy half-baked, I couldn't help but be flattered that he so much wanted my approval. I actually enjoyed our time together. Other than the card game I used to have with Jerry Nadir, my weeks hanging with Jim were the most sustained contact I'd shared with another man since my career fell apart. It's not like my writer friends dumped me. It was me who distanced myself from them. I could not bear their successes in the face of my failures; so, like a wounded animal, I crawled off to let my career die far away from the pack.

Jim was an eager listener and when he wasn't trying too hard to impress me, he seemed a pretty interesting kid. He was genuinely fascinated by my stories of New York and of my week-long coke-fueled benders. He loved hearing about the famous people I'd met. *Yes, Jim, Truman Capote did sound like that and I don't know if he was nicer when he wasn't drunk because he was always drunk.* The kid especially enjoyed the stories of the famous women I'd fucked. I explained to him that although I didn't have the scars to show for it, I'd faced death down a few times myself.

"My scar tissue's on the inside," I said, sounding like bad movie dialogue.

While I wasn't quite ready to get all teary-eyed over not having fathered a son of my own—Amy couldn't have kids and given my self-absorption and my own role model, I was ill-suited to fatherhood—it did stir some unexpected feelings in me.

After shooting, Jim would drop me off at school. After class, I'd head back home for another few hours of writing. Then the St. Pauli Girl would come by. She'd cook for me, I'd help her with her school papers, then write a little more myself, and we'd end the night in my bed. Last night, we didn't even fuck. I was worn out. We seemed to need a night of simply falling into sleep, our bodies twined together for warmth and comfort and nothing more. I woke up early and slipped into my office.

About an hour after that, Renee, wearing only what she was when she came into the world, showed up at my office door, a faded old accordion file tucked under her arm. "What's this, Ken?"

"What?" Still tired, I barely glanced at her. I kept peering through the curtains in my office, watching for Jim's truck. The St.

Pauli Girl walked over to me, pressing her body against my back, wrapping one arm around me. I heard the file land on my desk.

"Are you bored with me?"

"What are you talking about?" I sounded annoyed, but regretted it. I spun around and tried to hug her, but she pushed away from me and moved back by the door.

"Does Jim fuck like me?"

"What?"

"Look at me," she said, rubbing her right hand over her breasts, letting it brush over the trim triangle of dark blond hair between her thighs. "Are you more interested in Jim than me? More interested in that book? Aren't I enough to keep your attention?"

"Don't be silly. Come here."

She didn't hesitate. I kissed her softly on the mouth and then turned her around so that her bare, muscular back rested against my chest and abdomen. I threw my right arm around her breasts, pulling her so close that not even the Holy Ghost could have slipped between us. Brushing her lush blond hair away with the point of my chin, I ran my mouth over the light down on the nape of her neck, kissed her ears. I let the fingertips of my left hand trace the curve of her hip. I slid my fingers slowly across her flat belly and down into her soft, trimmed thatch of hair. Her breaths grew short and rapid and she was already wet as I ran my fingers gently along her folds. I nudged the tip of my finger into the split at the tip of her labia. Not wanting to rush her, I made lazy, gentle passes, increasing the speed and pressure just a little with each stroke. Finally, she grabbed my wrist and pressed my fingers hard against her. Her back arched, body shuddered. She sighed and relaxed, falling fully against me.

We stood there like that for a few minutes, the tension flowing out of her body. She felt small and vulnerable in my arms. It was dawning on me that I did in fact know far more about Jim than

I did about the St. Pauli Girl. I really had cut myself off from women. I'd sleep with them, but I didn't want to know them or anything about them.

"I'm sorry about before," I said, kissing her on top of her head. "I didn't sleep much last night."

"Why not?"

"Meg's supposed to be calling soon about the book deal and the tension's starting to get to me."

"Oh, the publishing stuff."

"Yeah, that." I kissed her again, let her go, and retrieved the file from the desk. "You were asking about this."

"I found it in bed instead of you," she said, wrapping herself up in an old quilt thrown over the back of my desk chair.

I brushed a loose strand of hair out of her eyes, tucking it behind her ear, and kissed her on the mouth.

"What about the file?" she asked, sitting down in my desk chair.

I reached into the file. "You've seen me writing lately."

"Yeah."

"I'm writing about what's in here," I said, handing her a tattered spiral notebook.

"What is it?"

"It's the diary of a murderer."

She got a sick look on her face. "A murderer?"

I told her about being sent to do a piece on the Troubles and detailed how I'd met the man who'd hunted me down in Deptford, how he'd given me that damned notebook.

"But why you?" she asked.

"He never said anything except he heard I was looking for a different kind of story. I don't know. Maybe he could spot a fellow lost soul."

"Didn't you ask?"

I laughed. "He wasn't the kind of man to ask."

"What makes his story so different?"

"Because he was like the slave ship captain who comes to see the tragedy of what he has done. But unlike the slave ship captain who writes 'Amazing Grace' because he believes there is a God to redeem him, McGuinn knows there is no God. McGuinn is so much more a tragic figure because he knows there is no redemption or forgiveness. What is done is done."

But the book wasn't done and when Jim called to say he'd be a half hour late, I went back to it.

There he was, the jumpy bollix, ten paces over his left shoulder and about as inconspicuous as a cunt in a cock shop. He was looking everywhere but at McGuinn. Short of stature, he was a mean-faced fooker with opaque eyes. No more than thirty with the bloated muscles and acne of a juicer, he was a real trouble boy, that one. The type of lad that was always spoiling for violence. Maybe, McGuinn thought, he would oblige the lad, as he possessed a knack for violence his own self.

But he had to make a choice quickly. He supposed he could vanish into the crowd like so much smoke and keep going. It wasn't as if this town held any particular fascination for him. To the contrary, he could recreate his lonely little hell in any of a thousand shite holes along the road. One factory or abattoir was much like another, one bloody and mindless job same as the next. Yet he found he was in no hurry to scurry. He'd been on the run his entire feckin' life and he was spent. This corner of nowhere was as fine as any other in which to make a stand. Besides, he was curious.

This set up smelled neither of the Prods nor the Brits. Although it had the feel of amateur night at Ralph and Jim's

Bar and Grill, McGuinn couldn't risk dismissing the possibility that there were forces at play here beyond his experience. Unlikely, for sure, but possible.

The man who believes he has seen it all is a blind fooker and more often than not, a dead one.

.

Weiler's writing was, for my money, always less than the sum of its parts. The novels were like long-form versions of Steely Dan songs: slick, well-produced, clever as hell, but rather soulless and incomprehensible.

—E-MAIL FROM HASKELL BROWN
TO FRANZ DUDEK

Twelve

Patty Duke

I'd broken the mile barrier on my run that morning and felt like Chuck Yeager. The euphoria was short-lived because when Jim dropped me back off at my house, I noticed the red message-light flashing as I walked through the front door. I recited the procrastinator's oath to myself—*Never do now what you can put off until you die*—but I wasn't a procrastinator by temperament or nature. If I was five minutes early, I felt ten minutes late. Even when I was writing *Curley Takes Five*, possibly one of the worst books ever written, I was weeks early for my deadline. An editor at Penguin once confided in me that her definition of a perfect author was one who hands in a brilliant manuscript and then gets hit by a bus. In my case, I think Ferris, Ledoux would have settled for the bus and considered themselves lucky. Those were dark days.

That was a long time ago and the red light flashing was now. The message was a terse *Kip, call me back. Pronto! Meg.* I knew Meg Donovan. Terse messages meant things had gone badly.

I dispensed with the chit chat. "How bad is it?"

"All is not lost."

"Said the optimistic surgeon to the triple amputee. That's a little cryptic even for you, Donovan."

"The rights deal is still on, no problem. They even upped the offer."

"But the new book is off. That's what you're telling me," I said.

"That's what I'm telling you."

"Fuck!"

"Don't take it out on me."

"I said fuck, Meg, not fuck you."

"Look, Kip, this isn't all bad. By us throwing a demand for a new book into the mix, we gave Travers Legacy an out, but they didn't take it and sweetened the pot. They want those books. If the new editions of your books sell well, they might be amenable to tossing you a bone next year."

"And this tossing me a bone notion is based on what exactly, my horoscope?"

"I had lunch with Mary Caputo last week," she said. "Mary Caputo is Franz Dudek's assistant at Travers Legacy. Franz Dudek is the publisher."

"And . . ."

"And Mary told me Dudek was definitely willing to give you a one-book deal, a small deal, but a deal. Before you go bonkers, Kip, you should know it wasn't a wholly artistic decision on his part. He loves your old stuff, but he was willing to take a flier on the new book for the same reasons he's including you in the rights deal."

"The dead kid."

There was a brief silence on Meg's end of the phone. "That's right, the late Frank Vuchovich. You understand the value of free publicity. Well, it's even more important now than it used to be. Publishing is about to get swept away by the social media/e-book tsunami just like the music industry got wiped out by digital downloads."

"So what happened?"

"Haskell Brown happened. He put the kibosh on the new book. He never wanted any part of you to begin with. He was pressured by Dudek to include your books in the retro package. That was as far as Haskell was willing to go and he wasn't very willing to go that far, if you get my meaning. He let Dudek know he would quit if push came to shove and Dudek wasn't going to push or shove any further for you."

"What the hell did I ever do to Haskell Brown? Did I bone his wife at a party or something?"

"Haskell's gay."

"What, he thinks I would have boned his wife if he were straight?"

"I told you, Kip, people here remember the Kipster. Haskell worked as an assistant editor for Moira before she died, so he heard all the dirt about you and how impossible it was for Moira to deal with you at the end. So I'll send the rights contract down for you to sign." It wasn't a question.

"Nope. Tell them I want two weeks to think it over."

"Two weeks! What the hell for?"

"Because I'm disappointed. Because I'm angry. Because I'm a foolish, self-destructive prick. Take your pick."

"Why not ask for two months or two years?"

"Don't give me any ideas, Meg."

"Don't be an asshole, Kip. You'll blow this."

"It won't be the first thing I've fucked up, will it?"

"The list is long and apparently still growing."

"You know the funny thing about playing chicken with me these days, Meg?"

"What's that?"

"I've got nowhere else to fall and nothing left to lose."

"Except this deal," she said.

"No, the rights deal is something to gain, not to lose. Seems like two different things from where I'm sitting. Tell them two weeks."

"If you promise me something."

"Depends on what."

"That if they call your bluff when the two weeks are over, you'll sign."

"I might."

"Fuck you, Weiler."

"I love you too, Donovan. Talk to you in fourteen days."

Click.

●

I was dead quiet during most of our ride up into the hills and, for the first time since we began this routine, Jim Trimble seemed off balance. He didn't know what to make of my sullenness or how to react to my silence. It reminded me that in spite of his big ideas and his prowess with guns, he was just a goofy kid who thought the world outside Brixton was what he saw when he surfed the net or what he'd read in the pages of my books—the poor dumb schmuck. He'd seen less of the world than Patty Duke: *But Patty's only seen the sights a girl can see from Brooklyn Heights . . .* For weeks now, I'd acted the prized pupil to his wise and benevolent master. It didn't feel that way today. Nothing felt the same. The falls and rapids didn't seem quite so majestic. Yet when the kid handed me the .25 Beretta, something changed.

I took off the safety, swung the little automatic around, and put the entire clip into the trunk of a tree about thirty feet away from me. If ever there were such things as angry bullets, I'd just pumped them into that pine. I tossed the gun down in disgust as Jim ran over to the tree.

"Holy shit, Kip! Come over here and look at this. Check this out!" he said, poking his index finger in and out of the tight grouping of holes in the flesh of the tree. "It's not like one bullet's on top of the next, but it's pretty damned good. Hell, you've never shot like that. What got into you?"

"Anger and self-loathing must do wonders for my shooting."

He tilted his head, staring up at me like a confused puppy. "What happened to piss you off so bad?"

I'd told him previously about my conversation with Meg and about my asking for a new book contract. Jim had been totally with me—a real shocker—and thought my risking all that money was further vindication of his choosing me as the focus of his hero worship. Christ, you should have seen him. In the blink of an eye, my standing up to Stan took a backseat to my taking on the big bad world of New York publishing.

"They turned me down."

"Who did?" he asked, still kneeling by the tree.

"Haskell Brown, the editor at Travers Legacy. They want my old books, but it looks like a new book's out of the question."

"He's crazy. How could he not want a new book from you?"

Jim wasn't putting me on either. He was utterly sincere and seemed bewildered and hurt about it. It was kind of sweet, really, to have him hurt on my behalf. Because I had managed to alienate everyone from my past who might have taken up my cause, it had been a long time since anyone felt connected to me in this way.

"It wasn't all bad news, Jim," I said, placing a consoling hand on his shoulder. "Brown's boss was actually willing to give me a new book deal, but he wasn't willing to risk losing his editor over me. I can't blame him for that."

"I guess not," he said, but didn't mean it. "So did you cave?"

"Not yet. I told my agent to tell them I needed two weeks to think it over, but I guess I'll take the deal in the end."

"Two weeks?"

"That's if they don't just call Meg tomorrow and tell the pair of us to go fuck ourselves."

The kid's face broke into a broad, goofy smile. "Cheer up, Kip."

"What the fuck for?"

"Two reasons."

"Enlighten me."

He stood and raised his right index finger. "One: I think you're ready for the chapel."

"That's a reason to run like hell, Jim, not to cheer up."

"You'll be fine."

"We'll see about that. What's the second reason? And, please God, I hope it's better than the first."

"Took seven days to create the world. Just think of how many things can change in twice that time. Things will turn out all right. You'll see."

Thirteen

Shroud

This time, we had only a cold wind to keep us company. When we got out of his pickup, I was distracted by the woeful groaning of the desolate hangars and by the creaks and shrill whines of the huts. Their complaints were like the laments of humpback whales. Jim seemed not to take notice. His flashlight cut careless holes in the blackness as we dragged the generator out of its storage spot. When it sputtered to life, the generator killed the mournful romance of the night.

Before we entered the hangar, Jim took me by the bicep. "Listen, this isn't like up in the woods. This is serious. Pay real careful attention to what I'm doing and the way I do it. You'll have to do it exactly like this or you can't come back."

"I understand," I said.

That wasn't enough for Jim. "I'm not kidding, Kip. The last time was a one-time-only thing. There aren't second chances. Inside here, the rules always apply."

"I get it, Jim. I do."

He nodded with confidence, but he looked worried. This meant more to him than I realized. He couldn't have known how important it was to me because I didn't discuss, except in the most vague terms, what it was I was writing about. I couldn't, not yet, maybe not ever. Haskell Brown wasn't the only potential obstacle blocking my way. If I couldn't get back inside the chapel, Terry McGuinn and I were fucked. Both of us would be remanded to the purgatory we'd only escaped from a month ago. Even I knew there were no words I could say that would reassure Jim. I had to perform.

We walked down the same lighted path the St. Pauli Girl and I had come down the night of my first visit. And I was once again struck by the incongruity of the white blockhouse in the midst of the huge hangar, and of the elaborate wooden door set against the concrete.

"What's with that door?" I asked.

"We scavenged it and the pews from the base chapel."

I had my answer. That's how this place got its name.

"Everything in here," Jim continued, "except the generator was scavenged from the base. Even the mattresses and white paint. There's all sorts of basements and tunnels and things underground here that people on the base either didn't know about or forgot about. You'll see, but first things first. Wait here a minute."

Once he stepped out of the light, it didn't take long for him to be completely swallowed up by the darkness. I followed the sound of his footsteps scraping grit between the floor and the soles of his boots. I heard him clambering up a metal staircase and in less than a minute, come quickly back down.

"Here," he said, coming into the light, holding out a white T-shirt so large it was like a shroud. "Put this on."

"Why so big?"

"It's going to be covering a lot of stuff," he said.

I did as he asked. Only after I got it on did I notice Jim had removed his jacket and was wearing the T-shirt he had worn the last time. It was covered in way more red crosses than I had realized. And there was something else. Tucked in his left arm, against his ribs, Jim held a helmet that looked like it was designed by a hockey-playing gladiator. What I assumed was the face mask was a curved piece of padded steel with only a tiny slit for an eyehole.

He said, "You'll wear this once or a few times at most, but either way it takes some getting used to."

"Once, if I fuck up?"

"Or if you get killed." He smiled sadly and handed me the helmet.

Heavy as it was, I understood why it might take some getting used to. I didn't put it on. "Ashes first, right."

And for the first time that night, Jim smiled at me with a bit of confidence. "The ashes represent the origins of the chapel and the practice we put in. Also reminds us of where we're headed if we make a mistake."

And there it was again, the repulsion/compulsion thing. Jim had alluded to death twice in twenty seconds and I should have run. Instead I stood there and let him dab ashes on my forehead. As we rehearsed the rest of the rituals, I asked what each one meant.

"You have to earn the right to understand them," he said. "And there's only one way to earn the right."

Fourteen

Red Fist

I rested my sweat-damp cheek on the cold porcelain rim, the sour stench of my vomit wafting up to me from the bottom of the bowl. When I had nothing left in me to give, I sat down with the back of my soaked-through shirt against the cool tile wall. My head was exploding. I was faint, shaking with the chills. I was afraid. I don't know.

Five days had passed since I'd put that tight grouping into the trunk of the tree, four since Jim had walked me through the dry run in the chapel. My shooting had since faltered. My writing too. My focus was gone and when I booted up my laptop I was back to staring at the screen, helplessly. I was disgusted by my own fragility and I'd asked Renee not to come back to the house until I got the shooting over with. I was also afraid for the first time in my life that I would be impotent. I wouldn't have been able to bear that, not now, not with the St. Pauli Girl.

Now, this was it: my first time shooting in the chapel. Jim came up to me, a bottle of water in one hand, a towel in the other. He poured half the bottle over my head. "Here, drink the rest," he said, handing me the bottle and pulling me to my feet. When

I was done drinking, he toweled me off. "Come on, Kip, it's time to get dressed."

I wasn't looking forward to this part of the evening. Jim had dressed me in full protective gear the day before so I could get used to the feel of it; but there would never be a time when I'd get used to it, especially, as he had warned, the helmet. Cobbled from Army surplus, sports equipment, and whatever had been lying around people's garages, the suit was bulky and stank of the sweat, vomit, and urine of the people who'd worn it before me. Jim slipped the giant white T-shirt over the padding, and I helped him do the same. The first time in the chapel, you shot against your mentor. That and the fact that Jim was dressed in a suit like mine were the only things that kept me from running. Armored as we were, it was unlikely either one of us was going to die tonight. Yet somehow, that was of little comfort.

Just as I was willing myself to calm down, I heard it: the eerie thunder of dozens of stomping feet and hands clapping in unison, echoing around the hangar. My knees got weak.

Jim grabbed me, steadied me. "Everyone goes through this. You'll be fine." Then, after a pause, "It's time. Let's go."

As we walked slowly out of the locker room and toward the chapel, the noise grew louder and louder, the foot stomping and rhythmic clapping blending into an indistinct roar. We paused outside the wooden door, Jim daubing ashes on both our foreheads.

"Remember to do the things I showed you the way I showed you how to do them," he said, staring me directly in the eyes. "Tonight, that's as important as anything else."

Jim entered first. When I squeezed through the space between the mattresses, it wasn't only the din I couldn't make sense of. There were more people there than the first time Renee brought me, but their faces were as a blur, like looking out the window of a moving subway at the faces in the windows of a passing train.

I heard Jim say, "Helmets on," from a million miles away and felt something on my head. Hands and fingers snugged the helmet to my chin. The face mask limited my vision to a small window straight in front of me. My hearing changed again, taking on a muted, windy quality. An arm, Jim's, looped through the crook in my left elbow and marched me exactly eight strides—one stride for each original member of the chapel, Jim had said—between the pews to a spot directly at the center of the chapel. As Jim had instructed, I touched my right index finger to a spot above my heart, and at the top of my lungs shouted, "Blessed are they who have not seen, and yet believe." I bowed quickly, then stood erect.

I turned right to face a mattressed wall and felt Jim's back against mine. I counted to five in my head and then took four slow, measured strides. Jim had explained that each stride was symbolic of the first four duels in the chapel by its eight original members.

"Stop!" The voice was a familiar one, the deputy sheriff's.

I halted, bringing both feet together and, as instructed, I took one more stride.

"Turn!"

I about-faced. Jim was about thirty feet directly in front of me.

The crowd noise grew less distinct, but my sense of smell became extraordinarily acute. My head once again filled with the rank traces of fear that people had left on the suit before me.

The deputy sheriff showed me the little Beretta. He showed me the clip, slid the clip into place, thumbed off the safety, and racked the slide. He placed it in my hand and once again my perceptions shifted. Now all I could hear was my heartbeat and my shallow, rapid breaths bouncing around the inside of the helmet. In my head, all I could see was my father's head flung backwards, his blind eyes seemingly focused on my mom's fussy white curtains. Then, just as suddenly as it had come, the vision of my father vanished. Now all I could see was Jim. Not him, his chest. I imagined I could see his heart beating in his rib cage like a red fist, clenching and unclenching. When he raised the .38, my world grew silent and still. I became unconscious of my heart beating, of my breathing, of the smells. I felt on an island at the center of the universe and knew that Jim was right: things were going to work out somehow.

The deputy asked Jim, "Do you believe?"

Jim answered. "Blessed are they that do."

"Do you believe?" the deputy asked me and the chapel grew absolutely silent.

"I will be blessed by gunfire."

"Then be blessed," he said, stepping back.

I raised my right hand and fired. That's when the freight train hit me.

Fifteen

Serrated Edge

Sissy loads, my ass! The bullet hit me like Paul Bunyan's axe. I'd been hit and hit hard. Rolling over, getting on all fours, I was still a little out of it—weak, shaken, kind of in a trance. Still, I was electric. The rush was like nothing that coke or pussy or fame had ever given me. I'd fired a bullet at another human being and, in spite of all the protective gear, it was as primal a thing as I'd ever done. I saw Jim coming my way, a smile as wide as could be hung across his rugged face. His mouth was moving, but I couldn't make out any words. The roar was back and it filled up my ears and the rest of my head.

Now he was standing in front of me, pulling me up, throwing his arms around me. He let go with one arm and kept the other flung over my shoulders. When he stepped back, it got quiet once again. He reached across and put his finger in the hole his shot had made in my shirt.

He asked. "Are you blessed?"

"I have been blessed by gunfire."

"Do you believe?"

"I believe."

"Blessed are those who have not seen, and yet believe."

"I have seen and I believe," I said.

Then the silence shattered in a roar. Jim's proud smile was so broad I thought his skin might crack.

"Look! You hit me! You hit me!" He was beside himself, poking his finger into a small hole in his shirt above his abdomen. "Virgins almost never hit anything but the mattresses. They're always so nervous and weak. People have a kind of built-in thing about not killing other people. It's one thing to shoot close to them up in the woods. It's really different to aim at another person and pull the trigger, no matter what they're wearing. But you did it, Kip. You did it."

We pulled off our helmets and shirts, the snaggle-toothed girl collecting the shirts from Jim and me. The St. Pauli Girl folded herself into my arms. Tears of relief streamed down her cheeks, but there was something else in her expression that I couldn't quite decipher in my numb euphoria. Whatever it was quickly vanished and she kissed me. It felt like my first kiss, the best first kiss. But when I looked up, I saw an unwelcome face, one that I hadn't noticed in the blur of preceding moments: Stan Petrovic's. There he was, standing at the very back of the crowd that had circled around us—that sneer on his battered face as cruel as a serrated edge.

I didn't have time to focus on Stan because Jim, Renee, and I were being carried away with the will of the crowd, our feet not seeming to touch the ground as we were swept along. Hands pulled at my protective gear and by the time we reached the beer coolers, Jim and I were naked from our waists up. He had a small red blotch on his stomach about the size of an old silver dollar. The splotch on my chest was similar in size. We were both going to be bruised and sore for a while. I could only imagine the kind of pain you'd be in wearing only the thinner vests.

Jim shook up a can of Bud. "Welcome," he said and showered me in beer.

Everyone else repeated the gesture until I was thoroughly soaked. I loved it. I had on a full body buzz and could have left earth's orbit under my own power. My fears and worries, my disappointment over the book, had all been washed away by the beer and evaporated with the gun smoke. There was definitely something transformative about coming out the other end of this. It had been maybe five minutes since Jim and I had fired live ammunition at each other, and fuck me if Jim wasn't right: I felt reborn. There was my total dunghill of a life beforehand and there was now. I grabbed a beer of my own, shook madly, and gave Jim a taste of his own medicine. When I was done, we hugged again.

It was like the rush from a roller coaster ride. When it's over, you want to go again more than anything else in the world. The rush didn't last. Nothing good ever lasts. The buzz drained out of me through the bottom of my shoes. Suddenly, my legs were rubbery and everything fell on my shoulders all at once. I was weak and I wanted nothing more than to lie down right there and pass out. Jim picked up on it right away.

"Come on, Kip, let's get cleaned up."

He fairly dragged me into the locker room and I lay down on the cold floor. I was vaguely conscious of Jim washing himself. I was utterly spent and my mind was as empty as it had been since the day I was born. My internal voice was asleep and I wanted to be. I think I nodded off there for a few minutes.

"Okay, Kip," Jim said, lifting me to a sitting position. "Drink this and then wash up." He handed me a cold bottle of water and pointed at three more bottles on the locker room bench.

I guzzled the water and made to stretch out again. "Just let me die here in peace."

He laughed. "It happens to everybody. It's the fear and the adrenalin. It gets to you, but we have to go back inside."

"Why?"

"We've got to watch the others shoot."

"I'll read about it in the morning papers."

He laughed again. I had my moments.

"But there's someone you've got to see shoot."

"Who?"

"Renee."

Sixteen

Fallen Queen

The St. Pauli Girl was barely recognizable in her protective gear, but it would have been impossible not to recognize the hulking figure standing across the room from her. Although the helmet and face mask obscured his pocked and scarred visage, Stan Petrovic stuck out like a malignant cyst. For the second time since we met, Renee seemed small and vulnerable. I realize that's an odd thing to say about someone with a .40 Glock in her right hand, but the menace that Stan Petrovic exuded couldn't be contained by all the padding in the world. Protective armor is meant to keep things out, not keep them in.

"I don't like it," I heard myself say.

"Don't worry about Renee. She's good. She can take care of herself."

"Thanks, Jim, but you'll excuse me if I find little comfort in that." I started to get up. The kid held me down in my seat.

Before I could get another word out of my mouth, the chapel echoed with gunfire. The next thing I was conscious of was kneeling over Renee, searching her shirt and suit for where the bullet had hit. I couldn't find an indentation anywhere. My mind was racing with the illogic of it. She was down, so she had to have been hit, but there was no hole, no blood. She was down, but she wasn't writhing in pain. The St. Pauli Girl was deathly still, and quiet. Frantically, I ran my hands along the makeshift leg armor. Then a disembodied voice called out: "Headshot."

And there it was: a thumb-sized hole in the front left side of the thick flak padding glued onto the Army surplus helmet. Before I could move, I was being shoved out of the way and Renee seemed to disappear behind a wall of bodies. They moved around her like worker bees attending their fallen queen. I think I was in shock and just stood there for what felt like hours. Then I heard something else and turned to see Stan getting up onto his hands and knees. He was grunting, struggling to pull off the face mask and helmet. I ran at him, rearing back my leg to kick the cocksucker in the face, but Jim tackled me before I swung my leg forward. He kept me pinned to the floor.

"Stop it, Kip," he whispered in my ear. "You're going to fuck everything up. You can't do that now. You can't fuck it all up now." He was almost pleading.

"That fuck shot her in the head. He killed Renee."

"It was Stan's first time too, just like you."

"I don't give a—"

"She's okay. She's okay. Calm down! She was just stunned and knocked her head when she fell back. Look."

I raised my head up as far as I could against Jim's mass and saw the St. Pauli Girl smiling at me in that way she had.

"Okay, okay, let me up."

When everyone was certain Renee was steady on her feet, they moved away from her. She moved toward Stan and repeated the same ritual Jim and I had performed only a half hour before. Then it was Stan's turn for the beer bath, for the adulation, and eventually for everything else I'd gone through earlier.

"Are you okay? Are you okay?" I was shouting at the St. Pauli Girl.

"I'm fine. I just feel stupid. Christ, you'd think I'd never done this before."

"But you're okay?"

"I'm okay, Ken. I promise," she said, pecking me softly on the cheek. "You really do care about me."

"What's that supposed to mean?"

She didn't answer, instead pulling me over to where Stan was the center of attention, his fat gut wet with beer, a small red mark blooming in the center of his chest. When he looked around, he noticed me at the back of the crowd. I smiled at him as he had smiled at me. Tonight I would make nice like everyone else, but this wasn't over between us.

●

The St. Pauli Girl didn't say a word as we drove back to my house. Maybe Jim was right about her and she could handle herself as well as anyone, but her silence was eloquent. I wouldn't have known what to say had she spoken. Renee had come very close to dying, *very* close; closer, I suspect, than she thought possible. I was more than a bit lost myself, caught in that post-adrenalin netherworld of my rush-crash-rush cycle and the panic and relief over her close call. I was trying to make sense of it, to filter it; yet I knew that even if I squeezed everything out of the events of that evening, leaving nothing but pith and peel, it wouldn't have added up. There are some things in life that can be reduced down to their molecules and yet yield nothing of their nature. Maybe it was all too raw.

Finally, Renee leaned over, resting her head on my thigh. I finger-combed her hair and she began softly sobbing.

"Does your head hurt?" I asked.

"That's not why I'm crying."

"Why then?"

"Because of what you did back there."

"I was worried about you."

"I care about you too, Ken."

"Shhhh. Relax."

Her tears dried up and she closed her eyes as if to sleep. As she rested there, an ugly thought came to mind. It was a question, really. One I thought I knew the answer to, an answer that, if correct, was more unpleasant than the question itself. I knew it was a question better left alone and unspoken, but when the St. Pauli Girl stirred it spilled out of my mouth.

"Why did you shoot with Stan?"

"Why do you think?" she said, pushing herself upright. "Why did you shoot with Jim?"

"Jim says the first time you shoot, you shoot with the person who trained you."

"Then stop asking me questions you already know the answers to, especially if you don't like the answers."

"But why would you train Stan?"

"He had to be trained by someone." Her voice was steady, cool, distant.

"But why you? Who picked who? Did Jim have anything to—"

"You sound jealous," she said, a mischievous glint in her eyes.

"Maybe a little."

"Only a little?"

I swung the steering wheel hard right and skidded to a stop on the shoulder. I undid my seatbelt, reached over, pulled Renee to me, and pressed my mouth onto hers, hard. My tongue was between her lips before she had a chance to breathe and my hand was undoing her jeans. She didn't fight, but she didn't help either.

I didn't care. Once I got my hand under her panties, she became decidedly less passive.

When we finished, the windows were fogged over and the car smelled intensely of sex. We sat back in our seats, half-naked, taking it all in. In Brixton, we could have been parked in the middle of the road for the lack of traffic. From the time I pulled over until the time I started back to the house, a half hour must have gone by and not one car passed us in either direction.

"I'm the third most experienced person, Ken," the St. Pauli Girl said as I put the car in gear. "That's why I trained Stan. That's all."

"It's okay, I was just being an idiot. Who's the second most experienced shooter?"

"He's moved on," she said, "so now I'm next in line."

We didn't say much more on the drive, but when we got to the house we let our bodies do the talking until we lost our voices.

I am sorry to inform you that due to a decrease in sales and a lack of demand over the past several years, we find it necessary to reduce and sell off our overstock of inventory of the following titles: *Clown Car Bounce, The Devil's Understudy,* and *Curly Takes Five.* Prior to reducing the inventory, I can make copies available to you at the special rate of $2.60 per unit.

—TRENA KEMPTON, LIQUIDATIONS MANAGER

Seventeen

Gun Cherry

I went back to writing with a head full of plot ideas and a new determination. The story of Terry McGuinn was going to get told regardless of what Haskell Brown had to say about it. It might never get read, but it was going to get written. There was always the option of sending the manuscript out under a pseudonym, though that was much less appealing to me. And if it came down to it, I could always self-publish the thing; but one way or the other I wanted my name on the book as a kind of *Fuck you!* to the critics who had eagerly shoveled dirt on my coffin. After the St. Pauli Girl drifted off, Terry McGuinn was all I could think about: McGuinn dealing with a fool like Stan Petrovic . . . McGuinn in love with a girl like Renee.

McGuinn could sense their eyes on him as he and the lovely Zoe made their way along the street. He'd only spotted the one, the acne-faced boyo, in the bar proper. McGuinn'd kept an eye on the lad. The others, he supposed, must have laid in wait outside Ralph and Jim's. He was being set up for sure, but for what? If this had been the Brits or Prods, if this had been some of his own come for him, Jesus would have already let go his hand that he might fall to hell. He would have been dead the second he walked out of the pub or into a shadow.

The fair Zoe stopped, turned, and kissed McGuinn hard. Her tongue was dancing inside his mouth, his in hers. It was soon hard to distinguish the one from the other. She stood back, took his hand, and led him down an alley. She stopped only a few meters in, pushed his back against a steel door, kissed him again, then dropped slowly to her knees. Ah, this skirt is a sharp one, McGuinn thought, smart enough to know he would never have followed her to the end of the alley where he would easily be boxed in.

As she undid him, he reached his right arm around behind him to where the Sig was stashed against the small of his back. He worked his fingers around the grip and slid the 9mm up from between his shirt and the waistband of his pants. He kept his gun hand behind him and waited for the ambush to be sprung. He didn't have but a few seconds to wait.

There were three of them surrounding Zoe and McGuinn, men all: the trouble boy, another lad of pale complexion—as fierce looking as a cripple-winged sparrow—and a well-built fellow with the look of an American footballer. McGuinn recognized the footballer's face from the slaughterhouse. Didn't know him by name, but had seen him about. He was the leader, this one, with bright copper eyes and a shrewd mouth.

Oh, and there was something else—each of the lads held 9mm's aimed squarely at McGuinn's head and torso.

"Seem's you lads have caught me with me pants down," he said to distract them.

It worked, for as they smirked, they relaxed their gun hands just enough to give McGuinn the time he needed. In a blur of lightning quickness, he pulled Zoe up from her knees, spun her around, and put the Sig Sauer to her neck. When he spoke, McGuinn spoke directly to the footballer, ignoring the other two.

"I don't know what you're playin' at, fellas, nor who you're accustomed to playin' with, but I'd advise ya to drop yer weapons and let me be on me way. And do me the courtesy, will ya, of not pretendin' the fair Miss Zoe is not a part of this? It will save us all a lot of bother."

"There's three of us," the footballer said, his voice cool as a late fall evening. "I like our odds."

"Then ya don't know shite, lad."

And with that, McGuinn shoved Zoe at the trouble boy, who stumbled backwards, shot the sparrow in his gun shoulder, and wheeled on the footballer. The footballer placed his automatic on the cobblestones and kicked it away, but as he did, he smiled the most disconcerting smile that McGuinn had ever seen.

"Well done," he said to McGuinn. "You've passed your audition."

"Now what kind of shite are you talkin'?"

"We'll be in touch," said the footballer.

"Like fook you will. Ya aren't goin' anywhere."

"Okay, Irish, have it your way. We'll wait for the cops and you can explain Joseph's bullet wound away and tell the cops all about who you are and where you come from." He smiled that smile again. The footballer had McGuinn and he knew it. "All right, son, take the juicer, yer wounded, the girl, and be gone."

"No," said the footballer, "I think we'll stay. I don't like being told what to do. Those sirens are getting louder, Irish. If there's any running to be done, I think you'll do it."

One of the ways McGuinn had managed to survive this long was by knowing when defeat was at hand. He didn't hesitate. He ran, hitching up his trousers as best he could while still holding on to the Sig. He turned to look back. They were nearly gone, but he did catch the briefest glimpse of Zoe. There was a sadness about her as disconcerting as the footballer's smile.

I was feeling so good about myself, about the chapel, about getting back to work, about the St. Pauli Girl. But when Jim came by for our morning run it was like he was determined to test my resolve, like he wanted to make sure I knew my place.

"We're not shooting today," he said almost before he got out of his truck.

"Are you kidding me? After last night, I am totally juiced to—"

"We're taking the day off. It's the rule."

"*Your* rule?"

"The rules aren't mine, Kip. Like I told you before when we were at the chapel and I was walking you through things, stuff will get explained to you as you earn the right. Last night you earned a ticket inside the chapel, but not the keys to the kingdom. The chapel isn't a game to us or a diversion. It's our thing. I know how excited you are to shoot again and to know everything, but it's not how it works. Like any discipline, there's stuff you've got to do first before you understand it. You either have to trust me or turn away. It's your choice."

He knew I wasn't going to turn away. I felt like the kite on the end of his string. He was a smart kid who knew a lot about me. Give the junkie a taste and then hold the prize just out of reach.

Watch him jump, beg, and crawl. I knew how that worked, but I didn't like it. Still, I knew there was a single word I could say that would chaff his ass. So I said it:

"But—"

"Your choice." He didn't like being challenged, especially by me, and his expression showed it.

I hid my smile from him, but he had another surprise for me.

"There's something else. Next time we shoot, you have to pick a new gun."

"I was just getting good with the Beretta."

"Good isn't the point," he said. "The chapel isn't about simply being competent. It's not a gun range. The chapel is about the essential nature of the gun and how we can use it to elevate us."

Christ, I thought, here we were again, back to that metaphysical bullshit. I wasn't happy about it or about switching guns, but I didn't want to push back too hard. We didn't talk much during the run. I knew I was being an ungrateful prick, that without Jim and the St. Pauli Girl and the chapel, I'd still be staring at those seven first lines, but I was disappointed. Oddly, that's when Jim chose to ask me a favor.

"Kip, um, I'm kind of embarrassed to ask . . . Oh, forget it."

Whatever anger I had for Jim seemed to vanish. It was easy for me to forget that in spite of his big talk, Jim was such a kid. He was so tongue-tied, so pathetic trying to ask me whatever it was he wanted to ask me that I felt sorry for him.

"Just ask, Jim."

"Can I borrow your Porsche this weekend? There's this girl I used to date who went away to school upstate and I'm going up to see her tonight—"

"Sure, Jim, anytime. Better an old red Porsche than an old F-150."

He blew out a big breath of relief. "I'll take good care of her. Fill up the tank and everything."

"Don't worry about it. I trust you, Jim."

I went inside and retrieved my car keys. When I handed them to Jim, he got that *Gee-can-I-blow-you* look on his face. Instead, he just thanked me and swore I wouldn't regret lending him my car.

I guess my generosity was good karma because things went wonderfully with Renee that evening. She'd spent the day getting things ready for a special meal to celebrate me losing my gun cherry—her phrase, not mine. Three things I already knew about her: she could cook, she could fuck, and she could shoot. What else could a man ask for in a woman? It had also dawned on me recently that she was a lot smarter than I'd given her credit for. Well, maybe smarter isn't the right word. She *was* smart. That much was clear early on, but more than that, the St. Pauli Girl was wise. She was the one who talked politics, and world affairs in a reasoned, nuanced manner. I really enjoyed listening to her. I'd stopped thinking about the world around the time it stopped thinking about me, but later that night Renee wasn't interested in the state of the world.

"What was Amy like?"

"Where's this coming from?"

"You can't blame me for being curious," she said. "Do you think about her?"

"Funny, I used to think about her all the time. Less so since … since September. At the end there, our marriage was just a massive compound fracture. That's when things were really bad for me."

"Bad with her?"

"Bad with everything. I was getting kicked to the curb by my publisher. Not that I didn't deserve to lose my contract. At least when Amy cut me loose, she told me to my face."

"What did your publisher do?"

"The liquidations manager sent me a letter offering me my novels at a heavily discounted rate before they sold off the remaining stock to clear space in the warehouse. Nice, huh? Not a word from my publisher or my editor. Not a 'thank you' or a 'fuck you.' Not even 'goodbye.' It was like getting a Dear John letter from your fiancée's third cousin."

Renee looked hurt on my behalf. "How could they do that to you?"

"I did it to me. Then I called my agent and she told me what I already knew. She's tough, Meg, and didn't sugar coat it. No velvet glove on her iron fist. I'd made her life pretty miserable with my bullshit. That's what I do to women, I make them miserable. Maybe you should run."

She ignored that last part. The St. Pauli Girl no longer seemed much in the mood for talk after that. Both of us were tired and after dinner, we went to bed. Neither one of us slept very long and for all the right reasons. In fact, we spent the entire weekend sleeping very little and in our own very little world.

Eighteen

The Fine Print

When Jim showed up for our first run following my very tiring weekend, I was really happy to see him. I could feel the big smile on my face. Downstairs, I put my hand out to him.

"I'm glad we're friends, Jim."

"Me too, Kip."

"Sorry I was cranky the other day."

"Everybody gets a little weirded out after their first time in the chapel. It's no big thing."

"We're okay, then?" I asked.

"We're always okay. And thanks for the car. She was totally impressed." His smile said what he no longer had to. Mission accomplished. He'd gotten laid.

Later that day, after class, it was back up into the woods as usual. As happy as I was for him, I still wasn't pleased about having to get accustomed to a new sidearm. No matter. I needed Jim as a friend, as the man who would keep me on the inside. Until I stood across from Jim in the chapel, raised my weapon and fired, I'd told myself it was all about writing again, about McGuinn. That was no longer true. It may never have been true. If I never wrote another word, I would've been hooked. I *was* hooked. I wanted that rush again so badly I could taste it. So when Jim said pick another gun, I picked another gun.

It was definitely the .38. The feel was very different from the Beretta. The Beretta was small and sleek—a woman's gun, Jim teased. It popped more than banged when you fired it. The .38 was no cannon, but it was a beast by comparison. Still, it fit comfortably in my hand and after only a few rounds I started to get a feel for it.

Things were going great and the tiny dose of bad blood between Jim and me seemed forgotten—forgotten until I asked if I could shoot the Beretta one last time for old times' sake.

"I told you, you're never going to see that gun again, so don't ask about it!" It wasn't a suggestion. It was the first time Jim's tone was unmistakably belligerent.

"Christ, kid," I said, using *kid* to tweak his nose, "you and your rules! Why not open up your own chapter of the NRA and leave it at that?"

For the hurt expression on his face, you'd have thought I'd just gut-shot him. His lips moved, but only wounded animal noises came out. Then realizing how stunned he must have looked to me, he turned away in embarrassment. Only after getting hold of himself did he face me. His expression was no longer stunned or wounded. I'd seen him angry once, when Vuchovich was holding us hostage. He was angrier now.

"Don't ever say that again, Kip. We're nothing like those gun queers."

"Gun queers?"

"It's the old-fashioned meaning of queer. It means like obsessed. We're not like that. We don't care about muzzle velocities and specs and shit like that. We're not queer for the guns themselves, not like the Colonel."

"Okay, but why hate the NRA? I mean, I'd think you would hate gun control advocates worse."

"Gun control is a misnomer. They don't want to control guns. They just don't want you to have 'em. I understand that and, let's be real, it is kind of hard to argue that we wouldn't all be safer if no one had handguns. The NRA types, man, they're the worst. They're the real gun control advocates because they want to control what you do with your guns: how to hold them, how to carry them, when to clean them, when to use them, and on and on. They're fascists. They couldn't give two shits about the Constitution. For them, everything except the Second Amendment is the fine print. They're just a bunch of gun queers."

I held my palms upward in surrender. "Sorry."

"All right," he said, but he was still red-faced. "Just don't ever say that. We've come a long way together, too long a way to screw it all up now. We're both in the deep end of the pool, Kip, and there's no going back now."

I kept quiet. The kid needed to have his say if we were going to move on. Besides, I was trying to figure out if there was something I was missing. This was the second time in only a few days Jim had talked to me this way. After I went after Stan Petrovic and Jim tackled me, he had said a very similar kind of thing. *You're going to fuck everything up. You can't do that now. You can't fuck it all up now.*

"No, Kip, I'm the one who should be sorry, not you. I shouldn't have gone off on you like that. Don't be mad at me, please," he said, his frightened inner child that he hid so well coming to the fore. "I just want you to like and understand me. I think sometimes I want that a little too much and I get worried is all."

"Jim, you're the best friend I've got in this world. Forget it. Let's just shoot."

And shoot we did, way longer than was normally the case. It was a race to see whether the sun would set before we ran out of ammo. I could tell Jim was getting bored, so I regaled him with some of my endless supply of stories. What I don't think Jim realized was just how hooked I really was. He didn't have to beg for my approval. By now, it was almost beside the point.

Nineteen

Monkey Suit

Ironic thing is, it took me standing there in the chapel a second time to realize it wasn't Amy's respect I wanted, but my own. Regardless of the forces that got me there, I *was* there, the .38 in my raised hand. Standing across from me was the security guard from the abandoned base, a Glock in his raised hand. Although I wasn't nearly as proficient with the .38 as I was with the Beretta, I wasn't going to complain or balk at another chance for the big rush.

"Even with all the practice, you're so nervous that first time that if you didn't just raise up and shoot, you'd probably kill someone in the crowd," Jim had said. "Ain't that different than being a real virgin, you just aim and shoot." We both had a laugh at that.

The second time was different. Gone was the profound nervousness, the panic that came with not knowing. The nauseating smells that had nearly caused me to swoon were expected, almost comforting, and the protective gear, though still cumbersome, didn't irk me quite so much. The sweat that poured out of me was from excitement, not fear. I moved out of the locker room to the chapel under my own steam. There was no change in my perceptions. My hearing was fine. I wasn't particularly conscious of my breathing or of the beating of my heart. What I felt was alive. I was fully in the moment maybe for the first time in my life. The ritual of the ash seemed to have the paradoxical effect of both heightening my sensations and calming me even further.

Through the door and padding, I stood shoulder to shoulder with my opponent, the security guard from the base. Our helmets were strapped on. We took eight measured strides to the center spot on the chapel floor. We did not bow or shout, "Blessed are they who have not seen, and yet believe." Jim had told me, "Only virgins do that."

I felt my opponent's back to mine. I counted out the four strides, stopped, then took the one last step and about-faced. I zeroed in on my opponent's chest. This time I didn't need to imagine a red fist pumping inside a rib cage. I simply focused on the center of his vest. Jim placed the .38 in my hand, placed a Glock in the hand of my opponent, and stepped off to the side. He asked the both of us if we were ready. When we nodded that we were, Jim told us to raise our weapons and said, "Begin."

"Each visit to the chapel is a different test," Jim had explained. "The second time is as much a test of wills as a matter of marksmanship. It's sort of like a game of chicken. How long can you stand there staring down the barrel of another weapon before one of you gives into the tension? Big balls won't do you any good if you miss and take one in the chest. It's a balancing act."

I had to constantly weigh the loss of accuracy, the gun getting heavier in my hand the longer I waited, versus the macho factor.

As we stood there, rain pelting the corrugated metal roof of the hangar, there was a palpable sense of anticipation in the dank air. Maybe the same energy was there the first time too and I had been so consumed by the experience I hadn't noticed. The longer I held back, the bigger the rush. I could feel the thousand little crosscuts in the textured grip of the .38. Then I saw or thought I saw a tensing in my opponent's stance, but I could not react quickly enough. A flash. *Bang!* Then I fired.

A second later, I was still standing, still breathing freely. Nothing hurt. The freight train missed me. Across the way, the security guard was down, writhing on the floor. I was staring at him, admiring my handiwork, buzzing inside my own skin like a total freak. I'd hit him, but I couldn't lose control. I walked over to him, gave him my hand, and pulled him to his feet. We removed our helmets and stood across from each other. He looked utterly dejected. His hand was on my shoulder, my index finger in the hole in his shirt above his heart. Only I spoke, "Stop doubting and believe." When the receiving line was formed, only I passed along from person to person, repeating the phrase.

Someone clapped me on the back. Jim. "Great shot, Kip. Maybe you *can* get as good as me. You okay?"

I didn't answer right away. I couldn't. Just nodded my head yes.

"Come on." His arm urged me forward. "Let's get a beer."

I unhitched all my gear. As it fell to the floor at my feet my energy level dipped, but it was nothing like the crash I experienced the last time. Renee kissed me on the cheek and we slowly walked over to the beer coolers. I was already fantasizing about my next time in the chapel, about how I wanted to try this without the monkey suit and helmet. Addiction isn't only about the here and now but about the buzz of anticipation. It may well be a physical phenomenon, but it's equally romantic. In a wonderfully perverse way, addiction is like falling in love.

This time, Jim didn't come back to the locker room with me. It was only me and the security guard washing up, mostly in silence. What would we have had to talk about, anyway? I was lost in thought, feeling good about where I was at in my life. I wasn't sure I had ever felt this way before, even at the height of my fame and talent. How completely fucking weird was that? Life was good. I was writing again. Things between Jim and me had pretty much returned to normal. My times with Renee were really pretty amazing. I wasn't nearly bored with her and more surprisingly, she didn't seem the least bit tired of me.

When we went back into the chapel, the next two shooters were the big guy from the BCCC maintenance crew and Jim. They were dressed only. in vests covered in white T-shirts. The front of Jim's shirt was covered in red crosses and black smears. The big guy's shirt bore about ten or so crosses. The St. Pauli Girl stood next to me, holding my hand. There was a very different kind of tension in the air and in the crowd than earlier. The pinging of the rain on the roof was foreboding, each drop the tolling of a bell. I could feel the change in atmosphere in Renee's grip as she could in mine. This was gladiatorial and it came with the very real possibility of blood or death.

Something else was different, too. Although both men acted out the same rituals the security guard and I had just performed, there was a marked change in how they were done. The both of them moved with such amazing grace and precision that it seemed like a pas de deux. Although they were different sizes and different ages, the length and timing of their strides was nearly identical.

The snaggle-toothed girl handed each man his weapon—the maintenance guy the .38 I'd shot earlier and Jim the Browning—and stood back. She asked if they were ready. They nodded that they were and then, just as Jim had done before, she said, "Begin."

I figured the maintenance guy had to be pretty good to have done this kind of shooting ten times and for Jim to risk his life facing him. Still, the BCCC maintenance man was clearly the more nervous of the two. Jim stood there, steady as a rock, weapon raised, seeming not to breathe. Sweat was visible on the big man's brow and he wasn't nearly as solid as Jim. His breaths were louder and raspy, probably a result of all those cigarettes he always smelled of. He fired. Jim fired. They both went down, but it was obvious something was wrong. There was blood.

"Oh fuck! Oh fuck!" the big man screamed in pain, clamping his right hand over his left bicep, blood seeping through the tight spaces between his fingers. "Oh, Jesus, it burns."

Jim lay still where he fell as he had the first time. Nearly everyone rushed to the blood. Renee and I ran to Jim. We pulled him to his feet, but he bent back over in pain. When he stood straight again, I saw the hole in his T-shirt. He'd been hit in his belly and it clearly hurt, Kevlar or not.

"How is he?" Jim asked, thrusting his chin at the maintenance man.

"You hit him in the arm. What happened?"

"Later."

Jim rushed over to his bleeding opponent, who had a white towel wrapped around the wound. The blood hadn't yet leaked through.

"He'll be all right," said the guy from the copy center. "The shot just sort of cut through his tricep. Good thing it didn't get lodged in there. It'll hurt, but we'll get him patched up."

Jim went over to him. That weird silence fell over the chapel and everyone stood back to form the line. Jim stuck his index finger onto the bloody towel. The big man stuck his bloody finger to Jim's belly and they recited. Then they moved along the receiving line. Unlike in the world outside the chapel, wounded or not, you were expected to finish what you started. A few weeks back, Jim told me that short of death, there were no excuses. Now I knew it wasn't just hyperbole.

Jim gave the wounded man the customary hug, but didn't apologize. The maintenance guy didn't utter an angry word, but there was obvious puzzlement in his eyes and hesitation in his demeanor. As he was led back into the locker room, his eyes met mine and he held his gaze until he was helped through the mattresses and out of the chapel. There was something in his stare that I couldn't understand and by the time he disappeared from sight, I stopped trying to comprehend.

Jim said it fell on the two of us to clean up, so I sent Renee on ahead as we waited for the place to clear out. I looked forward to having a chance to talk to Jim about what had happened, but I wanted Jim to be the one to bring it up. He had a slightly different agenda.

"So, how was it the second time around? Different, right?" he asked, tying up the last of the plastic garbage bags. "Not like your old life."

"Let me tell you something: guns and books, they're not as different as you think. The first book is all about excitement and anticipation. You just write the damn thing because you don't really know what you're doing. But the second book ... Watch out! Especially if the first book got people's attention. When the second book is published—that is if you can manage to write a second book—they lie in the weeds for you wielding their long knives or worse."

"Worse?"

"Much worse," I said. "They can ignore you."

"That's a bad thing?"

"The worst thing there is, to be ignored," I said. "Better to be despised. So what happened with—"

He shook his head. "I was off tonight. My head was someplace else and I waited too long to fire. By the time I squeezed, he'd already hit me."

"Shit!"

"He'll live."

"But what if he hadn't?"

"You know those rules you were complaining about? Well, we got them for that too. Are you scared about shooting now?"

"Pretty much the opposite, Jim."

He smiled proudly. "Good thing. Come on, let's go."

Outside the hangar, the rain had given way to an achingly clear sky and a chilly northeast wind. I loaded the garbage bags into the box of Jim's pickup while he went to shut down the generator and stow it. Without the rumble of the generator all I could hear was that eerie creaking of the buildings in the wind.

Twenty

Outlines

I was worn out and when Jim dropped me off, I dragged my ass upstairs and into the shower. Renee was nude on the bed, dead asleep. As I let the water run over me, I realized my grasp on the inner workings of the chapel wasn't as firm as I thought it was. But I'd survived this long without understanding most of the mysteries of the universe and one more, give or take, wasn't going to ruin my day. I would either figure it out for myself or Jim would reveal the knowledge to me one day when we were out in the woods shooting. He enjoyed that, doling out information in tiny doses. I think it helped him feel in control, which, I suppose, he was.

The St. Pauli Girl came into the bathroom just as I finished shaving and kissed me on the cheek.

"There's three phone messages for you," she said.

I laughed. "I wonder who died?"

She punched my arm. "Don't even joke like that."

"When you're my age, kiddo, it's not a joke."

Feeling re-energized by the shower and Renee's lack of clothing, I was prepared to ignore the messages, but I was too curious.

I hadn't received three messages in a single day since Janice Nadir had taken her act on the road. She used to call me all the time and tell me how much she wanted to suck my cock or how she liked it when I fucked her hard from behind. I didn't miss those messages. Suddenly, irrationally, my focus shifted away from Janice and I found I was thinking of Amy. Had something happened to her? Is that what those messages were about? If they were, what would I do? How would I feel? Where would that leave me? Even I was a little bit embarrassed by my thinking of Amy only in terms of myself.

I splashed my face with aftershave, rolled on deodorant, and slipped into my old terry bathrobe—a long-ago gift from Amy. I kissed Renee on the mouth, desperately—a kiss like a prayer— and told her I'd be back up in a few minutes. Now she looked worried too. My mind raced with a hundred scenarios, one worse than the next, as I took the stairs two at a time. I listened to the three messages—all from Meg. The brittle tone of her voice and the cryptic "You need to call me back" did little to allay my fears.

"What the fuck, Donovan? Is Amy all right?"

"Amy?"

"My ex-wife," I whispered into the mouthpiece. "You remember her?"

"Don't be a schmuck, Kip. As far as I know, Amy's miserable being married to that dickhead Peter Moreland, but otherwise fine."

"Then what's with the messages? Something's wrong. Are you—"

"I'm fine too."

"Then what's the matter?"

"You haven't heard?"

"Heard what?" I asked, not very patiently.

"Haskell Brown is dead."

"What? What happened, did the gerbil get loose and gnaw through his colon?"

"Not only are you a prick, Weiler, but you're a homophobic one," she said.

"I love you and *you're* gay."

"We're not talking about me."

"Okay, Meg, what happened?"

"He was robbed and murdered early Sunday morning in Chelsea. They beat him and shot him. The cops think it was more than just a robbery because of the brutality of the beating."

"I don't understand."

"A hate crime, you idiot. Gay bashing isn't as popular as it used to be, but it's still the sport of kings for some."

"Fuck. I mean I had no love for the guy, but . . ."

We stayed on the phone sharing a minute of uncomfortable silence. Neither one of us, I think, wanted to say aloud what we were both thinking. Then Meg, as she always did, gave it voice.

"If that new book of yours isn't just some bullshit excuse to blow your life up again, Kip, tighten up the pages you've got so far. With them, I want an outline and a story synopsis as well."

"You know I don't do outlines."

"You do now! You want this book published, Weiler, you follow the rules, my rules. Understand? Remember that in this business mothers eat their young and then use the bones for toothpicks. And it's worse now than it used to be. Remember also, you're not who you used to be."

"I'm not sure I ever really was."

"Don't get philosophical on me, Kip. It doesn't suit you. I want something on my desk a week from today, ten days, latest. I'm going to let stuff settle down some before I approach Dudek through Mary Caputo."

"Okay."

"One more thing. I'm going to send signals to Dudek that you'll take the rights deal if he even thinks about a new book for you. That's as far as I'm willing to push him and if his answer is ultimately no, it's no and we take the rights deal. This is our last chance with Travers Legacy and yours with me. Get it?"

"We're through if I fuck this up."

"Exactly. I love you, Kip Weiler. God knows why, but I always have. You shoot this down or screw it up and that's it between us."

"One week," I said.

"Ten days, latest."

When I got upstairs, the St. Pauli Girl was sitting up in bed, her arms folded around her knees and bare breasts. "Is everything okay?" she asked, the concern on her face still visible even in the semidarkness.

I answered by gently unfolding her arms, softly pushing her legs apart, and pressing my mouth onto her. But when I woke up hours later, the St. Pauli Girl's flavor still filling up my senses, I was again thinking of Amy. Even now, ten years removed from her, I didn't fully comprehend the attraction. Given how many women I'd had without hardly trying, I didn't understand the power Amy had that let her turn me inside out, but she could and with nothing more than a sideways glance or the pursing of her lips. After we were married, I used to tell myself that my straying into strange beds—and I mean "strange" in all of its *Oxford American* permutations—was simply a function of my petulance about Amy's sway over me. I loved her fiercely, yet I resented her for it. Go figure.

Amy had been forced to deal with the worst of the Kipster, especially his talent's long, slow death rattle and the thousand little aftershocks that followed in its wake. Still, the dissolution of our marriage wasn't all on me. Amy was neither a martyr nor saint. She had her hairline cracks and peculiar vanities. The woman was more complicated than a Chinese box and twice as hard to open. Even her demeanor came with a wind chill. She considered writers more craftsmen than artists, and was more than a little irked by just how easily money and fame had come my way. "At best, writers are McArtists," she was fond of saying. Oh, we were quite a pair: two wounded, complicated people who resented the shit out of each other. Now there's a formula for success, huh?

As I stood to clean up, it occurred to me that a new book might mean more to me than I could have imagined. I went to my office afterwards to follow Meg's orders. I typed "Outline." Yet in spite of the news of Haskell Brown's death and the blood in the chapel that night, nothing came to me. For the first time since starting the book I felt pressure. And there I was staring at the nearly blank screen, the cursor mocking me at the end of the "e" in outline. *E* as in empty.

Twenty-One

Cutthroat

I wasn't empty for long.

A blanket of autumn snow in a hardscrabble place like Brixton County had that falsely purifying picture-postcard effect. You could fool yourself that the snow somehow stopped the miners and loggers from getting shitfaced after their shifts and going home to beat the crap out of their wives. If you listened carefully enough, you could almost hear John Denver singing some cracker-barrel hymn to the simplicity of rural life. Simplicity, my ass. Life was no less complicated here than anywhere else. If anything, life in Brixton had a more desperate edge than almost any place else I'd unpacked my bags. It was the land of coal and pine, not milk and honey. Like Jim once said to me, the only options for kids who grew up here were the mines, the pines, or the military recruitment signs. So, no, as pretty as it all looked as Jim drove Renee and me up into the hills that Friday at dusk, I wasn't buying into the notion of Brixton's snow-white baptism.

We started out the way Jim usually drove when we were going to shoot, but somewhere along the route he took a turn away from the river and we were in unfamiliar territory. We weren't headed to the chapel either. Not even Renee seemed to know where we were going. The confusion in her eyes was manifest. Funny, I thought, how I barely noticed the beauty of her eyes anymore. I used to see her features as a collection of distinct physical assets—the suede blue eyes, her impossible cheekbones, that perfect ass—as aspects of herself, as the St. Pauli Girl, but not as a woman. It dawned on me that these days I thought of her less and less as the St. Pauli Girl.

Finally, Jim pulled off the pavement onto a pitted dirt road that bounced us all around like a mechanical bull in a honky-tonk bar. We drove through a gap in a slatted wooden fence that had seen better days. The sky was already turning darker when I noticed some familiar vehicles parked along the side of the road. Jim hadn't said what we were up to and I still couldn't be sure, but the sight of those other pickups relaxed me. It had quite the opposite effect on Renee, the confusion in her eyes morphing into worry. Jim didn't pull over until we emerged into a clearing about the size of two football fields placed side by side.

"Used to be a berry farm," he said. "Guy went bankrupt after they shut the base down."

When we piled out of the Jim's old F-150, people emptied out of their trucks too. This was a long way from the chapel, but it was the same ragtag cast of characters. The deputy sheriff was there. Stan Petrovic too, in all his pock-marked glory. In fact, the only one missing was the security guard from Hardentine. Guess he actually had to watch the abandoned base.

Jim asked, "Did you set up the logs like you were told?"

The fat kid said, "Everything is ready." He retreated to his 4x4, started it up, and turned it so that it faced the clearing. In the truck's high beams, I could make out several piles of logs. Some were stacked no more than one or two high, while others were piled maybe three or four feet high. They were set at odd angles to each other and there didn't seem to be a pattern to how they were arranged.

Jim was pleased. "Good, let's collect the equipment here, and then go and park our trucks at even intervals around the patch. Don't forget to leave them running and to turn your brights on."

I think that's when I started rushing. My head was spinning so that I barely noticed Renee go back to Jim's truck with him. I was vaguely aware of the displeasure in her voice as she spoke to him, but I was already too far gone to care. Things were starting to make sense, a twisted kind of Brixton sense. We were going to shoot, but it wasn't going to be done like the carefully choreographed Kabuki of the chapel. No, this was going to be very different indeed.

"We have four full suits," Jim said when he returned from his truck and dropped the Colonel's duffel bag to the ground. "If we do this fast, most of us can shoot tonight."

There was much rejoicing in Mudville, except from the maintenance man. Jim reached into his coat pocket and pulled out a handful of folded pieces of paper, which he dumped into his Carhartt baseball cap and shook around.

"Line up. I'm going to give you all numbers and then we'll pick from the hat." With that he pointed to himself, "One." Renee: "Two." Me: "Three," . . . and so on until he got to Stan Petrovic, "Seventeen."

Jim thrust the hat out in front of the maintenance guy from BCCC. If this honor was some attempt at reconciliation for Jim having wounded the man, it wasn't working. The guy glared at Jim as he stepped forward, rubbing the coat over his bicep where he'd been hit by the bullet. Jim seemed oblivious and told him to pick four numbers. He did without enthusiasm and handed the four slips of paper to Renee, who didn't seem at all pleased to be calling the numbers. The undercurrent was a far cry from the chapel.

"Eight. Three. Nine. Seventeen."

The fat kid, the deputy sheriff, Stan, and I stepped forward or maybe everyone else stepped back. I was now rushing so hard I couldn't tell.

"Here's the deal," Jim said, dabbing his finger into the now familiar coffee can and touching it to each of our foreheads. "Get your suits on. I'll load your weapons with four rounds each. This is Cutthroat: every man for himself. You take a hit anywhere, you're dead. You've got to stay within the confines of the clearing and the only things you can use for cover are the log barriers, the snow, and anything else that you can find out there. You can't hide behind the trucks and you can't sit behind any one barrier too long. When my truck horn blows, you have to move. You don't move: you're dead. You have fifteen minutes to kill everyone else out there with you. Got it? Good. Then get dressed. When you're suited up, pick up your weapon, walk out there, and select a barrier. When all four of you are out there, I'll blow the horn to begin."

Ten minutes later I was flat on my belly, taking cover behind one of the low log barriers. I had the .38 in my hand, my heart thumping. In spite of the cold, I was sweating through my underwear. This was going to be a test of so much more than marksmanship and machismo. The wind was up, and depending upon your position, snow might be blowing into your eyes through the slits in the face mask of your helmet. You'd have to think your way through this and I figured my brain was about the only advantage I had.

The deputy sheriff was far more likely to have been trained for situations like this even if the most dangerous thing he ever did was to chase pleated skirts. Stan may have been a surly motherfucker and a belligerent drunk, but you don't play special teams in the NFL for as long as he had without a giant set of balls and an incredible instinct for survival. And the fat kid had been good enough to have faced down Jim in the chapel.

Jim stood on his truck horn for the game to begin. Instead of running out from behind the barrier, I rolled to my left, made a bipod of my elbows and steadied the .38. I took the chance that one of my opponents would stand and run across my path. I figured right. The fat kid burst out from behind the tallest barrier. I took a deep breath, let it out slowly, and squeezed the trigger. He went down in a heap, grabbing his left thigh and screaming in pain. As usual, I spent too long patting myself on the back. Dirt and snow kicked up a few inches in front of my face, through the eye slits, and blinded me. *Shit!* My eyes filled with tears and I couldn't stop blinking, but I had to move and move fast.

I rolled back behind the barrier, which was probably against one rule or another. I couldn't afford to care. This was about survival and about winning. Fuck the rules, I thought. As my eyes worked hard to flush out the dirt, I realized that at least some good had come of what had happened: The fat kid was out of the game, leaving me only two adversaries to worry about, and one of those adversaries had wasted a bullet. I had three bullets to make two kills and so did one of my opponents. The other still had four, but I had to use my head for something other than math.

Figuring it was human nature for people to stay safely hidden behind one of the barriers until Jim blew the horn to move, I decided my best chance at survival was to go now, before the horn. Problem was, I had only a vague notion of where one of the others might be. Since the shot that kicked the dirt into my eyes had come from in front of me, I guessed that one of the shooters was behind the barrier about sixty feet ahead of where I was. I had no sense of where the other shooter might be. If I chose wrong, I'd probably be running straight into a waiting bullet. Having decided to go, I took a few deep breaths, but the equation changed before I could move.

Strange, I almost felt as if I wasn't thinking as me anymore, but as McGuinn. Early on I had made the decision not to confine McGuinn to a place like the chapel and now here I was struggling in a setting not unlike the one I was creating for McGuinn. Sometimes art imitates life and sometimes it's the other way around. Out here, it was both. Writers often inject themselves into their characters. Now, I was trying to inject my character into me.

Just as I stuck my head out from behind the logs, I caught sight of the deputy coming out from behind the barrier straight ahead of me. *So he was the one who almost got me.* He was making a mad dash for a low stack of logs thirty yards to his left. I guess he'd also thought the element of surprise was the smart play. Only it wasn't.

He didn't get five feet before Stan rose up from a prone position to the left of another barrier and blasted the deputy square in the back. He pitched forward from the force of the bullet and his own momentum. He lay there still for a few seconds, but didn't writhe in pain or scream anything except, "Goddammit!" The bullet must have caught him in a heavily protected spot and the only thing wounded was his pride.

Now there were two: Stan and me.

Stan stayed upright, making the same mistake I had, taking a lap of honor before he'd won anything. He was pretty far away from me and my eyes weren't yet totally clear of grit, but I doubted I would get a cleaner shot at a stationary target later on. Taking the shot right then is what McGuinn would have done. He'd written that you had to take your shot when the opportunity presented itself because second chances are never guaranteed. I fired. Splinters flew off the edge of the log barrier just at Stan's back. He turned his head my way. I couldn't see his face beneath his helmet, but it was easy to imagine his sneer. I ducked back behind the logs.

The rush was gone and in its place was fear. It didn't matter that the suit afforded me full protection or that I had two rounds left. I was being hunted and I was hunting. This was worlds apart from the controlled situation of the chapel. I'd been scared before, but not scared like this, not even when Frank Vuchovich stuck the Colt in my face.

The horn blew and I moved, combat crawling as fast as I could to a tall stand of logs to my right. I stopped long enough to rise up to try and catch a glimpse of Stan. I thought I heard something, but I'd lost him. I crawled again. Something crashed down loudly to my left. I sat up on my knees and aimed the .38. That's when the baseball bat hit me in the back of the head and I went to sleep, face mask down in the snow.

●

My head burned with pain and when the trauma room doctor shined his pen light in my eyes I thought my skull might literally explode.

"You've got a textbook concussion there, Mr. Weiler," said the doctor. "We'll get you something for the pain, do a scan to make sure it's nothing more serious, and we'll keep you here overnight."

I was in no shape to argue with the man. I didn't even know how I'd gotten there and wasn't a hundred percent sure of how I got concussed. The last thing I remembered was being on my belly in the snow behind a log and thinking about how scared I was.

"I'll let your wife come in while I arrange for your scan and get a nurse to bring you something for the pain."

Wife? Amy was here? Jesus, I *really* was confused.

Renee came into the examining room. She was red-eyed and shaking.

"The doctor says you're going to be okay in a few days, but you have to stay here tonight," she said, her voice brittle.

"What happened?"

"You don't remember?"

"Some of it, but not how I got hurt," I said.

"Stan threw a big rock that landed over your left shoulder. When you got to your knees, he came up behind you and . . . and . . . "

"And what?"

"He shot you in the back of the helmet from about twenty feet. The round got between some of the padding and the helmet took almost all the impact. If it was one of those old metal helmets . . . I told the doctor you fell off a ladder."

"Did anyone do anything about it? Did Jim?"

"We can't. It's against the rules. You get into this and you take the risk. Anything else would ruin the whole idea of it," she said, her heart not in it.

I knew. Jim had told me a hundred times. Didn't mean I had to like it.

"I'm going to kill fucking Stan. I'm telling you, Renee, I'm going to kill him."

"Who are you going to kill, Mr. Weiler?" It was a nurse, a small cup in one hand and a larger cup in the other.

"My landlord," I lied. "If he had repaired the porch like he was supposed to, I wouldn't have been up on that ladder."

"Here," she said, "take these. They should help with the pain. And please try not to get agitated."

When the nurse left the room, I repeated, "I'm going to kill that cocksucker." And I swear I almost meant it.

166

Twenty-Two

Fox Hunt

This time we met at 4:00 A.M. not at the chapel and not at the old berry farm, but at a long-abandoned logging camp about five miles east of where Jim and I shot in the woods.

Here, the surrounding hills were not so steep nor as prevalent, and whole swathes of forest had been logged into submission in the years before anyone had heard of Earth Day. At this point in its travels, the Crooked River ran a straighter, wider course and whispered in comparison to its roaring by the falls.

Renee had been sullen and silent as she drove my car up into the hills. She hadn't said so, but I knew she'd wanted me to stay home. I was feeling much better, though I wasn't quite over my concussion symptoms. We both sensed it wouldn't take much to send me backsliding. You have no idea just how awful concussion headaches are until you experience them. Considering my once prodigious consumption of cocaine and alcohol, I'd had some formidable headaches, but the ones I suffered through in the wake of Stan's shot to the back of my head were titanic. Legion were the joys of concussion because the headaches weren't the worst of it.

In the days following Cutthroat, I became depressed and disconnected, lost inside my own head. My internal voice was drowned out by a cloying and constant ringing in my ears and there were moments I found myself thinking life wasn't worth living like this, that it wouldn't take much more of it to send me following in my father's footsteps. A bullet through my brain, I thought, couldn't have been much worse than what I was suffering through. I suppose if the predawn festivities were just one more trip into the chapel for ashes and bullets, I would have stayed home, but the rush of something new pushed me to go. Even so, my head was a little cottony. I felt a beat too slow, a step behind.

Getting gingerly out the passenger door, it struck me that my red Porsche seemed completely out of place there among the pickups in a clearing above the river. It gave me pause, reminding me that in spite of all that had transpired since late September, I was just as out of place among these people as my car was among their trucks. It gave me pause, but didn't stop me. I'd crossed a line the first time I walked into the chapel and there would be no stepping back now.

The fog shrouding the treetops and crawling a few feet off the ground felt like it was pouring right out of my head. Whether it was the early hour or that the ride along the bumpy dirt road had worn me out, I couldn't say. What was obvious to me was that I was falling back down the well I'd only just crawled out of. I couldn't quite focus on the words Renee spoke to me as we trudged up a low hill to where the others were seated in a circle on old tree stumps around a small campfire. Everyone I'd ever seen at the chapel was there, Jim giving me a slight nod of hello. I was glad to be able to rest on a stump as an unwanted and familiar throbbing began in my temples.

Laid out by the fire was one solitary protective suit, the Colonel's duffel bag, and the can of ashes. I waited. We all waited for someone to come forward and when someone did, I was caught completely off guard. It wasn't Jim who stepped to the fore, but Renee.

"This is Fox Hunt," she said, looking everywhere but at me. "One fox. One suit. The rest of us are the hounds. Some of us have done this before, but I will explain it for everyone else. The rules are simple: The fox gets a fifteen-minute head start and we can't watch where the fox goes. The fox can go anywhere, hide anywhere, and use whatever tricks it has to to survive, but the fox has no weapon. After the fifteen minutes, the rest of us have until sunup to kill the fox. The hounds will have only one round in their weapons. If the fox eludes us, we all have to swim across the river and back as punishment. Then we will meet this Friday at the chapel and burn our shirts in a fire. All but the fox will be worthless once again, all of our blood erased. Those who are not original members may never be invited back in."

She nodded at the guy from the copy center who handed us neatly folded pieces of paper. That done, he retrieved the can of ashes and went around the circle, dipping his fingers into the can and touching them to our foreheads.

"If there is a mark on your paper, pick a weapon and walk down to the river, facing the water. Spread out far from each other. In fifteen minutes or so, a shot will be fired and then it begins."

There was a slash across my paper and as I rose off the stump to get my weapon, I wobbled slightly. Jim grabbed my arm to steady me and whispered in my ear, "When it starts, stick by me."

I was glad he made the offer, because as I moved down by the riverbank the fog only got thicker. The headache was worsening and I could feel myself retreating into that isolated place inside my own skull. Time lost all meaning as I stared into the black water. Then I thought I heard something and the world went crazy. People were running everywhere, but I was frozen. I looked for Jim, for Renee, to no good end. I couldn't make sense of anything.

Suddenly, I was being pulled away from the riverbank and saw that it was Jim who had me by the wrist. He was speaking to me. I could hear that he was saying things, but his words were just jumbled sounds in my ears. I kept tripping over things, falling over, and sliding back toward the river on the slick ground. Jim was good, never letting me lose sight of him, never abandoning me, but it was just no good. Once we got out of the clear-cut section of the forest and into the trees, I lost Jim. I thought I heard his sharp whispers cutting through fog. Yet I could not focus well enough to locate him. His whispers faded and then disappeared altogether.

With my completely fucked-up sense of time, I can't say how long I just stood there, deciding what to do and how to do it. Eventually I forced myself to move, taking small, measured steps to test the ground beneath my feet. I needed to find a place to wait the fox hunt out, to rest, but I had to choose wisely. These woods were dark under the best of circumstances and with the fog, it was impossible to see more than fifteen or twenty feet ahead of me. Bullets would be flying and there was always a chance of ricochet. The fox was actually in the least danger of any of us.

Walking did me no good, so I got on hands and knees and felt my way. I found a spot where some trees had fallen over each other to create a kind of barrier with a hollow just large enough to accommodate me. With a wall of big pines in front of the hollow, I felt I'd be pretty safe there until the sun came up. I lay down on my left side, the wet pine straw making a less than comfortable mattress. It didn't take long for me to stop noticing the discomfort or the dampness or anything else.

I didn't sleep, exactly, because I was conscious of occasional gunshots echoing through the trees, twigs snapping under foot.

I also heard voices, passing footsteps. How close by, I could not say. And though I wasn't asleep, I wasn't awake either. Each sound seemed to set my mind off in another direction. Mostly I confused myself with Terry McGuinn, envisioning him, us, in the hyper-reality I'd created in the pages of the book.

McGuinn's prayers were answered with the Almighty's usual mix of mercy and malevolence. There were no lurking branches beneath the waterline on which he might be skewered, but the current did conspire to twist his body in such a manner as to ensure his wrecked left shoulder would absorb the full brunt of the impact against the felled tree that lay across the river, pushing him to the falls. When his shoulder smacked into the tree, the explosion of pain stiffened him so fierce it near snapped him in half. He'd never experienced the likes of it before and when the agony subsided enough for him to snatch a breath, he realized his bladder had let go. He laughed through chattering teeth.

"That's right," he said, looking skyward, "why impale me, for fook's sake, when you can favor me with small indignities? This can't be the extent of me punishment for the trail of bodies I've left in me wake, can it?" The Lord, he thought, may have chosen the Hebrews, but his sense of irony was purely Irish.

Now that his little moment with God had passed, he had to get himself out of the water. As the pain of the impact with the tree lessened, he realized he could not feel his legs and that his good arm was leaden and stinging like a basket of bees. But this wasn't about pain any longer. Another few moments in the water would be his undoing, so he willed his right arm onto the tree. It was no good. Most of the bark had been stripped away by the pounding of the water and the exposed wood was as slippery as ice. Finally, his groping hand fell upon the jagged knob of a branch that had been torn away by the current. His hand anchored to the knob, he talked his near-frozen legs into feeling for a rock or some refuse he might use to propel himself up out of the water and onto the tree.

Bang! Something heavy—a smaller tree or orphaned canoe, perhaps—slammed into him, pressing the wind out of his lungs and nearly sending him back under. But Terry McGuinn, calling on whatever strength he held in reserve, kept himself up and eyed the flotsam that had almost cast him to his fate. He had been wrong, as wrong as he had ever been, for the thing that had hit him with such fury was neither a tree nor a canoe. It was the body of the poor footballer Zoe had lured out of the bar less than two hours ago. The bullet wound had destroyed the lad's once-handsome face, but the shine of his wet, rich black skin under the moonlight showed his beautifully sculpted muscles, muscles now as useless as the prayers of the Brit soldiers who had kneeled before McGuinn and begged for mercy.

McGuinn bowed his head over the body, not in prayer, but in frustration. It was his attempt to save the lad that had gotten his own self shot in the shoulder and caused him to go tumbling into the river. With a gentle pat goodbye, Terry maneuvered the lad under the tree and sent the body on its way. As he did so, a bullet bit into the pulp of the tree not a few centimeters from his hand. He had no more time to mourn the boy. It was his life at stake now and he was determined not to die on someone else's terms.

I'm not sure what roused me finally. It might have been the snapping of a twig, the echo of another gunshot, or the sound of soft steps on the forest floor. My headache was better, if not fully gone, and the fog had lifted both inside and outside my skull. The sky was lightening in preparation for dawn, but I was still a little disoriented and stiff from the awkward position I'd had to keep myself in. Then things got very real all at once.

I heard footsteps, rapid footsteps coming my way. I forced myself up out of the little hollow to peek over the fallen trees that had sheltered me. And there, two hundred or so feet away, running right at me was the fox. It was impossible to mistake that bulky suit. Bulky suit or not, the fox ran gracefully through the woods. One big problem with that suit was the eye slit in the face mask. It didn't allow for much peripheral vision and when running, it wouldn't allow for very good vision straight ahead either. The fox hadn't seen me.

I tucked my head back behind the trees, pulled the .38 out of my waistband, and checked that my one round was in the right chamber. I had to act quickly now as dawn couldn't be more than a minute or two away and the fox would soon be on me. Figuring the fox might try to take cover where I had passed the last few hours and that he wouldn't be able to leap over the top, especially not in that suit, I crawled around to the side of the felled trees that followed the downhill slope. That was the path of least resistance and even if the fox turned in the other direction, I would have a pretty clear shot at his back.

I did what I had done during Cutthroat and made a bipod of my arms, but as I took square aim at the fox, something struck me. There was a familiarity in the fox's gait, things about the way it moved that I recognized. *Renee!* Fuck, it was Renee and she was turning toward me. I clicked back the hammer and began to squeeze the trigger when the woods exploded with thunder. The fox wrenched sideways, then tumbled forward, landing right in front of me.

I yanked the straps and pulled off her face mask. I'd been right. She was breathing hard, her face wet with perspiration and twisted in frustration. Still, her mouth smiled a little bit up at me. But before I could say a word, another figure appeared, standing above us. Jim.

Twenty-Three

Dry Turkey

Meg called on Thanksgiving Eve, two weeks after the Fox Hunt. I had finally gotten past all of my concussion-related symptoms. In spite of the pain of playing Cutthroat and the disorientation of Fox Hunt, it was worth it. Both had opened my eyes to new possibilities for the book and the cursor no longer mocked me. I'd incorporated both experiences into the book and riffed on that scene of McGuinn in the river. I don't know if I dreamed it or hallucinated it, but whatever state I was in when I conceived it, I loved the idea of McGuinn caught in a deadly cycle of violence where he tries to stop the killing. The outline and synopsis seemed to write themselves and new pages poured out of me. The world I had created for McGuinn was paradise, a redemption of bullets.

The most difficult thing I had to do during those days was to call Meg and beg for an extension to her arbitrary deadline. I repeated the lies Renee and I told the ER doctor about my falling off a ladder and sustaining a concussion. Meg gladly gave me a week. Although I'd met the new deadline, I hadn't heard back from her since. I just assumed all my maneuvering to get a new book deal had fucked everything up. Surprisingly, I was okay with that. I kept on teaching my classes, writing the book, shooting with Jim, and playing house with Renee. I didn't start drinking again or looking for coke or someone new to fuck. I almost qualified for Zen mastership. *Om.* I guess the only un-Zen aspect of the new me was my desire to fuck up Stan Petrovic in the worst possible way. Not only did I want to kill the prick, I wanted to humiliate him while I did it.

I'd missed one turn in the chapel, but had shot once last week. Though the thrill wasn't gone, it was going. After playing Cutthroat and Fox Hunt, the chapel seemed tame and my rush was a bit less intense. The junkie's dilemma: I'd hit that wall junkies always hit. No matter what anyone tells you, all addictions are the same. You've got to keep upping the dose. Jim seemed to know it without being told.

"Another couple of weeks, Kip, and maybe you can try the real thing."

"The real thing?" I said, getting hard at the thought of it.

"Vests only."

"Like you and the fat kid?"

"Yeah, just like that, but don't say yes right away."

"Yes."

He laughed, but shook his head. "It's dangerous, Kip. You saw what could happen if everything doesn't go just right. I could just as easily have hit that guy in the throat or eye as his arm. If you get killed, we're just going to take you out in the woods and bury you somewhere you won't ever be found. Even if you're real seriously wounded, that's what we'll have to do. We can't risk everybody else to save one person. You understand?"

"Ever have to do that before, dig a hole out in the woods somewhere?" I asked, smiling.

Jim didn't answer, keeping his expression cool and neutral. "Just think about it," is all he said.

I didn't have to think about it. I wanted it. I suppose I'd wanted it from the moment I saw Jim and the fat kid in the chapel that first time. I could still smell the gun smoke in the air.

"I want it, Jim. I want it."

And then, for the first time in a month, I saw hints and flickers of that smile. The one that said: *I know you, Kip Weiler; I know you better than you know yourself.* But it quickly vanished, forced off his face by the proud mentor smile. He extended his right hand to me, and his grip expressed more pride in me and more love for me than my father had ever managed in his entire lifetime. Was it odd that I basked in the glow of approval of some twenty-year-old yahoo from Buttfucksville?

"Then let's start getting you ready."

But that was earlier and now Meg was on the phone. What she had to say made Thanksgiving seem so much more than an excuse to force down dry turkey and watch football.

"I don't know how you did it, Weiler, but this book is fucking genius."

"And . . ."

"And Franz Dudek thinks so too," she said. "It's a deal. I was going to send the contracts down, but I think you need to come up here next weekend. We should talk face-to-face."

"What for?"

"I miss you."

"That's horseshit, Donovan. If you missed me so much, why haven't I seen you in seven years?"

"I don't think you really want an answer to that, do you?"

"I suppose not, but you still haven't given me a good reason."

"Because Dudek wants to take us out to dinner and look you in the eye."

"What, he's going to read me the riot act?"

"I don't know, frankly, but it must be something like that. And if he does, you're going to sit there with your hands folded and take it."

"For this, yes," I said. "I'll take whatever he's dishing out."

"The hotel's on my dime, Weiler. I'll e-mail the reservation details to you."

"I'll be there."

"You better be."

Click.

Twenty-Four

Drama

Until Frank Vuchovich stuck his Colt Python in my nose, the toughest thing I had to tackle in Brixton was explaining subordinate clauses to the zombie-faced kids of coal miners and loggers. Well, that and marking their near-illiterate papers. Yet, as the West Side of Manhattan stretched out before me through the towers and cables of the George Washington Bridge, I found I was scared shitless. Suddenly, Brixton County felt like William Blake's Jerusalem, dark Satanic mills notwithstanding. From the night Meg called with the good news, I thought this was exactly what I wanted. Now, not so much. It hadn't taken long for the doubts to creep back in—the remembrances of things past, the bad things.

When I came out of rehab, Brixton was an easy place to land. One of the keys to breaking any addiction is to avoid the people, places, and things that help facilitate easy access to your particular poison. Well, let me tell you something about New York City in the 1980s: it was the mother of all enablers. I confronted my weaknesses on a moment-to-moment basis. Not confronted, really. I just sort of acquiesced. Every restaurant, every club and night spot was full of cocaine, cocktails, and willing blonds. And there was always an ample supply of Seven Sisters fangirls at the ready when I got bored of the blonds and wanted to have an intelligent conversation between orgasms.

Adoration is a universal addiction to which I was no more or less susceptible than anyone else. In the Manhattan of those golden years, nothing got the toadies, sycophants, and suck-asses going like success. Regardless of the abject dreadfulness of *Clown Car Bounce*, *The Devil's Understudy*, and *Curley Takes Five*, I would have continued to be hailed as a genius if those books had somehow managed to do good numbers. When anthropologists and historians want to study the Big Bang moment of our cultural demise, they will look back to 1980s Manhattan, the time and place when the singularity of substance and style exploded into a chasm of universal proportion. Didn't matter what the essential value of anything was as long as it sold.

So it was with no small amount of trepidation that I'd loaded a few things into the last vestige of the Kipster, his ridiculous 1988 Porsche 911, and headed for New York City. I'd come close to selling the car a hundred times. I mean, for chrissakes, the nearest Porsche dealership was fifty miles across the state line and simple maintenance cost more than a month's rent. Plus, in a calloused and chapped-hands place like Brixton, it marked me as a superior fucker and a total outsider. Oddly enough, as I drove out of town, I no longer felt like either one of those things.

And there were reasons for my skittishness about driving back into the lion's mouth that went beyond my worries about temptation. I'd swiped the .38 from the Colonel's duffel bag the last time I shot with Jim. I don't know why exactly. There was no inherent thrill in "borrowing" the .38. I nearly soiled myself at the thought of getting caught and then having to explain myself to Jim. The fear was not that I'd be exiled—it was pretty clear that Jim got as much out of our relationship as I did—but that I wouldn't have been able to express my reasons for taking it in a way that made any sense.

Fact is, I had gone shooting with Jim nearly every day since the end of September. It was part of my routine and writers dread the loss of routine almost more than anything else. I think I took the revolver because I wanted to carry a piece of that routine with me even if I couldn't shoot in the wilds of New York City. It was a rosary to pray on, a physical reminder of the thing that had made the book possible in the first place. But who knows? Truth is always more complicated than the rationalization.

And there was Renee. She too was part of my routine and don't think I hadn't been tempted to bring her, to show her my old world, a new world to her. Unlike the .38, which would be nothing more than a kind of semi-religious talisman, Renee would bring real comfort. It wouldn't have been the first time I'd sought convenient comfort in the company of a woman. The amazing thing is, I didn't want to disrespect Renee like that, to turn her back into the St. Pauli Girl. I'd even convinced myself that she didn't want to go. She hadn't asked to come, not with words. Yet, as the week unfolded, I could see *Please bring me, please* writ large in her eyes.

In spite of my recent un-Kipster-like behavior, I didn't fool myself that my default settings weren't still firmly locked on self-destruct. It would take more than a few months of writing, monogamy, and noble impulses to declare the Kipster fully exorcised. I liked drama. I mean, what else were the chapel, Cutthroat, and Fox Hunt all about if not drama? I liked to complicate things and I was less than confident that the new me wasn't more a function of lack of opportunity than a reflection of profound change.

No, as much as I liked the idea of having Renee with me, I knew leaving her in Brixton was the right thing to do. The right thing for me. For once, I needed things to be simple. I told Renee that I'd be going back to New York soon enough and that we'd make a vacation of it, over Christmas maybe. It wasn't so much a lie as a fantasy, one she seemed willing to go along with so we might both get through the week until I left.

●

Now, with the first dim rays of the sun filtering through the gaps in the skyline, it occurred to me that this was when I'd normally be wrapping up my first writing session of the day and climbing back into bed with Renee for a few minutes before getting dressed to run with Jim. Okay, so I knew I would miss them, miss my routine, but I didn't expect it to happen even before I got across the Hudson River. Hell, a few more minutes of this, I thought, and I'd be getting weepy for Stan Petrovic.

As I opened the door to the Liars Pub, a gaggle of chattering, Southern blue-hairs poured out past me and asked for directions to Radio City. Their tour bus to Branson must have missed a turn at St. Louis. But who was I to laugh at them, even a little bit? You teach at Brixton County Community College, you lose the privilege of looking down your nose at anyone but yourself.

"One for lunch?" the hostess asked, thumbing a stack of menus.

"I'm meeting someone. The reservation's under Donovan."

When the hostess looked down at her reservation sheet, I looked at her. Curvy, petite, and in her mid-twenties, she was dressed in a vintage clothing store cocktail dress—black, of course—over black heels that reeked of credit card debt. Her hair was jet black, her skin a shade of light mocha, her eyes almond-shaped but hazel. Her lips red and thick, her nose upturned, her breasts full, she was the most exotic-looking woman I'd seen in seven years.

"Yes, we have it, but I'm afraid Miss Donovan hasn't yet arrived. Would you care to be seated or to wait at the bar?"

"Actress, dancer, painter, or writer?" I asked. This might have been the only time I posed the question without a motive more nefarious than curiosity. After all, no one who looked like her came to New York City for a career in hostessing. Nobody.

"Writer."

I said, "You have my condolences."

If she was offended, she didn't show it. "Tell me about it."

"This place used to really be something once."

She sighed. "So I've heard."

"You would have liked it," I said.

"Not now."

"Of course not, it's a job."

"It's a corpse. No one likes working in a place that once was."

"Almost as unpleasant as somebody who once was. I'll be at the bar."

I'd been so exhausted when I drove across the GWB and down to the hotel on 44th Street that nothing had penetrated. Nor did I get teary-eyed and gawky on the cab ride over here. Only when I made my way to the bar did it begin to sink in. Standing there, taking it all in gave me a sense of just how long I'd been away, of how isolated and insulated I'd been, and what this weekend might mean to me.

The Liars—no one who knew better called it by its full name— was a stone's throw from the Flatiron Building and had been around for about a century. Back in the day, it used to be the kind of place where writers swapped stories about bigger-than-life characters like Runyon, Fitzgerald, Faulkner, and Hemingway. But now as I looked around I saw that the place was as artificial as Disneyland. It had become a theme park eatery that sold T-shirts and hot sauce. The banquettes bore the names of legendary writers on commemorative brass plaques. The Liars was a venue where gods and giants had been supplanted by tourists and the talentless. Even before I left New York, the Liars had become a bit of an insiders' joke. Now it was just a joke. Not so different from me, really.

Given that Meg had booked me into the Algonquin, it came as no shock that she'd chosen the Liars for lunch. She seemed not to know what to do with me, fearing, I suppose, that I'd somehow melt down at the thought of eating or sleeping somewhere not haunted by literary ghosts. And why not? "Literary ghost" was a pretty apt description of me. I might have considered telling her that I would have preferred to stay in a boutique hotel and to lunch at a restaurant that didn't sell souvenirs. The very notion of a chic hotel and three-star restaurant had broad appeal to someone from Brixton County. And while the Algonquin, a lovely old hotel, was more than several steps up in class from Hendrick's Motor Court or the Red Roof Inn in New Prague, it wasn't exactly hopping. The most exciting thing about the Algonquin was the cat that lived in the lobby. Maybe that was the point. Until I signed those contracts, Meg meant to keep me as far away as possible from hot new places and dangerous old haunts like the Chelsea Hotel. I didn't like it, but I guess I understood her reasoning.

I took note of many things as I stood there nursing a pint of ale. Meg was always late for our meetings. She liked drama too, but only of her own making. I noticed too that several additions had been made to the caricature sketches of writers, editors, and publishers lining the walls. I saw the sketch of Moira Blanco that hadn't been there seven years ago and the one of the recently deceased Haskell Brown. I wondered if the cops had made any headway on his murder, but didn't dwell on the subject. I wasn't a hypocrite and it was Brown's homicide that had cleared my path. I noticed sketches of Bart Meyers and Nutly and Marty

Castronieves. Mostly I noticed the one of me that wasn't there and winced at how much that hurt.

Nor did it escape me that the hostess wasn't close to being the hottest woman in the place. At the bar alone there were five women, most of them in their early twenties, who, even on a no-makeup–bad-hair day, would have been Miss Brixton County. And no two of them were attractive in the same way. I'd forgotten that New York City was a city of St. Pauli Girls. That at any one time in any bar, on a subway car, or in a movie theater line, there were women, young and old, whose varied charms and looks were even more alluring than Renee's. Renee had a kind of regional perfection, if that makes any sense. Yet, at that moment, I found myself missing her. Then Meg walked in.

When we first met, Meg's look was sex neutral: not androgynous, neutral. She was plain faced, brown eyed, thin lipped, and built like a pencil, so she depended on her black-on-black wardrobe and take-no-prisoners attitude to lend her an air of authority. We hit it off almost immediately, though, to this day, I'm unsure why. I liked that she was immune to my charms and me to hers. It was just healthier that way. Funny thing is, our taste in women was very similar: we liked them, a lot of them, and often. It was one of the few things we shared, actually. Meg was unknowable. I knew about her. I knew she was loyal and dogged, but not why. True, I'd earned her a lot of money once, but that was yesterday's news and in New York publishing, yesterday was ancient history. I never knew much about her upbringing, her family, or what was going on inside her head and she never volunteered information. Still, we'd somehow managed to love each other.

The Meg who strolled into the Liars was more severe looking than I remembered. Her thin brown hair had gone silver-gray and she wore it short, gelled, and spiky. She had on glasses with sharp rectangular lenses like microscope slides set in heavy black frames. In her black leather duster with upturned collar, she reminded me of Ming the Merciless from the old Flash Gordon serials, and her black bag was more Harley saddlebag than purse. She would have been as out of place in Brixton, I thought, as Truman Capote in Holcomb, Kansas. I watched Meg hungrily eye the hostess as she handed her the duster to be checked. That much hadn't changed. Meg wore a black silk blouse over gray wool slacks and pointy-toed black pumps. Around her neck and wrists she sported thick, uncomfortable-looking silver jewelry twisted at irregular angles. Sort of Cartier meets Home Depot.

"What are you smiling at, Weiler?" she asked, when I slid into the booth next to her.

I leaned over, kissed her cheek. "It's been a long time, Meg."

"You're not going to start sobbing, are you?" she said, even as she squeezed my hand.

"I promise. You?"

"Don't be an ass. I've wasted too many tears on you over the years."

"You look good, Donovan. And gray slacks, my god, it's heresy." She laughed or what passed for her laughing. "You could always do that to me, you know, make me laugh. You look older, Kip, but fit."

"I run."

"Talk about heresy! The only running you used to do was from bed to bed."

When the waitress came over and began reciting her prepared little speech, Meg cut her off and ordered a dry Ketel One martini with four olives. I held up my half-finished beer and said I was fine. Meg looked relieved.

"This was an interesting choice for lunch," I said. "What happened, all the tables at Applebee's and Ruby Tuesday's were booked?" She knew I didn't want an answer. "And the good old

Algonquin, thanks for that. Maybe I'll find an old pair of Dorothy Parker's knickers to sniff. Her crypt's in the basement, right?"

The martini arrived and Meg swirled the contents around with the olive-laden plastic sword. She sipped it, curled her lips, and slid an olive into her mouth.

"Look, Weiler, if I could have kept you in a straitjacket and leg irons until after dinner tomorrow night, I would have. But I figured the Algonquin and this dreadful joint were the most I could get away with without you acting out."

"It's fine. *I'm* fine. You don't have to worry."

"If you're trying to make me laugh again or reassure me, it isn't working."

"I guess I've given you ample reason to be skeptical."

"Ample? Since when is understatement part of your repertoire?"

That was my cue for a segue and I took it. "So, did you read the new pages I added to the original manuscript? What did you think of the plot synopsis?"

"I've read them both." Meg did that curly lip thing again, took another sip, and a second olive. She actually turned to face me, a very un-Meg-like thing to do. "Kip," she cleared her throat, "before we go to dinner tomorrow night, I have to . . . um . . . ask you a question."

Meg hesitating! Surely, this was the end of days.

"What's the question?"

"Is it your book?"

Of all the things she could have asked, I didn't see this coming. I was shocked and angry. "What the fuck kinda question is that to ask me?"

"Think about it, Weiler." She held up her right index finger. "One: You haven't sent me a manuscript in god knows how long and your last three books were, to put it mildly, disasters." Her middle finger. "Two: I call you with a big rights deal and what, magically there's new book?" Her ring finger. "Three: The voice in this new book doesn't sound like your old voice at all." Pinky. "Four: Your new characters aren't anything close to what your old characters used to be like. These people have souls." Thumb. "Five: The writing is done in pitch-perfect Irish dialects." Left thumb. "Six: And all of a sudden you're an expert on handguns?"

"Better stop now before you run out of fingers and have to remove your shoes," I said. "You forgot to mention that *Gun Queer* doesn't contain a dream sequence."

"That's not an answer, Kip."

"You want an answer?"

"Yes."

I would have told most people to go fuck themselves, but Meg had earned the right to hear the truth about where the book had come from. "Okay," I said. "Order another martini or two. I've got a story to tell you that you might not believe."

She took my suggestion and about forty minutes later she knew more about my life in Brixton County than she ever wanted to know. Meg gulped down her third martini and didn't bother fussing with the olives.

"Are these people dangerous?"

"Anyone with a weapon in his hand can be dangerous, but there's only one asshole in the bunch," I said. "Mostly they're harmless and just plain bored. There's a lot to be bored with in Brixton no matter what you do. This world they invited me into is the one place they can shine. It's like a cross between Kabuki and Catholicism."

"What is the significance of those rituals you were telling me about?" she asked, turning once again to face me.

"Some come from how the chapel was founded, like the ashes from the first tree they shot at. The number of steps you take to get to the chapel floor and to shooting position have their roots in how many people were originally a part of things. And the things we recite come from the Bible when Jesus is talking to Doubting Thomas, but there are other things we do that have to do with status."

"Status?"

"Look, Meg, I don't think you can appreciate what these people's lives are like. The people at the chapel, they've got no futures. They either work in dead-end jobs in a dead-end town or go to community college in order to get dead-end jobs. There's no way for them to derive any self-esteem or achieve anything worthwhile outside the chapel. The chapel is really their salvation. It's a way for them to prove themselves as something other than a clerk or a short-order cook."

"But how do they measure status?"

Now I hesitated. It was one thing for me to create a fictionalized version of the chapel, but I actually felt a pang of guilt. I was breaking the big rule. I was talking about the chapel openly, naming names, discussing it with an outsider. And I wasn't sure I wanted to give all the details about the shooting, especially the part about shooting with only a vest for protection. I decided to fudge a little.

"We get red crosses on our shirts every time we shoot. It shows how brave we are and how we trust each other. The higher the number of crosses, the higher the status. Each time we shoot, the test is different. Sometimes it's who's fastest, other times it's who's most accurate. It's even in how well we perform the rituals. For instance, when we walk four paces away from each other, stop and take one last step before turning to face one another, we strive to be as close to thirty feet apart as possible. When the real experienced people shoot together, they often are exactly thirty feet apart. I don't know all the nuances or intricacies yet because I'm still new, but it's all carefully thought out."

Meg shook her head. "Still, why don't you consider moving up here to finish the book? I would feel safer with you close by."

"To make sure I don't go off the rails, you mean."

"That too," she confessed.

"No need to worry, Mom. Staying down there is good for the book and good for me."

"And this blond, the St. Pauli Girl—"

"Renee."

"Renee. Do you love her?"

"I've been faithful to her probably longer than I was faithful to Amy."

"I was waiting for that name to pop up. She's miserable, you know."

"So you've said."

"You should call her," Meg suggested.

I didn't know what to say. Had I known, I don't think I could have managed to say it. No matter what Renee was to me, she would never be able to touch the way I felt at just the thought of hearing Amy's voice over the phone. Then it dawned on me—I guess it was a day for revelations, large and small—that I had nearly achieved the goal I set for myself the year before. With the book deal, the money from the rights deal, my keeping on the straight and narrow, and my newfound monogamy, I was nearly in a position to win back Amy's respect and my own.

"And one more thing, Weiler," Meg interrupted my reverie.

"What's that?"

"I ran the title by Dudek and as I anticipated, he thinks *Gun Queer* would be too controversial. It's got to be *Gun Church*."

"*Gun Church* it is."

Twenty-Five

Potato Farmer

The big powwow had been at a chichi steak restaurant in the Meatpacking District. There wasn't a T-shirt or bottle of hot sauce anywhere in sight. There were four of us for dinner: Meg, Franz Dudek, his trophy wife Amelia, and me. Meg was in a black silk cocktail dress over black hose and a different pair of pointy-toed pumps. She left her industrial-strength jewelry home for the night, wearing instead a silver-clasped black leather bracelet, pearl stud earrings, and a simple string of pearls around her neck. This was about as girly as Meg Donovan got in public.

Amelia Dudek, all curves, legs, and lips, was about thirty, give or take. She'd probably done plenty of both: giving and taking, I mean. Her features were not so very different from Renee's, though she wasn't as naturally pretty. But Amelia knew the tricks: how to dress, how to makeup, how to accentuate and obscure. Franz Dudek wasn't at all what I expected. I guess I thought he'd be slight and regal, the last viscount in a long line of vanquished Slavic nobility, shipped off to Eton and Oxford at an early age before surfacing in New York. Instead, he looked like a sixty-year-old potato farmer in a good suit. He was big-boned and broad-shouldered. His peasant hands were thick, his fingers gnarled, but he had a kind, handsome face. There were many such faces in Brixton and with a little coal dust on his cheeks and a hard hat on his gray head, he would have fit right in.

I don't know what Dudek was expecting from me, but the look on his face when I met him and Amelia at the bar was fucking priceless. He seemed almost disappointed that I wasn't some drunken monster with a drippy junkie nose and a blond on each arm. The late Haskell Brown had no doubt filled his boss's head with endless tales of the Kipster's debauchery and his exponentially diminished talent. It's not like I hadn't disappointed people before. I'd nearly turned it into a second career. It was that I hadn't ever done it in quite this manner before.

Earlier, when the wine steward poured glasses of the old Cabernet Dudek had ordered to accompany our steaks, I'd noticed the sick look on Meg's face. There'd been no need for her to say the words. *This is when he's going to fuck it up.* I knew I'd been on probation from the moment I agreed to come up to New York. That's why I had club soda and lime at the bar before we were seated and why, during dinner, I barely finished half a glass of wine. I was being watched, tested at every turn. The Kipster would have been glad to live down to their expectations by asking Amelia how much the prenup was worth or whether she'd had her boob job done before or after marrying old Franz. The impulse for self-sabotage was irresistible to the Kipster and he would have jumped at the chance. Why bother writing a crappy book that tanks, when you can just blow yourself up in front of your publisher? But *Gun Church* wasn't a crappy book and I wasn't the Kipster. His last vestige was parked in the Hippodrome Garage, directly across 44th Street from the Algonquin.

The hard part came later, after the contracts were signed and Dudek promised to have the checks cut to Meg Monday morning.

Publishers don't pay the author. They pay the agent and the agent pays the author after her percentage comes off the top. Nor do publishers fork over all the money at once. For the rights deals, it was half on signing and half on publication. For *Gun Church*, payment—like Caesar's Gaul—was divided into three parts: one-third on signing, one-third on manuscript approval, one-third on publication. But any way you carved it up, I walked out of the restaurant well over a hundred grand ahead of when I walked in. It wasn't about the money. I didn't even mind that the advance for *Gun Church* was less than the advance the Kipster had received for *Beatnik Soufflé* a million years ago. That was the Kipster's first book and *Gun Church* was mine.

No, the hard part wasn't about the advance, but about being left alone in a city that I no longer knew and one that no longer knew me. Meg offered to take me out for a drink, but her heart wasn't in it. I could always tell when there was someone keeping the bed warm for her at home. And frankly, I wasn't in the mood for trying to celebrate while simultaneously sitting on my hands. Franz Dudek might have looked like a farmer, but he well understood human nature and knew better than to press his luck. Instead of offering me yet another chance to fuck up, he just patted my shoulder and told me to go home and finish that book.

What I did was go back to the hotel. Success came so easily to the Kipster that he never quite trusted it. Hence, when things fell apart, he had no coping skills on which to rely. So this was new for me, achieving something through hard work that I wasn't willing to piss on or away. I didn't know what to do with that. In the jumble of feelings, the only thing I thought I wanted to do was to call Renee. I wanted to share the moment with her, but I couldn't pick up the phone. Maybe it was because I so regretted not bringing her or maybe because I didn't. Maybe to call her would have indicated she meant way more to me than I was willing to let on. I wasn't sure of anything.

And there I was, the .38 in my hand, looking at the bedside phone. I kept snapping the cylinder of the Smith & Wesson in and out the way some smokers flick on their old Zippos in one fluid motion. That I found comfort in this didn't much surprise me. Nor did it surprise me that I loaded a single round into the cylinder and spun it like a roulette wheel. I wasn't going to do anything stupid. That impulse had passed with the concussion. I just liked the *clickity-clicking*, the feel of its weight in my hand. Then the phone rang and I jumped. I hoped it was Renee, but I'd given up magical thinking during the first Clinton administration.

"Hello," I said, snatching up the phone, keeping the .38 in my other hand.

"Ken?"

The last time my equilibrium was this out of whack was during Fox Hunt, but this was more disorienting. The woman at the other end of the phone could cut me down faster than any bullet ever could.

"Amy, what are you—How did—"

"Meg told me you were in town."

I could not speak.

"Ken. Ken, are you there?"

"I'm here, but why are you calling?"

"Do you really have to ask me that?"

"It's been ten years, Amy. I thought you never wanted to speak to me again."

"I thought so too."

"What's changed?"

"I've been thinking a lot about you lately, about us, since the incident when you saved your class. I thought about calling a hundred times, but I could never find the right moment."

Funny, that September afternoon that Vuchovich took my
class seemed like a thousand years ago, almost like it never happened. I didn't understand how just hearing Amy talk about it
made it all real again.

"What made this the right time?"

"Proximity. Knowing you're in town. I'm not sure. Meg says
you've just signed a new book deal."

"Meg's been telling tales out of school."

"Is it true?" she asked.

"I'm surprised you didn't already know. I thought Peter would
have told you."

"Peter and I don't really communicate much. We just grumble
at one another in passing. Even if we did speak in full sentences,
I doubt he would have wanted to tell me anything positive about
you. It is positive, isn't it?" she hedged.

"It's good news, yes, but I don't think you'd recognize my writing. I don't feel enough like a god anymore to snicker down my
sleeve at my characters. You spend seven years in Brixton and you
see what real hopelessness is like. Living on the edge isn't having
to move into a Tribeca condo because you were forced to sell your
place in Amagansett. I couldn't write a book about Wall Street
now. I wouldn't want to."

"You sound different."

"I'm old, Ames," I said, before I could catch myself using my
pet name for her.

"No one's called me that in a very long time, Ken." Then she
stopped and there was silence, but something in her breathing
told me she wasn't finished. "Come see me."

"I—I can't. I'm leaving first thing and—"

"No, Ken, tonight. Right now."

This wasn't what I had envisioned. Of course, I had thought of
Amy constantly since I agreed to come up to New York. And I'd

fantasized about us bumping shoulders on the street or us hail-
ing the same cab, but not this. If I was going to see her again,
I wanted it to be when the book was out and I had something
tangible to prove all the pain I'd caused her, and myself, had come
to something worthwhile.

"I'm beat, Ames. I don't have it in me now. Sorry."

"That's okay. You don't have to go anywhere except to the
elevator."

"What?"

"I'm in the lobby."

Twenty-Six

Gun Math

Of course, in my fantasies Amy hadn't aged a day: her hair was black and cut in a simple bob, her face unlined, her sad mouth smiling only at the corners. Her gold-flecked green eyes, the most God-awful sexy eyes on earth, would glow in low light. Her breasts, always so firm and assertive, would be untouched by gravity and time. And the rest of her body, paradoxically lean and lush, would fit together with mine, as it always had even at our worst moments. Of course there would be speckles or smudges of paint on her jeans, T-shirt, and running shoes, on her hands, cheeks, and forehead.

The lighting in the Algonquin lobby is famously soft. Still, when she stood up from the sofa and edged around the marble coffee table, Amy's eyes did not glow green. Her hair was indeed black, but long and lined with threads of gray, and any hints of happiness in her smile had been buried deeper than Brixton coal. Gravity had been kind to her body, but she was too thin. It didn't suit her. She had abandoned her uniform of T-shirt, ripped black jeans, and duct-taped running shoes for a proper woman-of-means wardrobe: a tasteful white cashmere sweater, navy blue flannel slacks, and gray heels. Paint? Not a drop on her. Yet, when she came up to me, softly stroked my cheek with the back of her hand, and kissed me lightly on the lips, none of the rest of it mattered.

When I fell out of the moment, I noticed that I was kissing Amy and not lightly. I noticed too that she was kissing back. It was a stupid thing for both of us to do, really stupid. Then again, we had been stupid in love with each other. It was always like that between us: we knew better, but couldn't help ourselves. It wasn't like we'd had some blissful period together at the start before it all went south. We were trouble for each other from day one. Yet no matter what damage we inflicted on each other or, worse, on ourselves, we were completely and utterly stupid for each other. Even now, ten years totally removed from each other's lives, it was still there. That's why it had taken us so long to fall apart in the first place.

I grabbed her biceps and pushed her away. Not because I could feel everyone in the lobby watching us. Everyone but the cat. The cat couldn't give a fuck and neither did I. I pushed her away because this wasn't the way I wanted it to happen. I'd wanted her respect, not this. Falling into bed for us would have been as easy as falling down and if we were going to fall, I didn't want it to be about how unhappy she was with Peter Moreland.

"I'm sorry, Amy. I can't do this," I said, looping a strand of her hair behind her ear.

I moved her gently aside and made for the lobby door. I needed air, more air than was in the hotel lobby or maybe in all of Manhattan. Thank goodness she didn't follow me out. I couldn't have withstood a scene out there on the street. That was such a part of the dance of Amy and the Kipster. I so didn't want that to be part of my life again. Bent over, taking deep, slow breaths, I cursed Meg for doing this to me. And knowing Amy could not stay inside the lobby forever, I took my hands off my knees and walked east along 44th towards 5th Avenue.

As I walked, I thought I heard a familiar sound. It was the sound of a truck's ignition. *Jim's truck!* Jim's truck sounded like that. I was so fucked up that I actually started looking for his old F-150. I didn't find it, of course. Hearing it was a product of wishful thinking and a longing to be rescued. I needed more than just fresh air. I ran across 44th, headed back west and ducked into the garage where the Porsche was parked. From the entrance of the garage, I watched the front of the hotel. When Amy finally left, I went back up to my room and retrieved the .38.

●

There had been a time when I knew exactly where to find trouble and what kind of trouble I would find when I got there. But the trouble I had in mind would have a gun in its hand, a gun pointed at me, and there would be a gun in my hand too. There *was* a gun in my hand, a .38 with one bullet in the chamber. Then I put it away.

Having exhausted all the old familiar places in Manhattan, I drove the Kipster's Porsche to some of his former Brooklyn drug haunts. Brooklyn was where I went when I was desperate for blow, when I didn't give a shit about how many times the coke had been stepped on. What I discovered was that in my absence more than just the Liars Pub had been turned into a theme park. The whole of New York City, it seemed, had been scrubbed clean and neutered, turned into a silly Las Vegas hotel-like version of itself. Even Red Hook, once the toughest neighborhood in all of New York, had gotten its ass wiped and been forced to take a long soapy shower. I mean, it had an IKEA and cutesy little tapas bars.

Good thing about Brooklyn is that it's big and I knew there couldn't have been enough soap and disinfectant to scrub behind the ears of all its neighborhoods. About twenty minutes or so after I'd left Red Hook, I was driving up Linden Boulevard at a crawl. I pulled off Linden onto a side street and into the mostly vacant parking lot of a strip mall. It was the time of morning when it was either very early or very late, the time when too much alcohol, frayed nerves, and perceived slights led to blood. And the only business still open in the strip was what looked to be a third-rate topless joint. The lurid red neon sign flashed Black Honey. If I couldn't find trouble in East Flatbush at that time of the morning in front of a topless bar named Black Honey, I wasn't going to find it anywhere. Forget Red Hook. Much easier, I thought, to pick a gunfight at a topless bar than a tapas bar.

With the motor still running, I sat on the front fender of the Porsche. The .38 was in my waistband and tucked behind the bottom of my famous brown corduroy blazer. I could hear the muffled thumping of the drum machines through the door and walls of Black Honey. No one entered or left, but it was only a matter of time till somebody came outside to smoke a cigarette or a joint or tried to cop some drugs to keep them awake till the sun rose up. I didn't have long to wait.

Three hard-looking black men came staggering out the front door of the club. They were all in their early thirties. At first, they didn't notice me at all. They were just laughing a little too loudly, fist-pounding, jostling each other around: the same shit all half-in-the-bag guys do outside topless bars. Then one of the men noticed me noticing them.

"What you starin' at?" he said. The smile disappeared from his face.

The smiles on his friends' faces went to that same mysterious place. Except for the continued muted pounding of the drum machine, the world got eerily quiet.

"I'm staring at you. Something wrong with that?"

For a brief second I thought they might let it go at that: just dismiss me as some stupid old white boy who didn't know how to mind his business or his manners. And maybe if it had been earlier in the night, or if there hadn't been so much to drink, or if . . . But it wasn't earlier and I wasn't going to get dismissed, not easily, anyway.

"Will you listen to this cracker motherfucka?"

"Yeah, you get the fuck outta here, you know what's good for your ass."

"But I don't feel like going," I said.

The third man, the man who hadn't yet spoken, reached around behind him. That's when the rush went full throttle and I got that tunnel vision thing. But this wasn't the chapel and these guys weren't playing Cutthroat. They weren't playing, period. Jim's words rang in my head, "The Colonel used to say it wasn't a sport unless both sides knew they were playing." I had no vest, not even a white T-shirt to protect me. Never mind that I had only one round in the .38. I knew it was possible to divide one by three, but this was gun math and bullets didn't work that way. And suddenly my rush was overwhelmed by fear.

I moved my hand slowly under my jacket, feeling confident I could get to the .38 before the man reaching behind him could draw, aim, and fire. Then what? I was hot shit with a gun in my hand and bullets in my gun, but what would I be worth with an empty cylinder? A lot of my life had been a bluff, but bluffing wasn't going to get me very far after shooting a man through his heart in the parking lot of a titty bar in the armpit of Brooklyn. I froze for a second time that night. Good thing too, because when the man brought his arm back around in front of him, his hand wasn't holding a gun, but a badge.

"Get gone, motherfucka."

He didn't need to tell me twice and I got gone.

Twenty-Seven

Aftershocks

I'd been back from New York for about a week, and that week had been a tale of two lives: both mine. On the one hand, everything was exactly the same. On the other, everything was exactly different. It's fucked up and a little hard to explain because if you were looking from the outside in, from the vantage point when crystal clarity just begins to soften at the edges, you wouldn't have noticed the spectrum shift.

I got up early, wrote, crawled back into bed with Renee for a few minutes, went running with Jim, taught my classes, went shooting with Jim, came home and wrote, ate with Renee, wrote, fucked, and went to bed. That was pretty much my routine before I left for New York and it was my routine when I returned. The transition felt seamless, like the perfect pass of a baton during a relay race. I had handed off the baton on my way out of town and grabbed it back on my way in. I don't think I could have adequately expressed to Renee how happy I was to be, for lack of a better word, home.

But something had changed and, at first, I could only describe the symptoms of the change, not what they meant or what had caused them. Renee seemed pleased enough at my return, but she wasn't herself, or more accurately, she was like her old self. The fucking between us, which had undergone a steady transformation from ferocious and hungry to delicate and soulful, had turned back again. Since I'd gotten home, she had insisted on me taking her from behind and urged me to do it harder and harder still. When I'd crawl into bed with her in the morning, she wanted me in her mouth much more than she wanted my arms around her. She was back to making up and dressing like the St. Pauli Girl. Lots more makeup. Lots less clothing. It was almost as if she were trying to make me conscious again of just how young she really was and to make me wonder what it was we were doing together. If that was her intent, it was working.

Initially, I put it down to me. That I was sending out weird vibes because I regretted my decision not to take her with me to New York and worse, that I felt guilty for kissing Amy while I was there. Can you even believe it, Kip Weiler feeling guilty for kissing another woman? It was my ex-wife, for fuck's sake, and it wasn't like I initiated it. Compared to some of the Kipster's past antics, kissing Amy was like an act of atonement. Still, it felt like a betrayal. I'd never understood what that word meant before now, but I knew it wasn't the kiss that was the betrayal. It was the way I reacted to hearing Amy's voice on the phone, the way I got hard at the brush of her hand against my cheek.

I came around to see that it wasn't all me, that Renee had a little residual anger and resentment over my not taking her with me. Probably more than a little. But when I tried to discuss it with her, she either denied it or put the onus on me. "It's in your head," she'd say and give me a dismissive kiss. Whether it was her or me or both of us, at least I got to a point where it made some sense. None of that, though, could explain away Jim's behavior.

Jim's *I-know-all-about-you-Kip-Weiler* smile made an unwelcome comeback. I can't say that I liked it either, not for a second. I wasn't sure what had caused him to start flashing it again. I was pretty certain he hadn't noticed me pilfer the Smith & Wesson before I left for New York, and I made quick work of slipping it back into the Colonel's duffel bag the first chance I got. But even if he knew I'd nicked the .38, I couldn't really see him getting too bent out of shape over it. In fact, given the basics of Brixton logic, he should have been proud of me. Of course, he might have been a little less proud had he an inkling of how close I'd come to getting into a gunfight with an off-duty cop. But it was more than just his smile that caught me off guard.

When we got up into the woods that Monday, he had some unexpected news for me that was more unwelcome than his smile.

"Time to move up to a real weapon," he said, handing me the .45 Browning. "You're good with the .38. Better than I thought you'd be. Let's see what you can do with this."

I wasn't ready. I was barely used to the .38. I'd fired the Browning a few times over the last several months with very mixed results. It was a lot of gun for me. Even with sissy loads in the clip, it had wicked kickback. Jim was great with it, but he was great with anything he put in his hand. And if what Jim had said before I left was still the plan, I was about to step into the chapel wearing only a vest for protection, with an unfamiliar gun in my hand.

"But I haven't really gotten good with the .38 yet."

"Modesty doesn't sound right coming out of your mouth, Kip. You were good enough with it. Sometimes good enough is good enough. It's time to move on."

"Says who?"

I saw something in his eyes and in the shape of his lips that looked more cruel than wounded, but he caught himself.

"You know how it is," he said. "This isn't a democracy. Things get decided for you when we shoot in the chapel. You just have to trust we know what we're doing. We've been right so far, haven't we? Someday you'll be deciding things for yourself. Just not yet. I thought you understood that for us the chapel is life and we need the rules and rituals. It's what separates us from each other and from the rest of the world. I get that it isn't your whole world and that someday you might leave and not come back, but you can't be treated specially or it takes the meaning away for the rest of us."

He kept saying *we* and *us*, but it felt an awful lot like the decisions were his and his alone. I mean, fuck, I was already edgy enough about shooting with only a vest and this sudden shift in weapon gave me no comfort at all. Nor was I reassured by his vague promise of future choice. I'd have to live long enough to exercise that franchise.

Jim saw the apprehension on my face and was quick to reassure me. "Don't worry about it, Kip. I'll be in there with you and I won't let you kill me. You'll be fine like you always are."

I was glad he was so sure because I wasn't. After seeing him clip the maintenance guy in the arm, my faith in Jim's guarantees had been shaken a bit. So I took our practice sessions in the woods a little more seriously. They became a lot more businesslike and a lot less fun. Still, the potential danger of it gave me some wicked rushes.

The most unnerving moment since coming back to Brixton came in the dark and quiet of my bedroom. It was Friday night. Renee and I had just finished fucking our brains out. We were just lying there in the dark, me staring up at the ceiling, Renee still shuddering slightly. Soon she'd get up, go into the shower, and I'd follow. But that Friday night, Renee didn't immediately get up to shower and her shudders weren't the quiet little aftershocks of orgasm. She rolled over to face me. She was crying, her tears pouring onto the bed. I reached out to hold her, but she slapped my arms away.

"What is it?"

She said, "I love you and I know you don't love me."

I wanted to lie to her. It would have been hard not to want to lie to her, even for the Kipster, but I couldn't. "Being with you these last few months has been wonderful. Our time together has been the healthiest relationship I've ever had, but I don't suppose that's love. I understand that that's not enough for you."

"Kip, please go back to New York. Tonight. Right now! I'll send your things after you. Just get in your car and go before it's too late."

"Too late?"

I reached out for her again, but she was already rolling out of bed, heading for the shower. I stumbled after her, but she'd locked the bathroom door. Eventually, I went back to bed and passed out.

When I woke up early Saturday morning, she was gone. Renee hadn't packed up her things or left a note. It wasn't anything so dramatic as all that. By the next day, by the time I returned from my morning run with Jim, she was back. I tried asking her about what she'd said, about my leaving before it was too late, but she acted as if I were mad, that I must've dreamed it. I might have very well been mad. Still, I hadn't dreamed it.

Twenty-Eight

Terrible Twos

More had changed than the shifts in the tide among Renee, Jim, and me. *Gun Church* had taken a dark turn. Whether it was playing Cutthroat, Fox Hunt, my trip to New York, or the need to self-destruct, I couldn't say. Maybe the fear over having gotten the deal and the need to actually deliver a manuscript had pushed me over the line.

McGuinn's notebook was filled with bomb diagrams, drawings of booby traps, plans for ambushes. There were names and places, body counts, reports of how specific operations had turned out: some bloody and successful, some bloody and disastrous. By the time I'd read halfway through his notes, I was numb to the havoc, the blood, the destruction, the baby's arm lying in the road, hand still clutching a rattle. That was the horror I believe he was getting at: how even the slaughter of women, children, and friends had become as mundane as the image that looked back at him from the mirror every morning. But that was not the book I wanted to write nor the book I believe he'd wanted me to write. There was no deeper truth in the mundanity of violence. That truth sat on the surface and required no mining at all. That book had been written a thousand times over, and the truth of it had played out across the entire twentieth century and continued unabated into the next. There were other truths he wanted exposed, though he was vague about them.

The only deeper truth I'd ever exposed was that I was a fraud. My work, even my early good work, said almost nothing about the human condition. What it said a lot about was a particular time—the 1980s; a particular place—New York City; and a particular group of people—voracious yuppies who were nothing more than ridiculous children in adult bodies who had never grown out of their terrible twos. What is the deeper truth of a two-year-old? *I want. I want. I want.* My books were snapshots, cute snapshots, better than most of the period, perhaps, but not worth much more than an airing every twenty years so that people might say, "How nice. How quaint."

What happened to the man I thought of as McGuinn was that he lost his soul, not by killing. It wasn't about the killing itself. I don't think that troubled him, really. Nor was his giving me his notebook an act of a man who had found God or cared to find him. Religion wasn't the point. He had lost his soul and I think he wanted me to find out why and to retrieve it somehow, whether he was alive to see it or not.

McGuinn was numb with cold, exhausted, and bleeding from his shoulder wound, but he had found himself a place to hide that the others were unlikely to find.

He went back over it in his mind; how after the incident in the alley, a week had passed before they contacted him again—Zoe waiting for him outside the front door to his flat. How she had stayed that night and the next. How they had fucked until they were raw, only to do it again and again. How in spite of her orgasms, she seemed as far away as the streets of Belfast. Two days later, when she left him, Zoe gave him the ultimatum he was sure would come.

"If you ever want me again, you have to meet us tonight," she said, handing McGuinn a slip of paper. "We'll have company for you, an old friend of yours."

McGuinn would have gone regardless of that last wee bit of enticement. He had to know what these people knew of him, about who he really was, and how they had targeted him. What good would it do him to run if he was easily found out?

When he showed at the address that night, they were waiting for him and this time there were more of them and better prepared. He was asked politely at the point of several guns to join them in the back of a van. Before he got in, they took his Sig and a black bag was thrown over his head. It was taped loosely around his neck. He'd done this routine before, from both sides. They weren't going to kill him, at least not yet. It was very odd, for as they drove there was little or no chatter in the van, but McGuinn felt a familiar, almost comfortable presence that he could not make sense of. There was nothing and no one in this town he was familiar with.

As the van came to a halt, the doors opened and McGuinn was helped outside. He didn't need to see to feel there was grass beneath his shoes or to know he was at a river side. Someone else was being taken from the van, but with fewer manners than had been shown to McGuinn. There was a bit of a tussle, a body hit the ground at McGuinn's feet, and there was a distinct grunt. Again, McGuinn felt that familiar presence. The bag was removed from his head and when his eyes adjusted to the gloaming light, he understood. For there at his feet was Old Jack Byrnes.

The footballer from the slaughterhouse spoke first. "He came to kill you, Irish. That's what he told us after we spoke to him."

McGuinn looked down at his mentor, but Old Jack didn't bother to shake his head in denial. Whatever was left of McGuinn's heart sank. He'd known they would come for him eventually, but he never imagined it would be the man who was more father to him than his real da. Now it was Terry McGuinn shaking his head.

"He came snooping around work, asking about you about ten days ago. Your good luck we already had our eye on you for membership."

"Membership! Membership in what?" McGuinn wanted to know.

The footballer spread out his arms and gestured at the woods, the waterfall, and the running river. "In this. In our church."

"Church? And what church would that be, boyo?"

"Gun Church."

"Gun Church," McGuinn repeated. "One church has already failed me, son, and I've no heart for another."

"But we won't fail you, Irish, ever."

Terry McGuinn smirked. "And what proof would you give of that, son?"

"Fair question," the footballer admitted. Then he turned to the juicer and motioned for him to cut Old Jack's hands and feet free. He left the gag in.

Old Jack tried rubbing some feeling into his wrists and ankles, but couldn't bring himself to look at McGuinn.

After a few minutes, the footballer knelt down by Old Jack and whispered in his ear. With that, Old Jack Byrnes took off, running towards the woods. The footballer reached into his jacket pocket and came out with McGuinn's Sig in his hand. He gave it to McGuinn, handle first.

"He's all yours, Irish."

"What if I don't want him?"

"Well, Irish, someone's going to get hunted down tonight. If it's not him, then . . . "

"So that's how it is?" McGuinn asked.

"Consider it a tithe. Don't worry, though. When you're done with him, we'll clean up after you. Like I said, Irish, we won't fail you."

The Thursday after my return from New York, when Renee grew weary of my asking what had changed between us, she turned the tables on me.

"You're the one who's different, Ken. Since you got back, all you do is grunt at me if I come into the office while you're working."

"It's the pressure."

But it wasn't the pressure at all. It was that I had woven the fictional McGuinn so deeply into the fabric of my own life that it frightened me. That feeling I'd had out in the old berry patch and up in the woods during Fox Hunt, seeing things as McGuinn might, had grown stronger. Now, anything connected to the chapel was filtered not only through me, but me as McGuinn. When I stood in the chapel, I stood with McGuinn at my shoulder. When I was woozy during Fox Hunt, it was McGuinn I had dreamed as. *Gun Church* was proof that he was part of this before I was ever fully aware of it. I wondered how long it would be before I was found out. That the canvas on which I was painting *Gun Church* was a semi-urbanized permutation of Brixton County, and the characters thinly veiled grotesques of Jim and Renee and the rest of them.

Okay, it was true that the things I had my characters doing with McGuinn were nothing more than expressions of my own personal darkness. And yes, it had all come out of my head and my sense of the man I knew and wrote about as McGuinn. But I could not escape the sense that with a little push at just the right moment, the snaggle-toothed girl, the deputy, Jim, Renee, and the rest of them would gladly cross over from the real world into the world of *Gun Church*. That, maybe more than anything else, made up my mind for me. The time had come to see the chairman of the department.

Twenty-Nine

Buyer's Remorse

Jean-Jacques Beauchamp, the Engagin' Cajun, was chairman of the English Department at Brixton County Community College: a job nearly as prestigious as being the head shit-shoveler behind a circus parade. And while Beauchamp's fall from grace wasn't quite as precipitous as mine, it was plenty steep. Thirty years ago, he'd been hailed as the next Faulkner, which, in a literary sense, was like being hailed as the next Babe Ruth. What a curse to hang on someone. Now the only thing J. J. Beauchamp did like Faulkner was drink. He had once been quite a handsome man, but the drink had robbed him of more than his talent. Any shred of vanity had gone the way of his depleted liver. I liked J. J. and he liked me. We were kindred spirits. Neither of us bothered pretending we were anywhere but where we were or that a single thing we'd accomplished mattered more in the scheme of things than a swatted fly.

"Chairman Beauchamp will be with you shortly," said his famously unfriendly secretary, Miss Crouch. Her mien matched her manner.

"Fine," I think I said. I wasn't paying much attention.

The ground hadn't stopped shifting under my feet simply because Renee had returned to my house and to my bed. I still couldn't make sense of her veiled warning about getting out of town and, no matter how I prodded and cajoled, she continued to be disinclined to help me understand. I recalled that Renee had suggested I leave Brixton once before, a few months back when Meg had first called to discuss the rights deal. It hadn't seemed like a warning then. It did now. Look, it was easy to understand why she might think it a wise idea for me to get out of Brixton, but why would she want me to do it in the middle of the night, to just get in my car and go? That was the part I couldn't get my head around. Did she have a jealous ex-lover I didn't know about? Was Stan Petrovic making threats that hadn't yet gotten back to me? I didn't know what to think. Beyond that, I was worried that I'd hurt Renee by admitting I didn't love her, worried even more that she had come back to me knowing it.

Maybe some of the ground shifting had to do with the fact that we were coming to the end of the fall term. Final papers were due in a few days and the new term would begin in mid-January. Maybe the end of the term had something to do with Renee and Jim's recent confusing behavior. Were they worried that the end of the term would mean a severing of the bonds between us? Were they distancing themselves from me before I could do it to them? Maybe so and maybe they were right. For even as I sat there, trying to make sense of the last week, these past few months, the last seven years, it dawned on me that it was useless to pretend things hadn't changed. During my early morning run, I realized that no matter how little New York City felt like home, neither did Brixton, not really. It was clear to me that the subtle and not so subtle changes I'd noticed in Renee and Jim since my return were a kind of blessing. A blessing because it disabused me of whatever fantasies of domestic and rustic bliss these last few months had engendered.

How long did I think playing house with the St. Pauli Girl was actually going to last, especially after our little chat the other night? She was back now, but for how long? How long would it be until it wasn't enough for her? A week? Two? A month? Six, at most? Could I envision another seven years of shooting in the woods with Jim? Me, I never had to grow up—academia was Never-Never Land without Smee and Hook—but Jim would grow up. Brixton made its inhabitants grow up. Even if Cutthroat turned into a bimonthly event, it would become like any other high. It would flatten out, get old, get boring.

Frankly, Jim had scared the shit out of me with this change of weapons thing. I wanted to live long enough to finish my book, to spend my money, to see Amy again. When I thought about it, I just could not imagine facing another crop of student-zombies and their illiterate ramblings. I hadn't been much of a teacher to begin with and I didn't think I had it in me to fake it for very much longer, not now that I was a writer again. And finally, there was my own uneasiness about being found out, and the sense that the world I lived in and the one I created weren't really so far apart.

"The chairman will see you now, Professor Weiler."

When I walked into his office, J. J. Beauchamp was seated at his desk, pouring himself a tall bourbon of questionable heritage. Some of his straggly gray hair nearly got to taste the cheap whiskey before he did.

"Well, fuck me if it ain't the great man his own self, Kip Weiler," Beauchamp said, a broad smile on his face. "Drink?"

"No thanks, *Chef.*"

"*Chef! Mon dieu.* Kip, you call me *chef*, it mean you wantin' sometin' from me, *non?*" Beauchamp slipped easily into his childhood patois. "If not a drink, what it is, then?"

"A sabbatical."

"Next fall should be no problem. I'll have Miss Congeniality start drawing up the papers."

"Not next fall, J. J. Next term."

"Little late in the day for dat, *ami, non?*"

"I know, but I got it coming. More than that, I need it."

"Not to get too technical about it, Kip, but you're supposed to give me some more notice than this."

"I'm not fucking around with you, *Chef*. If I didn't need it, I wouldn't be here."

"*Porquoi?*"

"The truth or the horseshit?"

He laughed. "There's a difference? From where I sit it's hard to divine the one from the other. Why don't you say your piece and I'll cipher out what I need to know."

"I just signed a book deal with Travers Legacy."

"Is that the horseshit?" he asked.

"No, J. J., that's the truth."

He jumped out of his chair and threw his big arms around me. He kissed both of my cheeks. His breath smelled strongly of bourbon. "Well, kiss my fat Cajun ass. Congratulations. Do I get a free copy?"

"Two."

"Then you let ol' J. J. worry 'bout dat sabbatical. I'll say you requested it last term and I lost the paperwork. You may have to come back in and fill out some forms, but I know some folk who owe dis ol' Cajun *beaucoup* favor." He winked at me. "A man doesn't chair a department in a shithole like this without people owing him."

"Thanks, J. J."

"Forget dat. You go finish dat book, *ami*. Where you going to?"

"I'm not sure."

"Well, then, just go get there." He waved his hands at me to leave. As I turned to go, he was on the intercom asking Miss Crouch to come into his office.

●

It had snowed again that afternoon, lightly, but enough to evoke memories of the night we drove to the old berry farm for Cutthroat. Jim didn't take that turn away from the river and we were clearly headed to our usual spot in the woods above the falls. Jim wasn't very talkative and that suited me fine. I was feeling a little like a man who'd just pulled the rug out from under his own feet and found myself wishing that J. J. Beauchamp had been less amenable to my request for a sabbatical. I was okay until J. J. asked the question about where I was going.

I didn't think I could stay in Brixton and hope everything— my writing, playing house, running, and shooting—would somehow return to the way it had been before I'd gone to New York. It had already changed. *I* had already changed and recognized there was no going back. Once you learn how a magician does his tricks, you can't regain your innocence. There were a lot of places I could go to other than New York, but even I knew that going anywhere else would just be running away. In my gut I understood that if there was such a thing as destiny, I was going to find it there, not here or some other town or city in which I'd first be establishing myself.

Even when we got to the bluff by the falls and began our trek up the hill, we didn't have much to say to each other. That changed when we got to our usual spot. He asked me if everything was all right.

"Got a lot on my mind," is all I said.

"Like what?"

I wasn't going to mention the sabbatical, not to Jim, not now, but he had known Renee longer than me and, according to her, they'd dated a few times. I figured it was safe enough to ask him some questions.

"Do you know if everything's okay with Renee?"

"Why?" he said, pressing rounds into the Browning's clip.

"She's been acting a little different since I got back from New York."

"Maybe she's mad you didn't take her."

"No maybe about that, Jim. I wish I had taken her, but it's more than that."

"How do you mean?"

"She seems edgy."

That got his attention. "Edgy. Edgy how?"

"I don't know, it just seems like there's stuff she wants to tell me and when she hints at things, she won't explain them."

"What kind of things?"

"Jim, if I knew, I wouldn't have to ask you about it."

"I guess you're right. Here." He handed me the Browning. "We got a lot of work ahead of us today, Kip."

"Why's that?"

"We're shooting tomorrow night, me and you. Vests only."

My hand was shaking and I couldn't will it to stop. I wasn't sure I wanted it to stop. Jim saw it. I was glad he saw it. I was rushing all right, but it was the kind of rush that was going to make me puke.

"Don't worry about me," he said, that unwelcome smile rising on his face like a cold winter sun. "I'm hard to kill. You'll see."

"I'm not sure I'm ready for—"

"No one is ever ready for this, Kip. No one. Ever. Now let's get going."

Suddenly, I found myself imagining my body on the chapel floor, the blood spurting out of my neck, my limbs getting as cold as the concrete beneath me, my eyes staring up into the blue tarp. I imagined my last thought not being of Amy, but of Renee, tears pouring out of her like the blood out of me, telling me to get out of Brixton before it was too late. Of course, by then, it would be too late. I wondered if it was already too late.

Thirty

Ragged Little Tunnel

We shot last. Who the fuck knew why the rules were the rules? I mean, I had come to understand some of them. I knew why we did a lot of the things we did: the ashes, the number of paces, the hierarchy of crosses, et al. But I was at the point where I believed that some of the rules were just another name for Jim's fancies. Some of the rules didn't make any sense except in the worlds of the chapel and *Gun Church*; but this one, the one about shooters in vests going last, made perfect sense. After all, there was real drama when people were actually risking their lives and that's what Jim and I were doing. Given my penchant for drama, I should have been all for waiting, but waiting just made me want to run. I couldn't force myself to run. For some godforsaken reason it was still important for me to not disappoint Jim. Renee was different. I think she would have helped me run.

The usual cast of characters was on hand, with the exception of the maintenance guy from the college. While I wasn't exactly tearful about his absence, I couldn't help but wonder if there was lingering resentment about his getting shot by Jim. I remembered the look on his face when we were in the berry patch, how he stared at Jim. All that vanished: Any thought about anything else disappeared the moment we stepped out onto the chapel floor and counted out our paces. Suddenly, I felt naked without the security blanket of the protective suit. I even missed the stink of sweat and puke left behind by the gun junkies who'd worn it before me. I felt utterly stripped bare there in my white T-shirt and vest.

When Jim turned to face me, I began to shake, and the harder I tried to stop it, the worse it got. Even my attempts to summon up McGuinn's callousness paid no dividends. He'd abandoned me at the worst moment. There across from me, exactly thirty feet away, was Jim: rock steady, expressionless, calm as an executioner. It didn't help that Renee was the one to hand us our weapons. Felt like everything that could unnerve me had been heaped on me. My shaking hand did not escape her notice. Her eyes were wide, but not with fear. Her expression was unreadable and she did not say a word to me as she stepped back. Instead, she asked us if we were ready. Jim said that he was. I lied that I was.

Renee said, "Begin."

Then, as I raised the heavy .45 in my shaking hand, Jim did me a favor. He smiled that smile at me; the smile I had grown to hate, that smug, all-knowing smile. Suddenly, I didn't need McGuinn. My hand stopped shaking and what I felt in my heart for Jim was nothing like love. I squeezed the trigger.

●

The emergency room doctor—the same guy who'd treated me for the concussion—was, to say the least, skeptical. "You're getting to be a regular around here, Mr. Weiler. Let me guess, you fell off a ladder again."

"Amazing," I managed through teeth clenched in pain. "Do you. . . do . . . tarot card . . . readings . . . too?"

"I've worked trauma rooms for twenty years, five of them at Cook County in Chicago," he said, gently pressing his gloved fingers against the bruised and swollen area on my right side. "You develop a sense about people in this line of work. You might say I have a built in bullshit-o-meter and the needle's spiking pretty high at the moment."

"Really?"

"Uh huh. Funny thing about working in a big city hospital, you see a lot of gunshot trauma. In fact, on about five occasions, I treated cops who'd been shot at relatively close range. Lucky for them, they'd been wearing their protective vests," he said, pressing hard on the center of the bruise. I nearly passed out from the pain.

"Funny . . . what's . . . funny about . . . that?" I asked, gasping for air.

"Funny because your injury there looks exactly like damage a person might sustain if he were shot and the bullet was stopped by protective armor like a Kevlar vest, for instance."

Jim had been good to his word. His shot hit me squarely in the vest, a few inches below my right nipple.

"I don't . . . look good in . . . vests."

He ignored that. "See, the thing most laymen don't understand about protective armor is that it will usually prevent a handgun round from boring a ragged little tunnel through your body, but it can't stop the laws of physics. The energy from the bullet has to go somewhere. Sometimes the vest will dissipate the energy sufficiently so that the wearer only gets a bad bruise, but there are times the energy will crack the wearer's ribs or do even more serious internal damage. I'm sending you for X-rays, Mr. Weiler, but you've got some cracked ribs there. I'd bet on it."

"I fell on . . . the point . . . of a . . . wrought iron fence. I'm lucky it . . . didn't break . . . the skin," I said, the pain easing for the time being.

"And did you used to tell your teachers that the dog ate your homework? Did your teachers believe you? This is Brixton County, Mr. Weiler. There isn't a wrought iron fence for fifty miles around. Look, I don't know what you're playing at, but you better stop it before someone gets seriously injured. Have you ever seen what bullets do to the insides of the human body?"

"Yes . . . as a matter of fact," I said, remembering my father's blood on the fussy curtains. "Thanks, Doc, but . . . I . . . fell on the point . . . of a fence."

"Suit yourself, Mr. Weiler. I've got other patients to see."

Still, it could have been worse for me, much worse. The occasional broken rib must have been pretty standard fare for the chapel, but there was no escaping the fact that the margin of error between broken ribs and bleeding out was miniscule. I was finally experienced enough with a gun in my hand to know that very little separated a great shot from a miss. All it would have taken to turn a bull's-eye into a disaster was a momentary lack of concentration, an unexpected distraction, a cough or a sneeze, the buzzing of a mosquito. And as good as Jim was, he wasn't immune to any of those things. I'd seen as much when he hit the maintenance man.

Jim's own warning rattled around in my head. "You get killed, we're just going to take you out in the woods and bury you somewhere where you won't ever be found. Even if you're real seriously wounded, that's what we'll have to do." So as bad luck goes, I guess, I was ahead of the game. I meant to keep it that way. I was about a hundred grand richer than I'd been a few weeks ago and I had a book to finish. I was pretty determined not to step into the chapel again. Nothing like those rare moments of clarity in your life. Standing on the wrong end of a gun will make you focus like almost nothing else.

When the curtain around the examination table pulled back, I expected an orderly to come in, but it was Renee. She was positively jovial compared to the last time we were here. That night, she was red-eyed and shaking. Tonight, for the first time since I got back from New York, she seemed like the Renee I'd grown so comfortable with before I left. The edge was off, her smile broad. It lit up the room.

"How do you feel?" she asked, clasping my right hand in both of hers.

"Alive."

"Good to be alive." She leaned over and kissed my forehead.

"Very."

"How are your ribs?"

"The ... doctor ... thinks they're ... broken. They ... really hurt."

"Probably are broken," she said. "It happens to all of us sooner or later. Me too. They'll tape you up and you'll need to take it easy for a while."

"Thank ... you, Doctor Svoboda."

She blushed. "You hit Jim, you know. Almost everyone misses their first time shooting that way."

I was glad she was happy about it. All I was was relieved. Frankly, I didn't give a fuck if I hit Jim or shot through the tarp and hit the hangar roof, as long as I didn't kill him. I realized I was more frightened of that than getting killed myself.

"Renee," I whispered. "I don't ... think I ... want to do ... this anymore. Shooting, I ... mean."

If I thought that was going to upset her, I couldn't have been more wrong.

"Promise me you won't," she said, moisture forming at the corners of her fierce blue eyes. She kissed me again, only this time on the mouth. "Promise me you won't."

"I promise. Renee . . . there's something else . . . we . . . need to talk . . . about."

"*Shhhhh*." She placed her index finger across my lips. "Not tonight."

"Okay, Mr. Weiler," the orderly said as he strolled in pushing a wheelchair ahead of him. "Time to take a ride to X-ray."

He helped me into the chair. Renee promised to wait for me and when I turned back to look at her, she was still smiling, but there were tears too.

Thirty-One

No U-Turns

By the following Monday, I was able to get around again. If not completely without pain, then with much less pain than I'd had in the days immediately following getting shot. At least I could breathe again. Weird thing, I felt like I'd been holding my breath for the last decade and had only now exhaled. I'm not sure I can explain it or if I even want to, but that's just how I felt. I didn't much enjoy the tape job the doctor had done on me to stabilize the ribs while they healed, but there were a lot of things I'd liked less, things that hurt more and hadn't done a fucking bit of good for me.

Truth was, the broken ribs were another one of those unexpected blessings that had been coming my way lately. While it gave me many more hours of uninterrupted writing time, it also gave me an excuse to avoid discussing with Jim my decision to step away from the chapel. I was certainly in no shape for running or shooting, and I wouldn't be for at least another week or two. Jim did come by on Thursday morning to see how I was doing and to tell me how proud he was of my shooting, but I was still in a lot of pain, a little drug addled, and in no real mood to chat. He seemed to understand.

The weekend had been pretty quiet. Renee left on Friday night to go see her folks, who she said lived about ninety minutes north of Brixton in the middle of the state. I thought the timing of her visit, a few weeks before Christmas, was kind of strange, but she said she didn't know if she'd be going home for the holidays and that she wanted to make sure to spend a few days with her brother Jake, who was on leave from the Army. And while I was glad for the time alone, I had my newfound guilt to keep me company.

I'd pretty much lived with Renee for three months. We had fucked our brains out on an almost nightly basis. She'd endured my occasional foul moods and dealt with my legendary vanities and insecurities. She'd followed my routines, lived her life by my clock. Yet I'd never once asked what her parents did for a living or where they lived or even if they were alive; and, until she mentioned Jake, I didn't know Renee had a brother. The guilty part was not that I hadn't asked but that I hadn't cared to ask. I hadn't cared. Worse still, I hadn't yet told her I was leaving. This guilt thing was a pain in the balls.

Renee's absence also allowed me to call Meg without worries of being overheard. I hadn't spoken a word to Meg since our dinner with Dudek because I was still supremely pissed off at her for the shit she pulled with Amy. I was also displeased that my check from her was long overdue. Meg had her own ideas when it came to sending me large sums of money. Apparently, I hadn't quite erased all her doubts about the reformation of Darth Kipster. In the past, I'd appreciated her attempts to hold back funds so I couldn't purchase Costco-sized bags of cocaine. That was then.

"Kip!"

"Where's my check?"

"Fine, thank you, and yourself?"

"Sorry, Meg, I'm not in the mood for small talk, especially not after that stunt you pulled with Amy. How could you do that to me?"

"You needed to know there was something to come back to, you idiot."

"I know this is hard for you to accept, but I've finally learned how to tie my own shoes and everything. I can even manage the activities of daily living without adult supervision."

"Says the man who's shacked up with a twenty-year-old girl and lets himself get shot with live ammunition. Yes, Kip, I'd say that instills a lot of confidence in me about your recent maturation."

"Well, try this on for size: I'm moving back up there at least until the end of the summer. You need to find me a one-bedroom apartment close to Manhattan, but not in it. Maybe in Brooklyn or Long Island City somewhere and you need to find it soon."

"Are you fucking around with me, Weiler? Because if you are, I'm not laughing."

"No joke, Donovan."

"Is this with or without . . . what was it you called her . . . the St. Pauli Girl?"

"Without. I might have Renee come up for a week. I owe her that, but she won't be staying, no. And don't you dare call Amy."

"You needn't fret. She's as angry with me as you are. Angrier, probably. What did you do to her exactly that got her so bent out of shape?"

"It's what I didn't do, but that's not the point."

"I promise I won't let her know you're coming. I'd cross my heart, but I'd have to have one to make it a meaningful gesture."

We both had a laugh at that. I think I laughed a little too long to suit her, but I didn't really care.

"You haven't even cut my check yet, have you, Donovan?"

"Guilty as charged."

"Well, keep the funds until I get up there and use whatever you need for the apartment. But when I get into town, I expect the check that day. You with me?"

"Like a conjoined twin."

"There's an image I could have done without."

"So when's the big move?" she asked.

"The middle of January, I think. I can't be any more specific about it now, but I'll let you know."

"Look, Kip, I can't believe I'm even uttering these words, but do you think you'll be able to finish the book back here? You'll be leaving your cradle-robbing and gunplay behind, after all."

"I'll finish it."

"You're certain?"

"No, not really, but the chances are just as likely I'll finish in New York as here. Besides, if I feel myself slipping, I can come back to Brixton. I'm taking a sabbatical, not handing in my resignation. Burning this bridge would really be a bridge too far. In any case, I have a lease on this house that I'm responsible for for several more months."

"Okay, I'll have my assistant get to it on Monday. Will you need a parking spot for your car? You do still have that Porsche, don't you?"

"Renting a parking spot in New York would cost more than my rent on this house. It's moot anyway. The Porsche's staying here."

"Suit yourself," Meg said. "Ta."

And that was it. I was committed now, sort of. Sort of, because if there was one lesson being the Kipster had taught me, it was that there wasn't a commitment in the world that couldn't be broken. Well, I suppose once you've jumped out the window or pulled the trigger, there are no U-turns. I wondered if my father had time to wish he hadn't pulled the trigger. I was on my way to taking one more step away from Brixton and towards New York.

Thirty-Two

The Three-Doughnut Rule

The campus of Brixton County Community College was actually quite pretty. Lots of red brick and ivy, big live oaks and maples sprinkled in amongst the predominant pines, and a classic clock tower atop the library. It was easy to understand how some administration types mistook its looks for its quality. The former dickhead president of BCCC was wont to say that Harvard was the Brixton County Community College of the northeast. Was it any wonder he hadn't lasted very long?

The ever-popular Miss Crouch had prepared all my sabbatical paperwork for me to sign. There were tabs and little yellow Post-it notes with instructions on each of the forms. No wonder she'd survived seven department chairpersons. As warm and friendly as J. J. Beauchamp was, the Engagin' Cajun was no administrator. Disorganized and drunk a good deal of the time, he had his head stuck so far up his ass that he needed someone like Miss Crouch to steer the ship. Trust me, at BCCC, there was no political intrigue involved in landing the chairman's job. No one yearned to be English Department chair. It was a short-straw job that people accepted only because it came with a five-thousand-dollar per-term stipend.

The one thing Miss Crouch couldn't do was to fill in the section of the paperwork that asked for an explanation of the reason for the sabbatical. Not that anyone probably gave a shit, but you were required to fill it out before a sabbatical could be granted. This is where you were supposed to mention some lofty research study or scholarly project you were working on like a Cartesian reinterpretation of the Dead Sea Scrolls. I wrote simply that I was taking the time to finish a book. I didn't bother mentioning that the book in question was about as scholarly as the back of a baseball card and was sort of a cross between pulp fiction and an idiot's guide to existentialism.

"You'll be missed around here, Professor Weiler," said Miss Crouch as I handed back all the signed and completed forms. This was the most the woman had said to me in seven years.

"Really, why's that?"

"Because the female adjuncts will have to find a new form of entertainment in your absence."

I stood there, stunned. I wanted to say something but Miss Crouch had already moved on to other matters, dismissively turning her back to me. And what would I have said? I was just grateful she hadn't mentioned the co-eds I'd bedded during my tenure at Brixton. Although that particular form of "mentoring" was frowned upon by the current administration, our state university system was one of the last holdouts that hadn't formalized a ban on such relationships.

With the fall term having ended the previous Friday, the campus was very quiet. There were a few students around. Mostly there were squirrels, crows, and a few other faculty members. I much preferred the squirrels and crows. For the first time since the incident with Frank Vuchovich, I walked over to the southwestern corner of the campus, to the building where it had all taken place. The building had been closed for the term, but was scheduled to reopen for the spring semester. I was glad I wouldn't be there to see it.

I stood outside Halifax Hall staring up at the windows the police marksmen had shattered with their bullets. I turned to look at where the shots came from, imagining a straight red line drawn across the sky from the roof of the lecture center through the new windows of Room 212. I recalled the confused look on Frank Vuchovich's face. I wondered now as I wondered then about what the kid had expected to happen. He must have known he wasn't leaving the police with very many options, yet he seemed almost surprised by the spray of glass and blood, and the burning bits of metal ripping through his body.

There was another imaginary string holding together a narrative that led from the death of Frank Vuchovich to the chapel to Haskell Brown's murder to here. It was a line of perplexing coincidences and good fortune that I grabbed hold of to pull myself out of my perpetual tailspin. This line was red too. I didn't believe in God. I'm not sure I ever did, but if he did exist, I wondered if he would send angels and omens in the form of blood and bullet wounds.

"Gun Church, indeed," I whispered aloud and walked on.

I didn't get fifty feet before I felt a strong hand latch on to my bicep. I gasped and my ribs barked at me. It was the maintenance guy, rake against his shoulder, lit cigarette dangling from his lips.

"We need to talk, you and me, Professor," he said, letting go of me.

"What about?"

His head was on a swivel, looking around, behind him, over my shoulder. "Not here."

"Then where?"

"Not your house either."

"Okay, not my house," I said. "How about the Dew Drop Inn? I'm going over there in a little while to get something to eat. It's usually pretty empty this time of day."

"I'll be there in an hour or so."

That was it. He walked away from me without another word and didn't look back. I didn't know what it was all about, but I could guess. He had some nasty things to say about Jim and he figured I'd be a good audience. He was right, but I didn't give it much thought as I turned to the student union.

At the student union, I picked up the paper and threw my change on the counter just as I had that September afternoon when all of this began. I found I was no longer thinking of the late Frank Vuchovich or the maintenance man, but of shooting in the woods with Jim. I would miss it. I would miss Jim's company too. I would miss the sweaty-handed, heart-thumping rush of the chapel. I didn't regret my decision to walk away from it, but I had no doubt that the junkie in me would always be tempted to put a gun back in my hand. In the end, some of Jim's wacky notions about the essential nature of the handgun proved true. Although I tried to hold myself apart from the other people at the chapel, I had been seduced. I had proven myself in a way most people in the regular world never dare try. I was special. Staring down the barrel of a loaded handgun imparts a certain kind of wisdom unobtainable through most other means.

Even armed with that wisdom, the temptation would always remain. I once had a girlfriend who lived by what she called the three-doughnut rule. She had weird food allergies and trouble regulating her blood sugar, but knew she could safely eat two doughnuts without having her body go batshit. Still, on occasion, she would eat three. When I asked her why, she said, "Because sometimes it's just worth it." I'd come to realize that we all have our own versions of the three-doughnut rule. I knew that if I stayed in Brixton, I would eventually have ashes dabbed on my forehead to step back into the chapel, to eat that third doughnut.

On my way to the Dew Drop, I stopped at the hardware store in town to buy a package of light bulbs. My ribs were sore and I was short of breath, so I sat down on a stack of bags of rock salt. I guess I was too preoccupied by my pain to notice I had unwanted company.

"What's the matter, pussy, your ribs hurtin' you?" It was Stan Petrovic. He had a bag of screws in his hand and a cold, drunken stare on his face. "I played whole fucking games in the NFL with broken ribs and two wrecked knees."

"Good for you, Stan. Maybe they'll throw you a parade someday."

I wasn't in the mood or in shape for one of our little skirmishes, but since he'd hurt Renee and hit me in the back of the head, I had no patience for his bullshit.

"What's the matter, your asshole hurt from letting Jim stick his fist up there? You ain't such a hero without a gun in your hand, huh? Think you have the balls to vest-shoot with me?"

That got my attention. One thing I'd found over the last few months was that the people who showed up at the chapel kept their mouths shut tight about it. Over that period of time, whether on the street or in school, I'd crossed paths with everyone who had ever been to the chapel. The only time I'd mentioned it was to Meg and I felt guilty about that. Even the maintenance guy hadn't alluded to the chapel when he pulled me aside not twenty minutes earlier. Not once did any of them even hint at our connection. There wasn't a nod, a wink, or a gesture. Nothing. And now this drunken fool was standing in the aisle of the hardware store talking about the chapel like it was common knowledge.

"Keep it down, Stan. You know the rules."

"Fuck you and fuck the rules."

"Shut your mouth."

His saw-toothed smile was raw and cruel. "Why don't you do it for me, cunt?"

I thought to speak, but instead I planted my left fist into Stan's groin. It wasn't the hardest punch I'd ever thrown. It didn't have to be. Petrovic groaned, grabbed his balls, and fell to his knees. He teetered for a second or two and collapsed backwards into the shelves that held boxes and bags of nails and screws. A few of the boxes crashed to the floor.

"Don't fuck with me again, Stan," I growled, standing over him. "Fuck with me again and I'll kill you."

When I turned to leave, I noticed everyone watching. Half of them looked about ready to applaud. I just wanted to go get something to eat and read the paper in peace.

Thirty-Three

Redtails

The Dew Drop Inn was what you might have expected: a seedy and frayed hole in the wall, a working man's bar. There were two beer pulls, one for light beer and one for regular. There was one kind of scotch, one kind of bourbon, one kind of vodka. No one ordered mojitos. Even the burger choices were limited: with or without cheese, with or without fries. If you wanted avocadoes or roasted poblano strips, you were shit out of luck. As I anticipated, the place was pretty empty except for Richie the barman and a few stubborn flies that forgot it was December. Richie nodded hello. I nodded back.

"I'll have a burger with cheese and fries and a ginger ale," I said, making my way to a back booth.

I settled in and unfolded the paper. The *Brixton Banner* was birdcage lining, as local as local papers get. It featured articles on subjects as diverse as advances in coal-mining technology, belt tightening in the lumber industry, and who had won the charity pierogi-eating contest at St. Stanislaus Church. The war in Afghanistan was reduced to a few inches worth of body counts buried between the car ads and obits. At the end of things with

Janice Nadir, reading the *Banner* in bed became my way of telling her we were done for the day, that it was time for her to run along back home to Jerry.

My favorite things in the *Banner* were the letters to the editor. No highfalutin' horseshit in Brixton, just conspiratorial paranoia at its most rabid. Distrust and hatred for government—federal, state, and local—ran deep around here and with it came the usual substrains of white supremacy, anti-Semitism, xenophobia, et cetera. I loved the letters that tried to tie all of these things into one tidy, hateful little package. My all-time favorite had been this one letter from a woman who claimed that the area coal mining was just a government cover for digging secret shafts. That the shafts were to be used to protect the Jews' money during the nuclear war being instigated by the dark races in order to wipe out the Aryan peoples. Now, I'm sure letters of this nature get sent to the *New York Times* on a daily basis—the difference being that the *Banner* actually published them, and frequently.

Just as I unfurled the paper and began to scan the letters, Richie arrived with my ginger ale. He asked me how I was doing, why I hadn't been in lately. I said something generic about being busy and watching my weight. That seemed to satisfy him and he left, saying my burger would be up in a few minutes. When I turned back to the paper, my eyes drifted to a column to the left of the letters with a heading: *Murdered (continued from page 1).*

In New York City in the '80s, when homicide was a cottage industry, I would have simply ignored the headline. But these days, in these parts, murder wasn't usually part of the landscape. Premature death was common enough in a region where mining and logging were how folks earned their keep. There were plenty of hunting accidents and alcohol-fueled suicides too. There was the occasional migrant worker killed by a piece of farm equipment, but murder was rare. I could only remember two other homicides in seven years: one stemming from a barroom brawl. The other involved a woman who stabbed her husband through the heart with a kitchen knife because he'd pawned her Lladró figurines for meth money.

I skipped the letters for the moment, reading instead the continuation of the story from page one. The victim's body, it said, was discovered Sunday morning by two deer hunters just across the state line, along the banks of a tributary to the river that fed the Crooked River Falls. The victim was found in a car registered to his father, his body with three or four gunshot wounds. One of the hunters said, "We just figured he was drunk and sleeping it off, but when we got close you could see the bullet holes in the windshield and that he was dead."

The hunters were still pretty shaken and though they weren't considered suspects, they were being questioned by the sheriff's department. There was a hotline number to call, but not much else. It was only when I backtracked, turned to the front page and saw the full headline that I went cold.

REDTAILS RECEIVER MURDERED

A photo of a handsome African American kid with a white, self-assured smile stared up at me. He was wearing a football jersey over his shoulder pads, and holding his helmet tucked between his chest and his left arm. The logo on his helmet was that of a bird of prey, wings spread, talons unsheathed. The caption said his name was Lance Vaughn Mabry and that he had been a starting wideout for the Coggins and Hale College Redtails.

Coggins and Hale was a small school about twenty miles across the state line from Brixton. Academically, it was the four-year equivalent of BCCC: a place to jerk off while earning a degree of dubious quality and value. But for a school its size, it had a solid football program that had the reputation of producing good-quality, late-round, NFL draft picks. According to the first paragraph of the article, Lance Vaughn Mabry had been on just such a career path. Not anymore.

By the time Richie brought over my food, I'd read the story twice. I no longer had an appetite. I was upset for the kid's family, sure, but that wasn't what was affecting me. It was hard for me to ignore the incredible similarities between this kid's fate and the scene I'd written into *Gun Church* after my concussion-induced dream of McGuinn in the river during Fox Hunt. The victim in my book, just exactly like Mabry, was a young black athlete. In the book, he's lured out of a bar by Zoe, the character based loosely on the St. Pauli Girl and named after the woman who had been Peter Moreland's country club date all those years ago. Once outside, he's abducted, dragged out into the woods to be hunted down, and shot like a wild animal, his lifeless body left to rot out in the countryside.

Although they'd found Mabry's body in an area much like I'd described in the book, the kid was in his own car and there was no mention of his being lured by anyone to go anywhere. There were other differences too, but I still couldn't get my head around it. I threw a twenty-dollar bill on the table and left, taking the paper with me and leaving the burger for the flies. Richie might've nodded and said something. He might not have.

I was halfway home before I got my legs back under me and remembered about meeting the guy from the BCCC maintenance crew. I was too preoccupied to care and whatever he had to tell me would keep. In the car, I listened to the local news-radio station. The murder was the lead story, but their report was equally as sketchy as the *Banner*'s. Back home, I planted myself in front of the TV, something I almost never did. And though the TV news had remote pictures from where the body had been discovered, they had no fresh details to tell. I got out my laptop and read and reread and reread again the scene from *Gun Church*.

Levon Dexter felt as if he was gagging on his own thundering heart as he ran through the brush along the riverbank, his mouth as dry as the combs of the reeds he swept out of the way that snapped back in his face as he pushed on. The muscles around his eyes, his cheeks ached from the prolonged tension, yet he felt no pain in his legs despite the blood. He knew there was blood. There had to be blood. He'd felt the nicks and cuts from the coarse grasses and brambles as they chewed into the bare skin of his ankles, calves, and thighs. The only persistent pain he felt was the burning stitch in his left side. Coach wouldn't be happy about that. By this time in the season, Levon should have been in the kind of shape to play every down on defense and special teams without breathing too heavy.

"Coach! Shit," he thought to himself, "why the fuck I'm thinking about Coach now?" Even as he ran he fought the urge to stop and listen, to rest to catch his second wind. He also fought the anger in him and the desire to find a way to get that bitch who set him up. Part of him wanted a piece of her so bad he thought it would almost be worth it to sacrifice himself in order to get at her. But his instinct for survival and his daddy's words drove him forward.

"They can coach you stronger, boy, but they can't teach you speed and speed is what you got. Just keep running. The rest of it will take care of itself."

His daddy, a hardass ex-Marine sniper, had schooled him good, so Levon had been careful to leave false traces along the way. He'd torn his shirt up and left a shred of it only a few hundred yards from where them crazy gun motherfuckers had shoved him out of the van. He'd left other shreds of shirt and pants here and there in a clear path toward the hills before doubling back and working his way along the river's edge. They didn't have no dogs with them as far as Levon could tell, so he didn't worry about leaving a scent trail. He was a little concerned about the blood he guessed he was trailing as he went, but even in full moonlight it would be hard to pick up.

Damn the full moon! If it had been cloudy or if the moon had been just a slice of itself, he might've risked fording the river at the point where he doubled back. If, if, if . . . But like Coach said, "if" was a loser's word. Anyways, with that moon up there like it was, Levon couldn't dare cross the river: so wide and violent along this stretch. He would be way too vulnerable. Dark black skin affords you only so much of an advantage. The light coat of mud Levon had spread over his face and body to matte the shine of his sweat would wash right off the second he hit the water. Then there was his unfamiliarity with the area. What if he made it across to the other bank and it was flat and wide open over there? He'd be too easy a target.

No, he had come back by them, passing so close he could hear the crackle of dry grass beneath their feet. Only one of them spoke and loud, too: the old man with the Irish accent, the one that blond bitch called McGuinn. If Levon didn't know better, he'd have thought that McGuinn was helping him out, signaling their position. But no, Levon thought, that was bullshit, a trap. He just continued on, using the roar of the river to mask his sound. Was a windy night, too, so his stirring the cattails didn't draw any particular attention.

He figured he must have been near parallel to where they'd cut the tape off his wrists and ankles and kicked him out of the van, so he willed himself to slow his pace and quiet his breathing. Levon didn't stop, but his strides were careful now, measured and stealthy. He was no fool, realizing the river's roar that helped provide cover also prevented him from hearing any trackers that were more than a few feet away. Then, in the distance, a shot. Another. Another and another. *Pop. Pop. Pop, pop.* Each echo seemed to overwhelm the one before it.

A little ways farther along the bank, the river took a sharp twist and from there seemed to flow directly into a dense wood. He stilled himself completely, gathering himself as well as listening as best he could for sounds only humans make. Hearing nothing, Levon charged through the sedge and reeds for the bend in the river. By the time he made it, the stitch in his side was on fire and he could barely catch his breath. He thought about trying to cross the river here, but decided not to. He pressed his hand to his side where the stitch burned and knew immediately that the moisture on his hand wasn't just sweat. Blood. There was blood, a lot of it, pouring out of his side. It glowed black in the moonlight. The cold water would sap his energy and he didn't think he had the strength to make it. He needed a safe place to rest, to think.

His daddy's lessons came back to him again. "Most folks, they just plain lazy. Even most soldiers get that way. They just look straight on ahead of themselves or side to side. So you ever in a tight spot, boy, you get high or you get low. Most likely, they'll walk right on past you."

He picked out a big old oak tree with a few thick, low-hanging branches—a tree that had stubbornly held on to many of its leaves in spite of the season. Levon was pretty sure that if he could kick off the trunk of the tree, he'd be able to grab one of the low branches and make his way up. With all those leaves still on its branches and all those gnarled and crisscrossed branches, they wouldn't be able to spot him from the ground, full moon or not.

Levon took several deep breaths—deep as he could, wounded like he was—and took off in a dead run for the oak. He thought he heard something to his left, a rustling of dried leaves, but did not lose focus. He had picked out a spot on the tree trunk where he would kick off with his right foot to propel himself up to that low limb. He heard the noise again, but kept thinking about what all his coaches had taught him about tackling. Focus on the ball carrier's numbers. Stick your face mask right between those numbers, wrap your arms, and drive him into the ground. He focused on that spot on the tree and ran to it as hard as he could. This time, it wasn't the rustling of leaves that tugged at his focus. He saw something, a flash, out of the corner of his eye. If he had held on a little bit longer, he might have heard the accompanying thunder, but he was beyond hearing, beyond pain, beyond the reach of his daddy or his coaches.

Zoe and McGuinn heard the shots and came running. The others already had the kid's ankles roped to the limb of a big oak, his body swaying to and fro in the stiff breeze, his lifeless fingertips no more than two or three feet off the ground. Zoe and McGuinn hung back as the others used their cell phone cameras to snap pictures with the body as if it were a fourteen-point buck . . .

That was the last line I read when Renee walked through the front door.

I didn't have to say anything to her. "Kip, what's wrong?"

"That kid who was murdered."

"What kid? What are you talking about?"

I handed her the paper and watched her read the story.

"Oh, my god. That's terrible, but what's it got to do with you?"

And that's when it hit me, when Renee asked aloud the question that had been rattling around in my head for the last few hours: I had to get out of Brixton. I wasn't thinking straight. It was the old narcissism kicking in. A black kid who just happens to be a football player gets murdered out in the woods near here and somehow I turn that into it being about me. How did that work exactly? What, I wrote things down on my magic laptop and *poof*, they came to be? I was losing my mind. The pressure of having to finish the book and anxiety over moving back to New York must have been getting to me. The time had come to relieve some of that pressure. I closed my laptop, took Renee by the hand, and walked her up the stairs to the bedroom.

Night had fallen by the time we were done and the room was nearly pitch black. It's hard to use the term "old times" when you've only been with someone for a couple of months, but that's how it felt: like old times. She was relaxed in my arms and begged me to face her when we fucked. After each orgasm, she cuddled in my arms until one of us got an itch to begin again. This was the Renee I'd left behind when I went to New York. Being with her, inside her, felt so good and so right, I couldn't believe I was about to tell her I was leaving. I didn't get the chance.

I was trying to summon up the words to say as we lay there in the dark, her back pressed against my chest, my arms surrounding her. It was incredibly quiet, but for the occasional wail of a passing train.

"You're leaving to go back to New York, aren't you?" she whispered. It was perfectly loud against the utter stillness.

"I am."

"Good."

"Do you really mean that?"

"No and yes. You know I love you, but you don't belong here, Ken. This isn't your home. It never has been."

"It only ever felt like home with you here."

She spun around to face me. "Thank you for saying that."

"I mean it. This was a very lonely life without you."

"I know you mean it." She kissed me. "I know you do."

She let me hold her for a little while longer. Then she took me by my hand and led me into the shower.

Thirty-Four

Anything, Except Everything

The paranoia over Lance Vaughn Mabry's murder had faded away, but was never completely out of my thoughts. Even after the sheriff theorized that the death hadn't been anything more than a careless accident, my unease persisted.

"Been known to happen," the sheriff said at a press conference. "Deer hunters, 'specially young and inexperienced ones, they come down here thinking they're gonna bag a big buck their first time out. Most of 'em don't never even get to take a shot. So they get all bored and frustrated and have a little too much to drink. Then they go down by the river with their dumbass side arms, find what they think's an abandoned car, and shoot it up. My bet is they didn't even know what they done until they heard about it on the radio the next day. Now they're just scared. Don't worry, we're going through all the huntin' licenses and checking for suspects. What we're gonna find here is that it was just a terrible, stupid mistake."

But that next morning, other things were far more present on my mind. With only a few breaks for writing and eating, Renee and I spent that whole day and day after that in bed—sore ribs and all. The sense of desperation was heavy in the air. Although I invited Renee to come up to New York for a week when I moved, we both knew she wouldn't. Just as I was leaving Brixton behind, she had to let me go to leave me behind. Sabbatical or no sabbatical, we both knew it was unlikely I was ever coming back. This time we had together was all the time together we were ever going to have, and neither one of us seemed inclined to waste it.

Well beyond the continued intensity of my time with Renee, things that had been all wrong since my return from New York had somehow righted themselves. I hadn't crossed paths with Stan Petrovic again. That all-knowing smile of Jim's was gone and he seemed genuinely happy for me. He didn't even react badly when I explained about no longer wanting to risk getting my head blown off in the chapel before leaving town. It helped, I think, that I gave him and Renee a lot of the credit for turning my life around. I'd said it not only to be nice—something the Kipster would only do in service of pussy or cocaine—but because it was true. It may have started with Frank Vuchovich's gun in my face, but my urge to write again might have died with him that day if I hadn't gotten involved with Jim and the St. Pauli Girl.

The one thing Jim asked of me was that we keep up our routine until I was ready to leave. I was glad to oblige him. A writer's routine is more than just what he does in his office, at his desk. It's his life. It's his comfort. And while I knew I would have to create a new routine when I got to New York, I was thrilled at the prospect of having at least some more time with my old one. My ribs were healing, but not healed, so I kept our morning run under a mile. Even that made my chest feel like it was caught in a junk yard car-crusher. I wasn't complaining. With the term over, I had more time for writing. Shooting was fun again and when we were up in the woods above the falls, I regaled Jim with as many tales of the Kipster as I could remember. I was incredulous at the seemingly inexhaustible nature of those stories.

Knowing that I was leaving made Renee's decision about going home for Christmas an easy one: she stayed with me. One of my gifts to her was a clothes shopping spree at the regional mall in Stateline. We went to the movies afterwards and I treated her to Thai food for dinner. When the waitress asked if my daughter and I had enjoyed the meal, we just laughed it off. We fucked particularly long and hard that night.

Jim came over Christmas Day. Renee made a regional-style ham that featured an apple glaze and chestnut sauce. It was really good. I let myself drink a little bit, having a glass of champagne and a few beers. Renee and Jim both had a lot more than me. After the apple pie Jim's mom had baked for the occasion, we sat around listening to my vast collection of bad New Wave CDs and discussing New York in the '80s. Jim knew a lot about the era from my books and from our talks, and I swear I saw a little jealousy in Renee's eyes, but it quickly passed.

When it was getting late, I told them both I had gifts for them. Their eyes lit up at the sound of that and I could clearly see they were both still kids, really. The only thing I could have done to make it better was to have had a fat man slide down the chimney in a Santa suit. I handed a small gift-wrapped box to each of them. They hesitated.

"Go ahead," I said. "Open them up."

Jim was first. "Holy shit! These are the keys to your—"

"—Porsche. That's right. When I leave, it's yours."

For the first time since I met him, Jim Trimble was at a loss for words. He actually hung his head. Then he just held his right hand out and said, "Thanks, but I don't know how to—"

I shook his hand. "Just like my old golf clubs, the car's something I should have parted with a long time ago. There's no place for it in my life anymore. Take it. Enjoy it. Just beware, the repair bills and insurance will bankrupt you."

The three of us had a laugh at that, but I was glad to be rid of the Kipster's car. I very badly wanted to molt the last vestiges of the Kipster's skin before I went back to New York. I didn't know if there would be a future for Amy and me or, if there was one, that I wanted it. I did want to set things right with her. I wouldn't have been able to do that if the specter of the Kipster was looming. Funny how things evolve. For years after Amy handed me my walking papers and married Moreland, I told myself I would have sacrificed anything to have her back. Anything, except everything. I was as ready to give up my extracurricular activities as I was prepared to write a great new book, which was not at all. The lies we tell ourselves are always the most obvious ones, but we always believe them. I guess my road back started when I began to believe them a little less.

"Now yours, Renee," I said, pointing at her gift.

It held a key too, one she already had a copy of—the key to the house. She was a bit confused by it, I think.

"The house is yours, rent free until the end of the summer. I'll pay the utilities too. I'm leaving a lot of the furniture. It's not enough of a gift, but . . . " I couldn't finish the sentence. The one gift she wanted was the one I couldn't give her. If I could have only brought myself to say "I love you," it would have meant everything to her.

"Thanks, Ken." She kissed me softly, but hugged me tightly. When she relaxed her grip, I did not. I didn't let go. When I finally opened my arms, placing my hands on her shoulders, she stepped back slightly and gazed right up into my face. Gauging by her expression, that hug meant much more to her than a few months free rent.

Almost involuntarily, I said, "I lo—"

Renee stopped me, covering my mouth with her hand. "Don't! Don't ruin it. Thanks for the house."

Jim, looking a tad perturbed, cleared his throat and the spell was broken. He went out to his truck and came back in with a gift-wrapped package of his own. He handed it to me.

"Your turn." His smile was crooked, but pure. A gift to a friend and father figure, one he took pride in giving. When I caught a glimpse of Renee, she didn't seem nearly as happy or excited by it.

"Heavy," I said, tearing away the paper.

Under the paper was a lovely cherrywood case about ten inches by ten inches by three or four inches. The case, however, wasn't what gave my gift its weight. There was something inside, but it was locked. Before I could say a word, Jim held out a shiny key to me. It was a night for gifts of keys.

"Go on, open her up, Kip."

When I turned the key and lifted the case's finely crafted lid, I was as horrified as I was delighted. Inside the cherrywood case, resting in a molded foam bed that exactly matched its unique shape was a Royal Blue Colt Python with a six-inch barrel. It was the same type of handgun Frank Vuchovich had used to take my class hostage.

"This is amazing, Jim."

"We don't want anyone up in New York thinking they can fuck with Kip Weiler."

"Not unless they're carrying a Howitzer." That pleased him. It pleased him a lot. "Jim, this thing must've cost you a fortune." I didn't have the heart to tell him that there was no way I'd be able to carry the Python around. Getting caught with an unregistered handgun in New York City meant mandatory jail time. I'd been willing to risk it the last time I was there, but not again.

"It makes me happy to give it to you. Your books meant a lot to me after the Colonel took off and that we're friends . . . No gift I could ever give you would be good enough."

"Thanks again. Can we use it up in the woods this week?"

I didn't think it was possible, but his smile got even broader. "You bet."

"Oh, shit!" I said. "I almost forgot. Wait here."

I went upstairs and retrieved two packages. When I got back downstairs, I handed one each to Renee and Jim.

"What's this?" Renee asked.

"Open them up."

They pulled off the wrapping paper. Renee was working hard at choking back tears and for the second time in one night, Jim was speechless. Omitting the title of the book, I'd had mock dedication pages done up and framed by a specialty print shop and art supply store in New Prague. The paper was heavy book stock and was the same size as it would be in a hardcover. I took Renee's and read it aloud.

For Renee and Jim, who helped me find my way back.

Renee couldn't hold back the tears any longer and ran out of the room. Jim said it was time for him to hit the road.

Later that night I found myself downstairs in the darkened living room, the Python in my hand, thumb pulling back the hammer, finger squeezing the trigger. I remembered that time in Bart Meyers' house when I held a Python and how I had tried to grab one just like it out of Frank Vuchovich's hand. The world, I thought, was rife with bizarre coincidences, invisible threads that pulled together moments of our lives so many years apart.

Thirty-Five

Freak Show Roster

Leaving was finally at hand. The time since Christmas dinner passed with accelerating momentum: each day evaporating faster than the day before it until there was only one tomorrow left. I no longer gave much thought to the death of Lance Mabry and when I did, I felt foolish for ever entertaining my old narcissism. The day I went back to school to clear out my office, I'd hoped to run into the campus maintenance man to apologize for missing him that day at the Dew Drop Inn. I figured that what he had to say couldn't have been too important, that his wounded arm and wounded pride had finally recovered. Except for my bed and a few miscellaneous items, the van was packed. After the farewell party at the chapel, there would only be sleep. Then, early in the morning, State Highway 87 East and I-95 North.

This close to leaving, it would have been impossible not to look back at my life. Sometimes you look back at the road you've taken, but since September it was more like the road had taken me. That I'd simply been the passenger along for the ride. My time in Brixton was now divided into two distinct parts, BV and AV: *Before Vuchovich* and *After Vuchovich*. I thought back to how the St. Pauli

Girl, dressed in an unzipped brown hoodie and skin-tight jeans, had showed up at my house soon after Frank Vuchovich's death: how her nipples hardened in the crisp night air, how she'd given me a soft and solitary kiss and handed me a sheet of paper, an invitation into a world I could never have imagined. Now with Renee sitting next to me in the car, a fancy cherrywood case on her lap, I knew where I was headed. The road was no longer my master. I no longer needed an invitation or a set of directions to where I was going.

I turned to look at Renee as I drove over the last hill before reaching Hardentine. We'd spent New Year's Eve and New Year's Day at the MacClaren Arms, a rather grand old hotel across from the state capitol building. It was the most fun I'd had in a very long time. I suspect it was the first time Renee had done anything like it. We did formal dress-up and danced and overate and drank a little too much. When we fell into bed well after midnight, we fucked with half our clothes still on, and passed out. The next morning we finished getting undressed and went at it for hours. A room service breakfast never tasted so good. Being with her, watching her enjoy the things she'd only ever seen in movies made it all worth it. I hoped it would help motivate her to get out of Brixton, to show her there was a world of possibilities, and to want more for herself than to die by the inch as a miner's lonely wife.

Shooting with Jim using the Python was also a lot of fun. Okay, it wasn't like half-dressed, drunken sex with Renee, but it was good.

"Kicks like a motherfucker," he said, firing my Christmas gift and taking off a small tree branch at nearly fifty paces, "but it's a really accurate revolver if you know what you're doing. And, Kip, you know what you're doing. You're better at this than I ever thought you could be."

"Thanks, Jim. That's high praise coming from you." And it was.

We also talked some about what he was going to do with his life once he got his associate's degree in June.

"My mom works for Dixon Mining and I could get a job there anytime. But this life, this place isn't for me and I know that as much as the chapel is everything to me, it's a dead end, too. I'd die of boredom here, but don't worry about me, Kip. I've got a plan to get out of here that's working out pretty fair so far."

I waited for him to give me more details, but none was forthcoming. It seemed he'd said about all he wanted to say on the subject.

Along with shooting and running together, Jim came with me to do all the errands I knew Renee would have hated doing as I prepared to leave. You know, the stuff that meant goodbye was for real and probably forever. He came with me to my old local bank to close my account, to the nearby branch of a mega-bank to open a new one, and to rent the van I'd be driving north in the morning. He came with me to the post office when I filled out the change-of-address form to have my mail forwarded to my new place.

Meg's assistant had landed me a two-bedroom apartment on the top floor of an old Victorian house on a quiet street in the Ditmas Park section of Brooklyn. The rent, she said, was a steal at about the same rate I was paying for the house in Brixton. Only in New York City would it be considered a steal and I explained to Meg that her definition of quiet didn't remotely resemble the Brixton definition. There was no quiet in Brooklyn, ever.

Renee had been holding up pretty well until we got to the hangar at the abandoned base. There were no tears, not yet. I had no doubt they would come, but later, in the dark and quiet of my bedroom. That's when Renee always let down her guard. She was most comfortable letting me see her after I'd been inside her and with the dark obscuring my view. Now her mood seemed to fluctuate between melancholy and edginess.

"Why did you bring this?" she asked me about the Python, handing me the case.

"Jim wants me to show it to everyone. He's proud that he got it for me. I don't mind."

She didn't say the words, but her expression said them loudly enough: *I don't like it.*

There were bound to be many things about that night and the following weeks she wasn't going to like. The next few weeks were going to be full of painful transitions for everyone involved. I didn't think myself immune from missing her.

I put the gun case on the hood of the car and held Renee tightly in my arms.

"Come on," I said. "let's get this over with so we can be alone."

With the exception of the maintenance guy, they were all there when we walked in: the whole freak show roster including Stan Petrovic, and even he managed to be civil or what passed for his version of civility. Although it was clear he was already tanked up, he shook my hand and then ignored me. Jim and Renee notwithstanding, I wouldn't get teary-eyed for any of the chapel losers: not the fat boy, the skater kid, the girl with the bad teeth, the sheriff's deputy, the security guard, the grill man, et al. Only one thing tied us together and not very tightly, and not for very much longer. They meant no more to me than any other group of ghosts who'd drifted in and out of my life. No more than people who'd stood at the same subway platform with me.

Still, I didn't like that the maintenance guy wasn't here. It was one thing not to run into him again the few times I'd been back to campus, but I had fully expected him to be there. That said, I didn't mention it to anyone, especially not to Jim. He was such a stickler for the rules. How could I explain about the clandestine meeting that never happened? Besides, come the morning, I wouldn't need to waste an ounce more of energy on the rules or Brixton. The world of *Gun Church* might've gotten its start here, but now it existed on the page and in my head.

It was fucking bizarre. They'd strung a sign above the entrance to the chapel that read GOOD LUCK IN THE BIG APPLE. I didn't have the heart to tell them that New Yorkers never called New York the Big Apple. There were handshakes, a kiss or two, beers—lots of beers—and even a goodbye cake. The cake part of the festivities felt more surreal than shooting ever had. At least there was no piñata, nor was anyone suggesting we play Pin the Tail on the Donkey.

Once the cake was dispensed with, they began passing my Christmas present around. I was relieved to have their focus shift away from me and to the Python. They were loading it up and taking pot shots into the mattresses at the back wall. Fine by me. I half-hoped one of them would break the thing so I'd have an obvious excuse to leave it behind. As it was, I had arranged for Renee to keep it at the house in Brixton for me until I figured out what I was going to do with it. I knew that stalling for time wasn't much of a strategy. I figured if I procrastinated long enough, the situation might take care of itself.

Jim brought out a bottle of Laphroaig Single Malt—Kant Huxley's favorite scotch. He poured a round of thimble-sized shots for everyone. I thought there was some chapel rule against shooting and drinking alcohol stronger than beer, but who the fuck cared? The minute the bottle came out, Renee's demeanor changed again. No longer just tense or sad, she looked undone. She literally grabbed my forearm, urging me to leave.

"Please, Kip, let's go home. I don't know how much longer I can hold myself together in front of other people and I want time alone with you."

There was palpable desperation in her voice, and although I kind of dreaded the heartache coming once we got home, I agreed to leave. But as we made our move to exit, Jim stepped between us as if cutting in on a dance.

"Come on, Kip," he said, taking my arm as Renee had. "They want to see you fire the Python, then you can split."

I shrugged my shoulders at Renee and went with Jim.

Someone had set up a row of beer cans on a plank at the far end of the chapel. The deputy sheriff, who'd just finished loading the big Colt, handed it to me. "Go for it," he said.

"Go! Go! Go! Go!" the rest of them chanted. "Go! Go! Go!" It was the same thing the cop had shouted as my students escaped from the classroom after I grabbed Frank Vuchovich's gun.

I went, nicking the first can, then obliterating the rest, beer soaking the mattresses behind them. I opened the cylinder, dumping the spent shells to the ground. They clinked like off-key wind chimes against the concrete floor. There was a round of applause as I handed the Colt back to the deputy, but someone wasn't clapping.

"You're pretty fucking good with beer cans . . . for a cunt," Stan Petrovic snarled, the near-empty bottle of scotch in his hand. He had mean-drunk eyes and a red, feral face.

I didn't say anything and walked away. Once I was out of there, I thought, I would never have to deal with the asshole again. But it wasn't going to be that easy. He stepped directly in my path, putting himself halfway between Renee and me.

"What's wrong, cunt? Your bitch in heat? Gotta go home and fuck her in the ass before you leave her to the rest of us? I heard she likes it in the ass, the same way Jim's momma used to like it." He growled, hurling the scotch bottle at my head. I ducked just in time and it smashed against the chapel floor behind me.

I bit down hard on the inside of my cheeks and tried to think of anything else.

Stan wasn't close to finished. "Come on, faggot," he taunted. "Not so brave when you can't sucker punch me in the nuts, huh? You didn't think I was going to forget that, did you?"

"Shut up, Stan. Just shut the fuck up!" I heard someone screaming. It took a second before I noticed it was me.

"Shut me up, cunt!" He came up to me, put a gnarled hand on my chest and shoved me back. It wasn't hard enough to knock me down, but hard enough to let me know my leaving was going to have to go through him. "Shut me up."

I looked around and noticed no one was willing to get involved. Stan was trouble. I was going in the morning, but they would still be here and so would Stan. I knew better than most that he wasn't the kind of man you wanted angry at you.

"Shut me up," he repeated.

"You're not worth it, Stan."

Apparently, that was precisely the wrong thing to say. He shoved me again, only this time hard enough to send me sprawling backwards.

"Show me you got some balls, faggot. Shoot with me and this will all be over for good."

"You're fucking crazy," I said, scrambling to my feet. "You know that?"

"Crazy, huh? I'll show you crazy."

And almost before he got the last word out of his mouth, he turned and bulled his way through the crowd. There was a collective gasp, and by the time I had made my way through the wall of bodies, I saw what the gasp was all about. Stan had Renee, one thick forearm tight around her neck, his other hand twisting her arm behind her.

"Shoot with me and I'll let her go."

"You *are* crazy. Let her go, now!"

He didn't even answer, just smiled that ragged, saw-toothed smile, and twisted her arm so hard she screamed.

"Let her—"

She screamed again, tears pouring down her cheeks, and she went limp.

"Next time, her shoulder comes out of the socket, faggot. What's it gonna take? You wanna watch me fuck her? That it? Is that what it's going to take? 'Cause I'm all in for that: fucking her and killing you. Talk about hitting the daily double. She's so young, I bet her pussy's as tight as Jim's mom's asshole was." He moved his paw so that it reached Renee's right breast and squeezed it hard enough to make her wince. "Nice firm tits. I bet she's wet for me."

I looked at Jim, wondering why he hadn't reacted to any of this. He was frozen, an angry little boy, powerless and confused, a scowl on his face. He wasn't going to be of any help at all. I wasn't the only one looking at Jim. The rest of them were looking to him as well. Sheep, they took their cues from him. He was inert and so they were inert. There I was in a room full of people, all expert shots, and not one of them worth a good god damn. Not even the sheriff's deputy made a move. I was on my own.

"No, Stan, that won't do it," I said.

"Then let's try this." He let go of Renee's neck, reached a hand behind his back, and came up with a .40 Beretta. He made a show of thumbing off the safety. He released Renee's arm and she melted to her knees. He racked the Beretta, then got down beside her. He grabbed a fist of her hair and yanked it hard. When she reflexively opened her mouth to scream, he forced the Beretta's barrel between her lips and teeth. Her eyes were wide with terror and the crotch of her jeans turned dark with urine. "How about now, faggot?"

"That's it, motherfucker! I'm gonna fuckin' kill you. Let her go!"

"Not yet, cunt. Not until I see you step out there." He nodded to the place in the center of the chapel where we shot. "Get out there and stand ready. Then I'll let her go."

"Give me the fucking Python," I screamed at the deputy.

"Here," he said, handing me the Colt. "It's fully loaded."

"Good." I wasn't going to let Stan go with just one shot. No, once I knocked him over with the first shot, I was going to punish him. I was going to walk up close to him and empty the other five bullets into his vest. He wasn't going to have one or two broken ribs, but a chest full of them. Then, when the Python was empty, I'd kick his teeth down his throat. "Where's my vest? Get me a fucking vest."

"No vests!" Stan barked. "Let's see if you got any real balls in your shorts for doing anything but sticking your cock in this bitch." He yanked her hair again.

"But—"

"No buts. We both know the rules. One of us walks out of here. The other one gets buried out there in the woods somewheres. You say no and I'm gonna blow her tongue out the back of her neck. Then we'll shoot anyway. Now step out there and wait for me."

I didn't have much choice.

I went to tell Jim to take care of Renee as soon as Stan let her go, but he seemed to have vanished. He was probably so embarrassed by his cowardice that he couldn't face me. For him, I guessed, it was the Colonel all over again.

Then I stepped out towards the back of the chapel near where the beer cans had been lined up. I waited for Stan. It didn't take long for him to stand opposite me, but the deputy stood between us.

"Look," the deputy said, "make sure you want to go through with this before—"

"Get the fuck out of the way, asshole," Stan barked.

But the deputy didn't move, not immediately. "First, you both put your weapons down by your thighs. You're going to do this, you're going to do this fair. Now put your weapons at your thighs."

We did as we were told. I focused all my attention on the area of Stan's right shoulder. Sure, I wanted to kill the motherfucker and I wanted him to die slowly, but I didn't want to go to prison or get treated to a lethal injection courtesy of the state. And while everyone here liked talking about the rules of the chapel and how they all knew the risks they were taking, I didn't want to test the strength of their convictions.

"I'm going to step aside," said the deputy. "When I say go, the rest is up to you. Agreed?"

Stan nodded his head yes as I did the same. The deputy sheriff walked backwards towards the others. He took careful, measured steps, never turning his head.

"Go!"

It all happened in a single excruciatingly slow breath. I went deaf as we raised our arms. Then the silence was broken by Renee screaming. My muzzle coughed out smoke. I was not conscious of what Stan's Beretta did. My arm flew up so fiercely that I could feel the blowback in the hairs on my forearm. I suppose I might have squeezed my eyes shut, waiting for a bullet to cut through me. I breathed out. Something Stan Petrovic would never do again.

Even at thirty feet you could see he was dead. Everyone else was deadly still, the whispering of their rapid breaths like a hushed declaration of disbelief. But there is a vast ocean between stillness and death, and Stan—his shirt soaked with blood, his gun arm curled over the top of his head, his left leg twisted under him, his left arm and right leg splayed at ragdoll angles—was on death's distant shore. Only when I felt the ache in my hand from squeezing the Python's grip so tightly did I unfreeze and step forward.

Kneeling over him, I could see my shot had ripped through his chest where his heart once beat. I'd been focused on his right shoulder. I'd missed. Was it my rage or that I was scared? Was it that the ammo was different or that I had too much to drink or that Renee cried out just before I fired? I would never know. What hit me next was the awful cocktail of odors coming off his body: the metallic tang of spent gunpowder and blood, the sour must of sweat and scotch.

Then, as I breathed his death into my lungs, I saw it: that look of confusion and shock. That now too-familiar *this-wasn't-supposed-to-happen-to-me* expression that had been Frank Vuchovich's death mask. Though in life Stan Petrovic and Frank Vuchovich shared not a single similar feature, in death they were twins. I could make no more sense of it than either of them. They had to know there was a chance they were going to die, yet when death came they both seemed so utterly perplexed and disbelieving.

Someone, Renee, touched my shoulder and I crashed, inside and out. I swooned, nearly falling face-first onto Stan. I managed to veer to the side, my hands cushioning my fall. When I got back onto my knees, a wave of nausea slammed into me. I thought I might never stop throwing up. I was sick with terror, my panic spinning completely out of control. It was one thing to fantasize about killing a man. It was something else to do it. I was barely conscious of Renee holding on to me, her touch only faintly registering. I was soaked through, shaking with chills, still spiraling downward. I turned and looked up to see Jim standing over me, an open beer cooler in his hands. He'd dumped the ice and melt on me. He put the cooler down and lifted me up. He brushed back my wet hair and stared straight into my eyes.

"Forget this. We'll handle it. No one will ever find him or know what happened to him. You were home with Renee tonight. All night. She'll swear to it. Take these," he said, closing my hand around his truck keys. "I've already got the keys to your car. Go home, Kip. Leave for New York in the morning and never think about this again. We know the rules here and we'll stick to them. And I'll never forget what you did for me. Go."

"Okay," I said robotically, reaching out for Renee.

Jim stepped between us again. "She stays and helps. It's the rules."

"But—"

"No, Kip, go ahead home," she said. "It's easier this way."

"Are you okay? I mean, he—"

"I'll be fine. Please, just go."

I didn't have anything left in me to argue with. I was spent. I walked through the slit between the mattresses. GOOD LUCK IN THE BIG APPLE was the last thing I saw as I left. I didn't look back.

Thirty-Six

Auto-Mythology

One morning I woke up and Stan Petrovic wasn't the first thing on my mind. The man I thought of as McGuinn had written about it in the notebook: the process of forgetting the worst of things. He'd written that it got easier and easier each time he killed. I had no desire to find out if that was so. I was sure I'd done all the killing I was ever going to do. What did I know?

The month that passed since I'd arrived in Brooklyn had been the weirdest month of my life and, given my life, that was saying something. From one moment to the next, my guts churned with terror and relicf, paranoia and calm, rage and regret. I couldn't see an NYPD cruiser on the street without sweating through my shirt. Each time the phone rang or my landlord knocked at my door, I jumped back down the rabbit hole. I relived my last night in Brixton over and over and over again, killing Stan Petrovic a hundred times, a thousand times. I'd second-guessed myself at every turn and there were days my complete inner monologue consisted of two words: *What if.* About the only emotion I hadn't suffered was guilt.

Harder to get out of my head than the image of Stan's bullet-fucked body was the image of Renee. I still seethed, recollecting the terror in her eyes, her helplessness, and the dark humiliation of her urine-soaked jeans. No, I was without guilt over killing Stan. If ever a man was born deserving of a violent death, it was him. It was kind of hard to argue that the universe wasn't a better place without the belligerent prick. His death fueled my work. Whenever I found myself panicking, I would go back to reread or tweak some of *Gun Church*. Whenever I found myself missing Renee, there was one scene I would reread over and over again:

Everything was different tonight. Not because the world had changed, but because it hadn't. She had. Tonight would mark the sixth time she would lure someone to their death.

Cosmo's was different in name only from the other two bars in which Zoe had trolled for her prey: dark, smoke-filled, and crowded, with plank flooring rank with spilled beer, and the stink of toilet backwash. Good, she thought. Her aim was to attract attention without being at its center. She could not afford the spotlight and had so far been able to avoid it. The descriptions in the papers were always pretty vague. It was amazing what different color wigs and makeup could do.

Someone once wrote that God was his most cruel in his use of imperfection, in that he used it to such varied ends. So it was for Zoe—a dollar-store demigoddess with electric blue eyes, but unruly blond hair; pleasing curves, but a slightly thick waist; long legs, but one just slightly longer than the other. Yet her imperfections made her alluring in a way that unadorned beauty could not match. Unwanted attention and unwanted touches had been a part of her life for as long as she could remember. She didn't like thinking about that, about her father putting himself inside her before she'd even gotten to middle school. Now the touching, all the touching, was on her terms

The deafening music in Cosmo's that night was a bizarre intergenerational mishmash that blended into an emulsified roar. For Zoe, the louder, the better. Her prey would have to get in close to talk to her, and when the preliminary chitchat was over they would have to move on to conduct business elsewhere. She would press her way through the crowd, taking notice of who noticed her. Then she would work her way to the bar and order a drink. The first time, that was all it took. She was so nervous that she picked up the first man—a college kid, really—who approached her. He proved to be too easy a target. He came almost before she had him fully inside her, and then it took barely fifteen minutes for him to run himself straight into a killing zone. That's why she had chosen more wisely the next time. He proved to be a real challenge. Took him a long time to come and nearly two hours to kill.

Zoe dreamed of the victim's kiss. It had been different this week because she knew they were thinking of executing McGuinn tonight as well, that the prey was only meant as a distraction. She wasn't going to let anything happen to McGuinn. She didn't love him. She didn't have love in her. Her father had seen to that, but McGuinn was the only man whose touch didn't make her retreat into that dark place. So she moved through the bar, her face neutral as a spider's. Circling back through the crowd, she found her prey. They wanted a distraction and she meant to give it to them, only not the distraction they'd had in mind.

"Hi," Zoe said, moving in close to a petite brunette seated near the beer pulls. "I don't even know why I bothered coming here."

When the brunette looked up and took a close look, Zoe knew she was already entwined in her web.

The pages of *Gun Church* seemed to be my only retreat for those first few weeks and, like everything else in the surreal world I'd inhabited since September, Stan's death helped push me to take risks with my work, to edge the plot further out on the limb. That fusion of me and McGuinn that began in the berry patch was nearly complete. The lines between my life and my work were getting awfully blurry. What had started out as a vehicle to tell McGuinn's story was veering perilously close to autobiography and myth-making, to auto-mythology.

For the first week, I shut myself in my new apartment, unpacking only my laptop and toiletries. I even slept on the floor. Meg tried to get me to come into Manhattan for dinner, but I begged off, explaining to her that I needed time to adjust. Eventually, she stopped asking. I called both Renee and Jim so many times I lost count. I wanted reassurance that everything was all right, that Stan was buried and forgotten, that there was nothing that could lead from him to me. They never answered. They never called back. I found a kind of reassurance in their silence. Whether or not I wanted to put Brixton behind me was beside the point. It seemed Jim and Renee were determined to do it for me, and I stopped calling altogether.

Mid-February in Brooklyn isn't exactly Paris in the springtime, but that first morning I woke up without Stan Petrovic's corpse on my back felt like the best spring day ever, in spite of the snow. *That* was the morning I returned Meg's calls.

"So, you *are* alive, Weiler? I was beginning to get concerned."

"Concerned? No need to speak in code to me anymore, Donovan. I'm not using. The only thing I've put in my nose in seven years was a Kleenex and I haven't had a drink in a month. I've just shut myself in to do my work. You've gotten the pages I sent you, right?"

"I guess that's what alarms me," she said. "Very scary stuff."

"You have no idea, Meg. No idea."

"Want to talk about it?"

"No, and don't ever bring it up!" I snapped.

"No need to bite my head off."

"Sorry. It's just safer if you think of it as purely fictional, Meg."

"Safer? Safer for whom?"

"Just safer. Leave it alone," I said more to myself than to her.

"So I see the book is moving along."

"It's getting there."

"But where is 'there' exactly? You were pretty vague about the ending in your plot synopsis and I'm not sure where you're taking it."

"You're worried?"

"It's my job to worry."

"Well, stop it. You're my agent, not my editor."

"I'm your friend."

"The ending will be as good as the rest of the book," I said.

"I think that's what I'm afraid of."

"I didn't call to talk about the book."

"What then?"

"What's Amy's cell number?"

The question has been raised a thousand times: Would Romeo and Juliet's love have endured had they survived? In Kip Weiler's uproariously profane and deliciously cruel second novel, *Romeo vs. Juliet*, he not only restates the question, but uses the answer to absolutely flay the American body politic. Weiler takes to task all the parties insinuating themselves in the divorce proceedings. No group or individual is immune from his scathing wit. With demonic delight, he skewers the Knights of Columbus, ACT UP, Sinatra, Streisand, Jerry Falwell, and even poor Larry King.

—JACKSON DRUM, *THE MERTON REVIEW*

Thirty-Seven

Lot's Wife

She didn't bother hiding the anger. I hadn't expected her to and she was never very good at faking it. There was never any doubt about when Amy was pissed off. I'd given her ample opportunity to display her many and varied expressions of anger—from slow boil to rage—and by the end of our marriage, angry was her baseline state of being. But there was something else in her tone, a grudging joy at the sound of my voice that made me push her to see me again. I didn't have to say *Please* more than ten or fifteen times and I didn't try to explain why I'd left her standing in the lobby of the Algonquin.

We met on neutral ground, a coffee bar in the West Village. Dressed in paint-speckled jeans, torn running shoes, a back-to-front black Kangol cap, and the weathered Schott motorcycle jacket I'd given to her as a birthday gift twenty years ago, Amy looked more like her old self, more like the woman I fell in love with than the woman I'd fled from eight weeks ago. Just seeing her, her eyes afire, brought it all back—how stupid we'd been for each other, how much we still were. It was as obvious on her face as it must have been on mine.

"God," she said, taking her green tea from the barista. "I will never understand how you do this to me. Even when I hated you, Kip Weiler, I loved you. That night after the country club, when I told you I couldn't take it anymore, I would have stayed with you if you had persisted a little longer."

"I know, but you were right to push me away. I'd been scuttling my ship for a long time and you were getting pulled down in the suck. That last year together was terrible. I was empty and you didn't even want me anymore. That's how I knew we were over."

"Is that introspection I hear from the lips of the Kipster?"

"No . . . I mean, yes . . . I mean, it's introspection but not from the lips of the Kipster. He doesn't live here anymore."

"What's changed?"

"Everything."

"You used to be succinct."

"Believe me, that is succinct," I said, sipping my coffee. "Everything *has* changed. Let's walk."

"Walk? You used to take a cab to go to the bathroom. Do you have a fever? What have you done with my ex-husband and who are you?"

"Cut it out, Amy."

"Fine."

"I even run these days. Well, not for the last month, but I'm getting back to it this week."

"Not if it keeps snowing like this you're not."

We'd both heard the forecast for a lot of snow, but I guess we both sensed that we needed to get this first get-together over with as soon as we could. It was easy to ignore the snow before it started falling. Now, it was fairly impossible to ignore.

We turned south toward Tribeca, snow falling pretty heavily as we walked. There was already more snow on the sidewalk than the combined snowfall in Brixton over the last year. New

York City is beautiful in the snow, but it's a very transient beauty. Nothing stays pure very long in the city once it touches down.

"That night at the Algonquin, when you just showed up like that, what was that about?" I asked.

"I miss you. I've missed you."

"Ain't memory grand, how time sands off the bitter edges? But you couldn't miss the Kipster, not really. In the beginning of us, I acted like a sex- and drug-addicted fool because that's who I was. At the end, I was doing it to hurt you, to make you push me away."

"I know."

"So, I don't get it. I get why you dumped my ass. Best thing, really, but why marry Peter fucking Moreland?"

"I married Peter for several reasons, all good ones, I thought at the time, but none of them having to do with love. He was stable. He understood my work and—"

"—he wasn't me."

"Exactly," she confessed. "He wasn't you. I married him to punish you."

"Yeah, and how did that work out?"

"Somebody got punished."

"Not somebody, everybody."

She stopped in her tracks, playfully pulling my coat sleeve so that I'd turn to face her. "Okay, this is the last time I'm going to ask: What have you done with my ex-husband?"

"I told you, everything's changed. Weird thing is, most of it happened in the last few months. I got straight a long time ago, after my second trip to rehab. But I hadn't really started exorcising the Kipster until about a year ago. I finally got sick of all my old bullshit. In Brixton, I'd had a long series of one-night stands and loveless affairs just like at all the other schools. I had this one terrible affair with a colleague named Janice Nadir. One afternoon, we were lying around in bed in one of those motel rooms with mirrors on the ceiling and I was staring up at myself. I was thinking about you, wondering what you would think of me there doing what the Kipster always did."

"And what did I think?"

"You were sorely disappointed, but not surprised. I imagined you shaking your head and saying, 'Same old Kipster.' I got this notion in my head that I wanted to earn back your respect whether or not you ever knew about it. I didn't think I would ever write again, but I thought I could at least start acting like a grownup. Your unknowing respect became the central theme of my boring life in Nowheresville."

Amy stepped close to me, slowly worked her arms around me, and rested her head on the wet, snow-covered shoulder of my jacket. She let her tea fall to the ground. I dropped my coffee too. We didn't kiss. I didn't take off her cap and stroke her hair. She didn't brush her hand against my cheek. We didn't even move much. We just stood there like that, her head on my shoulder, ten years of hurt and longing condensed into a silent, snow-covered moment on the street.

Then a strange voice broke the trance. "You guys wanna go get a room or something?"

The first thing I saw when I turned around was his badge. The first thing he saw was the panic in my eyes.

"Yo, buddy, relax," he said. "I was only busting your chops."

"Sorry, officer. You startled me."

"No problem, but I think you and your girlfriend better get going anyways unless you wanna become Mr. and Mrs. Snowman. It's coming down pretty good. S'posed to get at least two feet."

"Thanks."

"And you might wanna pick up these cups. Love ain't an excuse for littering. You know what I mean?" He winked as he walked past us. "Have a nice day."

We watched his dark blue figure disappear into the snow. Finally breaking our embrace, Amy scooped up the cups and threw them in the corner trash basket. I used those few seconds to get my heart out of my throat. My breathing was almost normal when Amy got back to me, but she wasn't fooled.

"What was that about, Kip? You nearly jumped out of your skin when you saw the cop. I could feel your heart pounding through your coat. You're not carrying, are you?"

Carrying? I panicked again, then realized she was talking about drugs, not guns.

"I told you, I've been clean for a long time."

"Then what? You can't tell me that reaction was nothing. You were scared to death."

See, about a month ago, I killed a man. Shot the motherfucker right through his heart in front of witnesses.

No, somehow I didn't think this was the appropriate time or the place for that confession, but I had to tell her something.

"This sheriff's deputy in Brixton used to harass the shit out of me because I slept with a woman he was hot for. It was years ago and it didn't last, but he could never let it go. So when he found out I was moving back here, he promised to make sure the bullshit would follow me north."

"Same old Kip. At least you're consistent."

That cut me, deep. I don't know what I expected her to say. I told her a lie I knew she would believe and she did, without question. I realized then it was going to take more than her missing me or one embrace to make her see the Kipster was really dead. She did, however, seem to read the hurt in my eyes. I think she apologized. Her mouth was moving and she hung her head slightly, but I was too distracted to hear her. My focus had already shifted elsewhere.

Just like that night at the Algonquin, I heard a noise I thought I recognized. *Jim's truck.* I was sure I heard Jim's truck. I'd been in that old pickup nearly every day for four months and knew its idiosyncrasies like I knew my own. Its exhaust system had come loose. Jim had jerry-rigged a clamp by twisting together a few wire hangers, looping the hangers around the pipe leading to the muffler, and then hooking the makeshift clamp over the rear axle. When the truck accelerated quickly, the pipe kind of rattled and scraped against the hangers. I snapped my head around, but the snow was now coming down in blinding, wind-whipped sheets. I caught a glimpse of a taillight disappearing around a corner, the snow turning its glow from red to pink.

Was it Jim's taillight? Of course not. Just like with the Mabry kid's death, it was the Kipster's narcissism rearing its ugly head once more for old times' sake. Amy and I were right by the Holland Tunnel and even in a snowstorm, thousands of cars poured out of its exits, spilling onto the cobblestoned Tribeca streets. I was already off balance from being with Amy, from holding her again, and I was still reeling from the scare I got from the cop. I didn't know that I would ever be able to see a cop again without going into full fight or flight, or thinking of Stan Petrovic's body moldering in a grave somewhere in the backwoods of Brixton.

"Kip, are you all right?" Amy asked, pulling me along.

"I should have worn a hat."

"Come on, my studio's only three blocks away."

But even as we walked towards Amy's warm, dry studio and all the possibilities it had to offer, I could not help but play Lot's wife and look behind me.

Thirty-Eight

Molecular

I hadn't turned to salt, but in some sense I was still looking behind me.

It was three in the morning and I'd yet to shake the afternoon's chill. It was a chill not from the cold or the wet of the snow. That chill was gone fifteen minutes after we got to Amy's studio. No, the chill I carried with me was in my marrow, a feeling that the specter of Stan Petrovic would not be so easily buried as his body. If the day had taught me anything it was to not trust what you think you know. It went beyond imagining the scrape and rattle of Jim's pickup. It extended all the way from Brixton into Amy's bed.

When we first met, Amy was just beginning to taste the fruits of success. And that early success was more about critical kudos and good press than paychecks. In those days, she was sharing cramped studio space with a bunch of other painters in the basement of an old factory building. The light sucked and she didn't really care for some of the people with whom she shared the space. Worse, she despised their work. I bought her the loft studio as an engagement present. It was a stretch then, before I got my big contract, but I was in love. It might have been the first and last selfless thing I'd ever done. Until I met Amy, the concept of love-inspired art of any kind made me gag. Once we were together, I understood it was possible to love someone so much that promises of the moon and the stars weren't just a load of crap. But I never was a guy to hang the moon or promise the stars; and in Amy's universe, a spacious loft with natural light was more valuable than all the lofty promises and metaphysical conceits of a thousand ardent poets. Did that love stop me from fucking around? Not for very long, no. To be human was to be a contradiction, and in that way I was more human than most.

Of course, as I sank further and further into living out the myth of the Kipster, the loft became less Amy's workplace than retreat. Finally, it was where Amy moved when she left me. I think maybe that accounted for some of the discomfort I felt here. Coming here had started well enough. First off, it was dry, warm, and—even ten years removed—familiar. We talked a lot, mostly about how her marriage to Moreland had fallen apart.

"With you, Kip, there was always lust to fall back on. With Peter . . ." The shrug of her shoulders as her voice faded was quite eloquent. "We started drifting apart after only a couple of months and we've been living fairly separate lives for a long time now. I guess we should have gotten divorced years ago, but neither one of us has felt the urge or had the energy to pursue one." Again, she didn't say the words, but the forward lean of her body and the smile in her eyes spoke for her. *Until now*, they said.

We discussed her work and she showed me her latest paintings. Her recent work had taken a turn away from twentieth-century abstraction toward a kind of hyper-realism, which, as Amy explained, was simply another form of abstraction. Looking at those paintings, I think, was when the real discomfort began to set in. She had done a series of *in situ* portraits of us as a couple at different stages of our marriage. She had based the paintings on photographs taken of us by her friends at various parties. Some of the paintings were of posed group shots. Some were candid shots.

In the paintings from early in our marriage, Amy and I were painted in full color, so vivid they almost hurt my eyes. Our features, as were everyone else's, were so subversively subtle and cruelly perfect that to stare at them too long was to look into the invisible light of an eclipse. In these first portraits, only Amy and I were done in color. Everyone else was done in shades of black, white, and gray. But as the series advanced with our years of marriage, the pattern gradually reversed until only Amy and I were black, white, and gray. In the last in the series, I was nothing more than an outline. To look at them was far more painful than my broken ribs or concussion.

"I can't bring myself to show these yet."

"Why not?"

"The series is incomplete," she said, as if that explained it all. Maybe it did.

It was after Amy showed them to me that I realized she wasn't all forgiveness and light, that memory hadn't sanded off all the sharp and bitter edges of our time together. I had done a lot of damage to her. There was a warehouse of residual anger in Amy that couldn't be wished away into the cornfield. I guess I always understood that much even when I was tilting at the windmills of regaining her respect. What I wondered was, did *she* understand it?

That question or its answer didn't stop either one of us from fucking our brains out. We both knew where we were headed the second we walked back into her studio. That my subway line back to Brooklyn wasn't operating because of the snowstorm made it that much easier for us to pretend our first hungry kiss wasn't inevitable. Both of us orgasmed almost immediately. That was easy. Lust and hunger always are; although, the remainder of the night did not pass blissfully. I know it's crazy for someone who once fucked everything that wasn't nailed down to say, but I'd always believed Amy and I, together or apart, were mated for life. It was molecular. From the moment I tasted her again, I felt I was home. Yet, when I moved inside her the second time, I felt a wall between us, not a welcome mat. Even as we came again, Amy seemed as far away from me as she'd been when I was in Brixton, maybe farther. And as the night wore on, with each new clench the distance grew.

That's why I was standing here in the middle of the night, looking out at the still-falling snow through the arched windows of the loft, the streetlights turning the flakes an eerie pale red. With the subways shut down, street traffic at a standstill, and only the occasional distant rumble of a snow plow, it was as near to silent as Manhattan ever gets. My head was a jumble of love and regret. Remembering how far away Amy felt from me even when I was deep inside her made me think about what I had sacrificed in Renee. Though I knew I would never feel that sense of being mated to her, Renee had opened herself up to me. In bed, neither one of us carried old baggage along nor put up walls. I hadn't inflicted enough hurt on her to build barriers between us. She couldn't get enough of me and I couldn't get enough of her. I thought that if I had only managed the same amount of monogamy for Amy in the beginning as I had for Renee, there wouldn't be a series of sad portraits in the room keeping me company.

Then I heard something from down in the street and looked to my right. There, coming right up West Broadway, were a man and woman cross-country skiing. You had to love New York. I followed their progress as they glided past the loft building. But as they passed and I turned my head left to follow their progress uptown, I caught sight of a lone, dark figure across the street, half in shadow and partially blocked by the corner building. I cupped my hands around my eyes and pressed them to the glass for a better look. The ambient light, the windblown snow, and the tricks the shaking streetlights played with the shadows made it difficult to focus. By the time my eyes finally locked on to the figure across the street, it was turning away and I caught only a fleeting glimpse of a partial profile and a tuft of blond hair. My heart stopped for a beat. *Renee.*

Thirty-Nine

Tom Wolfe

A snail's pace would have been an improvement. With a pair of snowshoes, I think I could have made it back to the Avenue H station a lot quicker than the Q train. We were doing okay in the tunnels, but once we hit the above-ground portion of the trip, forget it. The big drifts and deep snow had been cleared away, but the wind was still howling, creating new drifts, blowing downed tree branches across the already slick tracks. All I wanted to do was to get back to my apartment and retreat into the pages of *Gun Church*. I understood the motives of my characters far better than the reasons for the knot in my gut.

In some sense, of course, I was quite relieved that the subways were running and to have escaped the increasingly claustrophobic atmosphere in Amy's loft. Apparently, I wasn't the only one who'd noticed that the fantasy of Kip and Amy, part two, had sprung a leak. Even when I quietly crawled back into bed at around four thirty, I knew Amy was in that same bad place I was in. She was as awake as I was, but feigning sleep. That was okay by me. It saved me from having to be the one to pretend. I passed out eventually and woke up as Amy was closing the door behind her. She hadn't bothered to leave a note. I was glad of that. What could it have said? I showered and got out of there in less than fifteen minutes. As I walked out the front of Amy's building, I looked across the street to where I thought I'd seen Renee. She wasn't there. She had never been there. I wasn't hallucinating, just projecting: seeing who I wanted to see, hearing what I wanted to hear.

I was losing it. I knew what that felt like. You do as many drugs and consume as much alcohol as I had on a regular basis, you're going to have episodes when you lose it. Sometimes it blindsides you and you wake up in the psych ward crawling out of your own skin, but then it's over, like a twenty-four-hour virus, and you move on. It's far worse when you can feel it coming on, when you're an impotent witness to your own deconstruction. When you feel the stitches holding the illusion of yourself together begin to stretch and pop, and you can't sew fast enough to keep the stuffing in. In the end, you just stop trying and let the seams rip. That's what this was like.

For fuck's sake, I knew the transition from Brixton back to New York was going to be a difficult proposition under the best of circumstances and these were far from the best of circumstances. I don't recommend killing a man, even a world-class asshole like Stan Petrovic, the evening before you begin life anew. But that wasn't all of it, not nearly. Beyond conjuring up the sound of Jim's truck and hallucinating Renee, there was Amy, and there was me.

Then, as if to put an exclamation point on my tenuous grip on things, a plug-ugly, thick-necked guy got on the train at DeKalb Avenue: Stan Petrovic. Maybe it was the way he hobbled to his seat on bad knees or maybe he really looked like Stan. He sat directly across from me on the near-empty subway car. On closer inspection, as ugly as he was, he didn't look like Stan all that much. Though his attitude wasn't far different.

"What the fuck you staring at?" he said to me, menace in his voice.

"Sorry. I was just lost in thought there for a minute." I walked to the opposite end of the car to wait for my stop.

•

The entrance to my apartment was around the rear of the house and my landlord was out clearing a path with his snow blower, the whine of its gas motor an unpleasant reminder of the generator we used at the chapel. The blower was shooting out a cloud of already graying snow onto Avenue H. When he saw me coming, he powered down the blower and walked towards me.

"Good morning to you, Mr. Weiler. You don't look so good. Long night?"

"Too long, yeah. Got trapped in the City. Train ride home took forever."

"I got a package for you inside."

"Package?"

"Yeah, my daughter found it on the front porch yesterday afternoon. She brought it up, but you weren't in. Come, I have it in my apartment."

I followed him through the door and up the backstairs. He lived on the second floor, his divorced daughter and her five-year-old daughter on the first. As we went, Isaac made small talk about the weather and his wife's bad back. Apparently, any kind of precipitation made her pain that much worse.

"Wait here," he said, disappearing into his apartment.

I stood on the landing, the floorboards creaking under my feet. The old place had charm, but it needed a lot of work. The appliances and fixtures in my flat were museum pieces and the paint on the walls so thick, it was thicker than the walls themselves. My house in Brixton was much the same. I wondered how Renee was doing there, alone, and if she was old enough to appreciate charm. Renee, it seemed, was much on my mind lately.

"Here we go," Isaac said, handing me a yellow nine-by-twelve envelope. It was less than an inch thick and not very heavy. "I got to get back down there and finish clearing the path. I don't want no one slipping and breaking their *tuchus* on my sidewalk. Lawsuits, I don't need."

As I trudged upstairs, I noticed that although it was a mailing envelope, it hadn't, in fact, been mailed. My name was scrawled across the front of the envelope in black marker. I didn't recognize the handwriting. *Handwriting!* Who handwrote anything anymore? It was no doubt several copies of some document—a foreign rights contract, I hoped—from Meg or Dudek that required my signature. I squeezed together the metal prongs of the clasp that held the flap closed, pulled the flap back, and slid the contents out.

My heart missed a beat for the second time that morning. Bound with a flimsy rubber band, it wasn't a contract at all, but a photocopied copy of a chapter from a typewritten manuscript. Not only did I recognize the pages as having been typewritten, I knew the exact machine—a portable Smith Corona—on which they had been typed. I immediately recognized the editorial notes as Moira Blanco's. Although the writer's name appeared nowhere on the pages, I was intimately familiar with his work. His name was Kenneth James "Kip" Weiler and the chapter was from the original manuscript of *Flashing Pandora*. There was just one problem, a daunting one at that: the copy of the chapter I was holding couldn't possibly exist.

I needed to sit down.

All previous indications I was losing it—the sound of Jim's truck, the faint glow of a taillight, my building a vision of Renee out of a fleeting glimpse of a profile from three stories up through a driving snowstorm, seeing Stan Petrovic's look-alike on the subway—had been ethereal at best, products of my wishes and worries. These pages were something else again. They were tangible proof I was skating along the razor's edge, about to fall off. And this wasn't just any chapter from any book. This was the chapter from *Flashing Pandora* that Moira had had me completely rewrite, the chapter in which Harper Marx had pulled a Colt Python on Kant Huxley and Pandora outside CBGB. I was freaked and ready to throw my recent Boy Scout behavior right the fuck out the window. Brooklyn didn't lack for bars. I called Meg Donovan instead.

"Kip Weiler, how are you?"

"A long way away from good, Meg."

"What's wrong with your voice? You're not high, are you?"

"Not yet."

"Not yet! What do you mean, not yet? You promised me you—"

"Did you have a package messengered over to me?"

"Package? What package? No, I didn't have—"

"How about your assistant? Did she—"

"No, Weiler, there was no package, at least not from us. What are you talking about?"

"Maybe from Dudek?"

"I can check, but he wouldn't have anything to send you at this stage of things. You know the drill, you won't get anything from him until you hand in the manuscript and they generate galley proofs. In any case, no one's messengering anything to anyone in this weather. What's this about?"

"I think I'm going nuts, Meg."

"Wouldn't be the first time."

"This isn't funny. I'm imagining things."

"What kind of things?"

"It's not important. This package is what's important."

"We're back to that again. You want to play Twenty Questions or tell me what's in the damned thing?"

"Something that can't be in it."

"Look, Kip, I'm a fucking agent, not a mind reader."

"Did you keep a copy of my manuscript for *Flashing Pandora?*"

"Of course not. You remember how crazy Moira was about loose copies of manuscripts. These days, it's all done electronically. In those days, Jesus, Moira was always so paranoid about anyone seeing a book before it was ready. But you know all of this, Kip. What's this got to do with anything?"

"Inside this package there's a copy of a chapter from *Flashing Pandora* that Moira cut out of the book."

"The chapter with the gun, when Harper Marx kills Pandora?"

"How could you possibly know that?"

"Because it pissed you off to no end. You said you knew Moira was right, but you were a kid genius then and didn't like being overruled, not even by Moira. It took me two weeks to talk you down from the ledge and to get you to rewrite it."

"That's right. I forgot that part. Some kid genius, huh?"

"So what's the big deal?" she asked.

"Because there's only one copy of it and it was mine."

"I still don't see why the fuss. Someone must've gotten a hold of your papers and made a copy of that chapter."

"They couldn't have."

"Why not?"

"Because when Ferris, Ledoux remaindered *Flashing Pandora,* I did a Tom Wolfe. I got totally fucked up and made a bonfire of my vanities. I burned the original manuscripts for all my old books and cooked hot dogs over the fire. I particularly enjoyed feeding this chapter to the fire one page at a time."

For once, Meg didn't have a snarky, sharp-tongued answer. "I don't know, Kip," was the best she could do. "Did anyone see who delivered it?"

"I don't think so."

"Well, maybe you better make sure before you get fitted for a straitjacket and reserve a padded room at Kings County."

"Okay, Meg."

"This probably isn't a good time to ask, but how did things go with—"

"Not now, Donovan. I can't talk about Amy now."

I hung up before she could ignore me. I put the pages back into the envelope and walked down the backstairs to the first floor. Isaac's daughter, Rachel, was in her mid-thirties and like her dad, she had a friendly demeanor. She was cute in a chubby, earth mama kind of way, but raising her kid on her own was taking its toll on her and she was fraying around the edges.

"Mr. Weiler," Rachel said, pulling back the door, her daughter clutched tightly to her leg. Her daughter stared up at me with skepticism and disdain. Sharp kid. Rachel immediately started finger combing her dyed blond hair. "My goodness, I'm a mess. Sara, say hello to Mr. Weiler." Sara shook her head no. "Sorry, she gets shy with people."

"That's okay."

"What can I do for—" she cut herself off, noticing the yellow envelope in my hand. "I found it on the porch yesterday, but you were out."

"Your dad told me. I wanted to thank you."

"Not a problem. All I did was take it in off the porch."

"I wanted to ask you, did you happen to see who delivered it?"

"I'm sorry, no. I was in the kitchen and heard something on the front steps, but by the time I got outside . . ."

Sara started tugging furiously at her mother's faded Brooklyn College sweatshirt.

"What is it, honey?"

Sara waved to her mother that she had a secret to tell and Rachel leaned over. When she did, Sara cupped her hands around her mouth and whispered into her mother's ear.

"Thank you, honey. Is it okay if I tell Mr. Weiler? It might be important to him."

Sara thought about it for a second and then nodded a reluctant yes.

"Sara says the girl who put the package on the porch had hair like Mommy's. So I guess that means she was blond."

"A girl. Was she a little girl like you?" I asked in a quiet but serious voice. I was often terrible with adults, but I was good with kids. Amy used to say that was because I'd never actually grown up. I repeated the question. "Was she a little girl like you?"

Sara clamped her mouth shut and shook her head no. The girl who had delivered the package was not a kid. This was progress of a sort.

"Was she a grownup lady like your mom?"

Same response.

"Was she pretty like your mom?"

Rachel blushed and even Sara's disdain abated a bit, but she didn't answer. Instead, she ran into the apartment and came back holding a magazine. She held it out to me. It was a woman's magazine like *Elle* or *Vogue*, and the cover girl was a neutral-faced blond, her skin masked in elaborate makeup. She had soft blue eyes and the cheekbones of a goddess. I got lightheaded, but tried to hold it together.

I asked, "The girl who put the package on the porch looked like this?"

Sara nodded yes, finally smiling with pride.

"Sara, if I showed you a picture of someone I think might be the girl, would you recognize her?"

"Uh huh." She spoke directly to me for the first time.

It took me about fifteen minutes to dig through the boxes and find what I was looking for. It was a copy of the *Brixton Banner* from the day after Frank Vuchovich had held my class hostage. A reporter had taken a shot of my students as they emerged from Halifax Hall. It wasn't the greatest photo, but you could make out their faces well enough. By the time I got back downstairs, Rachel had managed to brush her hair and put on some makeup.

"Listen, Sara, I really appreciate this. You're a smart girl. I'm going to show you a picture from a newspaper. If you see the girl in the picture, point to her. But if you don't see her, that's okay too. I mean it. You've done a great job whether you see her or not."

I folded the front page in half to hide the headline and held it out to Sara. Without any hesitation, she pointed at the picture.

"That girl," she said, tapping her finger on the paper.

Indeed, it was the girl, the St. Pauli Girl.

"Thank you, Sara. Thanks, Rachel. I really appreciate the help."

"Is anything wrong?" Rachel asked.

"Not at all," I lied. "Just an old friend playing a practical joke on me."

"Okay, then, is there anything else we can do for you?" There was both hope and disappointment in Rachel's question.

"Not right now, no. Thanks again."

My walk back upstairs was a long and shaky one. So I hadn't been imagining things. Well, at least not everything, though I wasn't sure that was necessarily a good thing. Renee was here. Maybe Jim, too, and I was being followed. Their presence suggested all kinds of questions that were making my head pound, but the questions worried me a lot less than their potential answers.

Forty

Pascal

A week had come and gone since the chapter arrived and only I seemed to have taken notice. The world kept spinning and no one, as far as I could discern, was losing sleep over the yellow envelope on my kitchen table. After three days of frying my brain with wild scenarios and conspiracy theories, I too moved on. What choice did I have, really? I'd finally unpacked all my boxes and set up shop like a man who meant to stay put for a little while. I had cable TV and Internet installed. The snowstorm that had paralyzed the area for days was no longer a subject on everyone's lips. All that remained of the two feet of snow were soot-blackened lumps where great mounds of it had been piled up and compacted by the plows. The rest of the snow had melted away, Jim and Renee receding along with it.

It's not like I hadn't searched for them at every turn and around every corner. God, my neck was sore from snapping my head about to look behind me. Sometimes, usually after a few hours of writing, I'd purposely go for long, leisurely runs to make myself an easy target for prying eyes, but it was a wasted effort. I didn't hear the scrape and rattle of Jim's truck or catch sight of a mysterious blond lurking in the shadows. No one on the street or in Prospect Park particularly reminded me of anyone else.

I'd nearly convinced myself that Sara had gotten it wrong and that she'd picked Renee in the newspaper photo because she looked like the model on the magazine cover. I knew enough about little kids to realize that they have trouble separating fact from fantasy—me too, apparently—that kids can be suggestible, and that they sometimes do what they think grown-ups want them to do. Still, there was no explaining away the chapter. And though I'd done my level best to ignore the damned envelope, it, unlike Renee and Jim, hadn't melted away with the snow.

Meg called several times to check in with me to see if I was still at loose ends or if I'd broken my promises to her. One of the ways I knew I'd killed off the Kipster was that it hurt me now to hear the expectation of disappointment in Meg's voice. It had once been a point of pride with me, my ability to disappoint those closest to me beyond their wildest dreams. I'd disappointed so many people in my lifetime, but only a few of them mattered. I wondered if there were some debts so large they could never be paid off, if I would ever again be able to prove myself worthy of trust. It was easy to understand why some people in my position would just give up and slide back into their weaknesses.

One weakness of mine that had been rearing its head lately was my addictive nature. I think my running again, combined with my writing and re-establishing a sense of routine, is what caused it. I missed shooting. I did. I knew it was fucked up, that I'd shot a man dead only five weeks before, but since when did knowing count for anything? When I was putting enough white powder up my nose to keep a small town sleepless for a week, I knew it was bad for me, that I was probably killing myself. Junkies are God's greatest rationalizers, but they know the truth of what it is they are doing to themselves. They see their sunken cheeks, sallow complexions, bloodshot eyes, the blood dripping from their noses. They know. *I* knew. It just didn't matter. It didn't matter then. It didn't matter now. I missed shooting. And fuck me if I didn't miss Renee too.

Of course, it was at that precise moment, the moment I let myself fully consider what I'd given up to come up here, that Amy called. I didn't much believe in God and the things people labeled as miracles did little to convince me otherwise, but it was at times like these that made me consider which was the more cruel: a cold and random universe or a god with a perverse sense of humor? With all due respect to Blaise Pascal, I chose to believe that no god was better than a cruel one.

"Hey, Ames, what's up?" I asked as if last week hadn't happened, as if the last twenty years hadn't happened.

There was silence at her end, but a noisy and weighty silence. Then she said, "I need to see you."

"It didn't work out so well the last time. I seem to remember you sneaking out of your own studio."

"I know," she said. "It's more complicated than I thought it would be. I love you, Kip. Like my art, it's like an affliction. I was so happy to see you and be with you again that I never realized how much it hurt, all the shit you pulled when we were together. When you were inside me . . ." There was silence again. "It never felt that way before, even when I was furious with you. Last week it was as if I was orgasming in spite of myself."

"I felt it too. Fucking was always easy for us, but it's different now. We aren't who we used to be. I don't want to hurt you anymore, Ames. I don't want to hurt anyone anymore."

"Then come to dinner with me tonight."

"Just dinner, right?"

"Just dinner. Just talking," she said.

"Just dinner. Okay. Where?"

"I don't know. What would you like?"

"Chinese food. I haven't had good Chinese food in seven years."

"I know the perfect place. It's on Lafayette in the Village. I'll get the exact address and text it to you. Be there at eight."

She hung up before I could have second thoughts. Too late. Second thoughts were all I seemed to be having lately.

Forty-One

The Remains of the Day

It had been so long since I had good Chinese food that I forgot how good *good* could be. I mean, the only Chinese food in Brixton was in the frozen food aisle of the supermarket and it was about as Chinese as frozen pizza was Italian. But the restaurant Amy chose was more than just good. It wasn't the standard Chinatown noodle shop or corner take-out, not by a long shot. No gloppy chicken chow mein on generic porcelain plates at The Peking Brasserie. The dining room was totally upscale, the service impeccable, with a menu consisting of gourmet variations on familiar dishes from many regional Chinese cuisines. In Brixton and its surrounding counties, regional cuisines were defined in terms of beef jerky and chewing tobacco.

Amy was already seated when I arrived and our hellos were so awkward and uncomfortable we might just as well have been on a blind date. We managed a fairly neutered embrace and chaste kiss. On the one hand, that made me want to run and not stop until I got back to Brixton and crawled into bed with Renee. No awkwardness or pretense with Renee. No need for apologies or penance. Just sex. On the other, I wanted to pull Amy to the red-carpeted floor and fuck her right there in the restaurant to show her how silly it was for her to hold my past against me. For chrissakes, the Kipster was as dead as Stan Petrovic. Then it struck me: maybe that was the problem. She was stupid for the Kipster. For me, maybe not so much. I could not help but wonder if Amy saw my transformation into an adult as a betrayal, as turning my back not only on who I used to be, but on who she had been, as a damning of our shared history. The waitress's arrival prevented me from wondering aloud.

"Drinks?"

"I'll have a Chardonnay," Amy said, anger as plain on her face as her nose.

"Ginger ale and oolong tea for me."

"Ginger ale?" Amy raised her eyebrows in mock surprise.

"I drink a little bit, but drinking was never the big issue for me, was it?"

"No, Kip, it was more cunts and coke."

I nearly spit out my water. I'd heard her use the word before, but I was taken aback by the bitter edge in her voice.

"Come on, Ames, that was a long time ago."

"Not for me," she said, patting her hand on her chest over her heart. "In here it was yesterday."

"Then what was last week all about: standing in the snow, resting your head on my shoulder? You think I'm such an ass that I couldn't read your code? First thing you brought up was your failing marriage. You did everything but announce your intention to finally get a divorce and then there were the portraits. And Jesus, Amy, you couldn't fuck me fast enough once you got the preliminaries out of the way."

"I didn't notice you resisting."

"Because I wasn't. Because I've missed you for ten years. Because I didn't want to lose you in the first place."

"You got a funny way of showing me you didn't want to lose me, because you fucked just about every—"

"Your Chardonnay," the waitress said, interrupting Amy's rant. "And your ginger ale and tea, sir. Would you like to hear our specials this evening?"

I raised my index finger and gave a slight nod at Amy. "Just give us a minute."

"Very good, sir. I'll be back shortly."

Amy and I pretended to study our menus and when the waitress returned, we listened to her description of the specials as if she were reciting the lost teachings of Christ. We ordered without much enthusiasm. In fact, what had been billed as an evening of just talk, and began as an evening of Amy airing old grievances, had become an evening of anything but talk. Amy seemed to have lost her zeal for upbraiding me and I was at a loss for exactly what to say. We waited for our food in uncomfortable quiet, the both of us looking anywhere but at each other.

At least when dinner was served, we had something to keep us occupied. Amy made polite conversation about things I forgot as soon as she said them. I was equally polite in my responses. *Do you really think so? I see. Yes, he's very talented.* It was all so terribly stilted and soulless that I felt like we were trapped in cutting-room scenes from *The Remains of the Day.*

"For fuck's sake, Ames, stab me or something, but I don't think I can take much more of this civility."

And for the first time in eleven years I heard Amy laugh. In a sense, to hear it brought me low, lower than her rage and disappointment ever could. Because in her laughter came the realization of what all that empty space in my life had been since I ran away from New York. It made me ache with guilt and regret— neither of which I was wont to do—because I had so wantonly and foolishly pissed away the only deeply loving relationship I'd ever had. Yet, at the same time it filled me with a strange joy to know I had made her laugh again, that I still could evoke in her something more than just rage. Her laughter encouraged me there might be enough left between us to build on, enough for me to hope.

"Wrong kind of restaurant," Amy said, her laughter calming. "Writers have thick skins and it would be too much trouble to shove a chopstick through your heart."

"At least you give me credit for having one."

"Oh, I never doubted your heart. I still don't. Your heart wasn't the organ that caused our problems."

"You think?"

"You're such an ass, Kip Weiler."

"True enough. So, Amy Anne Sanger-Weiler-Moreland, how would you like to date again?"

She didn't answer right away, distracted by something over my right shoulder. Then she said, "Date? What are you going to do next, ask me to the prom?"

"It's a thought. I do look good in a tuxedo. No, I don't want to lose you again is all, and clearly there's some stuff between us that we've got to deal with. I never want to feel the way it felt the other night and—" I cut myself off, noticing Amy's eyes drifting away once again. "Amy!"

"Sorry. What were you saying?" But even as she asked, her eyes wandered.

"What are you staring at?"

Her eyes remained fixed over my right shoulder. "All through dinner, there was a woman standing at the window behind you. At first, I hardly noticed her, but she's still there and I'm pretty sure she's staring at us."

I went cold inside and forced myself not to turn around. "Amy, do me a favor and stop looking at her, okay?"

"All right, sure."

"Look right at me, please."

Amy turned her head so that she locked her eyes on mine. "What's going on, Kip?" she asked, a false smile on her lips.

"Is she twenty, twenty-one years old, athletic build, about five eight with long, straight blond hair, high cheekbones, and blue eyes?"

"Who is she?"

"Is that her, the woman I described?" My whisper was as cold as my blood.

"That's her. She's really quite beautiful. Who is she?"

"I can't explain it, Amy, because I don't understand it myself. I'm going to get up in a minute as if I'm going to the bathroom, but I'm not coming back. Pay the bill and I'll send you a check tomorrow."

"What about your coat?"

"Leave it here and tell the waitress I'll come back for it later."

"What's going—"

"Amy, please just do it."

"Okay, okay." She relented, if not happily.

"What's she wearing?"

"What?"

"What's she wearing, the woman outside?"

"A ski vest, blue maybe, over a brown hooded sweatshirt, sweatpants … I can't tell much more. It's dark outside."

"Good."

"Is she a stalker?"

I smiled involuntarily. "I guess, in a way. I don't know for sure." I stood up, making a show of asking the waitress where the restrooms were. When the waitress left, I turned back to Amy. "I'll call you soon. Tomorrow, if I can."

With that, the false smile on Amy's face collapsed completely.

I walked towards the bathroom, but shouldered my way into the kitchen. At first, no one reacted, the chefs and sous chefs too busy fussing with clanging woks, cleavers, and cutting boards to worry about yet another asshole tourist who'd stumbled into their domain instead of the men's room. It was only when I didn't say "excuse me" or turn back around that anyone paid me any mind, but by then it was too late. There was an open side door about ten paces to my left that let cold air into the steamy kitchen and led out onto East 4th Street. I didn't hesitate and ran out through the door. No one came after me, but I slammed into a parked car. When I looked up, Renee, thirty feet away, was staring at me. She ran and I ran after her.

Forty-Two

Cats

What Amy couldn't see, what she couldn't have seen, was that Renee was wearing running shoes. I noticed because she put distance between us almost immediately. If I hadn't started running again, she would have lost me after a block. Even so, I wasn't exactly outfitted for a mad dash through the East Village. I was dressed in a sweater, sports jacket, flannel slacks, and beat-up old dress shoes, which, like the rest of my wardrobe, were desperately in need of euthanasia. And one thing I knew about Renee from seeing her nude, from feeling her powerful clench, was that she was in incredible shape. If I didn't catch her quickly, I knew I would lose her.

I called out to her, pleading for her to stop, but she kept her eyes looking forward, never wavering. We attracted some attention from other people strolling along Lafayette Street, but not an undue amount. This was New York City, after all. I stopped calling to her, not only because it didn't seem to be having an effect, but because it made me swallow big gulps of near-freezing air that hurt my throat and threw my rhythm out of whack.

Suddenly, Renee veered off her dead-straight path, cutting a jagged line through sparse but oncoming traffic across to the east side of Lafayette. Instead of trying to lose me she continued uptown along Lafayette. It was only when she got to Astor Place that she turned east and then south by Cooper Union where Bowery splits into 3rd and 4th Avenues. I'd lost sight of her for a few seconds after she turned onto Astor. When I picked her trail back up again as I turned right onto 4th Avenue, she was almost exactly the same distance ahead of me as she had been the entire time. It was at that precise moment I realized that Renee wasn't trying to lose me at all, that she would have actually had to wait for me on 4th to maintain the same distance between us. It all made a perverse kind of sense, the same kind of twisted sense my last few months in Brixton had been about. Renee's lingering in plain sight outside the restaurant, her running shoes and sweats, her steady pace, her easy-to-follow course weren't about escape, but capture, my capture. I was being led somewhere, hopefully not to slaughter.

I had a choice to make and not much time in which to make it. Knowing that I was being baited, I could have just stopped running, about-faced, and headed back to the Peking Brasserie. I could have taken control of the situation. Briefly, I fantasized about the stunned look on Renee's face if, when she turned, I was no longer there. Would she then start chasing me? I thought about the surprise I would see on Amy's face at my return, but I didn't stop running. I knew I wouldn't. I didn't even hesitate. There was no hook in my mouth, no line attached to the hook, no reel pulling me in, though there might as well have been. There was only the bait and that was enough.

Writers are curious bastards, more curious than cats. Besides, even understanding as little as I did about what was really going on, I knew that any attempt to seize control of the situation would be temporary, a delaying of the inevitable. Bad news is better than no news and I didn't feel up to sitting around waiting for the next time Renee would show up unannounced, nor did I want to risk upping the ante. If she'd been willing to appear outside a restaurant when I was with Amy, there was no telling what she might be willing to do the next time.

Seeming to sense my deliberations, Renee picked up the pace, widening the gap between us, willing me forward. If I couldn't decide, she would help me choose. She couldn't've known the decision to keep following her had already been made. I matched her speed and followed her past the entrance of Cooper Union's Foundation Building and down East 7th Street. We kept at it across 2nd Avenue, across 1st, but between 1st Avenue and Avenue A, Renee slowed her pace considerably. I began making up the ground between us in big chunks. Finally, when she was just west of Avenue A and Tompkins Square Park, she stopped completely, turned, and waited for me to catch her.

I didn't quite accept it was Renee until I was a foot away from her, her chest heaving, a panting cloud of white vapor in front of her face. Her cheeks were raw and red from the cold and her eyes watery, but, god, she was lovely. Screw me if, under the anger and confusion, I wasn't excited to see her. Even this close, I couldn't accept it was really her. Then her face turned from neutral to dead serious.

"Your wife is beautiful, Ken. She has the prettiest eyes."

"What's going on, Renee? What's this all about?"

"I miss you all the time. It really hurts."

"I miss you, too. I think about what I gave up to come here, but—"

"He's watching us, so be careful."

"He?"

"Jim."

"Hug me."

"Hug you?"

"Please, hug me. I need you to hug me."

I did as she asked. Her body was so terribly familiar in my arms. Everything about her—from the feel of her hair on my face, the floral scent of it, to the heat of her breath on my neck—all seemed so natural, but something was wrong. She tensed in my embrace and put her lips close to my ear.

"Go along with him," she whispered. "Do what he asks. Things aren't what they seem and they never have been."

"The package with the manuscript chapter, did you—"

"Forget that. It's too late now. I hoped you would understand."

"Understand what?"

She didn't answer, but I felt her hand slide beneath my jacket, along my belt line, and down into my back pocket. She let her hand linger there in my pocket for a moment before removing it. It was an odd little moment of intimacy between us.

"What was I supposed to understand about the chapter, Renee?"

She untangled herself from my arms and stepped back. "Renee! Don't you mean Zoe?" And before I could react, she slapped me across the face. "Which one of us were you fucking all those months, Ken, me or Zoe?"

I was stunned and cold again inside and sick to my stomach. I was being pulled in so many directions it rendered me immobile. But there must have been a question on my face, because Renee answered it.

"That's right, Ken, *Gun Church*. I've read every word of it and so has Jim. You should have changed your password. Pandora was just too easy for me to guess."

"Fuck!" I heard myself say.

"Jim's in his truck on the corner by the park. I don't know why I care, but I do, so don't upset him. If he gets pissed, you'll put Amy in danger."

With that, she walked back in the direction we'd come. I was reeling, barely conscious of the passage of time and when I looked up, Renee was completely out of sight. I was so unsteady, I might not have moved at all, but her warning about Amy had gotten my attention. Somehow I put one foot before the other and made it to the corner.

Forty-Three

Fanboy

And there he was, Jim leaning on the front fender of his F-150, a broad and goofy smile painted across his face. Again, as with Renee and in spite of myself, part of me was joyful at the sight of him. Seeing him there—his quirky, rough-hewn looks, remembering our morning runs, shooting together in the woods above the falls—made me acutely aware of what I'd sacrificed and how lost I'd been since returning to New York. The St. Pauli Girl's dire warnings notwithstanding, there was a measure of warmth and comfort in Jim's being here. Although I knew it wouldn't last, it freed up my limbs enough that I might approach him without completely freaking.

Yet even as I crossed the street, the warmth and comfort flowed out of me, down through my legs, out the soles of my old shoes, and onto the cold and pitted pavement of Avenue A. As I crossed the street, Jim Trimble's goofy, boyish smile morphed into that knowing, superior smile of his. From the day Jim first walked into my classroom and tried to be the teacher's pet, I'd had my niggling little doubts, doubts that I'd willingly, even eagerly, overlooked. But there was that smile again and my doubts were now full blown. I could feel my limbs seizing up on me. I was within a foot or two of him when panic fell like a shroud. Angry horns blared as I stopped dead still in my tracks. I was buffeted by the winds of passing cars and self-doubt. A cab was bearing down on me. I winced, bracing for the impact. A strong hand pulled me out of the way and I thumped into the side door of the old pickup.

"Are you crazy?" Jim was shouting at me. "Christ almighty, Kip, I didn't go through all this shit for you to end up road kill."

I wanted to speak. I really did, but the panic was choking me, making it impossible for me to string thoughts together. Jim had no such trouble.

"The way you wrote about this park in *Beatnik Soufflé*," he said, "I thought it would be a real dump, but it doesn't seem so bad."

I managed a syllable. "What?"

"You described Tompkins Square Park as a kind of a hellhole. I watched an interview you did once where you said you meant the park to be allegorical. That since Moses Gold's most famous poem was called 'Rumors of Purgatory,' it was only fitting he winds up living here as a homeless junkie."

"What?" It seemed to be the extent of my vocabulary.

"Get in the truck, Kip." Jim's voice was inhuman. I'd disappointed him already.

When he pulled away from the curb, I heard the familiar scrape and rattle of the exhaust. I once again lost track of time and place, my mind racing with myriad scenarios, one worse than the next. I wasn't conscious of where Jim was driving to or what would come next. I remembered Renee's warning not to piss him off, how it would be bad for Amy, and I rediscovered my voice.

"Our books live in our readers' heads, Jim, not ours. Writers forget their books after they've written them."

That explanation seemed to meet with his approval and the temperature inside the Ford's cab rose a few degrees.

"What's going on, Jim? What's this about?"

"You," he said. "It's always been about you."

"Me?"

"Sure, who else?"

"I'm a little confused," I confessed.

He shook his head. "You know, when I set this all in motion, I thought you'd have figured it out by now. From everything I'd read about you, I knew you were a sharp guy."

It. This. What the fuck was he talking about? Renee had said something similar about the chapter from *Flashing Pandora*, that she had hoped I would have understood. I was ready to mention that to Jim, but I stopped the words before they got to my lips. I knew Renee was involved in whatever *it* or *this* was. What I didn't know was the extent of her involvement. She had warned me about Jim, after all, and I wasn't looking to hurt her anymore than I had already.

"These days I'm about as sharp as a bowling ball. Too old. Too many drugs. It catches up to you." I took a deep breath, a long pause and said, "So, you've been reading *Gun Church*?"

I didn't think the question was particularly amusing, but Jim apparently found it quite wry and witty. "Yep," he said, still sort of chuckling. "Started reading it after I borrowed your car that weekend. What a great book. It's inspirational and—hold it!" He tugged the steering wheel hard right and we skidded to a stop, my head nearly slamming into the dashboard. "Got to belt yourself in there, Kip. I can't afford to lose you now."

I held my tongue, asking instead about the unexpected stop.

"Look." He pointed at a red neon sign, Maggie's Joint, above a bar.

It took me a second to time travel, to picture the place without the red neon, when its façade was very different, and I was a much, much younger man. "The Hunt Club," I whispered almost involuntarily.

He seemed surprised. "You remember?"

"This was my life, Jim. I'm not likely to forget this place. Most of the stories I told you up in the woods started with me here."

"You, Bart Meyers, and Nutly, right? Bet you couldn't measure how much pussy you got here over the years," he said.

"I wouldn't even know where to begin."

I kept forgetting about just how much Jim loved hearing those stories of the Kipster's exploits and how much he loved my books. I'd had so little respect for myself for so long, I found it difficult to fathom his fanboy obsession. *Fanboy!* Fuck me, so that was it, I thought. Maybe that's what this had all been about, Jim's obsession and Renee's hurt and anger at my abandoning her. Maybe Jim was just as angry as Renee at being abandoned, maybe angrier. It was easy for me to forget sometimes just how young and naïve Jim and Renee actually were. Weak with relief, I felt I could breathe again, finally.

"Come on," I said, slapping Jim's shoulder, "let me buy you a drink."

You'd have thought he'd just won the lottery, and he was out of the truck like a shot.

Forty-Four

eBay

Maggie's Joint was pretty empty and pretty much what I expected: an Upper West Side bar dressed up, no doubt at great expense, to look like a shithole dive in Sheepshead Bay. You've got to love Manhattan. No wonder everyone was moving to Brooklyn.

"Barstool or a booth?" I asked Jim.

He was so wide-eyed, he didn't answer. I found us a booth by the retro jukebox. Jim ordered a Bud because he didn't know any better. The barmaid nodded her approval of his low-rent chic. I ordered a Laphroaig neat, to blur the lines between Kant Huxley and me. I figured to play into Jim's obsession, hoping it would make it easier for him to explain himself to me. I waited for Jim to settle down a little and for our drinks to be delivered before asking him about what he and Renee had been up to.

"I guess you're pretty upset at me about my basing some of the book on you guys," I said.

He looked at me like he didn't quite understand what I was saying. "Why would I be upset about that? It's more than I could have hoped for when I started this whole thing, Kip."

And with that, the grip I thought I had on the situation slid right out of my hands. I inhaled my scotch and twirled my index finger at the barmaid for another round. Jim, following my lead, polished off his Bud in a gulp.

"I'm sorry, but you just lost me. What did you mean when you said it was more than you could have hoped for?"

"Man, Kip, you weren't fooling before about being slow on the uptake."

"Apparently not."

Our second round arrived and I told the barmaid to keep the drinks coming.

"Okay," I said, "we've established I'm missing something here, but what?"

He ignored the question, answering one I hadn't asked. "I liked it better when the book was called *Gun Queer*. That came from me. How could you change it without asking?"

My stomach clenched at the subtle malevolence of his tone and the proprietary nature of his question. As the seconds passed, it was becoming increasingly difficult to cling to the notion that whatever Jim and Renee were up to was fairly innocent and innocuous. There was nothing innocuous in Jim's voice, nothing innocent about his expression.

"Changing it wasn't my decision. It was about marketing. Writing is art. Well, at least sometimes. Publishing is a business. In that battle, business almost always wins."

"You shouldn't have let them change it." Jim sucked down his second beer and waved at the waitress for another. He seemed disinclined to continue chatting until he got his third beer, so I finished my drink as well. The barmaid was catching on, bringing over two Buds and my third scotch. Jim made short work of the third can and started on number four.

"You know, Kip, I get the feeling you don't appreciate what I did for you."

"But I do. Being with you guys, the chapel, it changed my life. I had this book I wanted to write forever, but I never got past the first line. Without you guys, I'd still be at the first line. That's why I dedicated the—"

He cut me off. "It wasn't easy for me to give her to you like that."

"What? Give who to me?"

"Renee," he said, his voice cracking ever so slightly.

"What do you mean, Jim?"

He chugged his fourth beer, his expression turning dour. "Brixton's not like here. There aren't so many beautiful girls everywhere. Anyway, it's different for a guy like you. Girls, they can't help themselves with you. I've seen it for myself. They get all flustered around you. It's not like that for me. Do you have any idea how hard it was for me to get Renee to even talk to me? I practically had to beg her and I don't like begging."

"No, I bet you don't."

"Fucking A." He was really feeling the beers now. "The Colonel used to want me to beg him to stop hitting me, but I wouldn't, not once, no sir. But I gave her to you and now she won't have me back."

"What do you mean you gave her to me?" I signaled to the waitress for another round.

"You still don't see it?"

"Don't be surprised. The last few months have been more than a little disorienting for me."

He smiled, but it was a maudlin smile I didn't know he had in his repertoire. "She thinks I don't know about the trip she made to your apartment in Brooklyn the day of the snowstorm and the package she left for you, but she can't fool me." His smile drooped into drunken self-pity. I knew that look only too well. I'd seen it in bathroom mirrors a thousand times. "I know how much she loves you. She'd do anything for you, even risk her life by defying me."

I didn't want to go there. The more Jim said, the less I understood. I was having trouble getting my head around any of it. I was light-headed, blood rushing in my ears, and the scotch wasn't helping. I tried to get him to focus on details, so I could latch on to something, anything.

"How did Renee get that chapter? I destroyed all the copies."

His face turned to stone. Christ, he was all over the place, emotionally. That made two of us. "Renee didn't get shit." He slammed his palm on the table, the few people in the bar turning to look. "The only thing she did was steal it from me. *I* got that chapter. Me! That's how this all started. Without that chapter . . ."

The waitress brought our drinks. Jim grabbed the can from her hand and not gently. Out of his line of sight, I waved my hand at the waitress to stop bringing drinks. She nodded that she understood and left, rubbing her hand as she went.

"Sorry. So how did you—"

"eBay."

"eBay what?"

"I always scan eBay for stuff of yours. I have signed first editions of all your books, signed paperbacks, uncorrected galleys, promotional bookstore posters, videos of your TV appearances, all kinds of shit. One day last March I saw that Moira Blanco's daughter was selling some of her stuff on eBay and I bought it cheap. It was mostly crap, but there were these envelopes with chapters from your manuscripts. How cool is that?"

"Pretty cool," I said, not wanting to set him off again. "But I'm still not seeing the connection between the chapter and—"

He annihilated his beer and squashed the can against the table. "Let's get the fuck out of here. I don't like it here as much as I thought I would."

"The Hunt Club is gone, Jim. Humans are sentimental. The universe doesn't give a shit."

"Fuck the universe."

"Doesn't work. I've tried."

He kind of snickered at that. "Yeah, well, we'll see." And he was out of the bar as quickly as he'd come in.

"Your friend okay?" the waitress asked, sliding the credit card receipt and a pen at me.

"Not sure," I said, adding a twenty-dollar tip.

"Not sure of what?"

"Of anything."

I think she said thanks, but I wasn't even sure of that.

Forty-Five

The King of Coincidences

It had been a long time getting to Coney Island—a long time and a lot of beers. Jim had it in his head to do the stations of the Kipster's cross. After buying two six-packs of Bud at a deli, we criss-crossed Manhattan, paying homage at sites Jim Trimble had determined were significant in my life or the lives of my characters. The drunker he got, the greater his reverence, the blurrier the lines between the Kipster and his characters, and the longer he prayed at my various altars. The only person for whom these places held any meaning was him. When we stopped at the building Kant Huxley had lived in, Jim nearly wept. *Flashing Pandora* was his favorite book ever, a point he repeated so many times during the course of our pilgrimage I wanted to scratch my own eyes out. He said he had a particular affinity for Kant Huxley. Did I know why? Did I care?

As the night wore on, it got more difficult for me to keep a lid on my emotions. Clearly, something was going on with Jim that was straying pretty far from the center line. I kept cycling through a spectrum of feelings, from anger to worry, from disappointment to fear, from boredom to disdain. At points, I even felt pity for Jim that he was so heavily invested in a writer whose time had come and gone. Still, there had to be more to it than this magical and miserable tour. Renee's warning was never far from my thoughts, but by about one in the morning, I'd pretty much had it. I was so drained and so tired of indulging his fanboy adventures that I exploded.

"That's it, Jim!" I yelled, slamming my hand down on the dashboard. "I want some fucking answers and I want them now. If you don't start explaining what you're playing at, I'm getting the fuck out of this truck."

But if I thought my outburst would push him to melt down or to give me the answers I wanted, I was wrong. He just floored the truck, flew through a red light, and turned down Chambers Street.

"Amy's loft is beautiful. I really like the portraits she's done of the two of you."

Words formed themselves in my head to say, but they caught in my throat like shards of bone. Fuck, he'd broken into the loft.

"You don't want to yell at me," he said, his voice feral and menacing. "The last person to do that to me was the Colonel. No one's gonna do that to me again. Stay or go, it's up to you, but all sorts of bad things happen when pets go off leash."

Fuck! Now he was quoting Satan to me, literally. Although what I'd said to Jim earlier in the evening was true, that I'd forgotten my books once they'd been written, I hadn't forgotten everything of my old work and I certainly remembered that line. In a chapter in *The Devil's Understudy*, Satan discusses the dangers of free will with his future replacement, a young investment banker. I never thought I'd have it thrown back in my face. Where only seconds ago I'd been nearly paralyzed with fear, I was now furious. If Amy weren't part of the equation, I might have smacked Jim across the jaw for using my own words to compare me to a dog on his tether, but Amy *was* involved and getting in one good shot wouldn't have been worth it.

"Staying?" It wasn't a question, not really, and ten minutes later we were across the Brooklyn Bridge, heading to Coney Island.

●

Jim was insistent. "Which bench was it that Romeo used? I want to sit on that bench."

We'd come to the end of the line, the terminal station of the Kipster's cross. In *Romeo vs. Juliet*—as Jim kept reminding me on our way here—Romeo bones his divorce lawyer on a bench in Coney Island. For reasons known only to Jim, he'd chosen this as our last stop.

"It was *that* bench," I said, picking one out at random.

He didn't question it and sat down on the cold moist slats, a beatific smile on his sloppy, drunken face. For all his bluster and menace, he'd believed me like a lost little boy believes the nearest grownup. I didn't join him on the bench. It was damp and raw by the ocean, a cold fog hanging over the boardwalk like a gray veil. The wind blowing in off the Atlantic had jagged edges, the salt air cutting right through my sports jacket and sweater. I turned my collar up against the cold and damp to no avail.

"So this was the bench Romeo fucked his lawyer on, huh? I loved *Romeo vs. Juliet* too. I used to jerk off imagining what it would be like having a hot girl like Romeo's lawyer straddling me, her panties torn and her skirt flared over my lap. I asked Renee to fuck me like that once, just like in the book, but she wouldn't. She thought it was weird. Did she ever fuck you like that, Kip?"

"I can't remember."

"I bet you can't."

"You in the mood to talk now?" I asked. "I'm freezing to death out here."

"I don't . . . feel so . . . good. I got . . . to . . . puke."

He ran unsteadily across the boardwalk and down onto the sand, fell on his haunches and emptied his guts. I stood at the rail on the boardwalk above him, facing the last vestiges of the amusement park. Those rides that remained were ancient beasts, hibernating through another brutal winter. Coney Island was a hopeless place, a place for dying. Jim trudged back up onto the boardwalk, a sheen of sweat covering his ashen face.

"Let's walk," I said. "It's too cold to stand still."

Jim didn't argue and followed me as I turned away from Coney Island and toward Brighton Beach.

"What was that crack before, Jim, quoting Satan back to me about pets off the leash?"

"I'm sorry I said that. I really am, I swear." I thought I saw tears welling up in his eyes.

What, I thought, did a few tears matter at the edge of the ocean? His tears worried me, though. Jim was mercurial. Sure, he was sad now, but manic and belligerent too. He was the kind of drunk who beats the shit out of his wife, then tearfully swears his undying devotion to her as she spits out broken teeth. Those kinds of drunks are sorry only for themselves and that makes them dangerous.

"We're way past sorry. What did you mean by it?"

"Did you know I got accepted into the best state university, but I stayed home in Brixton just so I could take your classes?" he said, as if he hadn't heard the question.

"I'm honored."

"You got me through high school. You did, you really did. I used to wish you were my dad. You would have been the coolest dad, not like the Colonel."

"I've always been barely able to be responsible for myself. I would have been a nightmare as a father, Jim, but I appreciate the sentiment."

Still choked up, he gathered himself before answering. "I wanted to give something back to you for what your books had given me, for what you meant to me. I could swear that sometimes you were writing the words in your characters' mouths just for me."

"Why not just come by and introduce yourself? I would have liked that."

"Because that's what anyone else could've done, but me and you, our connection is different. I knew that when I repaid my debt to you, it had to be something more than adoration. It had to be worthy of what you'd given me. When the chapter from *Flashing Pandora* fell into my hands, it was a sign. I didn't understand it at first, what it meant, but God is like that sometimes. He gives us the tools and signs, only we have to figure out how to use them. It was just like with the Colonel's handgun collection; I had it, but I needed to figure out what to do with it to give it meaning."

"God, Jim? I guess he's moved on from burning bushes to eBay."

"It doesn't matter if you don't understand," he said, wiping tears and sweat off his cheeks. "As long as I did, that's what mattered."

"Understand what?"

"I kept reading the chapter over and over again until I knew what I was supposed to do, how I could use it to give as much back to you as you had given to me. You'd saved me and now I would save you."

"Save me? Save me from what?"

"From your fate."

"My fate?"

"Are you kidding? Look at where you were, Kip. You were once one of the most famous and admired writers in America and you ended up teaching writing to kids who didn't give a shit and who had no idea of who you were. You didn't give a shit either. It was like you weren't alive anymore. Now look where you are and what you're doing. Did you think that all just happened? Brixton was no place for someone like you. Brixton is for people like me."

"But, Jim, by definition, you can't save someone from his fate."

The tears vanished as quickly as they'd come, replaced by that smug smile. "But I did save you from your fate and from Brixton, didn't I? That's why the chapter I found was so important. I used your own ideas to save you, to put you on a different path. Of course Frank going crazy helped too."

"What are you talking about?"

"Come on, Kip, did you really think it was just coincidence that Frank Vuchovich used a Colt Python with a six-inch barrel and a royal blue finish? I knew Frank his whole life. He was one of the original members of the chapel. I showed him the chapter from *Flashing Pandora* last spring. He wasn't the smartest person and he didn't read much, but I knew he would love the gun stuff. I couldn't believe it when he showed up in class that day in September with the Python. That's when I knew."

"Knew what, Jim?"

"Knew it was the final sign that I could save you. Don't you see? Frank was never the shiniest lump of coal in the bin, always moody and a little nuts, but I didn't think he would ever just snap like that. I knew it had to be a sign. After that, I used the chapter like a script. You were Kant Huxley and Renee was Pandora."

"And Renee just happily went along with this?"

"Renee was the easy part to begin with. She was always hot for you and she never loved me like I loved her. I broke up with her and told her to go for it, to invite you to the chapel. She didn't have to think twice about it. Later when she caught on, I had to persuade her to help me to help you."

"You're not serious."

His smile disappeared. He grabbed my arm and yanked me around to face him. "Serious? Why else would the chapter have fallen into my hands?"

"What if Frank hadn't snapped or if he had used a different gun or—"

"But he did snap and he did use that gun and he did get killed. What more proof do you need, Kip?"

"Get out of here." I pulled free of his grasp, rubbing my arm where his fingers had held me. "This isn't funny anymore. You're really scaring me."

"Did you know that when Jesus raised Lazarus from the dead, Lazarus smelled pretty bad because he'd been in the ground for a while?"

"And what the hell is that supposed to mean?"

"Nothing," he said, "but before you laugh at what I'm saying, you should think about it."

"I don't have to think about it. This is crazy."

"Crazy? I guess that Haskell Brown guy who wouldn't touch your book just conveniently got himself murdered to suit your career."

"What are you telling me?"

"Just that you must be the king of coincidences, Kip. Bad things happen to other people so good things happen to you. Is that the way the universe works?"

"Jim, come on, you're a sharp guy. Now you're stringing together unconnected incidents into a wishful narrative."

"And you're whistling through the graveyard."

"Very cute."

"It's not meant to be."

"What do you think you're going to get out of this, Jim? You don't need to build yourself up in my eyes. You taught me how to shoot, how to handle my fears. All that, your friendship, getting me back in shape, helping me write again, isn't that enough for you?"

"That's like me asking you if you'd mind someone else putting their name on your book. Without me, there'd be no you, no *Gun Church*."

"When you say those kinds of things, it worries me. I'm worried about you."

"I don't need your worry." He shoved me down and stamped his feet on the boardwalk. "This wasn't how things were supposed to turn out."

"How were they supposed to be?" I asked, pushing myself up onto my knees.

"Not like this. You're supposed to understand about how smart I've been and be happy and thank me for everything I've done for you." More tears, but this time he was sobbing, loudly. "You're . . . disappointing me . . . Kip."

I almost told him to go fuck himself, but Renee's warning about the danger to Amy, of disappointing Jim, was never far from my mind. "But I do see, I swear," I said, if not very convincingly.

"Don't lie to me. Don't fucking lie! I couldn't take that. I've killed for you. I can kill to hurt you too."

"Stop it!"

His chest was heaving and he was raging. He was on me before I could move, threading his hands around my jacket lapels and pulling me to my feet.

"Stop it? I'm just getting started. Think about the weekend Haskell Brown died. Remember, I borrowed your car to see—"

"—a girl who went away to college."

"That's right, Kip. Too bad that wasn't the truth, but I couldn't tell you what I was doing because you would probably have stopped me."

"Stopped you. Stopped you from what?" I asked although in my belly I knew what he was going to say.

"I wasn't visiting any girl. I was up here doing what had to be done, getting rid of the one thing standing in our way: Haskell Brown. I enjoyed beating the shit out of that guy. He kept asking me why I was doing it. He kept asking until I broke his jaw. You should have seen what he looked like before I put a hole in him."

"Bullshit!"

"The truth. Did you ever bother checking what kind of gun it was that killed him? You didn't check because you didn't want to know, did you? You still don't want to know, but I'm going to tell you. It was a .25 Beretta and your fingerprints are all over it. Don't worry. I got it tucked away in a nice plastic bag for safekeeping. No one will ever have to see it unless you get some stupid ideas about going to the police. And there's a record of your car's trip from Brixton to New York and back. I bet you didn't know all the states along the East Coast accept our state's electronic toll pass. So it would be real stupid for you to go to the police. I used all this to get Renee to let me read your book, to help me. She really loves you and would do just about anything not to have me turn the evidence over. I mean anything."

"Let go of me," I screamed, trying to break his grasp. "Let me go!"

"Not until I'm done."

I couldn't hold it in any longer. "Fuck you!"

"Fuck me? No, Kip, you're the one who's fucked. You're the one with all the blood on his hands. You grabbed Frank's gun. Haskell Brown, he'd still be alive if you didn't want to publish again so bad. And poor Lance Vaughn Mabry . . . I forget now, did you plant that idea in my head or did I plant it in yours?" Jim was no longer crying and the rage had calmed to an unsettling whisper. "I guess that was your idea. You're full of good ideas."

"You're telling me you killed that kid?"

"Your books are the blueprints. Don't you see, we're only the instruments in a bigger plan. It took me some time to understand it."

"You killed Mabry?"

"Just like in *Gun Church*. Renee dressed in a black wig, short skirt, and real high heels. I waited outside the bar in a stolen van. When they came out, I followed them to where I told Renee to take him. I shot him right through the windshield."

"Renee wouldn't do that," I said, struggling to breathe against Jim's fists tightening around my collar.

"You're not listening to me, Kip. I told you, she had to do it to save you. She knew I had the Beretta with your prints on it. I made her choose between you or some kid she didn't even know."

"Fuck you!"

That didn't go over well. He let go of my lapel with one hand and buried his fist in my gut. Gasping for breath, I collapsed. I hugged my belly, my cheek flush against the wet boardwalk planks.

"Look what you made me do! Look what you made me do! *Fuck. Fuck. Fuck.* I don't want to hurt you, Kip." He sat down next to me, arms around his knees, rocking. "I saved your life. Don't make me take it away."

I ignored that and the pain. "You're lying. Renee was visiting her family upstate the weekend that kid was murdered." My voice was strained and cracking. "She was visiting her brother Jake back from Afghanistan."

"She doesn't have a brother Jake or any kind of brother, and she's not from upstate."

I struggled to my knees for a second time. "I suppose you're going to tell me that Stan Petrovic isn't dead and buried."

There was that smile again. "No, he's dead all right. I made sure of that. I guess I sort of neglected to put live rounds in his gun. I set most of it up, but you played your part without even realizing it. Man, Kip, when you threatened to kill Stan in front of folks at the hardware store, you made things that much easier for me. Be tough for you to explain away him turning up dead, shot by your gun after threatening him. Like I said, Stan's dead. On the other hand, he's not exactly buried."

The world wobbled beneath me as I willed myself to my feet. My ability to function since killing Stan had been based on the belief that Jim, Renee, and the rest of the people in the chapel had acted honorably, that they had done as promised, burying Stan's body in a place in the woods somewhere he would never be found. Now I couldn't be sure of anything.

"You better start treating me with the respect I deserve," Jim said, getting right up in my face, his breath stinking of vomit and beer. "And you better not think about going to the police."

I walked over to the beachside railing to help keep me upright. He followed close behind.

"Go to the police! With what, some cockamamie story you dreamed up? They would think I was the crazy one."

"Don't say that."

"Jim, I don't know what you're getting out of this or what you want. Is it money, do you want some money?"

He was horrified, hurt. "Money? You think I want your money?"

"Then what?"

"I told you."

"What, my love and respect? You think stalking me, lying to me, hitting me, and threatening me is the way to go about earning it? You got some funny ideas about love and respect."

"Don't say that! Don't say that!"

"Or what, you're going stomp your feet some more? Grow up, kid, and stay the hell away from me." My head spinning, I pushed off the rail and made for the staircase to the street.

"Don't call me kid."

"Then stop acting like one."

"I wasn't lying," he called after me. "Don't make me prove it to you."

"Grow up, kid," I repeated, not looking back.

"I'll prove it to you."

Now I turned and shouted at him across what was almost the entire width of the boardwalk. "Whatever game you're playing at, you leave Amy and Renee out of it. This is about you and me."

"My game," he said. "My rules."

"They've always been just your rules, haven't they, Jim? All that stuff about how things were supposed to go in the chapel, that was a load of crap. I know a narcissist when I see one and I'm looking at one right now. This isn't about me. It's about you."

"I didn't wound Ralph for me, Kip."

"Ralph? Who's Ralph?"

"The guy from the grounds crew at school. I clipped him in the arm to get a rise out of you. I wanted to see how you would react to blood, to see what you'd do with McGuinn in *Gun Church* after that. Ralph was pretty mad at me for that. I had to kill him too, you know, before he could talk to you."

"Stop it, Jim. Just stop this, whatever this is, now."

"Too late for that. Too much blood spilled already to stop. Watch for signs, Kip, and you'll see clear enough what this is. Then we'll talk."

And with that, he turned his back on me. He walked down the boardwalk toward Coney Island until his figure was swallowed by the fog. I stood there, frozen. My hands were shaking, but not from the cold.

Forty-Six

The Price of Blood

Three days later and nothing. No headlines, no obits, no proof that Jim Trimble's twisted boardwalk tale was anything more than a fantasy narrative born of desperation. Poor Jim, I thought, so damaged by the Colonel, so in need of affection and approval he was willing to have me as a surrogate father. Yet, as bad as I felt for Jim, I no longer wanted any part of him. Even if every word he had said was utter crap, there was stuff he'd done, words spoken that could not be taken back. I wondered if he was in a motel room somewhere trying to figure out how he might unscramble the eggs. Maybe he was in his old pickup, driving back home to Brixton. I hoped Renee had found her way clear of him. There had been no sign of her either. Whether his story was real or imagined, the fact that he could take very profound tragedy and pain and weave it into such a warped chain of events scared the shit out of me. He needed help, a lot of help, but he wasn't going to get it from me.

To Amy's credit, she'd been pretty understanding about my disappearing act at the Peking Brasserie, but there was no getting around telling her about Renee. I didn't go into too much detail over the phone and I was careful to avoid the big picture. There was no need to worry her unnecessarily. It was bad enough that Jim had me looking over my shoulder. I didn't see the point in infecting Amy with my paranoia and nagging fears. Still, I was pretty sure Jim had broken into her loft and I wasn't prepared to roll the dice with her life. The morning after I walked down the boardwalk steps, I asked Meg to find me someone to keep an eye on Amy.

"What is this, Kip, stalking by proxy?"

"I wish I had the time to explain the irony of what you just said, but I don't. It's not about that. Please, just do it."

"What are you looking for?"

"Someone with a carry permit who can handle himself, but someone who won't stick out in a crowd. He's meant to be insurance, not a deterrent. I don't want Amy or anyone else to know he's there."

There was a pensive silence coming from Meg's end of the line. Then she gave voice to her worries, "Are these those gun nuts from—"

"Yeah."

"What's going on? Is Amy really in danger?"

"I'm not taking any chances."

"Why not call the NYPD?"

"No cops, Meg! No cops."

"All right. Don't bite my head off. You realize this kind of thing can get very expensive."

"Do it, Donovan. Just do it, please?"

"Okay."

I didn't give her time to ask more questions I wasn't going to answer anyway, so I clicked off. Within two hours of my call to Meg, I received a call from Tom McDonald, a retired NYPD detective who ran a private security firm. He explained that when they were on the NYPD, he and his team had helped safeguard everyone from the mayor of New York to the president of the United States and that they were expert at blending into the background if that was what the client required. That was exactly what I required. I gave him accurate descriptions of Jim and Renee, and Jim's truck. I gave him all I thought I knew about them. He said he already had all the information on Amy he needed to begin and promised that he and his relief, another retired detective, would give me regular phone updates.

He asked one last question. "You wanna tell me anything that maybe you didn't mention before?"

"They're both experts with guns."

"Hitting paper targets don't make you an expert."

"I'm not talking about paper targets, Mr. McDonald."

"Ex-military, huh?" he asked, his voice suddenly more serious.

"Something like that," I said.

"Good thing you told me, but don't worry about it. My partner, Tony Dee and me, we got her back. Nothing's gonna happen to your ex-wife on our watch."

"She can't know you're there."

"We know. Believe me, we'll fade so far into the background, no one'll know we're there unless they have to."

In spite of McDonald's reassurances and regular updates, I didn't sleep much that night or the following night. It was far more unnerving not knowing how much, if any, of what Jim had said was reality based. Not knowing made it really difficult to determine what else I could do to protect Amy; but even if I could have been one hundred percent sure of Amy's safety, I had plenty to keep my nights sleepless. There was no avoiding the truth of Jim's narrative even if he had nothing to do with most of it. Frank Vuchovich and Haskell Brown's deaths were facts. My rebirth as a writer and as a man had come at the price of blood, a lot of blood, and, so far, none of it mine.

It was all pretty exhausting and I got to the point where not sleeping was no longer an option. I could feel my body shutting down, but stubbornly hanging on to wakefulness. I just needed something to dull the edge of my own mania. There was nothing in my apartment to drink. I considered going downstairs and paying a visit to Isaac's daughter. For me, nothing took the edge off quite like fucking, but the Kipster was still dead and using a woman that way was his MO, not mine. Then I remembered the painkillers the ER doctor had prescribed for my broken ribs. I snapped one of the two remaining pills in half and swallowed it dry. I don't know when the sun was supposed to set on the rest of the world, but it set on me pretty damned quickly.

Forty-Seven

The Holdback

I jackknifed up in bed, eyelids snapping open like cartoon window shades, my clothes soaked through with cold sweat. The last time I woke up in a cold sweat, I was in detox. Christ, it was so fucking clear to me in my sleep that I couldn't understand how I hadn't seen it before. I had the proof or, hopefully, the disproof of Jim's version of events right there in the apartment with me.

The clock read 3:02 A.M. when I stepped onto the bare wooden floors and stood, stretching the knots out of my muscles. The room was utterly dark and still, but not quiet. The traffic noise from Coney Island Avenue and Ocean Parkway was like the buzzing of a sleepy hive and with the Avenue H subway station only two blocks away, the *cha-chum cha-chum, cha-chum cha-chum* of passing subway wheels was the rhythm of the night. Transfixed by the sounds, I let the darkness wash over me.

The trance was quickly broken and I found the metal file box where I stored my monthly bills. The beat-up old file box was the only thing of my father's I'd kept. I could not help but think of Jim, the scars on his back, the Colonel's handgun collection, and again feel pity for what had become of him. I felt a little sorry for myself too. Sorry that I had been broken for so long, that I had denied to myself that finding my father dead by his own hand had helped ruin me.

I sat at my desk looking through all my recent bills. If what Jim had said was true about driving my Porsche to New York and back, my CompuPass toll bill, which was automatically charged to my AmEx card, would be much higher than usual. In fact, for nearly a year before this last September, I had no toll charges at all. Until the day Frank Vuchovich held my class hostage, where did I have to go, really? But my AmEx statements for the two months prior to my departure from Brixton were nowhere to be found. I had my most recent one, but not the two previous ones. There was nothing particularly surprising in that. I just moved and I was never the neatest of record keepers.

I booted up my laptop. While I may not have been able to check my toll bills, I could look back at the media reports that followed in the wake of Haskell Brown's murder. When I Googled "Haskell Brown homicide," I got a boxcar full of hits. But the only thing any of the reports said about the bullet that caused his fatal wound was that it was from a handgun. Another dead end. Then I had an idea, one that even my sloppy record keeping couldn't thwart. I got my phone and scrolled down to the newest number on my contact list.

"McDonald here."

"This is Weiler. Everything all right there?" I asked.

"Fine. Quiet. She went out to dinner at nine to Otto's over on Fifth Avenue and Eighth Street. I can tell you what she ate, if you're interested."

"No, that's okay."

"She was home at ten fifty-one. Her lights went off at eleven forty-seven and no one's been in or out of the building since one-thirteen. My relief should be here in about an hour."

"Very thorough. Thanks."

"You're up kinda early, no?"

"Nerves, I guess, and I'm a writer. We work at odd hours sometimes."

"A writer, huh? Whatchu workin' on?"

"That's sort of why I called. I was wondering if you still have any contacts inside the department? I'm doing preliminary research for a book about the murder of a famous book editor. He was beaten, then shot to death. Happened a few months ago in Chelsea. Might've been a hate crime."

"Whatchu need?"

"I've read every report on the homicide, but there's nothing about the caliber of the handgun the killer used."

"What's the vic's name?"

"Haskell Brown."

"Gimme an hour. I'll make some calls."

While I was on the phone with McDonald, part of me must have been trying to figure out where the missing credit card statements had got to. No matter how hard I tried, I couldn't remember paying those last few bills or ever having seen them. Yet, I hadn't received any late notices or phone calls inquiring about overdue funds, and there was no old balance showing at the top of my new bill. I got a sick feeling in my gut as I thought about playing house in Brixton with Renee. "Mail's on the table," was her daily refrain. Renee would always smile when she said it, and her smile made me smile, but I wasn't smiling as I reached for my checkbook.

I used to pre-sign checks for her to use at the local grocery store or the campus bookstore or to buy some clothes. I never really paid much attention to what she spent money on or used the checks for. It felt good to be good to her, to want to be good to her. When my life consisted of boning every adjunct in a skirt, I had such disdain for myself that it subverted any pleasure I might find in the bedroom. My sex life was a version of Groucho Marx's famous line about not wanting to be a member of any club that would have him as a member. I didn't want anyone who wanted me, and when Janice Nadir and I were involved it was worse than that. I used her own love and desperation against her. So, yeah, when Renee came into my life, I was happy to do things for her. And she balanced my checkbook: a process as mysterious to me as quantum physics.

When I looked at the checking account register, I was heart-sick. Renee had written checks for those two AmEx bills. The amounts weren't outrageous given that I'd done some splurging since getting the book deals. I was no forensic accountant and without the actual list of charges to work with, I wasn't going to be able to back my way into the toll bill amount. But there was no getting around the fact that Renee, in spite of having four months of unfettered access to my checkbook, had paid only these two bills. Was she covering Jim's tracks or was it a coincidence that the accompanying statements were missing? *Coincidence.* I could hear Jim laughing. I hadn't wanted to believe she could have been complicit in Jim's crazy schemes—real or imagined, whether she was being forced to or not—but it was getting harder to convince myself of that.

I guess I was pretty old-fashioned in some ways. Mostly, I used my computer like a fancy word processor. I never banked online or did any of the other sorts of things online the rest of the world did. But this was different and I was frustrated; so armed with my most recent bill, I typed in *americanexpress.com* and followed all the prompts until I accessed my missing statements. I was scrolling through the individual charges when my heart stopped, then raced. There it was: a CompuPass charge for over a hundred bucks, about twice what it had cost me in tolls to drive up here when I moved. Before I could breathe again, the phone rang.

"How long before this book a yours comes out?" It was Tom McDonald.

"Years, if ever," I said. "Right now I'm just looking to see if there's a book here at all. Why?"

"Because the caliber of the weapon used is part of the hold-back and you can't share this information with anybody, at least not yet."

"The holdback. What's the holdback?"

"It's standard operating procedure for detectives to withhold certain details from any serious case. It's so they can make sure a suspect isn't bullshittin' them or wastin' their time. It's a way to eliminate false leads or confessions."

"I get it. A guy turns himself in and says 'I used a .38' when it was actually a .25. Something like that, right?"

There was a few uncomfortable seconds of silence on McDonald's end of the phone. Then, "Why did you say that?"

"What? Hold on."

I didn't really hear what he said. No, I heard it, but it didn't quite register because as I stretched my neck, my eye caught sight of something that didn't belong. "Wait a minute," I told him. I walked over to my door, the cell phone nestled between my right shoulder and ear. I popped on the floor lamp and froze. An envelope, not unlike the one the missing chapter had come in, had been pushed through the gap between the floor and the bottom of the door.

"Weiler, what's going on?" McDonald shouted in my ear.

"Just a second."

I forced myself to kneel down and scoop it up. This envelope was thinner, lighter, with nothing written on it. The flap was taped shut. I tried to pull it open, but that didn't work. I retreated to my desk to find scissors or a letter opener.

"Hey, Weiler."

"Sorry, McDonald."

"About the gun," he said.

"What about it?"

"Why did you mention a .25?"

"I don't know," I lied, finding an old X-ACTO knife. "It was random. Why?"

"Lead detective says your vic was killed by one shot to the back of the head. The bullet was pretty smashed up, but they're pretty certain it was a .25, probably from a Ruger or a Beretta."

My head was pounding, sweat once again rushing through my pores, my world wobbling severely on its axis. None of this, the toll bill or the caliber of the bullet, proved anything for certain. I told myself—even if I didn't quite believe it—that Jim could simply have stolen my toll pass and run up my bill. That the police holdback wasn't top secret. Hadn't I just found out what caliber bullet had killed Haskell Brown without much trouble? Jim was a resourceful kid, more resourceful than me. I'm sure he could have found out the holdback information.

"Weiler!"

"Give me a second," I barked, emptying the contents of the envelope onto my desk. And when I saw the item the envelope held, my world stopped wobbling and spun off into the void. It was the front page of the *Brixton Banner* and the headline read:

MABRY LURED TO DEATH BY DARK-HAIRED BEAUTY

"Weiler! You okay?" I could not find it in me to answer. "Weiler, are you all right?"

"Far from it. Get Amy out of her apartment. Get her the fuck out of there right now and take her someplace safe."

"What's wrong?"

"Everything."

Forty-Eight

The Oracle of Brixton

McDonald told me to sit tight, that he'd get back to me with their location after they'd gotten Amy safely away from the loft. I asked if he wanted me to call her to warn her he was coming.

"No, for chrissakes!" he screamed. "You'd only scare the shit out of her and make my job ten times harder. I'll handle it. Go take a cold shower or knit a fuckin' sweater and wait for my call. Should be a few hours."

In spite of wanting to crawl out of my own skin, I heeded some of his advice and took a shower. Afterwards, I sat in the living room of my lightless apartment, waiting for whispers of dawn to shine through my windows—whispers that came as dark clouds and the pinging of rain drops. I barely moved. My mind raced. I'd been so diligent at rationalizing away the obvious that I never let myself fully entertain the possibility that what Jim had said on the boardwalk might actually be a factual accounting of what had happened. Addicts are superb at denial, but there was no denying it, not any of it, not anymore. The bloody symmetry of it came crashing down on my head.

If it was true—and it was—that I had been remade as a person and as a writer, it had been largely at Jim's hand. There was no escaping it. I may have started the change to win back Amy's respect of my own accord, but the rest of it was more easily traceable. All the red lines led back to that September day when Frank Vuchovich came to my desk to retrieve his first assignment and stuck a Colt Python in my face. Or did they? Did they lead back to the day Jim found the *Pandora* chapter or did they lead back to me, to my writing it? Were my ideas the blueprint for the nightmare that ensued? Was Jim simply the Oracle of Brixton, deciphering the signs, making my wishes come true? Did it matter? The net result was the same. Did the body count stop at two or three or four? Jim's question about killing Mabry rang in my ears: "*Did you plant that idea in my head or did I plant it in yours?*" The incidents leading up to Stan Petrovic's death no longer seemed random or unconnected. I could see Jim's hand in everything.

I was going mad, waiting, raking myself over the coals for my blindness about Jim, worrying about the bodies left in my wake that could be tied to me. I'd had it up to my eyeballs and retreated to the safest place I knew: *Gun Church.*

McGuinn had had his fill of blood: blood in the name of a cause, blood in the name of boredom. None of it seemed to matter to anyone. He took ice cold comfort in that he could nigh count the bodies he left behind him at home, but he could well count the bodies he and those of the church had snuffed out like the lit ends of still-burning fags over these few short months. There was Old Jack, of course, the two black footballers, the cop . . . He'd once read a book where the writer wondered what was the cost of another body or two in a world awash in blood. Amen, brother. Amen. So it was that McGuinn threw his gun in the river and tightened the tourniquet around the jumpy bollix's leg wound.

"Listen, to me, boyo," McGuinn said, putting his face up close to the wounded man's. "Yer friends are dead and it stops here. Do you catch my meaning?"

He nodded yes.

"You let Zoe be or I'll come back here and kill ya so slowly you'll beg me to murder yer whole fookin' family just so's I'll kill you. Ya gettin' me?"

He nodded again.

"I'm takin' that van and I'll call fer help as soon as I can. Any questions, boyo?"

He shook his head.

"Good. Now, ya just lay there quiet and still fer help to come."

McGuinn stood, turned, and walked back to the van. He was tempted to fetch Zoe, whom he'd left unconscious on the other side of the river, but decided against it. No good would come of that, he thought, the mating of two spiders with nary a human soul between them. He certainly had nothing of his remaining and he'd no notion of where Zoe's soul had got to. She wasn't one for talking about such things and McGuinn wasn't sure he would have believed what she told him in any case. A lot had passed between them in these last months, even something akin to love, but very little truth.

As he drove out of the woods, away from the church, McGuinn looked in the rearview mirror. He feared all he'd see there were the faces of the dead he'd left in his wake. What he saw instead was the inky blackness of an unlit road. If blackness was all that lay behind him, he supposed he could make do with that.

Bleary-eyed and nearly spent, I closed my computer on *Gun Church* and Terry McGuinn for the last time. Then, at about 6:15 A.M., the phone rang.

"She's safe, but she's pretty pissed and not a little freaked." It was a voice I didn't recognize.

"Who is this?"

"Tony Dee, Mr. Weiler. I work with Tommy Mac."

"She's upset?"

"Wouldn't you be?"

"I guess. Where are you guys?"

"Check your email."

"What?"

"Just do what I tell you."

"Okay."

"And, Mr. Weiler . . ."

"Yeah."

"However you get to where you're going, keep alert that you don't have company. You notice anything or anyone suspicious, you turn in the wrong direction and call this number. Got it?"

"Got it."

The line was already dead before I could think to say anything else. When I checked, there was an email waiting. They were keeping Amy in the Whitestone section of Queens. I didn't know that part of the city very well and hoped Jim didn't know it at all.

●

God knows why, but my landlord, Isaac, let me borrow his car. I think maybe he knew I'd once been a famous writer. Even if I were still famous, I thought, who would care? In a country that values the ballroom dancing talents of washed-up actors, writers were less than afterthoughts. At least Amy was safe. That was the most important thing, but I couldn't quite see my way to making sense of all this for her and I didn't have much more time to figure it out.

Rush hour driving in New York is a nightmare under the best of circumstances and, with a steady rain falling, it had taken me two hours to get this close to where they were keeping Amy. My phone started ringing just as I was coming off the ramp from the Van Wyck onto the Whitestone Expressway. When I saw it was Renee's cell number flashing on the screen, I almost smacked Isaac's right fender into the concrete railing. I wanted to pull over to talk to her, but there was no place to do it. I flipped the phone open and put her on speaker. That's when I got even a bigger surprise.

"Hey, Kip."

"Jim? What are you doing on Renee's—"

"You'll find out soon enough. Why do you sound so funny? You better not have other people listening."

"No one's listening. I'm in a car. You're just on speakerphone."

"You better not be lying to me."

"I swear. No one else is listening."

"You shouldn't have done it, Kip."

"Done what?"

He ignored that. "Why couldn't you have just gone along with it? Why can't you just be happy? I gave you everything you ever wanted."

"You murdered people in cold blood, Jim. How could I just be happy with that?"

"What if you didn't know?"

"But I do know."

"But what if you didn't?"

I didn't answer. I said, "You mentioned that I shouldn't have done it. Done what? What's the *it* I shouldn't have done?"

"You went to the police. They're watching Amy."

With the mention of Amy, I lost focus and nearly rear-ended the car in front of me.

"They're not cops. They're private security. And what did you expect me to do after you threatened her?"

"I wouldn't have hurt her . . . not directly."

"How could I know that, Jim, especially after the things you said to me on the boardwalk?"

"You love her that much?"

"It's more complicated than just love. I owe her."

"How about Renee, Kip? What would you be willing to risk for her?"

"Let me talk to—"

"Don't give me orders. Why couldn't you have done what you were supposed to?" It was a rhetorical question and I thought I could hear him crying on the other end of the line. "Why did you have to ruin everything?" He *was* crying. "Why?"

"I'm sorry, Jim. Can I please speak to Renee?"

"What's that word . . . indisposed?" I could hear him fighting back his tears. "She's indisposed."

"Did you hurt her?"

"Not yet, but I'm going to." He was crying hard now. "Unless you do what I say, I'm going to do things to her that made the beating I gave that fag editor seem tame. She'll be begging me to kill her, Kip. That's a promise."

"How do I know you haven't already hurt her?"

"You don't. You'll just have to believe me. You didn't believe me the other night, but you believe me now, don't you?"

"Yes. I saw the headline. You really did make Renee lure that poor kid out of the bar."

"She did it to protect you."

"What did Mabry ever do to you that you had to kill him?"

"Your idea, Kip, not mine."

"Remember, I'll hurt Renee if you don't do what you're supposed to."

"I'll do whatever you want."

"I'm almost as mad at you for pissing her love away as I am for the other stuff. She risked her life for you." His crying had calmed, but the tone of his voice was a toxic mix of anger and self-pity.

"Don't hurt her, Jim. Please. I'll do anything you want me to, but don't hurt her."

"We'll see about that."

"I'm listening. Tell me what you want me to do."

"Don't worry, Kip. Amy will know."

"Amy? What's she got to do with this?"

"Maybe everything."

"Jim, this is—"

"Shut up! Just shut up and listen. Don't tell those security guys we spoke. You tell them, you'll be signing Renee's death certificate. Someone else's too. That will be more blood on your head, Kip."

"Someone else?"

"You just worry about Renee for now. Promise me you won't tell those guys."

"I promise."

"Say it to me. Say the words."

"I won't tell them. I promise."

"You ruined everything, Kip. This wasn't how it was supposed to be."

"I know you think that, but what's Amy—"

"Get to wherever she is and you'll understand. See you in a few hours." And with that, he hung up.

I never felt more pressed for time than I did at that moment. Every foot gained took an eternity. Flashing brake lights taunted me. I weaved the car in and out of traffic just to give myself a sense of progress, to stop me from completely losing my mind and bolting from the car in a dead run. I called Amy's cell four times, only to get her voice mail. I thought about breaking my word and calling Tony or Tom McDonald, but Jim had put the onus on me. Up until this point, the blood on my hands was naïve blood, blood that Jim had put there. Not anymore. The illusion of deniability, such as it was, had been stripped away. From here on out, if there was blood to be spilled, I would not be able to keep its stain at arm's length.

Forty-Nine

The Last Easy Thing

The address belonged to a red brick building. Only the knowledge that Amy was inside distinguished it from the other houses on the block. There was a silver Chevy Malibu parked in the driveway. I drove around the block a few times before parking and going up the front steps. My heart was pounding as I forced myself to knock.

"Who is it?" I thought I recognized Tom McDonald's voice.

"Kip Weiler."

The door pulled back, but there was no one standing on the other side. I'd taken a step forward when a hand latched on to my wrist, yanked me hard inside, and forced me face-down onto the carpet. My arm was being held immobile by a wrist lock when the door slammed shut behind. I was pulled up onto my feet, arm still behind me, something hard—the muzzle of a gun, no doubt—stuck in my neck. A thick-necked, middle-aged man with salt and pepper hair, dark, suspicious brown eyes, and a neutral mouth stepped out of the shadows. He patted me down so thoroughly that there would never be secrets between us. He removed my wallet from my back pocket, opened it, and alternated his gaze from my face to my driver's license. All of it, from the knock on the door to this, took no more than twenty or thirty seconds.

"It's him, Tommy. It's Weiler. Let him go." My arm was freed. "I'm Tony Dee," said the man in front of me, offering me his right hand. I shook it. "And that guy behind you with the map of Kerry on his face is Tom McDonald."

I turned around to see a silver-haired man about my size with sparkling blue eyes, a ruddy complexion, a disarmingly crooked smile, and a Glock pointed square at my belly.

"What was the name of the woman who contacted our firm?" he asked, politely but firmly.

"Meg Donovan."

He holstered the Glock.

"How do you like your coffee, Mr. Weiler?" he asked.

"Hot."

"Tony, why don't you get him some coffee while we have a chat."

We sat down at an unremarkable kitchen table. It was wood, had four legs, and four chairs. The entire house, at least the parts of it I could see, was decorated in like fashion: functional, not fancy. Tony Dee brought me a cup of coffee and told McDonald he was going to catch some sleep while he could. I took a sip of the coffee. It was hot. That was the best thing I could say about it.

"How is she?"

"She's a little freaked and pissed, but that's normal. She's in the other bedroom resting."

"Can I go see her?"

"In a minute," he said. "First I want to know what happened that made you push the panic button. And before you answer, remember that if the danger to your ex-wife has increased, the danger to me and my partner has increased too."

"I understand." And I did, but I had to be careful not to say too much until I saw Amy. "I came across some information that led me to believe that the threats made against Amy were real."

"Have you considered going to the authorities? Our firm can make that easier for you. We can hook you up with a top-notch lawyer, have someone meet you here if you're afraid of being spotted contacting the law."

"I'm thinking about it, but I can't do it yet. I need to see Amy, okay? I need to discuss this with her first."

"I see. Go ahead. Down the hallway to the right."

"Thanks, Tom."

"Wait until you get the bill before you thank me."

I stood up from the table, taking the coffee with me. I didn't want to drink it, but it made a good prop, made me seem more relaxed than I actually was. I walked down the hall past the bathroom and the bedroom Tony Dee was using. I knocked on Amy's door, but didn't wait for her answer. The time for acting cool and relaxed was over and I didn't want to waste any more time than I had to.

Amy was sitting on the bed, head in her hands, an unwatched TV playing in the background. When I approached, she looked up. Her face was completely drained of color and her skin showed every wrinkle, line, and mark. It was as if she were aging before my eyes. As I opened my mouth to speak, she put her index finger across her lips to quiet me. She tapped in something on her BlackBerry, then handed it to me.

"Listen," she whispered.

I put the phone to my ear. "Amy, this is Peter. Please do as I ask and do it the way I tell you to do it." It was Peter Moreland. He spoke breathlessly, his voice was cracking, struggling to say the words. "You must get out of wherever you are and come with Kip or I'll be killed. When you get on the road, start heading north on the New York State Thruway. When you get close to Stewart Airport, call this number. If you go to the police or are followed, he'll kill me and he says to tell Kip he will also kill Renee. He's serious, Amy." Then there was some static.

"That's right, Amy, I'm not kidding," Jim said. I pictured him grabbing the phone away from Moreland. "Do what your sorry excuse for a husband said to do. How could you leave a guy like Kip for a cowardly piece of shit like this guy? My respect for you has taken a nosedive. Oh, yeah, to prove to you I'm serious . . ."

There was a brief pause, a gunshot, Peter Moreland screaming, then nothing. I handed the phone back to Amy.

"How long ago did you get that message?"

"Half an hour ago."

"I've got to get out of here," I said.

She didn't move. "Is Renee—"

"Yes, the girl from the restaurant."

"Do you think he killed Peter? It sounded like he—"

"No, not yet, but he will. He's killed before."

"I don't want anything to happen to Peter on my account."

"Too late, Amy. We need to try and make sure nothing else happens to him."

"Kip, who are these people? What the hell is going on? What does Peter have to do with—"

"Jim, the guy who's got Peter, was a student of mine. He and Renee were in the class when the other kid took us hostage. We got close after that. Jim got me back in shape, taught me how to shoot. It's complicated. I thought he was harmless, but . . ."

"Harmless! He has Peter and god knows what he's done to him."

"I know. I know. That's why you're here. He threatened you and I had Meg hire these guys."

"They got me out of bed at four in the morning, knocking on my door, saying they were the fire department."

"I had to do something to protect you."

"You want to protect me? How about staying the fuck out of my life?"

"After today, I'll do whatever you want."

"Fine."

"I have to get out of here, Amy."

"I'm coming too."

I knew better than to argue. "Just follow my lead," I said.

We came out of the bedroom and found Tom McDonald still sitting at the table. He seemed surprised to see us and a bit wary.

"Everything all right?" he asked, getting to his feet.

"No, the guy, Jim, who's after us, he just called me." McDonald tensed. "Yeah?"

"He says he's got a rifle trained on the back of the house and I don't think he's lying. He described how far the shades were pulled down, their color and everything."

"Did he mention the girl, Renee?"

"She's there with him. She got on the phone after he was done talking."

His hand went right to his holster. "There's only the two of them, right?"

"Just Jim and Renee, that's right," I said.

"Okay, you and Amy get down low and stay here while I get Tony Dee up. Don't move. You got me?"

"Clear as a bell." Amy nodded in agreement.

As soon as McDonald tapped on the bedroom door and stuck his head inside to wake his partner, Amy and I took off. We had a little trouble with the front lock and that gave McDonald time to figure out what was going on. He screamed for us to stop and as we finally got outside, I heard his footsteps coming up behind us.

The door closed in his face and that gave us the time we needed to get down the stairs and into Isaac's car ahead of him. We were pulling away just as he reached us. I took a peek in the side view mirror. McDonald looked pretty pissed off.

I waited until we were nearly back to the highway before speaking. "Listen, Amy, Jim's dangerous and he will do the things he says he will. He killed Haskell Brown."

"Oh, my god!"

"None of this is about you, really. You and Peter are involved only because you are connected to me and Peter to you. Saving Renee is only part of why I'm going. Jim is my personal nightmare. I have to go. You don't. I can go by myself. Maybe I can talk Jim down. He does have this worship and adoration thing about me and maybe—"

"Will he kill Peter if I don't go?" she asked, her voice sharp as a razor. "The truth."

"Maybe, but he might kill him anyway."

"I'm coming."

"Are you sure? All you need do is say the word and I'll drop you off. You'll be safe."

"Of course I'm not sure. Who would be? But I'm coming just the same."

The rain had let up and the traffic had thinned. I pulled onto the Whitestone Expressway and moved easily into the flow of traffic. It was probably the last easy thing I would ever do.

Fifty

Headstones

It was around noon when I pulled off the main road and onto the thin strip of crumbled blacktop leading to the abandoned bungalow colony. Overgrown hedges, their leafless and twisted branches like tangles of natural barbed wire, scraped against both sides of the car. The approach was eerily similar to that of the old berry farm down in Brixton. I had a sense that whatever was about to happen would produce more damage than a concussion and wounded pride. Writers have a knack for the endgame. That's how many of us begin our books, knowing the end. Then we write to it. There was no scenario I could envision that left any of us— Amy, Renee, Moreland, or me—alive, let alone unscathed. Jim had painted all of us into a corner, himself most of all.

Up to that point, we had done exactly as we'd been told. As we approached Stewart Airport—like Hardentine, an old Air Force base—Amy called her husband's cell. It was Jim who answered, and Amy got hysterical when he refused to let her talk to Moreland. She had been okay during most of the ride, her fury directed at me keeping the bleakness of the situation at bay.

"Did you hurt Peter? Please don't hurt him. Please! I'll do any-thing," she was screaming when I pulled to the shoulder and took the BlackBerry out of her hand.

"Jim, we're not driving another inch until you tell me whether or not you killed Moreland."

Amy gasped at the bluntness of my ultimatum. I could almost hear Jim thinking through the phone. I knew he hated to be bossed around, but we had leverage. He needed us and he had gone through too much trouble to ruin it now.

"I blew off two of his fingers. What a pussy. He cried like a baby. I had Renee wrap up the wound." He then gave me direc-tions to get onto Old Route 17 leading into the Catskill Moun-tains and another landmark from which to call. "After you get there and I give you that second set of instructions, toss your cell phones. You show up here and I hear a ring or a buzz, Moreland will lose more than a few fingers. And Kip," he said, "no more threats." Then there was a gunshot, more screams. I clicked off, hoping Amy hadn't heard that last part.

I handed the BlackBerry back to her and told her that Peter was alive, but scared. I neglected to mention the gunshot and the screams. She was already wound so tight, I didn't want to risk her completely unraveling. If there was any chance at all of us coming out the other end of this, we needed to hold it together as long as we could.

The sun had broken through the clouds by the time we made the second call and the temperature had to be around forty degrees. It was then, after Jim had given us the new set of direc-tions, that I had a decision to make. I knew I still couldn't risk calling the cops. They might get to where we were going before we could and that meant I would be sacrificing both Renee and Moreland. There was no doubt Jim would murder them before the cops got within a hundred yards. And if they killed Jim in the process, I was fucked. There was the issue of Haskell Brown's murder. I could no longer pretend that Jim was blowing smoke about having the Beretta he had used stashed away. My fingerprints were all over that gun. I'd fired it so many times, gotten my skin caught in its slide, that it probably had my DNA on it as well. The gun, the toll record, no alibi, and my publishing contract made me look like suspect number one. I didn't even want to think about what he'd done with Stan's body.

On the other hand, how could I just stroll Amy and me into Jim's game without letting someone else know? To do that would allow Jim to make sacrificial lambs of us all. With us dead, he would just walk away from it, if only temporarily. At the very least, I wanted someone to find our bodies, but I was so stressed and worried about Amy, Renee, and what lay ahead of us that I couldn't think straight. In the end, I was Prufrock and did not dare to eat the peach. I did nothing and threw the cell phones away as instructed.

About a quarter mile up the crumbling, single-lane road, we came upon the area where the bungalows had once been situated. They had long ago collapsed from neglect or been bulldozed. All that remained of them were the cracked concrete footings on which they once had rested. The slabs were overgrown with blankets of moss and weeds shooting through fissures in the cement. Aligned in rows as they were, they looked like toppled headstones in a long-forgotten graveyard. At least Jim had developed a sense of irony along the way. This was the spot where we were supposed to get out of the car and walk down the hill toward the maintenance shed.

"Last chance, Amy," I said. "You can take the car and go for help. But if you walk down there with me, he's not going to let you turn around and walk away. Once you're in, you're in."

She closed her eyes, swallowed hard, paused. "But if you walk down there alone, he'll kill you and Peter."

"Probably."

"Let's go," she said. "I can't have all that blood on my hands."

During the drive here, I had tried to explain to Amy the series of events that had led us to this place. I hadn't gotten very far. She was too frightened, too distracted, and it all seemed so absurd. Eventually our conversation was reduced to me giving her false assurances, ones she seemed too eager to believe. Now all of that was done with and there would be no turning around.

The sun had disappeared back behind the clouds and a nasty wind had come out of nowhere. Old leaves and dirt blew into our faces as we walked through a stand of trees. The big pines, oaks, and maples leading down the hill felt oddly familiar. Then, hearing the low rumble and rush of moving water as we came through the trees to a clearing, I saw a small waterfall in the distance. It was no accident that this place felt familiar. It was not so different than the spot in the woods where we used to shoot outside Brixton. Jim had apparently scouted it out—which meant he knew the lay of the land, and that scared the shit out of me.

A mess of flaking paint and rotting planks, the maintenance shed was on a flat spot in a small clearing fifty yards above the falls. It was surrounded by the woods on three sides. Only the spot the shed was on and the broad downhill path to the river had been cleared of trees. A small access road, just wide enough to accommodate a tractor, led out from the shed into the woods. Jim stood with his back to the shed, Renee at his side. He held a Colt Python, the one he'd given me, in his right hand, a Glock in his left. The familiar butt handles of the Smith & Wesson .38 and the Browning .45 stuck up from the waist of his jeans. Peter Moreland, his clothes soaked in blood, both hands swathed in gauze mittens, was kneeling in front of Jim. Jim pressed the nose of the Glock to the back of Moreland's head. Amy made to run to him, but I grabbed her arm.

"Don't!" I whispered. "He's an expert shot with every one of those weapons. Don't give him any excuse to use them."

As if to prove my point, Jim fired a round into the dirt a few inches from my feet, and we were still a good ten yards away from the shed. The round kicked dirt up onto my pants and running shoes. Amy dropped down and covered her head with her arms. Then, looking up, noticing that I hadn't even flinched, she stared at me with a mix of awe and horror.

"That's close enough, Kip. Throw me your car keys." I did as he asked. "Amy," he said, waving the big Colt at her, "you come over here by me and see to your husband."

I helped lift her to her feet, but held on to her arm, and stepped directly in front of her. "She's not going anywhere, not yet, Jim." Renee shook her head no at me, but I was determined. "You let Peter, Amy, and Renee walk back to my car and then you can do whatever it is you have planned for me."

Jim fired a second shot. The round bit into the dirt no more than an inch from my left foot. I may have blinked, but that was about it. Renee shook her head even more insistently. Jim didn't say a word. Instead, in one graceful motion, he moved the muzzle of the Glock away from Moreland's head, lowered it, then fired into Peter's left calf. Moreland convulsed in agony and screamed so that I thought someone *had* to hear it. Amy dropped to her knees and threw up.

"I told you, Kip, no more threats. Amy, come here now unless you want Peter to lose the use of his other leg."

She didn't need prompting and fairly ran to Moreland's side. "You bastard. You fucking bastard!" she yelled at Jim.

He just smiled. "Tell your ex-husband to do as he's told or your current one is bound to keep suffering."

Renee removed her hooded sweatshirt and wrapped it around Moreland's leg above the wound. She used a branch to torque the sweatshirt tight. Amy made a pillow of her coat, resting Moreland's head on it as she stroked his hair.

"Was that really necessary, Jim?" I said.

"You tell me."

"What now?" I asked.

"Hard choices."

"Hard choices?"

"Who lives? Who dies? They don't get much harder than that, do they, Kip?"

"This isn't a game."

"It is if I say it is."

Amy interrupted. "He's going into shock. Let me get him some help."

"It's not my fault," Jim growled at her. "It's him. If he hadn't ruined things, we could have all been happy. Now, this is all that's left. So shut up. All of you just shut up!"

Amy didn't argue, but I could see she was seething underneath the surface. Good, I thought. There was that notorious rage. She wasn't going to surrender.

"What's the game, Jim?" I got him to focus on me again.

"Cutthroat meets Fox Hunt, New York–style," he said, pulling the .45 from his waistband and tossing it at me. "Go ahead, pick it up."

Fifty-One

Too Damned Smart

As I took slow, steady paces approaching the .45, a hundred things went through my head. Chief among them was that Jim was fucking with me, testing me. Why, of the four handguns he had, did he throw me the one I was least comfortable with? It wasn't coincidence. I'd lately grown very skeptical of coincidence. No, there was a reason he'd thrown me that gun. I only wished the fuck I knew what it was.

"Go ahead and pick it up," he called to me when I was standing directly in front of it. "Pick it up!"

I kept my eyes fixed on him as I knelt down and placed my palm around the gun's grips. I rocked it in my hand to reacquaint myself with its heft. The design was a century old and it was a pretty heavy weapon. I just held it, pointing the muzzle at the ground. I had no intention of provoking him.

"So, it's going to be me and you," I said.

He didn't answer directly. "Somebody's going to walk out of here alive today. Who that is depends on what you do in the next few minutes."

"What's that supposed to mean?"

Again, he didn't answer. Instead, he bent at the knees and placed the Glock and the Colt on the ground to his left. He took the .38 out of his jeans and dropped it by the other handguns.

I didn't move. I kept reminding myself that with Jim, nothing was as it seemed.

"What are you waiting for, Kip? Take off the safety. It's loaded. See for yourself. Go ahead. Do it, Kip, but hurry up. Moreland's lost a lot of blood and time's wasting. Tick, tock, tick, tock, tick, tock . . ."

I undid the safety and racked the slide. A bullet ejected, spinning in mid-air and then, hitting a rock, tumbled harmlessly in the direction of the shed.

"If I go for any of these," he said, gesturing at the guns at his feet, "you'd be able to blow a hole in me before I even got close."

"Probably."

He smiled. I really hated Jim's smiles. "You were asking about how you determine who gets out of here alive," he said. "This is how. You have the edge now and you better use it. You won't have it again, Kip, not ever."

"Shoot him for chrissakes!" Amy shouted, jumping to her feet. "Shoot the crazy motherfucker. Peter's dying. What are you waiting for?"

I looked to Renee for a sign, for some indication of what I should do, but she kept mute and noncommittal and that scared me. Did she know something that she couldn't say or wouldn't say?

Just as I put my finger on the trigger, Jim grabbed Amy by the hair much the way Stan Petrovic had done to Renee that last night in the chapel. He twisted it so hard that Amy fell to her knees. She was clawing at him, flailing at his legs. When one of her wild punches landed too close to his groin, he tugged her hair harder, snapping her head back. She stopped flailing and screamed in pain.

"Shoot!" he said.

I raised the muzzle, aiming at the center of his mass.

"Come on, Kip. Amy's right, what are you waiting for? You're not very good with the Browning, but you're good enough. You couldn't miss me from here . . . or could you? What if I moved suddenly?" Mocking me, he feinted his shoulders left, then right. "What if you flinch? What if the wind comes up?"

"Shoot him! Shoot him!" Amy was unraveling. "Shoot him, please. Get this over with. I can't take it anymore. Shoot him, for chrissakes! I don't care if you hit me."

Jim said, "But Kip does care. Don't you, Kip?"

I lowered the gun. "Sorry, I'm not playing that game." I put the safety on and tossed the Browning back to him. "You just wanted to see if I would shoot, whether I would risk Amy's life. Besides, the rest of the clip is either empty or loaded with blanks. You chambered one live round as a decoy. Well, I'm a little bit brighter than Stan was, Jim. I won't let you screw with me the way you did him. What was supposed to happen? I pull the trigger, you get a big laugh, and then what? You pick up the Glock and pump one into my kneecap?"

"You're a smart man," he said, dragging Amy with him to collect the Browning. "That was one of the things I admired about you and your writing. Your protagonists were really smart. They could figure out all the angles, but by the end of the book they were always victims of their own overthinking. They were too smart for their own good. Like in that chapter from *Flashing Pandora* when Kant schemes with Harper Marx to win back Pandora. He doomed himself. You're just like that, Kip, too smart for your own good. You should have taken the shot when you had it. He who hesitates is dead. Blanks? Empty clip? Let's see."

My guts churned as Jim pushed Amy face-first to the ground, turned to his right, and, without a second's hesitation, put two bullets into Moreland: one in the chest, the second shot blowing off part of his skull. Blood, shards of bone, and clumps of tissue sprayed all over Renee and the shed. Renee fell back, horrified. She furiously wiped the tissue and blood off her face. Amy raised herself up, turned to see the damage, and completely freaked. She was crying madly, pulling at her own hair. As she crawled over to Moreland, her hands slipped on his blood and she toppled forward onto his body. Her face was covered in blood and viscera.

"*Now* it's empty, Kip," Jim said, the slide locked in the open position. He hurled the empty Browning over the shed and toward the falls. "Like I said, too damned smart for your own good."

Fifty-Two

Ice Cream

Frozen for a moment, I rushed at Jim, but I didn't get two feet before he'd picked up the .38 and drew a bead on me.

"That's not how this is going to play out. No, sir."

I stopped dead in my tracks and threw up my hands. "Okay. Okay, but let me check on Amy."

"Go ahead, but don't get any ideas."

Keeping the .38 on me the entire time, Jim collected the guns he'd placed on the ground and stepped away. By the time I got to Amy, all the fight and hysteria had gone out of her. She was done, spent, in shock. I used my sleeve to wipe the blood off her face. She barely noticed. Her eyes were so distant I wasn't sure she even recognized me. If things turned worse than they already were, that distant place was probably a better place for her to be.

"Jim, how could you do that, shoot him like that?" Renee asked, still wiping blood off her own face.

"Ask your boyfriend. He had a clean shot at me. He had the chance. I gave him a chance. It's his fault, not mine."

"Amy's done, Jim. Let Renee take her somewhere and you can do with me what you want."

Renee agreed. "Let Amy go. This is about the three of us anyway."

"She stays. And you're wrong. This isn't about the three of us. It never was. It's about me and Kip, about him pissing away all the good things I gave him, you most of all."

"This isn't a game," I said.

"But it is, just like in *Gun Church* with McGuinn. He wanted out and to save Zoe. I don't see that happening today, Kip."

Jim maintained a safe distance from us. He tucked the Glock in his pants, took the .38, unhinged the cylinder, spun it, then snapped it shut. When that was done, he did the same thing with the Colt. He tossed the .38 at Renee and the Python at me. He put the Glock back in his shooting hand.

"See," he said, "Amy's going to stay here with me while you and Renee go into the woods. Only one of you is going to come out alive. Then you or Renee gets to go back in there with me. If you or Renee gets lucky, Amy gets to go home. If it's me that walks out of there, I'm going to kill her and I'm not going to do her the kindness I did her husband. I'm going to kill her an inch at a time, piece by piece."

I didn't move. "I'm not McGuinn and I'm not playing."

"Well, I am," Renee said, placing her fingers around the .38's handle and standing up. "I want to live and I'm tired of sacrificing for you, Ken Weiler. I loved you even before I met you and all you've ever done is hurt me and shit on me. You never once asked me about where I came from or my family or anything. You never even asked me what my major was or if I wanted to go on with school after I got my degree. The only thing you know about me, I mean really know about me, is that I shave myself instead of wax and I spasm when I come. You think you've changed, but you haven't. You're worse now than you used to be."

"That's not true," I said, even though most of it—maybe all of it—was.

"Okay," she said. "If you answer this question right, I won't play either. I'll toss the .38 away and die right here with you. In your arms, if you want."

"What question?"

"What's my favorite flavor ice cream?"

Jim's smile grew broader and smug. "Yeah, Kip, what flavor? *I* know Renee's favorite. I know her parents' names, where she grew up. Someone's favorite flavor isn't the kind of thing you should have to think about if you love somebody. I bet Amy knows your favorite flavor."

"Butter pecan," Amy said in a voice as far away as her eyes. Then, thankfully, she seemed to retreat back to that distant place.

"See. Go on, answer Renee. You don't know, do you?"

"I don't. You're right, I should, but I don't."

"It's strawberry," Jim said. "Now pick up the Python and let's get this over with."

I reached for the Colt. "You won't get away with any of this. Even if you kill all of us, you'll get killed yourself or spend the rest of your life in prison."

"Getting away's not the point anymore. I'll give myself up. I'll be alive and you'll be dead. *Gun Church* will be published and the only one left to tell the tale of how all this came down will be me. I will be your legacy and you'll be mine. Our names, our lives, and our blood will be bound up together forever, Kip. *Gun Church* will be as much mine as yours . . . maybe more."

"You're assuming a lot, Jim."

"Maybe, but I don't think so. Step away from Amy. Now! You too, Renee. I'm tired of talking."

We did as he asked. As we stepped away, he came toward Amy, the Glock aimed at her head. When he reached her, he gently pulled her to her feet, keeping her between us and him.

"Both of you have two live rounds." Jim looked at Renee and then at me. "It's Kip versus Renee, just like Cutthroat. Only this is the real thing. Only one of you is coming out of those woods alive and don't think you can fool me. I'll be counting shots, so don't get any fancy ideas about combining forces. Just remember, as good as you are with those weapons, you know I'm better with this." He waved the Glock. "And I've got a lot more ammunition. The one of you who gets out of the woods alive takes their chances against me. It's not much of a chance, but it's something." He checked his watch. "You've got one hour starting now. Kip, you go that way." He pointed to his left. "Renee, that way." He pointed to his right. "Remember, you try and fuck around with me and Amy suffers the consequences. Begin."

I walked back into the thicket of trees to my right. As tempted as I was to turn around to look, I couldn't risk it. Jim had gone over the edge. It wasn't that he had so calmly and coldly murdered Peter Moreland. I think I accepted that Jim had the potential for violence in him that very first night in the chapel. His potential violence was part of my rush and what inspired *Gun Church*. No, what let me know he was really gone was his talk of blood and legacy: my blood, his legacy. When I was several yards into the woods and protected by shadows, I dropped to my belly and looked back. Renee was gone, and Jim and Amy were nowhere in sight. Only Peter Moreland's wrecked body remained, but even as I got up and ran deeper into the woods I knew that Peter's body would have others to keep it company. It was only a matter of who, how many, and when.

Fifty-Three

His Monster

Between the darkening clouds and the canopy of the trees, I could not use the position of the sun to judge direction or the passage of time. My internal sense of time was utterly distorted by the alternating rushes of panic and calm. Much like that day in class with Frank Vuchovich, the world would suddenly speed up so that I felt I would almost fly off into space and then, just as suddenly, slow down so that each of my breaths and heartbeats seemed to have distinct histories. Only in the woods can you understand that shadows are as much a product of state of mind as light and the things that stand in its way.

I had no intention of killing Renee, but I couldn't be sure of her intentions. She seemed angry enough down in the clearing to kill me right then and there. I didn't blame her really. My narcissism was apparently so insidious that I was like a man who jumped a puddle and thought he'd crossed the Atlantic. I had never asked Renee anything about herself and the only things we shared were things about me. From the moment I walked back into the woods, I was determined to play keep-away until I could get a handle on what Renee had in mind.

Stopping every few yards to listen for her, I'd done a kind of zigzag pattern through the horseshoe-shaped woods. I was no outdoorsman, not by a long shot, but all my time with Jim in Brixton had taught me some important lessons. For one thing, forests can be very noisy places in their way. Swaying trees creak and crackle like old bones and wind whispers as much as it howls. Animals chatter, chirp, bark, rustle leaves as they scurry. Birds do more than sing and call. They make a hundred different sounds with their wings, claws, and beaks. Insects buzz and whine. Human sounds, however, are distinctive. They are clumsy and unnatural. The forest floor is littered with fallen branches and people can't seem to walk without snapping them beneath their feet.

Only when I followed the slope of the hill down to the river and the falls did I have any trouble hearing. So I moved about forty yards back into the woods, twenty yards on the river side of where the access road from the shed cut a swath through the trees. I should have known that Renee would be lying in wait for me there. I was sitting on a log resting, listening for the telltale snapping of branches when I felt a ring of cold metal press against my neck.

"Go ahead, Renee, just pull the trigger and get it over with. But please try and save—"

"Shhhh! Quiet." She removed the muzzle and fired a shot into a tree on my right. "Wait a few seconds," she whispered, her breath hot on my ear, "then shoot at something on your left."

I understood. To Jim, standing outside the woods, it would sound as if we were firing at each other. After I fired, she fired again. That left one round between us. She moved quietly around in front of me, putting her face close to mine so that we could speak more freely.

"Renee, I'm sorry. I have pissed away my time with you. If I had it to do over, I would—"

"Forget what I said back there. I had to make Jim believe I was really mad at you or none of this would work. I love you and I guess, in your way, you really do love me."

"Strawberry," I said. She smiled so that I barely noticed the absence of the sun.

"We don't have much time. One of us has to walk out of the woods and the other has to—"

The sound barely registered above the wind and the rush of the water. It was only when Renee's eyes got big and she coughed blood that I understood what was happening. There it was again. She slid sideways against my knee and to the ground, the left side of her sweater dark and wet. White bubbles formed in the blood at the corners of her mouth as she struggled to breathe. Her lips were moving and I pressed my ear to her mouth.

"Your back pocket," is what I thought she said. *Your back pocket?* If I survived, I'd worry about it then. I pulled away to check on her wounds, but it was moot. The St. Pauli Girl was dead. Of all the possible sounds in the woods, crying was the most distinctly human.

Jim was on me before I could raise the Colt, not that I could have seen him clearly through my tears. I tried to make the heaving in my chest stop by taking big gulps of air, but it would not stop. Even breathing became difficult.

"If I thought it was your idea to trick me, Kip, I would have killed you just the same as her," he said, his voice strained and woeful. "She thought she could fool me with that angry act down there, but I knew how much she loved you."

"Why did you kill her?"

His tone reverted to form. "Don't ask stupid questions. You killed her just like you killed Haskell Brown and Mabry and Stan

Petrovic. If you had accepted her love and my other gifts to you, she'd still be breathing."

Jim's cold nature put me back in the moment. "What did you do with Stan's body?" I asked.

"He's rotting in your Porsche in one of the old buildings at Hardentine. I used him as added leverage to get Renee to come up here with me. She would have done anything to protect you. And now . . ."

"I'm going to kill you, Jim."

"Good, that's what I like. You're not going to be a pussy and just lay down and die. If I counted right, you've got one round left. Let's see what you can do with it. Now when I tell your story, I won't have to make anything up about you dying like a man. Go ahead, I'll give you—"

I wheeled and fired, but if I thought I would catch Jim sleeping or in mourning, I was wrong. He fired too. I was down and my right side burned as if there was a white-hot sword sticking through me. My shirt was wet under my jacket and I didn't need to look to know it wasn't sweat. Jim had stumbled several feet backwards and I couldn't quite see him, but I could hear him howling in pain and rolling around on the forest floor. The thing about it was, Jim wasn't dead and I wasn't going to stick around to see how badly wounded he was. I got up and ran for the falls.

For some reason I held on to the Python, but a low-hanging branch smacked me in the cheek and I dropped the gun. For about twenty yards, I thought I might get to the river. But when another branch on a tree a few paces ahead of me was sheared off at its base and the shot echoed through the woods, I knew I was probably going to die.

I looked back and, in spite of the shadows, saw Jim dragging himself through the underbrush. His right wrist and thigh were wet with blood, his arm dangling off his shoulder like a useless piece of rope. He carried the Glock in his left hand. Jim was good with his left, but not nearly as good as with his right. He was probably losing a lot of blood and in pain, and adrenalin would carry him only so far, so fast. None of that was apt to help his marksmanship. The same was as true for me.

I weaved in and out of the trees trying to keep as many between Jim and me as possible without letting him get too close. Shots came in fast succession so that their echoes seemed to catch up to one another and overlap. I tried counting the shots—one into Moreland's calf, two into Renee's side, one for that first branch . . . and so on—but I gave it up. For all I knew he had ten clips on him and I stopped looking back altogether. I focused my energies on the opening up ahead and the ever-increasing noise of the river.

I came through the trees, caught my foot on the edge of an exposed tree root and tumbled head over ass into the river. The icy cold water sapped my strength and will, but oddly it did little to extinguish the fire burning in my side. It would've been so easy to surrender, to let myself be swept away over the falls and downstream. If Amy was already dead or if Renee were still alive, I might have given myself over to the water. But when I felt the sting of something bite into my left arm, I gave up any thought of surrender. A bullet whistled right overhead. Looking up and behind me, I saw Jim at the edge of the woods where I'd tumbled into the water. As I was pulled downstream I lost sight of him behind some dirt mounds and weeds. I willed my way to the riverbank and fought my way out of the water.

The bullet had taken out a small chunk of my bicep and it was bleeding, but not as badly as my side. As I came up over the bank, I could see the maintenance shed ahead of me, off to my right. Jim was nowhere in sight, but I decided not to take any stupid chances. Instead of making a dead run at the shed,

I combat crawled. I wasn't paying much attention to the damp, winter-hardened ground under me. About halfway to the shed, my leg brushed over something metal with angles and edges. I rolled on my side, the pain ripping me apart. There was the old .45 that Jim had thrown over the shed towards the river after killing Moreland. I laughed to myself. Unless Jim was willing to toss the Glock away and stand still while I beat him to death with the Browning, an empty gun was useless to me. I stopped contemplating the Browning when the ground kicked dirt into my cheek.

I looked behind me over my right shoulder and saw Jim about forty or fifty yards away, his head, shoulders, and left arm extended over the rise of the riverbank. If he made it up the bank he would have a clear shot no matter where I went or what I did. Now I understood what the term no man's land meant. But he was seriously wounded and wouldn't be able to work his way up those last few feet to more level ground without expending a lot of energy. Another shot kicked up more dirt. It kicked up something else with it: an idea. The odds of it working weren't very good, but I was out of other options.

Jim had been a little too comfortable and in control for too long. It was time to see how he would act when he didn't have all the advantages. Besides, I had to buy myself some time. I picked up the empty Browning, stuck it in my pants and rolled to my left. Christ, it felt like my side would split wide open. I was light-headed. Jim wasn't the only one losing blood.

"You're a fucking pussy, Jim, a coward," I screamed at him, crawling as fast as I could in the direction of the shed. "You going to shoot an unarmed man hiding behind a riverbank like a total pussy? What about all your high-minded bullshit about two people facing off across a room? I thought you were special, but when push comes to shove, Stan was right about you. You're just a scared little boy. You disappoint me, kid. No wonder the Colonel used to beat the shit out of you. He was trying to make you a man. I guess it didn't work." I took a big breath and rolled as quickly as I could.

He fired wildly. "Shut up!" He fired again, the bullet passing over my shoulder. "Shut up!"

"Did you know that Renee used to tell me about the two of you fucking? She said you were so clumsy and awkward she had to stop herself from laughing at you. I get it now, why you used to love to hear me tell you about all the women I'd fucked. Renee was probably your first and last. You were a disappointment to me and to her and to the Colonel. It's what you do best, kid, disappointing people. You're just a fuckup."

That did the trick. I could see him struggling to get up the bank. This was my chance. I stood, taking off for the shed, but I wasn't as quick as I'd been in the woods. My legs felt like soaked logs and I had to fight to keep my feet. I didn't look back. I had one chance, only one chance, and it all hinged on me finding a shiny metal object smaller than my thumb.

I as much fell as dived to hiding the wall of the shed and tried to gather some strength. Moreland's body was around one corner and Jim somewhere around the other. I knew that regardless of how badly Jim was hurt, I couldn't afford to split my focus. I fought the urge to free Amy from the shed, but I called to her, warning her.

"Amy, keep yourself as low to the floor as you can."

"Kip? Kip, is that you?" Her voice was weak and the wall between us made her sound like she was speaking to me from beyond the grave.

"Just keep yourself low and you should be all right."

I took my own advice, keeping low, and searching with my hands out in front of me. Wood splintered above my head and again and again and again. The Glock had a pretty long effective range. Jim could have been five feet away or a hundred feet, but I couldn't waste time checking. I had to find that fucking bullet I'd ejected from the .45, and there it was, under my left palm. I snatched it up and kissed the damned thing. I wiped it off and pulled the old Browning out of the waist of my pants. Fuck! The gun was filthy. It had thumped into the wet ground when Jim hurled it over the shed and had sat there with its slide locked open. My rolling around in the dirt hadn't helped either.

I brushed as much soil off the gun as possible and furiously wiped down the exposed barrel and slide grooves with my jacket sleeve. I blew air through the barrel to little benefit. It was just too dirty. I tried spitting on the gun to help loosen some of the grit and wash it away, but my throat was cotton. Until that moment I wasn't fully in touch with just how amped up I was. I was soaked from the river but covered in mud, so I opened my jacket, peeled back my shirt—trying not to look at the wound—and used the water- and blood-saturated material to wipe the gun down. A bullet, then another, pinged off the concrete behind me and I thought I could hear Jim close by, dragging his leg along the ground.

It had come to this. I released the clip. Hands shaking, I pushed the bullet into it, replaced the clip, and racked the slide. I tried not to think about the grit in the firing mechanism or how my rushed loading might jam the gun. I stopped breathing and listened. I hadn't imagined it; Jim was coming. I heard his foot dragging on the concrete slab on which the shed was anchored.

"Amy," he said as he passed the shed door, "I'll be coming for you any time now."

He wasn't worried about giving away his position. Why should he worry? He was the one with the loaded weapon. What could I do to him?

I saw the Glock come around the corner first. I raised the .45 into shooting position. Now Jim turned the corner. I squeezed the trigger. In that frozen split second that followed, I saw on Jim's face a familiar look of surprise. I'd seen it on Frank and Stan's faces as well; it looked a little bit different on Jim somehow. His surprise seemed tinged with a mentor's satisfaction and pride. His knees buckled and he fell backwards, his head smacking down hard against the concrete. I crawled over to him, my hand around the barrel of the Browning, ready to bring it down on his head. No need. His eyes were open and unseeing. He was deadly still. I tossed the .45, grabbed the Glock. Before I mustered the energy to get Amy, I just sat in silence with Jim: Frankenstein and his monster.

Fifty-Four

Miami

Even eighteen months later, I don't really remember much about what happened after I pried open the shed door and found Amy face down on the concrete floor, shaking. She says I never lost consciousness. I disagree. My eyes may have been open. Words may have spilled out of my mouth, but I wasn't there. The first clear memory I have is of waking up in the hospital in the dark, alone. I was so woozy that the pain, and there was a lot of pain, felt like it belonged to someone in the next bed. I didn't press the call button. I didn't want to see anyone or speak or hear another voice. If I could have quieted my own internal chatter, I would have. I fell back asleep.

The next time I woke up, there were state troopers outside my door, detectives and a doctor at my bedside. I didn't know what day it was or what hospital I was in, nor did I care. It didn't take a rocket scientist to figure out what they wanted. The doctor told me my wounds weren't life-threatening, that the shot in my side was a clean through and through. Jim's bullet had hit me below the ribs, traveled in a relatively straight line, and exited out my back without chewing up any major organs or blood vessels along the way. The shot in my arm had just notched out some tissue.

"It will leave a little scar, but that's about it," he said.

Little scar? There could be no such thing as a little scar from anything connected to what had happened.

The detectives bought my story, as far as it went. They didn't mention Haskell Brown, Lance Vaughn Mabry, or Stan Petrovic, and I sure as hell wasn't going to broach the subject. Not yet, anyway. No one offered me a lawyer. No one read me my rights. When they asked me about Jim and Renee I tried not to be expansive. They were both ex-students of mine, I said. I'd had a relationship with Renee that had ended on good terms. Jim was a friend and fan whose attitude towards me changed when I moved back to New York. He had been stalking me, threatening me and my ex-wife. I guess that pretty much jibed with what Amy had told them and with the physical evidence. None of this is to say I was free and clear.

The media were all over the case. It had all the red-meat elements they lived for: famous victims, overlapping love triangles, stalking, small-town strangers lost in the strange land of the big city, and violence, lots and lots of violence. Best of all, it was easy and distracting. Since many of those involved were dead and the rest of us weren't talking, the media could speculate themselves into multiple orgasms.

After I was released from the hospital, I stayed in a hotel in Manhattan under an assumed name. It was the only way to avoid being hounded by the press. Amy fell off the face of the earth after Moreland's funeral. I didn't blame her. Meg arranged for me to get daily visits from nurses who dressed my wounds and made sure my healing was progressing. I alternated between sleepless nights and days when all I could do was sleep. I cried a lot. I thought about Renee all the time, about her last words: "Your back pocket." After wracking my brain for what she could have meant, I convinced myself that I must have heard her wrong. Of course I'd checked my back pocket, and of course it had been empty. I seldom, if ever, thought about Amy. Her respect, which I had made the centerpiece of my ambition for the last year, mattered little to me.

For weeks I considered going to the authorities in New York and Brixton to explain the full and bloody extent of Jim's obsession, but I could never quite get my own head around it. *You see, this student of mine was obsessed with me and my writing. He bought an unpublished chapter of my work off the Internet and hatched a plan that involved him giving me his girlfriend and getting me involved with a place where we used to fire guns at each other with live ammunition in order to restart my writing career.* How the fuck was I supposed to convince the police when, in spite of everything that had happened, I still couldn't quite believe it myself?

I should have done less considering, because it was much worse when the NYPD and the Sullivan County DA, with the Brixton County sheriff in tow, showed up at my hotel room door. I greeted their appearance with a kind of martyrly relief. I'd been carrying around a lot of guilt, and part of me felt like they couldn't punish me enough for what I'd done or what had been done in my name.

The sheriff had found the Beretta in a plastic bag in the glove box of my old Porsche. They found Stan in my Porsche too, what was left of him. The sheriff made a point of telling me that his wife couldn't get the stink out of his uniform.

"Had to burn those khakis, son."

Now, what had for weeks looked like a nightmare perpetrated upon me and my ex-wife by a couple of crazy and lost kids, seemed much more like a joint venture gone utterly wrong. My prints were on the gun. Stan's body was found in my car. States all along the eastern seaboard had toll records of my Porsche's travel to and from New York City on the weekend Haskell Brown was murdered. Anyway you sliced it, I was fucked. Not only because the one person who could support my version of events—Renee—was dead, but because even if I could explain away every other aspect of the case, I had, in fact, killed Stan Petrovic and had stood by while others covered it up. In a grave somewhere, Jim was wearing that smug smile of his.

The last card I had to play was the sheriff's own deputy. He had been witness to much of this, especially to the events surrounding Stan Petrovic's death. But when I laid the deputy card down on the table, the sheriff just kind of smiled at me and said,

"Glad you brought him up, son. I was wondering where he got to."

Meg got me a lawyer—two hours too late, in his opinion. I had already talked too much. He was right, of course. And while I wasn't arrested that day, my lawyer said it was going to happen and sooner rather than later.

"They're probably just waiting for the other sheriff, the one from the jurisdiction where Mabry's body was found, to fly up to New York. Everybody involved in this case will want a piece of the press conference."

He suggested I get myself back to Brooklyn to find some clothes to make me look presentable in court and to scour my papers for anything that might aid in my defense. He didn't sound particularly hopeful. That made two of us.

Just enough time had passed since the murders at the bungalow colony so that my apartment in Brooklyn was free of news vans and reporters. And, apparently, no one had yet leaked word to the media of my impending arrest. My landlord wasn't thrilled to see me given that his car had been impounded by the state police. I think I apologized, but I wasn't exactly in full possession of my faculties that day.

I wandered around my apartment like a zombie. I knew there wasn't a single fucking thing in there that was going to exonerate me, so I settled on looking for a decent outfit to wear to court. I had a few suits that would work, but I couldn't help but feel like a condemned man worrying about shitting himself at the end of a rope. What would it matter what I wore to court? Rolled up in a ball at the bottom of my closet were the clothes I'd worn the night I met Amy at the Peking Brasserie. That was the night it had all started going terribly wrong: Renee showing up outside the restaurant, leading me on a chase to Jim, slapping my face on the street. It was also the last time I'd held her. I remembered the fragrance of her hair, how it felt against my face. I could almost feel her arms around me, her hand sliding down into my back pocket. *My back pocket!*

●

I refused to allow *Gun Church* to be published. It's not like Franz Dudek didn't want to publish it. I mean, in spite of Haskell Brown's murder, you could never get free publicity like this in a million fucking years. Franz had even convinced himself—but not me—that the book needed to be published or Haskell's death would have been in vain. He offered to raise the advance into the high six figures. In any case, the publicity would help sell the reprints of my old books. Maybe, if Brown had been the only victim, I might have consented to the publication of *Gun Church*. But there were more victims, many more—some dead, some still living—for whom the book's publication would have been the ultimate symbol of disrespect. And then there was Jim. If ever there was a book written in blood, *Gun Church* was it. I couldn't give Jim that victory. I tried to return the advance I'd received. Dudek refused it, so I sent it to Renee's family. I didn't fool myself that the book would never be published. Meg and Dudek had electronic copies of most of the pages and I would die eventually.

One thing I was sure of was that I no longer wanted to live in New York City. On the other hand, I didn't want any part of Brixton either. I didn't want to see the forest or the trees or to hear the sounds of rivers running or the din of quaint waterfalls. I never wanted to see the inside of another classroom or mark another paper or discuss Kant Huxley or Moses Gold. I did, however, like the notion of a mining town. Mining towns, as long as they don't have a community college nearby, are about one thing: mining.

Miami, Arizona, is a copper mining town east of Phoenix in Gila County. I'm one of about two thousand residents, none of whom gives a shit about who I am or who I was. I like it that way. If anyone's recognized me, I haven't heard about it and, believe me, in a place as small as Miami, I would have heard. I spend my days in an office doing data entry for one of the few remaining active mines in the area. At night, I go back to my rented house and work on my new book. I've been able to shake almost everything else from my past, but not writing. From the moment I was sprayed with Frank Vuchovich's blood, I knew the affliction—which is what writing is, an affliction—was back. My current work has nothing to do with guns or yuppies or New York City or disaffected members of the Irish Republican Army. It's about a man's journey to find something. He just doesn't know what that something is. So it's kind of a book about two journeys. I know something about that.

What Renee put in my back pocket that night was a life preserver. The life preserved was mine. The address in Queens was for one of those franchise package-delivery service stores. *You bring it . . . We pack it . . . They ship it.* The box, as the police confirmed afterwards, had been rented by Renee. When, in the presence of my lawyer and me, the NYPD opened the box, they found two yellow mailing envelopes not unlike the one Renee had used when she delivered the Pandora chapter to my apartment in Brooklyn.

About a week later, the police and the DA from Sullivan County—where the abandoned bungalow colony was located— asked my lawyer and me to come in to "chat." All I knew for certain until that point was that I hadn't been arrested and there had been no press conference.

"Mr. Weiler, would you like to tell us your version of—" The Sullivan County DA never got to finish his question.

"My client isn't going to tell you anything unless you reveal to us the obviously exculpatory nature of the evidence you retrieved from that box. Even then, I may not advise my client to discuss matters with you."

The Brixton County sheriff sat there silently, glum as could be. I guess he wasn't in the mood to call me son anymore.

"Counselor, what if I were to tell you that your client is no longer a person of interest?" said the DA.

After a few seconds of stunned silence, my lawyer said we'd be very pleased.

I started to get out of my chair, but my lawyer clamped his hand down on my shoulder.

"That would be lovely, but there is the issue of the late Mr. Petrovic. I can't very well let my client walk out of this room thinking he's clear of this mess only to have you boys change your minds next week and prosecute him."

The sheriff said, "We know for a fact your client didn't kill Petrovic. Fact is, the only person your client did kill, deserved killin' and that was Trimble himself. Seems it was Trimble that killed Petrovic and my deputy too. All we want is for your client to tell us his side of things so we can corroborate some details."

I didn't wait for permission and just started talking.

About a year ago, I heard from my lawyer. It seems that the evidence Renee left behind included hours of voice recordings she'd made of herself and Jim in which Jim, in the course of their conversations, confessed to just about everything but the Brink's job and the sinking of the Lusitania. She'd also left behind a written statement detailing her role in things and explaining why she'd made the voice recordings—to protect me—and to fill in any gaps in the narrative.

"I can probably arrange for you to hear the tapes and get a copy of the statement," he told me.

"No, thanks," I said.

For a long time afterwards, I'd wanted to give Renee credit for being smarter than either Jim or me. That she was brilliant for seeing how badly things might turn out. Just lately, however, I've had a change of heart on the matter. One day it struck me that voice recordings and hidden evidence had Jim's signature all over it, that he must have known he was being recorded, that these recordings were a testament to him, an insurance policy to make sure he got credit one way or the other, alive or dead.

But who knows anything, really? Did Jim know Renee was making those tapes? Was it Jim's idea in the first place? These days the only looking behind me I do is in the rearview mirror. I try not to look too far ahead either.

The End

Acknowledgments

Special thanks to my friends Jim Born and Fred Rea. It was a comment passed between them at a weapons demonstration that planted the seed for *Gun Church* in my head. Along the way, the following people helped grow that seed into a novel: Simon Wood, Sara J. Henry, Peter Spiegelman, Ellen W. Schare, Judy Bobalik, and Declan Burke.

I owe a great debt of gratitude to Steve Feldberg at Audible .com for finally seeing the potential in *Gun Church* and displaying a willingness to push me to reach it. Same for David Hale Smith, my agent, who always believed. Thanks, too, to Jim Fusilli for his generosity of spirit and guidance.

My biggest debt is to Rosanne, Kaitlin, and Dylan. For some reason they continue to believe. Without their love and support, none of this would be worth it.

About the Author

Called a hard-boiled poet by NPR's Maureen Corrigan and the noir poet laureate in the *Huffington Post*, Reed Farrel Coleman has published fifteen novels. Reed is a three-time recipient of the Shamus Award for Best PI Novel of the Year and is a two-time Edgar Award nominee. He has also won the Macavity, Barry, and Anthony Awards. He was the editor of the short story anthology *Hard Boiled Brooklyn* and co editor of the poetry journals *Poetry Bone* and *The Lineup*. His short stories and essays have appeared in *Long Island Noir*, *These Guns for Hire*, Mulhollandbooks.com, *Wall Street Noir*, and several other publications. He is an adjunct professor of English at Hofstra University and lives with his family on Long Island.